COLUMNS
&
CATALOGUES

PETER
SCHJELDAHL

THE FIGURES

For Brooke

Cover & author photographs by Mary Schjeldahl
Grateful acknowledgements to the editors of *The Village Voice*, where all of
the columns were first published; *Artforum*, where "Introduction" was first
published as "Critical Reflections," summer 1994; and *Art Issues*, where
"Notes on Beauty" was printed as "Beauty," May/June 1994; and to the
museums & galleries for which some of these essays were initially written.
The Figures, 5 Castle Hill Ave., Great Barrington, MA 01230
Distributed by Small Press Distribution, Inland Book Company, and by
Paul Green in the UK.

This book was made possible by the generous participation of The Saul
Rosen Foundation, of Wayne, New Jersey, whose directors A. G. Rosen
and Martin Rosen have been supportive from the book's inception, and
by a grant from The National Endowment for the Arts, a Federal Agency.
Copyright © 1994 by Peter Schjeldahl
ISBN 0-935724-68-0

TABLE OF CONTENTS

COLUMNS
&
CATALOGUES

B<small>ACK IN THE</small> 1960<small>S AND</small> '70<small>S</small> when I was a poet and did art criticism for money and bonus prestige, I superstitiously feared that if I took the criticism too seriously I would be ruined as a poet. But working beneath one's ability is depressing. After a dozen years of it, I got fed up with my own preciousness. I decided to write about art as well as I could and let the poetry see to itself.

My fear proved correct. Art criticism ate my poetry. Thus fed, my criticism came along nicely. I had a career in work I liked. Art-world parties were better than poetry-world parties. Doing something both more noticed and less naked than poetry steadied my self-regard. Art criticism may have saved my sanity. The poet I was had pitiful coping skills. Meanwhile, it helped that I loved art.

I believe that the story I have just told is true, but (and?) I do not understand it. I do not know what being a poet is or what being a critic is. As I have learned by experimenting, I do have feelings that go with each notion. The thought "me-as-a-critic" stirs a sensation of thin excitement in my chest and a state of watchful worry in my brain. The effect of the thought "me-as-a-poet" is somewhat the same, but more intense. The chest-excitement is profound and seems to run down my arms, as I understand heart attacks do. I have a sexual tingle. My mental state is like that of a horse in a burning barn.

As a critic I may project the poet-condition onto artists and experience it vicariously from a safe distance. I cast my soul out on a line and reel it back in, seeing what has stuck to it. When I am in good form, every artist I write about may be me-as-a-poet having a better or worse run. I try to remember that I am just visiting where the artist has to live. But if I would be sorry to have done what the artist is doing, I reveal that.

"Why would I have done that if I did it?" is one of my working questions about an artwork. (Not that I *could*. This is make-believe.) My formula of fairness to work that displeases me is to ask, "What would I like about this if I liked it?" When I cannot deem myself an intended or even possible member of a work's audience, I ask myself what such an audience member must be like and beguile the column inches with social-political conjecture.

9

The purely critical instinct aims to chop up, reduce, and explain away any object. An object with integrity resists. I am thrilled when something defeats my best efforts to break it down. Then I can surrender with thankfulness and praise. So pleasant is such surrender that I have sometimes forced it, fatuously, at the cost of catching hell from my conscience (if not a scornful colleague) later.

It is not quite that in judging art I prefer to err on the side of generosity. I prefer not to err. But I am spooked by the complacent or bitter pride of critics who make an enemy of enthusiasm. I wonder what, if any, appetite or personal use for art such critics have.

I get from art a regular chance to experience something — or perhaps everything, the whole world — as someone else, to replace my eyes and mind with the eyes and mind of another for a charged moment. I do not think this is unusual. I believe that anyone can use art for the same transport, and that many do. To cast one's soul outward is normal. Then to examine the experience and communicate about it to others is the extra operation of a critic.

As a journalist for a living, I have rarely been afforded the luxury of writing obscurely. I have written obscurely when I could get away with it. It is very enjoyable, attended by a powerful feeling of invulnerability. Writing clearly is immensely hard work that feels faintly insane, like painting the brightest possible target on my chest.

To write clearly is to give oneself away.

My fall from poetry into criticism was like Adam's and Eve's into sin, only the fatal tree was not of Knowledge but of Ideas. My notion of poetic temperament is reflected in somebody's remark about Henry James that he had "a sensibility so fine that no idea could violate it." The violences inflicted on the sentience of language by abstract thought and on sincerity by rhetoric can cause a poet physical pain.

To have ideas at all times and to come up with opinions on demand is part of the critic's contract with readers. I may have overcompensated. Someone recently said to me disapprovingly, "Peter, you're so decided." Does it count that I decided to be decided? That it's a game?

It is a game of masks: an "I" tricked out differently for each performance. Criticism at best is a performing art, a minor, lively art like musicals or stand-up comedy. It makes something out of something, unlike the major arts that make something out of nothing.

To avoid being enslaved by any one idea, I try to have a thousand of them.

My nightmare audience is of people who do not laugh or, if they do, give no value to laughter. How does one negotiate the ridiculousness of criticism without jokes? One does not. Jokes are a lubricant without which the machine seizes up and breaks down. I choose to think that people who expect unrelieved gravity in a critic are crazy, hence deserving of wary compassion.

Art historians, more knowledgeable than I, and theorists, more intellectually adept, work for me. I stripmine such of their information as might matter to someone and such of their ideas as can survive translation into regular English.

If I had one passionate reason for doing art criticism early on, it was to meet and know — and to serve — artists, whose positive responses to me I took as angelic blessings. I got used, of course. What else is an artist supposed to do with a smitten critic? Artists get to be selfish in compensation for the likelihood of their failure at an enterprise in which they stake everything. It is foolish to trust artists, disgusting to condescend to them.

"There are people who are too intelligent to become authors, but they do not become critics," W. H. Auden wrote.

Intimate friendships between artists and critics, as such, are tragicomic. The critic may seek revelation from the artist, who may seek authentication from the critic. Neither has any such prize to give, if each is any good. To be good is to give everything to one's work that is givable, with nothing left over but the ordinary or sub-ordinary person.

A critic who feels no anguish in relating to artists is a prostitute. A critic who never relates to artists, fearing contamination, is a virgin. Neither knows a thing about love.

Experience is the only book of art.

I will never accept that art criticism is a profession like dentistry. It is rather a zone of overlap between journalism and literature like sportswriting. My heroes are Charles Baudelaire and Roger Angell.

Also William James, Oscar Wilde, D.H. Lawrence, Auden, Frank O'Hara, and Dave Hickey.

Pigeonholes can be good sport: male, Midwestern-raised, Nordic-American, middleclass/bohemian, college dropout, etc., etc. "That's me." "Me" ("you" or "him" to you) is the costume rack of the public "I." To be, decidedly, all that one may be thought to be makes for versatility. The decision consists in embracing one's descriptions (stereotypes).

Only I get to say "me" as regards myself. That exclusive right is a great thing that I (and of course "I") could not do without. It marks my one field of hard-to-challenge expertise. Need I add that "me" is not me, the personality I always seek to escape? Some people enjoy being themselves. They do not become critics.

Recently I came across something I scribbled on the endpaper of an exhibition catalogue in 1979. I present it without changes. I am shamed by my 15-years-younger self, knowing how often I have failed his principles:

> What do I do as a critic in a gallery? I learn. I walk up to, around, touch if I dare, the objects, meanwhile asking questions in my mind and casting about for answers — all until mind and senses are in some rough agreement, or until fatigue sets in. I try not to think about what I will write, try to keep myself pried open. My nemesis is the veer into mere headiness, where ideas propagate fecklessly, and the senses are reduced to monosyllabic remarks now and then. I try to chasten my intellect with the effort of attention, which in intellectual terms is doubt — doubt being the certainty that you're *always* missing *something*. To stay as close as possible to confusion, anxiety, and despair and still be able to function is the best method I know.

It is a poor culture, careless of its common language, that pays a poet to be a critic and not to be a poet. But at least it pays.

I became a critic for the opportunities.

Columns

THE AUCTIONS

MONEY AND CONTEMPORARY ART got married in the 1980s. The couple was obnoxious and happy. Money brought the allure of power to the match, and art brought the power of allure. They had the meaning of life covered for the people who mattered, who were kin of money. Once embarrassed by money's crassness, the people who mattered saw with delight how, since espousing art, previously filthy lucre showed up fresh as soap flakes. Where did the dirt go? It was smeared on art's angelic body, which gained thereby a raffish piquancy. Like all leading couples, art and money understood their responsibility to model style and manners for society's improvement. Their style was nakedness, and their custom was to have sex in public.

The word from the pair's latest grapple, a round of contemporary auctions at Sotheby's and Christie's, is *pfft*. Money, perfunctory, clearly had its mind on something else, and art appeared listless. Toward the end of the evening bout at Christie's, the hammer of exasperated auctioneer Christopher Burge fell ever faster as the bidding on one piece of art after another failed to generate so much as a delicate sweat. ("Fair warning," he would snap. Then, glaring at the penultimate bidder: "Not yours. All done." *Whack*.) It was my second Christie's auction, and it had to put me in mind of the first, two years ago, when money and art lit up the joint.

In 1988, the Roy Lichtenstein painting of the guy looking through a peephole and saying, "I can see the whole room! . . . and there's nobody in it!" drew a nervous comment from usually no-comment Burge: "*I* can see the whole room, and there are many people in it." Right he was. (The Lichtenstein cleared its high estimate of $1.2 million by $700,000, and a Jasper Johns went for $7 million; 24 hours later at Sotheby's, a Johns fetched $17 million.) That was then. This being now, the peeper would have had it his way. Exactly nine works, out of 57, drew bids above their presale low-end estimates. Of these, three topped their high estimates. Several of the works that did well were picked up by dealers heavily invested in the late-'80s bubble: for example, a terrific 1956 de Kooning to Larry Gagosian (bidding by telephone from the third row of the auditorium) and an as-good-as-he-gets 1961 Cy Twombly to Thomas Ammann (defending a recent spooky run-up of prices for this artist). Twenty-seven works fell short of their secret "reserves" (minimum prices set by the owners) and went unsold.

The *Times*'s figures for the week at both Christie's and Sotheby's revealed that, of 554 art works that were expected to bring between $119.6 and $160.7 million, 332 sold for $70 million. As regards relatively recent art, results were much worse than the numbers suggest. A very large chunk of the $70 million went for a handful of blue-chip paintings that, like the de Kooning and the Twombly, are "contemporary" by only an elastic definition. The auctions' verdict on art post-1962 or so was, with a few exceptions, dire. For almost everything of the '80s, it was strictly from bloodbath. I had the thought that collectors must now find something new to do with their amassments of art, such as look at them. And yet . . .

"What are you talking about? That was great!" snapped the first dealer to whom I extended commiseration after Burge's lickety-split windup. Spin control was the order of the hour, as dealer after dealer, with optimism that could winkle a silver lining out of a lead mine, called attention to solid prices for "good things" and disparaged the quality of the other offerings.

The market, they insisted, is simply becoming selective after a period of indiscriminate inflation. Occasional bitterness was vented, as when someone righteously denounced certain dealers for not buying, or at least bidding up, work by their galleries' artists to shield the artists from humiliation. (Want to know what the '80s have done to our ethics? I remember when the slightest hint that a dealer engaged in such manipulation would scandalize.) But the overall schmooze on the street outside Christie's was defiantly bouncy.

I found one element of the odd euphoria credible: relief. In contrast to the stomach-churning tension of 1988, the mood in the room this time had been notably relaxed, as the well-heeled attenders — radiating mellow wealth, as ripe as pumpkins — looked on mildly. Plainly no one was going to jump out a window on account of an unbought Julian Schnabel. (I was told that when a Schnabel failed to sell at Sotheby's the night before, people laughed.) And there may have been nostalgic moral satisfaction among art folk who remember the relatively scruffy and idealistic 1970s, when a fair number of people were in the art game for love or for nothing. Here was a market, still vastly lusher than that of a decade ago, that had to feel reasonable, coming after a frenzy whose insults to common sense could seem to traumatize even some of its beneficiaries.

What I do not believe is that the euphemisms "adjustment" and "plateau," being bandied by wearers of rose-colored glasses, begin to describe what is afoot. All through the '80s, people anticipated a rational ceiling for the soaring art prices. There wasn't any. Now they seem to think there has to be a rational floor, and I don't see how that figures. Given a commodity whose appeal is strictly subjective, it defies logic to expect that an insane up will give way to a sane down. More probably, the contemporary art market will flash a momentary illusion of sanity as it swings from one extreme toward its opposite. The art craze was a herd phenomenon, and I fancy that the sound we hear is a returning thunder of hooves.

I take no — or almost no, or just some — schadenfreudish pleasure in the spectacle of art and money on the rocks. I've tried not to be distracted, in my attentions to art, by the money mania, and I'll try the same apropos the money blues. Moreover, a truly hard time in the art world will be yet another body blow for our reeling city. But there is hope in it. The recession ahead should foster a desperately needed rethinking of what art is and what art is good for. Seduced and abandoned, contemporary art may recover with poignant difficulty its old virtue, which was to be, among all things of no use, the most useless and perhaps despised and, for those who prize the edges of experience above the middleness of security, the supremely valuable.

CARROLL DUNHAM   *Sonnabend Gallery*

CARROLL DUNHAM'S LARGISH NEW PAINTINGS are personable baccha-
nals of swabbed-on intense colors and black-outlined polypus
shapes writhing in goofy hermaphroditic ecstasies. They bespeak
revived confidence for a notably sweet-tempered and audacious
painter who, like many other painters lately, has appeared to be
faltering. Gone are the early '80s, in which Dunham's art ma-
tured, when summer nights downtown smelled of turpentine and
it seemed hard to make a bad painting even on purpose. Nowadays to make a painting at all may be indiscreet.

Painting, symbol as well as unbeatable medium of individual
consciousness, thrives when people are interested in, and revere,
the reality of their own and other people's minds and hearts.
Painting can't *make* anyone interested and reverent. It can only
reward interest and reverence that are brought to it, in a social
milieu respectful of persons. When such a milieu is lacking —
or, as now, is embittered by market cynicism and political rancor
— painting ceases to be a locus of communion and is raked by a
crossfire of anxieties.

Dunham takes on the crossfire with a stylistic twist that, in
line with current talk of "high" and "low," may be termed the
New Low: a resurrection of debased models (Funk art of the
'60s, Peter Saul, Zap Comix, and subway graffiti are suggested)
whose haplessness expresses the pain of devalued personality,
even as painting's formal resources, liberated by such candor,
flavor the expression with joy.

Dunham, 41, made a small but solid hit in 1985 with his first
solo show, of paintings on wood veneer, that was part of a reaction against the strident pictorial rhetoric of Neo-Expressionism.
Like Terry Winters, though with more ebullience than that artist of somber grayed seed-like and pelvis-like forms, Dunham
combined a classically New Yorkish sense of abstract-painting
aesthetics with organic, sexually charged imagery, investing formal decisions with an air of emotional vulnerability. Cy Twombly
was one apparent inspiration. Another was Elizabeth Murray,
since the middle '70s a champion of abstraction and sincerity in

an artistic climate of figuration and irony. Though mostly male, the new painters like Dunham and Winters were plainly affected by feminism, cultivating androgynous symbols and tones.

Dunham's wood-veneer pictures featured rambunctious clusters of biological-looking abstract shapes and miscellaneous marks, sometimes derived from the wood grain. They felt radically dis-composed. They were like sex: agreeably concentrated chaos. They reminded some people of Hieronymous Bosch with their accumulations of strange incidents all shouting, "Look at me!" It was a marvel that someone could endure a state of such internal turbulence, sustained only by bedrock formal conventions. The effect was a shot in the arm for painting, confirmed as a public guarantor of Eros and freedom.

The shot wore off quickly, for Dunham as for others. A variously brutalized art culture has had increasingly little empathy for anybody's tender feelings. The typical American painting of the last couple of years, by anyone sensitive, exudes the mood of a duck in duck-hunting season. Dunham's show last year at Sonnabend, his first since eschewing wood veneer for canvas, certainly looked like the work of a rattled artist.

It was a series of paintings — ranked chronologically by his diaristic device of prominently scrawling all the months and sometimes dates of their production on his pictures — that subjected a polypus motif to strenuous compositional and figure-to-ground adjustments, as if anything so inherently awkward could or even should be gotten *right*. That show gave the impression of a defendant trying to apologize for unspecified crimes to a hanging judge.

With practically audible relief, the shapes in Dunham's most engaging new paintings are *wrong*. They are so wrong, so gross and ungainly, that they may initially repel. They defy you to contemplate them with pleasure. They promise you, word of honor, that no formal harmony or other aesthetic elevation is forthcoming. But they are not messes. They display a wonderfully refined talent that, precisely in being willingly traduced, spills forth its felicities as unselfconscious bonus gifts, without pretense or demand. These works throw themselves unstintingly on the mercy of the court.

Far from trying to resolve figure and ground — between pop-out cartoony shapes and patchworks of feverishly bright colors in plastic paint — Dunham seems fascinated by all the ways that the balance can collapse in one direction or the other. Sometimes the ground is overwhelmed by the shape, yielding the effect of a three-dimensionally shaded doodle like bubble-lettered graffiti. Sometimes the shape is skeletized by the teemingly advancing ground. The stain-painting of the ground is often very tasty. The hairy-knees-and-genitals style of the drawing is relentlessly tasteless. The paintings can be like head-on collisions of Helen Frankenthaler and a toilet joker.

What I'm calling the New Low, here exemplified by Dunham, is on the rise in American art as a strategic embrace of abject personal feeling between the devil of judgmental politics and the deep blue sea of commercial imperatives. The New Low's doyen is an only sometime painter: Los Angeles artist Mike Kelley, recently honored by the N.E.A. with the rescinding of a peer-panel-awarded grant for a show of his in Boston. Kelley, 36, is a master at giving offense — subtle offense, extraordinarily hard to characterize — with finely calibrated eruptions in art of stuff *so* low (thrift-shop stuffed dolls, for instance) as to be off any existing chart. The art culture is swinging his way.

I don't know if Dunham has been influenced by Kelley. As a New York painter — in a city that, unlike Los Angeles, is still and always a painting town, even when both it and painting are in a recession — Dunham may simply be seen to continue an intermittent local tradition of swandiving from chilly heights of formalism into warm gutters. (Philip Guston is the tradition's main hero.) In any case, Dunham's new paintings fit in with a convulsive movement of American artists toward emotional truth, however unbecoming the truth may be. The New Low is an evolving set of emergency measures for the sustenance of besieged souls.

THE ROMANTIC VISION OF CASPAR DAVID FRIEDRICH: PAINTINGS AND DRAWINGS FROM THE U.S.S.R.
The Metropolitan Museum of Art

In Berlin a year ago December I was happy about repaired but ineffaceable World War II bomb damage to the Charlottenburg Palace, where I saw a wonderful collection of paintings by Caspar David Friedrich. The feeling took me by surprise, unconsciously called forth (I later decided) by my own and everybody else's euphoria at the Wall coming down. Old misgivings about a unified Germany, which go without saying, surfaced as a sudden macabre pleasure, at that site of great German art, in residual rough handicraft of B-17s. The pleasure was a way to forestall anguish, I think, and to let me keep being glad about current events. I didn't have to brood on past events about which my nation had expressed its feelings so satisfactorily at the time.

Once again, now, I have been looking at paintings by Caspar David Friedrich — in a tiny and spotty but absorbing show of work from Soviet collections — with an adrenalin level pumped up by the day's news. U.S. bombs are involved again, this time dropped not so much in righteous anger as with a horrible smug pragmatism, and this time anguish is unevadable. As it happens, I have thought of Friedrich occasionally these past months when seeing the regular recourse of news photography and television to the artist's signature motif of a lone figure, back turned, confronting a barren expanse at sunset or dawn. Now it is a GI and the expanse is sand, not a poetical fellow surveying Baltic waters. But the pictorial structure is the same, as is part of the evoked feeling: heroic melancholy. (The contemporary additive is patriotic goo: lonesome young American pining for yellow-beribboned hometown.) And just to make a connoisseuring approach to Friedrich truly tough, there is another historical matter.

Like Richard Wagner, Friedrich (1774-1840) has long had something to answer for in some estimations, as Hitler's favorite old master. He is associated with the Nazi participation mystique, the immersion in supra-human pathos that, considered as uniquely Germanic, encouraged Germans to do as they liked

21

with other racial denominations. A foreboding of it is there to be seen in Friedrich, whose heroes wander their bleak landscapes defiantly sporting German medieval garb that was officially banned under the Metternichian new world order of that time. Friedrich thus mixes up spiritual abandonment to nature with resentful nationalism as if they somehow entailed each other, and the retroactively sinister presumption can make one want to turn his moony characters around and slap them.

Nor is there a lot to be said for the artist's ideals of human relations. A big painting at the Met, in which two men stand out on a rock beholding a moonrise over the sea while their women watch them adoringly from the shore, becomes hilarious when you notice its allegorical equation of the men with two sailboats and the women with a pair of anchors. Likewise wacky is a picture of two women looking across a nocturnal harbor at a looming phallic forest of masts and spires. One of the women touches the other's shoulder as if to say, "Steady, girl."

And yet Friedrich is great. Even the unfortunate pictures just mentioned may sneak up on you with the artist's slow-acting disembodied color. The buzz of a Friedrich occurs when what have seemed mere tints in a tonal composition combust as distinctly scented hues — citron lights, plum darks — and you don't so much look at the picture as breathe it. He is an artist of pale fire, of twilight that scorches. His Romantic innovations, notably in emptying landscape of form to fill it with emotion, retain the edge of their radical novelty, still fresh after nearly two centuries. As for his frequent awkwardness, that is characteristic of any flat-out symbolizing art. Edvard Munch is often awkward. So is Edward Hopper. Really ambitious and sincere symbolism always drives art's communicative capacity to the breaking point, discovering exact frontiers of the inexpressible.

Born to a small-industrialist family in Pomerania and living most of his fairly sheltered life in Dresden, Friedrich was one of "the surplus of over-educated, highly ambitious, under-employed, and deeply frustrated middle-class young men" who fueled the explosion of Romanticism around 1800. (The quote is from a recent book, *Caspar David Friedrich and the Subject of Landscape*, by Joseph Leo Koerner.) Goethe was an early champion of his, though the scientific-minded great man eventually got fed up with Friedrich's doomy free-floating religiosity. ("One ought to break Friedrich's pictures over the edge of a table; such things must be prevented," Goethe remarked with that moderation we so admire in Germans.) Friedrich was touchy and shy. "In order not to hate people, I must avoid their company," is one of his rare recorded sayings. He was convinced of being a genius on the new Romantic law-unto-oneself model, and a lot of younger people were quick to agree in Germany and other Northern countries, including Russia. He was a star.

Friedrich despised France, which returned the sentiment. (The Louvre recently acquired its first painting by him.) After fashion ran against him in Germany, turning to Naturalism and genre well before his death, he fell into near-oblivion unrelieved until the early 20th century in Europe and little relieved in the U.S. until the 1972 appearance of Robert Rosenblum's vastly influential *Modern Painting and the Northern Romantic Tradition: Friedrich to Rothko,* which corrected the previously blinkered francophilia of American modern art history. Since then his spirit, given a certain allure by its very disreputability, has flickered through a period marked by, among other things, numerous triumphs of new German painting. In the '70s and early '80s, Anselm Kiefer made specific references to Friedrich in some profoundly resonant works exploring ghastly ironies of German Romanticism, which was a liberal movement that happened to have some shadowy aspects that, under later peculiar circumstances, engulfed the world.

No end of dark ironies may occur to one in the spell of Friedrich (ideally in Germany, which has nearly all his best works as well as the right associations). For instance, Friedrich's fondness for ruins, seen at the Met in some of the sepia drawings that are this show's strongest suit, can seem to anticipate a century notable for producing ruins wholesale. (Tune in CNN for the latest models.) We are not apt to think that about other painters of ruins.

It is Friedrich's fate, as in many ways it was his aim, to represent the most convulsive potentials of Romantic consciousness. He did it with pictures that are to the ultimate degree hushed and static — as charged with unseen incipient power as those shots of soldiers in camouflage gazing across a vacant desert. Thinking of Friedrich, I feel close to an essence of sick excitement, of pleasure in immolation, that is war's spiritual lubricant.

23

THE DRAWINGS OF JASPER JOHNS
Whitney Museum of American Art

JASPER JOHNS WAS MISTER ART for several generations of the U.S.
art world (Europeans tended not to get it) starting in the late
1950s. He isn't any more. Opinions will vary on what his last really
successful body of work was. I think it was the "cross-hatchings"
(which ought to be called "hatchings," because their clusters of
diagonal marks do not cross) of about a decade ago. Those spiky
fields in paintings, prints, and drawings sing. They have the old
Johns magic of a schematic, impersonal, dumb motif coaxed to
ecstasies of light and color by his patiently stroking hand. They are
palimpsests of a thousand small urges and discoveries, alive in direct proportion to the motif's deadness. The taciturn motif gives
the pictures a brooding irony, as of Saturn presiding at a baccha-
nal. I kept returning to the hatchings in the current retrospective
of 117 drawings from 1954 to 1989, trying to puzzle out what used
to be so right about Johns and has gone so wrong since.

The rightness and wrongness I am talking about go beyond
an individual talent's rise and fall. They involve historic circumstances that invested tremendous meaning in a talent and then
withdrew the meaning. Johns was the great American artist of
the Cold War. He was the first to take for granted an American's
prerogative to alter the course of Western aesthetics (then still
presumably a mighty mainstream) at will and by right.

His American flag was a sign of history proper dropped on
the toes of art history. It laid nonchalant claim to something
momentous that everybody knew, if they knew what was good
for them. Its tender fuss of brushwork in vulnerable encaustic
cozied up to this thing, this manifest destiny, like a pet in the lap
of an indulgent giant. Young Johns astonished with his air of
having nothing to prove, though perhaps something to conceal.
Concealment was only sensible, as well as racy, in the days of spy
novels and real spies.

For a while, the Cold War was the U.S.'s Apollonian age, its
time for Roman virtues, and again Johns was the artist for that,
though with a Dionysian velleity playing in his determinedly

public images — suggesting the license of a Roman private life. He charged with libido symbols of libido's discouragement: numerals, maps, color names. His was a volcanic reticence that translated in the art world as avant-garde professionalism, setting a master tone for the '60s and beyond.

Leading by example, Johns refurbished for general use the then badly disarrayed old beaux-arts panoply of disciplines: painting, drawing, printmaking, sculpture. He created discrete and magisterial bodies of work in all those metiers, exhaustively exploring the technical possibilities and limitations of each — incidentally helping to establish orderly values in the art market, where his product lines were perennially supreme. (He maintained a sardonic edge toward the market, for instance by making expensive paintings that looked cheap and cheap prints that looked opulent — a game that got demolished in the '80s by a grotesque run-up of prices for everything bearing his signature.) Persisting from medium to medium was only a repertoire of dourly mute images whose message was: don't ask. Some artists play hide and seek with viewers. Johns's game was hide and hide, or hide and no-seek.

That was early Johns, whose sensuousness and intelligence — his penchant for beauty (beauty that seemed to happen to him by accident, every time) and his skeptical pragmatism ("Take an object. Do something with it. Do something else with it.") — felt as definitive to the art world as, to a devout peasant village, somebody's sighting of the Virgin in a grape arbor.

Johns gave the vocation of art a spiritual glamor of workaday exaltation. Looking at his work, young artists got intuitions of what they wanted to become, and art people of all castes had surges of self-esteem. The sensation was no less convincing for proving incredibly hard to talk about. It was a baffled love. I am only a bit surprised to realize that in 26 years as a critic I have never before written on Johns.

Johns's seraphic effect persisted, while fading, through the variously recessionary '70s. It was briefly revived by the hatchings, which appeared at a moment when the art world was embracing unbuttoned expressionistic figurative painting. The most abstract work of Johns's career, the hatchings opposed the moment with a pure distillation of his habitual values of passionate detachment and fierce restraint. It was a parting shot. Perhaps rather than be trapped in humiliating disagreement with his times, the ever strategic Johns succumbed to self-expression.

Johns's work of the '80s, with its autobiographical bric-a-brac and thematic conceits, isn't bad. It's just weak. The standard line of praise for it, in accord with an era of obligatory unclosetings and the spilling of guts, is that it "reveals" the artist. I suppose it does. Only, what it reveals is banal.

Johns's heart, laid bare, is ordinary — he worries about aging, we discover — in most ways except its extraordinary fondness for idle intellectual sport on the order of puns and anagrams. In this he follows his hero Marcel Duchamp, but without the pointed refusal of conventional seriousness that made Duchamp provocative. Johns's bagatelles are as insouciant as a dentist's appointment.

How many people are enthralled by the allegories of Johns's bathtub, Swiss avalanche warning sign, Picasso cribbings, optical teasers, George Ohr pots, Leo Castelli jigsaw puzzle, Grunewald altarpiece, *The Seasons,* and so on? I'm not. When looking at Johns's recent work, I may use the bottoms of my bifocals to get my eyes a close-in massage from his still frequently ravishing touch. But I am bored at any greater distance, reflecting on the basis of Johns's merely eccentric recent imagery that the personal, whether or not it is political or anything else, is overrated.

People who compulsively hide their feelings naturally excite curiosity. The curiosity is often misdirected, seeking to know what is hidden — which can hardly help but be banal and ordinary, or sub-ordinary, because so unnourished by interplay with the world. The true fascination of such a person is the highly developed, complexly nourished drive to conceal, itself. That's where the juice is. That's what we should want to know about.

Johns was more emotionally communicative when he brazened his elusiveness. By shifting the emphasis of his art from what it withholds to what it tells, he has fallen into all sorts of traps — among them, seeming to take himself seriously — that he used to avoid. His present futility is disheartening both in itself and for what it says about our culture at large. This is a culture that sloganeers for a "right to privacy," for instance, even as it demands to know, and to make known, everything about everybody. Some delicate collective agreement, which made Johns's halcyon greatness possible, has broken, perhaps irreparably.

THE TIMES THE CHRONICLE & THE OBSERVOR
Curated by Douglas Blau   Kent

THERE IS A NEW ART MOVEMENT. It is emerging 20-some years ago in one of the loveliest and smartest little group shows I ever saw. Assembled by Douglas Blau, an independent curator whose literary and connoisseuring sensibility is among the rarer orchids lately blooming in the art-world rain forest, the show addresses the question of why things must always happen in the boring present: why can't they happen in the more exciting past? Blau's answer is that of course things can happen in the past. What a dumb question.

The show's 15 photo-based paintings, most from the middle 1960s, represent the taste of a science-fiction writer and belletrist named Richard Archer (1937-1970). The artists are Richard Artschwager, John Baldessari, Vija Celmins, Malcolm Morley, Gerhard Richter, and Andy Warhol. In his catalog essay, Blau recounts coming across articles and prose poems by Archer in English magazines of the period, bought from a thrift store in Los Angeles. The texts are not quoted, for a reason perhaps suspected by readers noting that Archer's dates yield the Jesus age of 33. Richard Archer — "an aesthete who preferred the naturalistic" and who "wrote in monochrome" — is Blau's invention. But Archer's clairvoyant hipness, in a show that jolts my sense of a moment in art that I thought I knew well, is retroactively and henceforth real.

Archer was an American living in England whose projects included "a study of Reuters and other news photography services." He was intimately familiar with the time's scattered variants of photo-involved avant-garde painting — in London (the Independent Group), New York (Pop art), Dusseldorf (the self-styled Capitalist Realism of Richter and Sigmar Polke), and Los Angeles (Celmins, Baldessari, Ed Ruscha). No mere art critic then, or really until the 1980s, could boast such comprehension, which saw through national and stylistic differences to a new haunted sense of reality shared by artists who often were ignorant of each other and not always alert to the implications of their own work. The result was a major movement that, illumi-

27

nated only by a writer who did not exist, could hardly coalesce to realize its possibilities. How successful is Blau's fiction? Contemplating it, I found myself raging at the wasted chance.

The principle of the show's selection is that all the works were used by Archer to illustrate his texts, which ran to such things as "a detailed description of a contemporary city viewed through the window of a moving car. Each sentence was a snapshot." "There was a certain crispness to everything and a softness everywhere" in Archer's evocation of scenes "too dull to be called enchanting but enchanted nonetheless." A cultivated state of "psychological dream-time" made, in relation to the art, for "a form of mimetic criticism, something like what dance is to music," written "from the perspective of a complicit witness" whose matter-of-fact perusal yielded "a sensation of absolute identification, an empathy so complete it was as if [Archer] weren't really there." (And what do you know, he wasn't.) Where was "there"? "The exit sign we were passing might easily have said Twilight Zone, but instead read 'Alphaville.'"

The Times The Chronicle & The Observor is visually what Archer's writing seems to have been prosodically: flat and dreamy, astringent and sensational, coolly hot. It is colorless but for the cerise ground of an electric chair and the tangerine ground of a car crash by Warhol (also represented by a tabloid shot of a leaping suicide) and the mysteriously listless garish hues of ocean-liner postcards meticulously rendered by Morley. Otherwise, grisaille reigns in Artschwager's paintings on nubbly surfaces of Lefrak City and two high-bourgeois interiors, Baldessari's grainy treatments of street-scene snapshots captioned with their banal subjects (e.g., "Ryan Oldsmobile National City, Calif."), Celmins's densely painted crepuscular pictures of a bullet-riddled car and two World War II bombers in trouble (also one of her windshield-view paintings that I think are the all-time definitive art about the experience of L.A. freeways), and Richter's blurry crowd of hunters and dogs in his ravishing *The Hunting Party*. Rounding out our sense of a stillborn movement (Archerism?) are reproductions in the catalog of exactly relevant works by Robert Bechtle, Claes Oldenburg, Ruscha, and James Rosenquist.

Revisionist art history adds weight to the entertainment value of Blau's conceit (a variation on the fantasy of betting at a racetrack yesterday with today's sports section under one's arm). It is of course an exercise in hindsight, backdating an idea explored by critical theorists in the '70s: roughly, that the most intense register of postindustrial reality is *the picture*, medium of wandering subjectivity and elusive objectivity ideally symbolized by degraded photographs. But it's hard not to feel, at Blau/Archer's show, that artists a quarter-century ago had already gone straight to the heart of the matter, surrendering the poetry of painting to the prose of photography and making the consequent pictorial Alphaville a zone of subtle new connections between the inhere of disaffected souls and the out-there of a denatured planet.

Yet none of these artists except Richter — the German master at last recognized in the U.S., of late, as maybe the most challenging painter in the world — rang further important changes on the theme, which around 1970 was usurped by the illusion-happy, brainless movement known as Photo-Realism. The fiercely intelligent proto-Photo-Realist pictures of Celmins and Morley (see the childish signature on Morley's pristine *Empress Monarch*, a note of hilarity and anguish in face of tyrant photography) promised something better, but both painters soon distanced themselves from photographic models. Baldessari quit painting. Artschwager continued to make airless and intoxicating grisaille pictures, with steady results. Warhol continued to exploit his own innovations, with diminishing returns. Other artists would arise, as different as Chuck Close and Anselm Kiefer, to reinvigorate the frontier of painting and photography. But until ideas about picture-ness became cliches of the '80s there would be no concerted development along these lines.

Things happen the way they have to. You can go nuts thinking otherwise. But then, what is art good for if not organizing vacations into temporary insanity? In effect, Blau combines weary knowledge of the present with innocent energy of the past to produce an illusion of energetic knowledge floating outside time like a luminous thought balloon. It's crazy and quite wonderful, especially since the show's premise does not muffle but sharpens the mystery of the art involved. We are in better hands with the apochryphal Archer than with many a flesh-and-blood guide. "He spoke of how he loved to lose himself," Blau writes by way of explaining why, "to give himself over to that all-embracing awe."

ANNETTE LEMIEUX   *Josh Baer Gallery*

I HAVE A PROBLEM WITH ANNETTE LEMIEUX. Actually, it is a problem I have with dozens of avant-gardish young artists emergent in the last five years — a cohort sometimes vaguely termed Neo-Conceptual that has crept to international prominence with the mild inexorability of a morning ground-fog — but I choose to focus on Lemieux, who by being one of the best of these artists may occasion a fair test.

Briefly, I have been looking — staring, blinking — at Lemieux's elegant and laconic assemblies of found objects since about 1986 with a sullen heart, waiting in vain to feel something strongly particular. Is this because a deadpan tone is essential to her art? Or am I just disaffected? The answer is a bit of both, I think, and I want to sort it out with an eye to understanding something about a present art culture steeped in several flavors of malaise.

Lemieux — now 33, from Connecticut — belongs to what I have heard called the Assistants Generation, meaning several noted young artists who commenced their careers in the studios of art stars of the early '80s. In her case the star was David Salle. (Other successful former assistants and their respective assistees include: Ashley Bickerton/Jack Goldstein, Mark Innerst/Robert Longo, and Michele Zalopany/Julian Schnabel.) Though not as spectacular as the mid-'80s debuts of contemporaries in the movement known as Neo-Geo (Bickerton along with Jeff Koons, Peter Halley, Haim Steinbach, and others), Lemieux's subsequent rise was solid and bore hallmarks of the time.

Lemieux appeared often in group shows at the hipper Lower East Side galleries (Cash/Newhouse, International with Monument, etc.). She hatched a subtle theatrical manner — that of an artist without style, whose exhibitions were like one-person group shows — that delivered a *de rigueur* cool riposte to declining Neo-Expressionism and stood in dignified contrast to the product lines of Neo-Geo. Lemieux became, and remains, a fixture of the present far-flung circuit of galleries, museums, and kunsthalles, here and abroad, that like air-traffic control towers supervise the regular takeoffs and landings of squadrons of showmakers.

Lemieux's best known works fastidiously deploy such things as antique-shop furniture, world globes, second-hand books, old picture frames, and gnomic verbal messages, sometimes with paintings of bland stripe or dot patterns or with blown-up found photographs evocative of lost childhoods. One senses in the background of her art, as of much Neo-Conceptualism, the looming shamanistic influence of Joseph Beuys, whose oracular show-and-tell with worn objects led the way to our epoch of blackboards, funky fabrics, laboratory equipment, and vitrines. But not for her is Beuys's pungent humanity.

Her most discerning critic, Rosetta Brooks, once compared Lemieux's approach with Japanese flower-arranging: a little of this put intuitively with a little of that, and it looks perfect. It is important that her materials, like the ikebana master's flowers, are aromatic with previous, undisciplined lives of their own, and crucial that they be subjected to an artificial order. Her art of denatured nostalgias celebrates artifice.

Lemieux has the pluses and minuses — here comes the problem — of artists formed by an art world that for some years has been what you could call a mature industry, with a predictable market, hosts of promotional specialists (only sometimes to be confused with art critics), and protocols of acceptable attitudes. A friend of mine compares the typical career on this scene to that of a rock star, issuing an album of new songs each year. With respect to Lemieux's refined approach, a nicer analogy might be that of a poet putting out an annual slim volume (if one could imagine a world in which poetry is professionally viable). Her work has the silky tone of someone whispering in full confidence that her audience will lean in to catch every word.

Like a good poem, a good Lemieux arrays specific elements that keep their identity while radiating associativeness. In line with current intellectual fashion — such fashion being the very fluid in which Lemieux's kind of artist swims, a medium of assured communication — the associations of her new work tend to be political. She is abreast of the news with *Hell on Wheels*, an aggressive-looking mass of 100 steel helmets mounted on little rubber tires: a spectacle that is funny and, yes, faintly hellish, as is *Spit and Image*, twelve toddler suits in desert camouflage pattern hung on a gnarled Adirondack coat rack. Also touching a nerve of present unease is *Bread Lines*: twelve leaning planks plastered with wrappers of French and Italian bread from New York bakeries. (Lemieux told me that she delivered the bread from the wrappers to local soup kitchens — an oddly pragmatic act of charity, giving the work an anecdotal extra resonance.)

At times I don't know what Lemieux is driving at but am pretty sure I wouldn't like it if I did. An exceedingly handsome big canvas titled *Devouring Element* looks like a painting but was made with a branding iron: even rows of a brown Beuysian Maltese cross yield negative space that is a white network of swastikas. It is hard to escape the impression of a cheap shot. (Callow apocalyptic references are a standard mishap of Lemieux's generation. I recall a piece by the Starn Twins that incorporated a photo of Holocaust corpses and was titled, I promise, *Absence of Compassion*. Not that only the young offend in this way. Take Robert Morris, please.)

Occasionally shaky taste aside — though not entirely aside, because it points up the current fallacy of vesting mere artists with some kind of moral leadership — Lemieux is extravagantly talented. Her deceptive simplicities bespeak rigorous creative economy. She merits comparison with the finest other current installation-makers who likewise deal in dire content — for instance, the German Rosemarie Troeckel, with her stitchery of ominous heraldic patterns, and the New Yorker Cady Noland, whose strewings of all-American detritus are bleak epics of post-everything angst. Lemieux's works can linger in memory, percolating new meanings.

My favorite work in this show, *Interrupted Sleep*, consists of a huge grainy photograph of the artist apparently asleep under a rumpled sheet, bare feet protruding, and an actual burning lightbulb hanging in front of the photograph. Suggestions of dream and brainstorm mingle with airs of vulnerability and humility. The composition is reminiscent of something: a Philip Guston — the great painter's abject rapture recycled as cerebral theater. All these hints remain in suspension, weighing on the mind with snowflake lightness.

Why don't I feel, then, that Lemieux's art has anything to do with me? Probably because it has nothing to do with anyone in particular. It has to do with "the spectator," with "the audience," with institutionalized imagination. It is about showing up on schedule, showing off as required, and moving on. It takes for granted all sorts of assumptions about what an artist is and what an artist does, the common sense of a generation prematurely wise. (Another friend of mine tells me that if he hears one more artist say of art, "Look, it's a job," he will scream.) Those assumptions are due for some serious review.

JUDITH SHEA: MONUMENT STATUARY
Max Protetch Gallery

An INTERESTING THING ABOUT SKIN IS that it has two sides. The same goes for clothes (which might be considered elective skin, as skin is compulsory clothing). Inside, there is the important stuff that skin protects. Outside, there is the world. (My insides are "world," too, I suppose; only I don't believe it.)

I think most people feel mainly that their skin is the outer limit of themselves. It follows that most people are lousy dressers, unalert to meanings of clothes beyond comfort and concealment. (I am this type to an extreme. I never know what I look like and so rely on friends to inform me, gently.) But I am convinced that some people feel, in effect, that their skin is the inner boundary of the world, whose pressure — a pressure above all of gazes — they sense acutely. They dress great. Mutual incomprehension between the two types constitutes one of the fundamental misunderstandings without which social life would be rational and boring.

Is it possible to be both types? I fancy that Judith Shea is, reversible in her own skin, and that this makes her a terrific sculptor. A fashion student who turned artist in the mid-1970s, Shea over the years has created a body of work (or work of bodies) electric with an alternating current of self-consciousness and world-consciousness, a dialectic that she extends to problems of sculpture after Minimalism, sexuality under feminism, and everybody's being-in-the-world all the time. She has a frequent flaw of forcing more discursive meaning into sculpture than that mute medium can manage gracefully. Her current show of four bronze figures or figure-fragments creaks a bit with ponderous philosophizing. But Shea's sensitivity to the metaphysics of skin, a sculptural equivalent of perfect pitch, never fails her, unless perhaps by making her think she can get away with anything.

Shea cleanly fulfills the promise of this show's title, "Monument Statuary." Without being much larger than lifesize, her statues are as satisfyingly monumental as the classical precedents they headily comment on. I would want one for my formal garden, if I had a formal garden.

Shea emerged in an artistic tendency of the late '70s, known as New Image, that strove to insinuate figuration into painting and sculpture that had been caught in a cul de sac of abstraction by '60s formalism and Minimalism. She made a sensation with empty bronze or iron casts of articles of clothing — part of a blouse on the wall, a one-piece bathing suit front-down on the floor (*Crawl*), a pedestaled "little black dress" — swelled by the bodies of invisible wearers. Earlier she had sewn or constructed subtle caricatures of generic garments, a lexicon of fashion in odd materials. I well recall the kick of free-standing "checked pants" made of square-meshed wire fencing. (Shea is never not witty.) But the cast clothes were her major coup. They were, and still are, genius-touched. They brought a wealth of content and pizzazz into sculpture faithful to the self-evident literalness of Minimalism.

If nothing by Shea since then has had equal impact, it is because big changes in the art world drained urgency from her preoccupations. In retrospect, New Image was the last truly New York-generated modern-art evolution, eclipsed in the early '80s by the rangier agendas of German and Italian painters, English assemblage sculptors, French-theoried photographic artists, and international-circuit installational show-offs. Shea's once definitively New Yorkish characteristics of modernist idealism and stylistic erudition (for instance, in a startling bronze of a pair of shorts alluding at once to Brancusi and break-dancing) passed into a blind spot of contemporary taste. There she has struggled to reground her enterprise with reference to an ancient classical past and to present-day social and psychological vicissitudes.

Opus Notum Galateae Unum (The Only Known Work of Galatea), in the present show, is a gustily romantic bronze of classical drapery swathing a striding male figure from neck to ankles. The shape of one arm is visible beneath the fabric, held against the figure's chest. There are gaping holes where the other arm and the head would protrude. Metal posts in place of feet anchor the figure to a marble pedestal inscribed with the work's Latin title, which wryly surmises that Pygmalion's famous creature had her own fling at magic-making sexual obsession. The presence/absence of an idealized man is indeed magical, as a symbol of longing. Does the man long for the creator who longs for him? Able to manifest himself only through what contains him, he cannot say.

Like Shea's earlier work, the Galatea plays on the fact that, while fitting and projecting the human form, clothing breaks it up into parts. (Skin has no edges. Clothes do.) Here, clothes make the man, but only as much of him as they can reach. The same trope appears in *Post Balzac*, another pedestaled empty garment featuring a sex reversal. Here the robe of Rodin's mighty author gapes on the void of a body whose narrow shoulders, apparent in the drape of the sculpture's wonderful cascade of heavy bronze, indicate that it is (was? would be?) female. (This is the imaginary being I want installed in my imaginary garden.) While verging on smart-alecky, the sex-reversal motif is not a problem when I am looking at the work, to which it gives a decisive skew: the artist finding an efficient way to take personal possession of intimidatingly grand models.

Relatively troublesome, though still enjoyable, are the show's two other pieces, tableaux of statuary and fabric. *Apollo* is a splendid naked male torso (Shea can really sculpt, delivering exotically archaic pleasures of academic modeling) with, hung on the wall behind it, a schematic overcoat in stiff black linen. (This coat form, folded double lengthwise, recurs in her work; she has said it derives from seeing men on commuter trains fold their coats that way, in a gesture of peculiarly masculine fastidiousness.) You know what? I am disinclined to analyse Shea's *Apollo*, balking at a semantic gap between the work's halves that could be filled in, I suspect, only by an explaining-the-joke kind of exegesis. To put it another way, the classical torso and the abstract coat categorically repel each other, and to force them together strikes me as an uneconomical use of mental energy.

Shea's ambition to communicate can overstrain her means. The problem is interesting, in addition to distressing, because symptomatic of a present artistic climate that demands much of artists in terms of socially engaged meaning while giving them only the vaguest orientation in terms of style. As it happens, exactly that kind of dilemma — between responsiveness to the world and loyalty to self, between outside and inside — has been the dynamic of Shea's best work. Her case merits patience.

BALTIC VIEWS

LAST WEEK ON A BUS TO Leningrad I got angry for Finland. The Finns aboard found it very funny. For three hours we jolted on atrocious roads through Karelia, former Finnish heartland gobbled when Stalin deemed the border too close to Leningrad; Finland was in the wrong place. Amid forests of birch and pine, I surveyed the effects of a long disaster. This was my first time in the USSR (my fourth in Finland). I was unprepared for the brokenness of every human thing, the old Finnish farmhouses and lakeside villas collapsing or collapsed, the travesties of agriculture (apart from neat kitchen gardens), and other signs of avalanching dysfunction. The once famously cosmopolitan Baltic port of Vyborg (Viipuri in Finnish), which could be the prettiest small city in the world, felt postnuclear, its citizens listlessly wandering. Some gaped as our fancy tour bus wallowed by. The single purposeful activity I saw in Karelia was a man painting an ornamental fence around a roadside ammunition bunker. The contrast to Finland's grace and bustle was unbearable.

"Vyborg," I said to Helsinki art critic Markku Valkonen, who has a Karelian background. "You want it back."

"Sure I would like it back," he said softly, "but I do not want to spoil my life with bitterness."

"Then I'll get it back for you!" A military truck passed. "Bastards!"

That the American was going to fight for Finland made the rounds, hilariously. Finns have the absurdist humor of a people less than five million strong who, Markku told me years ago, "are very warlike and have lost 36 consecutive wars," mainly with much larger Sweden and very much larger Russia. They tend to be outwardly diffident, inwardly stubborn, and wonderfully soulful. "We are Scandinavian in politics, economics, and everyday culture," another Finn said to me, "but underneath is . . . ." She hummed *Volga Boatmen* with super vibrato. Finns have a dramatic and sad musicality. I love to hear Finnish, which I understand not at all, spoken. With its vowels that go on for days, that language of mysterious origin is devoid of cognates (except in Hungarian and

Estonian) and hardly resembles speech. To my ear its softly rollicking sounds are like water over rocks or wind through trees.

Of course I did a proper sauna, leaping parboiled and starkly into a Baltic Sea whose fantastic coldness registered intellectually while regarded with indifference by my body chockful of coziness. A sensation of invincibility is the secret of the sauna, I decided. I recooked and, in the translucent blue midsummer dusk that deepens toward midnight, wahooed off the pier again.

I like Finland and it seems Finland likes me, if only for comic relief. The Foreign Ministry hosted me for the reopening of the country's national gallery, the Ateneum. Six years under renovation, the beaux-arts building housing classic and contemporary Finnish art is a local pride and joy. Its design is a blend of meticulous restoration and understated high tech, a structure of engineered quietnesses that is also, as a social site, lots of fun. Happy thousands of Finns swarmed it on opening day. I turned out to be the western hemisphere's only representative in a press contingent otherwise European, including an Estonian, a Lithuanian, and two Latvians. You think the USSR isn't over? The nationalist tempered steel in those careworn but fearless Baltic art people would make Gorbachev cry. No one having hinted to me of a quid pro quo, this quid is gratuitous. To salve my independence, I will deliver a couple of nips to the hand that flew me Finnair Executive Class.

Helsinki is horribly expensive. A present recession, due to collapsing trade with the destitute Soviets, has yet to weaken a currency so mighty that, what with social-democratic taxes, everything costs twice what it does in New York — unless you want a drink, in which case take out a bank loan. Finns do drink, with an almost sacramental self-consciousness, intensified by the priciness of the beverages, that you must adore, even as you move about gingerly the next morning. More disturbingly, the country has a xenophobic streak, especially toward the world's Southern peoples. A recent presence of Somalian refugees has occasioned overt racism. And I was astounded by an omnipresent Finnish licorice ad featuring a Sambo-like cartoon of a black African. I decried it to Finns, who answered that this logo goes way back in time. I said so does cholera. I think I won those arguments, watching Finnish pride beat one of its practiced orderly retreats, this time in face of a p.c. American. It seemed fair return for the sense of being spiritually flimsy and superficial that, as an American, I experience in the sweet dark gravity of Finland.

One of the best public performance works I ever saw took place in front of the Ateneum on opening day. It involved African drumming, gamely approximated by Finnish musicians. Choreographer Reijo Kela arrayed 28 teenagers from the city's theater high school on oil barrels. Dressed in black and white and shamanistically wielding pine branches, they danced free-form for seven hours. That's right, seven hours. I heard and believe that the local philosophy of theatrical education emphasizes physical conditioning. Full of themselves above the passing crowds in Railway Square — against a great installation of 364 rippling green-and-white striped flags by Daniel Buren and the sublime National-Romantic-style train station of Eliel Saarinen — the kids were strictly over the top, but they were so gorgeous and their energy was so unreal they made me crazy. Having taken individual breaks now and then, all of them and all the drummers went flat out for the last hour, and you could see bystanders going to pieces. It was like a cavalry charge. I felt, "Stop, stop; no, don't stop!" I sensed a subterranean connection to the all-time peak of Finnish art, the gloriously neurotic turn-of-the-century National Romantic paintings centerpieced in the Ateneum (where resides one of history's strangest images, Hugo Simberg's 1903 *Wounded Angel*), and also to a currently dawning turn of the century marked, again, by surging nationalisms, apocalyptic intimations, and a general precipitation of everything.

I thought of it in Leningrad, where apocalypse is now. That city is huge and grand beyond anything I expected. Its early-19th-century structures by the amazing C. L. Engel, who worked also in Finland, help make the initial impression of a giganticized Helsinki, with aspects of Paris and Amsterdam thrown in. But, besides skin-deep, the beauty is a patch that unravels within a block of the Winter Palace, revealing palimpsests of squalor. The tour I had lucked into — of art people convened for the opening of a Rubens show at the Finnish lake-country resort of Retretti — went to the Hermitage. There I was overwhelmed, naturally, by the Rembrandts, Gauguins, and Picassos and by a room of

Matisses that nearly forced me down on my knees. Like most other lovely things in Leningrad, the staggering modern holdings, amassed by some of the most creative collectors who ever lived, end abruptly in 1914. Meanwhile, in a separate exhibition building of the Hermitage, there was a show of, get ready, Peter Max. I wish I could find that amusing. But the evidence of near-term Soviet vulnerability to Western hustlers is too ghastly. With its stupid Revolution finished, the USSR may be in for a revolution of imported stupidities.

I can't prove it, but I think the solutions, good and ill, for that part of the world will entail magic, especially of old ethnic and national mysteries. I thought this during yet another Ateneum performance, at official opening ceremonies attended by Finnish president Mauno Koivisto. Charismatically mournful-looking Koivisto, his hangdog features over excellent bone structure evoking a thousand forest nights, sat in the front row of the auditorium alone with his wife Tellervo. The evening ended with two bearded Danish veterans of Fluxus, sculptor Bjorn Norgaard and composer Henning Christiansen, on stage wearing huge hooked plaster cones as hats and as codpieces and feathered chicken wings all over. Lurching around the stage and sometimes climbing a ladder, they made caveman noises, baby noises, animal noises, bird noises, and mineral noises, a racket from a primeval Baltic of the mind. What a terrific culture! Imagine George Bush thus regaled — not that the U.S. has qualified shamans. From where I sat, Koivisto looked exceptionally mournful. But Christiansen told me afterwards that Tellervo had laughed throughout. I like to think she comforted her husband later.

MARCEL BROODTHAERS: THE COMPLETE PRINTS
Michael Werner Gallery

I KEEP WAITING TO LIKE Marcel Broodthaers. The Belgian poet-artist, who died of a liver disorder in 1976 on his fifty-second birthday, has become known in the U.S. by fits and starts since the early 1980s, when many of us first caught wind of his charismatic reputation (not exactly a cult, but assuredly a following). Broodthaers made his name on the Dusseldorf-Cologne scene of the '60s and early '70s, a milieu emerging in retrospect as one of the great creative crucibles of the century. (Joseph Beuys, Sigmar Polke, Gerhard Richter, and Anselm Kiefer, among others, hit their strides there.) Like the also prematurely dead Blinky Palermo (an inventive abstract painter), he is cherished by influential veterans of that scene who may agree on little else. His apostles to America range from fire-breathing Marxist-oriented critic Benjamin H. D. Buchloh, who edited a Broodthaers issue of *October* in 1987, to heavyweight Cologne dealer Michael Werner, currently showing the artist's prints and multiples in his New York space. Such variegated enthusiasm makes me feel I am missing something and, increasingly, that I will continue to miss it. Maybe you had to be there.

Or maybe you have to be European, at least vicariously — identifying with trans-Atlantic romances of an aristocratic or vanguard (or both) intelligentsia embattled by bourgeois and/or American vulgarity. Something like that percolates in the interminable interpretations imposed by certain critics on Broodthaers's subtly satirical texts, objects, films, and installations. For Douglas Crimp, writing in the catalogue of a retrospective at the Walker Art Center in Minneapolis two years ago, Broodthaers represents "the necessary stance of the artist working under the conditions of late capitalism." For Buchloh, the Belgian artist mournfully prophesied the cooptation of the rebellions of 1968 (in which Broodthaers somewhat gingerly participated) and "the complete transformation of artistic production into a branch of the culture industry."

That's a lot to lay on a gnomic poet who announced his

midcareer switch to art with a wry statement in 1964: "I, too, wondered if I couldn't sell something and succeed in life. For quite a while I had been good for nothing. I am forty years old. . . . The idea of inventing something insincere finally crossed my mind, and I set to work at once." But the critics' determination to make Broodthaers one of their honorary team captains (tipped off by ritual references to Walter Benjamin) is as inexorable as Michael Werner's drive to promote him.

The target of these projections seems to have been a most appealing character, not to be understood too quickly. As a young poet, he tended toward dreamy Symbolism. His heroes were Baudelaire, Mallarmé, and his older countryman Magritte. A biographical essay by Michael Compton in the Walker catalogue (published by Rizzoli) turns up some fetching anecdotes, including one about Broodthaers's youthful service in the Belgian wartime Resistance: he blundered badly when, on account of who knows what crossed associative thoughts, he delivered a secret message to an address on a street named Lake instead of a street named Valley.

In postwar Brussels, Broodthaers penned verse bestiaries, did some art criticism, worked as a publisher of small-edition books, and struggled to raise a family in bohemian poverty. In 1962 he met the Italian avant-gardist Piero Manzoni, who wrote his signature on Broodthaers and declared him a work of art. That was an era of explosive development for European avant-gardes, set off by the shock of American Pop art. With anti-American disdain then common among European intellectuals, Broodthaers wrote at the time that Pop was "only possible in a context of societies devoted to publicity stunts, overproduction, and horoscopes." But it goaded him.

"At the end of three months," Broodthaers continued in his 1964 statement, "I showed what I had produced to Philippe Edouard Toussaint, the owner of the Galerie Saint-Laurent. 'But it is Art,' he said, 'and I shall willingly exhibit all of it.'" His early work included assemblages in the vein of French New Realism with a sweet redolence of domestic life: pots of mussel shells, arrangements of eggshells, faces cut from magazines and displayed in canning jars. In a key gesture, he encased copies of his latest book of poems in plaster, musing on the destructive transformation of his unsaleable life's work into a surefire art commodity.

By 1968 Broodthaers was accompanying his flow of works with a series of "open letters" tweaking the art game, light-handed texts flavored with a delicate cynicism and offering Zen advice on the order of "don't feel sold before you have been bought, or only just." (Broodthaers's careful ambiguity, suspicion of politics, and allergy to jargon do not, of course, conceal from his exegetes that he agreed, or would have, with their ideas.) His most ambitious works were imaginary museums, installations combining art reproductions, common objects, obsessive images (eagles a multisymbolic specialty), intricate wordplay, and much museological paraphernalia: labels, display cases, vitrines.

Mingling satire on commercial and institutional culture with nostalgia for the disinterested passion of premodern collectors, Broodthaers's art-world actions established him as a sort of drier, unmystical Joseph Beuys (Beuys Lite, perhaps), a thinking person's shaman.

The 27 multiples at Werner reward contemplation, which is lucky because they demand it. (This is a show for one of those summer afternoons when, finding yourself in an airconditioned pleasant place, you are not eager to face the streets again and have a commensurately enhanced attention span.) Most are book-printed (letterpress or offset) compositions of words and pictures. The words are by Broodthaers and the pictures are from magazines, encyclopedias, comic books, postcards, old illustrations, and so on. There is some drawing, revealing that this artist couldn't draw worth a darn.

His forte was layout-and-design, bringing parodic order to deliciously cracked concepts. In one work, a poster chart of cattle breeds is labeled with the brand names of automobiles. Another is a money-exchange chart in which so many signed initials of the artist are taken to equal so many Deutschmarks or dollars. Most of the rest, including a deluxe-packaged wine bottle making obscure reference to Edgar Allan Poe's *The Manuscript Found in a Bottle*, defy description in one or several sentences, but each work packs a peculiar tickle. Some mildly haunt, such as the postcard image of a violent storm at sea titled with the opening of a message scribbled on it in 1901: *Dear Little Sister*. Rebus-like puzzles abound. Written verbal riffs (in French) have lyric bounce: "The man of letters. . . . The woman of letters, the boy of letters. . . . The woman of letters and her son."

There is a sense of being let in on the energy, though not the content, of an intensely private sensibility, in ways reminiscent of early Jasper Johns. Broodthaers communicated the fun of having secrets, a fun that telling the secrets would spoil. Still, the show is thin, overall, and a mite grueling.

In relation to Pop's lively vulgarization of fine art, Broodthaers's enterprise was essentially reactive rather than responsive. That is (unlike his contemporaries Polke and Richter, whose self-styled "Capitalist Realism" competed with American Pop and, being tougher and smarter, led to art that eclipsed it), Broodthaers was content to ironize in the margins of cultural change. That is his main limitation, though also his charm, as an artist. A conservative European at heart, whatever radical sympathies his mind may have harbored, he seems to have been offended not ideologically but spiritually and personally by the brash new art culture of commerce and entertainment, but he was not about to let it ruffle him.

The upshot is a slightly smug self-withholding, a refusal of feeling — the mask of injured superiority. Of course, this quality is the very thing that recommends Broodthaers to critics likewise nettled in their intellectual pride by the mindlessness of contemporary culture. They view his stoniness as "resistance" (and have little use for the wit that softens it). For myself, I quite prefer Broodthaers the Resistance worker who went to the right address on the wrong street because, I speculate, his fastidious poetic taste revised the overly general "valley" into the more specific "lake." My Broodthaers smacks little of Walter Benjamin, much of Don Quixote.

THRIFT STORE PAINTINGS
Organized by Jim Shaw   Metro Pictures

You LIVE A FEW DECADES. You figure you know quite a bit, at least in your chosen field. Then something makes you wonder if you know even what your chosen field is. I feel this way — blindsided, beggared — as an art critic at the moment, fresh from my third befuddling visit to an exhibition called "Thrift Store Paintings." You have probably heard of the show already. It is an event. Go with a friend for moral support and fun. Nearly 200 ragamuffin paintings — hobbyist and hack work bought for prices never exceeding $25, we are told, from thrift-store bins, flea markets, and other penultimate stops on the way to landfill — make for a great walk-in conversation piece. Being able to talk as you look also may reassure you that you are not going crazy or anyway not going crazy solitarily.

"Thrift Store Paintings" is mostly from artist Jim Shaw's collection, augmented by loans from fellow picture-scavengers. It seems there are many such scavengers, comprising a sect of the garage-sale cult, and I expect that the vogue for this show will inspire others to go public. (Just wait. By Christmas we will see a wave of such paintings in boutiques, and forget about paying $25.) However, Shaw's collection, which was shown to acclaim in his native Los Angeles last year and is featured in a delectable picture book (Heavy Industry Publications), differs sharply from that of your normal trash maven, and not just in quantity and, so to speak, quality. (Shaw has stated his criterion of value this way: "I am looking for something strange, or driven, in the mind of the artist.") "Thrift Store Paintings" amounts to a conceptual art work on the cutting (or at least abrading) edge of contemporary sensibility, which increasingly seems to mean sensibility tempered in some spiritual microwave of Southern California.

Shaw is best known for an ongoing voluminous series, "My Mirage," of many-styled small narrative works documenting the febrile inner life — compound of sex, drugs, rock-'n'-roll, art, and Catholic guilt — of a late-1960s adolescent named Billy. Shaw's teeming output, of which "Thrift Store Paintings" must be seen as a part, exemplifies an emerging trend that last year I termed the New Low. (Nobody out there picked up on this coinage. I will give everybody one more chance.) The New Low pertains to work, worthless-looking in form and abject in content, that tends to be about "inarticulation, failure, and rejection," to quote critic Ralph Rugoff's announcement of a prophetic group show he curated a year ago in Los Angeles. (Rugoff's proposed name for the movement: "Just Pathetic.") The New Low consolidates a generational turn against the variously inflated art culture of the 1980s, a defiant reveling in creative sheer fecundity suggesting a philosophy of gardening keyed to producing not cucumbers and lilies but compost. "Thrift Store Paintings" is a compost Giverny.

Nothing in the show is for sale. It is a gesture of disinterested lunatic connoisseurship, painstakingly arranged by Shaw according to genres of portraits, animals, cityscapes, abstraction, nudes, psychedelia, etc. Shaw's descriptive titles for the works evince exacting scrutiny: *Girl with Cigar-Like Flute and Goats, Moody Jerry Lewis-Like Boy, Scared Brunette Woman Looks at the Moon.* All artists guaranteed unknown, despite frequent signatures. (Shaw told me he regretfully declined the loan of a picture when informed that it was by the owner's grandmother.) A few of the paintings approach the glib finish of kitsch, a few might be termed "outsider" for their compulsiveness or "folk" for their charm, a few are obviously commercial illustrations (with something twisted about them), and some display enough trained self-consciousness to qualify as third- or fourth-rate high art. But these are all exceptions, or parameters, to a predominant mass of uncategorizable and, because so nebulous in style, effectively indescribable lumpen expression. What to call it? Painting. It can only be called painting. Very, very bad painting, but answering needs that also drove Velázquez.

As orchestrated by Shaw at Metro, the passions of bumbling amateurs to make worlds in rectangles, just like the old masters did, give an art critic vertigo by seeming to dissociate taste and quality, triggering delight that thumbs its nose at judgment. Badness — in any art, a palpable slippage between intention and result — usually forestalls pleasure by producing an unstable situation where one cannot relax into contemplation. Of course, the choice to contemplate can be perverse. It can be camp. But camp does not apply to "Thrift Store Paintings," in which one takes straightforward joy in work more or less straightforwardly lousy. The work's disjointed intentions and results are stabilized by Jim Shaw's selection and presentation. The upshot is a lesson in the power of curatorial aesthetics, which is where Shaw's real subversiveness rears its head.

Shaw's orchestration of the paintings — each chosen for a psychological quirk, "something strange, or driven, in the mind of the artist" — is loaded with subliminal cues to "artistic experience" and carefully insulated from distracting information. His aversion to learning anything about the artists is a tipoff, as is a compacted hanging that scrambles formal consistencies, period styles (whiffs of zeitgeist from Surrealism to Neo-Expressionism), and other potentially objectifying handles on the stuff. Shaw plays the quirks of the pictures against each other to a mutually intensifying effect that, when you are in tune with the show, can be like one of those pop-scientific demonstrations of a nuclear chain reaction with pingpong balls and mousetraps. (I am not mentioning individual works, because their synergy, not their identity, is what matters. You have to be there.) The show ends up being not about worlds in paintings but about paintings in the world.

"Thrift Store Paintings" is a serious travesty about genres, pictorial lexicons, connoisseurship, and markets of painting. We are invited to do with this art what experts and aesthetes do with any art. We can classify structures, identify influences, psychoanalyze motives, savor and compare qualities, and appraise relative worth, experiencing these conceptual operations free of high-cultural baggage, for the hell of it. Anonymous amateur painting serves Shaw less in its own right, perhaps, than in the way genetically uncontaminated white rats serve laboratory experimenters. It is a means for him, not an end — a means with the New Low cynosure of naked abjection safely beneath the reach of market rationality, academic intellect, and other oppressions of culture. His end seems to be an assault on those oppressions, humiliating them in order to comfort the already humiliated — the inarticulate, the failed, the rejected — among us and inside us. Shaw plots an art-world coup led by a boy named Billy.

THE INTERRUPTED LIFE
Curated by France Morin   *The New Museum of Contemporary Art*

Upstate recently I enjoyed the autumn foliage and was riveted especially by a heartbreaking little trick nature plays with trees whose leaves turn pale yellow. Seen from afar when an exact mix of yellow and late-summer sullen green is reached, the trees are ringers for trees in springtime, alight with the tender green of May. So in the moment before its extinction the landscape flashes this illusion of new life, which you could say either mocks hope or holds out a consoling promise, or both, if you want to indulge in the pathetic fallacy, and why not? I am for grasping metaphors wherever possible, because one cannot live without metaphors.

The New Museum's much-discussed "death show" begins with a work by Donald Moffett that efficiently combines metaphor and moral exhortation. Installed in the museum's lobby, it comprises 100 identical small round light-boxes, each bearing a gorgeous photograph of a fleshy white rose overlaid with the printed word "MERCY." The rose is a metaphor of life's sweetness and fragility, life's deservingness and need of the special consideration — deference of power to the powerless — that is mercy. The repetition of the word all over the wall evokes the harmonized shout of a gospel choir. Addressed to the AIDS catastrophe (each light-box, we are told, represents 1,000 deaths), Moffett's piece suggested to me that after all these horrible years we may be developing a public rhetoric of mourning that consoles, even as it confronts, relentless loss.

Then I saw the rest of the show and changed my mind. This is a ghastly show, on purpose but with a purpose deeply addled. It is masochistically numbing — deadening, in fact. I came out of it with my sensibilities thoroughly on the fritz, except for a rebellious urge to hilarity. What can you say about the tone of a lurid exhibition about death titled ever so daintily *The Interrupted Life?* Isn't that like calling something about plane crashes *The Inconvenienced Flight Plan?* This show and its overdesigned catalogue (with dense theoretical essays printed, to nicely funereal but hardly readable effect, on dark gray paper) manage to be alternately gross and fussy. Still, the organizers must be credited with bravely raising a subject so important that the occasion for having a go at it should not be wasted.

France Morin, the curator in charge, starts from the unexceptionable premise that Western, and especially North American, culture is fucked up in its dealings with death. She proceeds unwittingly to demonstrate why, taking an approach that, like the culture's, is oblivious to our need for serviceable rituals, availing metaphors, and other common ways to avow while allaying our fears. In this society we die as we live (and as we make art): pretty much alone, or in fragmentary communities. We quite sensibly keep the brute phenomenon of death out of sight and out of mind, because under the circumstances contemplation can hardly be other than a useless ordeal. Morin seems to think that unflinching scrutiny — a "long hard look at death," in her words — is the solution. More likely it is an aspect of the problem, or would be if it were even possible.

No one has seen death. It is a concept, not a thing. You can look only at such evidence of it as corpses or yellowed leaves, and if emotional coping is your aim you probably had best start with the leaves, or maybe dead small animals if you are really tough. Like many of the artists incautious enough to submit their individual expressions to the charnel spectacle of *The Interrupted Life*, Morin goes straight to dead humans, often mutilated, and thus makes an excellent case for repression.

(I thought of a friend who had to tell her little daughter that the hamster had died overnight. "Where is he?" the girl asked. "Well," said my friend, mind swimming with metaphysical conundrums, "his body is in the cage." Her daughter wailed, "Where's his head?")

There are morgue photos galore. There is an interestingly repulsive continuously projected film by Peter Greenaway, *Death in the Seine*, that uses an erudite historical pretext (mortuary documents from post-Revolutionary Paris) to justify innumerable avidly slow pans of naked actors playing dead. And jaded aesthetes may savor a collection of mostly 19th-century sentimental photographs of dead children in doll-like poses. Good works by Christian Boltanski, Andy Warhol, Bruce Nauman, and others don't stand a chance here, their subtleties drowning in the ambient Grand Guignol. The point of it all, for anyone less inured than a coroner, can only be morbid titillation: aesthetic sensation taking over from feeling in a last-ditch responsiveness to horror, after which all the hatches of the heart shut down tight.

How to keep the heart open in face of death? Other cultures know how. They do it with festivals — always at least partly religious, of course. Without quasi-religious balancing of fear and reassurance, if only in a metaphor's suspension of disbelief, thinking about death at all may be a mistake. It will only make you feel bad. (It may incline you to make others feel bad, too, on the misery-loves-company principle that possibly explains this show.) The festival with which I am a bit familiar — the Mexican, especially Oaxacan, Day of the Dead — tells me what a successful cultural integration of death can be like: funny, frightening, and profound. It works by blurring distinctions between the living and the dead. In Oaxaca on November 1 you get that the dead are not exactly dead. You also get — as I didn't right away, having it sink in dismayingly when it was too late to withhold my emotional participation — that the living are not exactly alive. It's a trade-off: some of our life for them, some of their death for us, and laughter to seal the bargain.

Death is embarrassing. It is radical disempowerment, you could say. The dead require mercy that may include the mercy of humor to cover the awkwardness of their situation, in which we will join them soon enough. While alive, to rehearse being dead — with propriety, with panache — seems a secret of death festivals, of which our culture is grotesquely bereft. (Maybe the saddest thing at the New Museum is a section of blank books in which visitors are invited to write their thoughts on death. Whether earnest or flip, the several dozen entries I read were uniform in all-American crashing banality.) Art might partly and intermittently make good the lack, but only with extreme tact. To anesthetize fear with shock — building up callouses on painful nerve ends — is a tactic properly left to horror movies. We want something else from art, something that publicly nourishes deep roots of feeling.

BRICE MARDEN: COLD MOUNTAIN
Dia Center for the Arts

VALENTINE'S DAY COMES EARLY for me this season. What follows is a great big red paper heart with doilies for Brice Marden.

How good is Brice Marden? Brice Marden is so good that there is no present way of judging how good he is. He is off the charts for fresh, convincing new abstract painting. Of course, those charts are limited. In the three decades that coincide with Marden's career, abstraction on canvas has declined from the living end of modern art to a respectable but often sleepy suburb of the contemporary. We have masters big and little, too many to start naming. And a few gifted recalcitrants in every generation continue to enlist in the cause, if it is a cause — as I am afraid it is for many, at times taking on the forced, tinny overtones of a minor cult. But only Marden reliably makes me, for one, feel that abstract painting is not only still possible but absolutely necessary. Only Marden, lately, has created a new style that — as individual talent is supposed to in T. S. Eliot's famous idea — recharges the tradition that nurtures and burdens him.

Dia has on long-term display six huge paintings, each nine by twelve feet, and many drawings and prints. Done over the last three years, the works are collectively titled *Cold Mountain* after an ancient Chinese poet known by that name, a crotchety Taoist wanderer. Here are two typically laconic and luminous lines from a Cold Mountain poem, translated by Gary Snyder: "Freely drifting, I prowl the woods and streams / And linger watching things themselves." That might almost be spoken by the abstract protagonist of Marden's current art — an animate line that prowls picture-space, bringing it everywhere to enraptured life. Marden's webby, tensile linear networks, fitting into the canvas edges like springs slightly compressed, derive from years of experiment with Asian-inspired calligraphy, and their thinly painted atmospheric textures give more than a whiff of classical Chinese landscape painting. The cross-cultural references are finally — though also pointedly — incidental to an experience of pictures that are very Western, very New York. Painter Gary Stephan has remarked to me that, of course, Asian stylistic influences were crucial in the formation of Abstract Expressionism in the 1940s.

With the *Cold Mountain* canvases, Marden recasts the New York-type big painting invented by Clyfford Still, Mark Rothko, Barnett Newman, and especially Jackson Pollock. The formal key of such painting is a double scale: enveloping, virtually boundless, allover image and discrete, matter-of-fact, local mark. When it works, you get extremes of generality and specificity — field and touch, disembodiment and bodiment — simultaneously, and they take you out of yourself. What makes it work is not mere command of the form. That was Clement Greenberg's mistake, thinking that great art could be reduced to a recipe. (He will say he didn't do that, but there is no other way of interpreting his embrace of dismal rote-following Color Fielders.) The big painting needs a metaphor. It needs poetry that grounds its aesthetic doubleness in a doubleness of life. Pollock realized a metaphor that is right up there, in American culture, with Melville's white whale — symbolizing misery and bliss, terror and mad joy, of existing. When you really look at a great Pollock, you get, inextricably, a dog peeing on a wall and the music of the spheres. It still feels radical, even shocking, if you give yourself over to it.

Marden has always worked within that tradition, though in ways cooled down and wised up by the collapse, in the late '50s, of big-painting metaphor into empty rhetoric, on the one hand, and tepid formalism, on the other. (By the early '60s, the most convincing big paintings, such as those of Andy Warhol and Frank Stella, were brutally and sensationally unemotional — degree zero, freeze-drying the form.) Along with Agnes Martin, Robert Ryman, Ralph Humphrey, and a few others, Marden kept the old Abstract Expressionist poetry barely alive — with a "barely" radiating poignance — in middle-sized paintings that stirred middle-sized emotions. The doubleness of his oil-wax monochromes went like this: disembodiment of ineffable color and embodiment of fleshy surface. The effect was hypersensitive, seductive, aching. It had an edgy sensual sophistication, like Manet, and a raffish romantic bleakness, like Lou Reed. Likewise rawnerved were Marden's densely gridded bleeding-line ink drawings. His complete separation of painting from drawing as activities, seeming to sacrifice wholeness for survival, communicated a sense of unresolvable crisis in art — a sense vouching for his pained authenticity.

From the mid '70s to the mid '80s, Marden's painting got bigger and less good as he rigged monochrome panels into post-and-lintel architectonic arrays whose evocation of Greek temples and so on rang hollow. Then his drawing took off, in hundreds of spiky-doodly ink calligraphs. It was an intensive exercise in stream-of-consciousness improvisation like nothing since Willem de Kooning's self-renewing burst of drawing, often left-handed or with eyes closed, in the '60s, and it would pay off in a similarly reinvigorated painting style. Marden was loading his hand with remembered possible mark-making gestures, which he then transferred, awkwardly at first, to his arm. His drawing-like strokes with sword-length brushes deployed paint thinned with turpineol (a powerful solvent enabling watery consistencies still dense with pigment) on gesso sanded to speedy smoothness, making for a risky process in which his slightest muscular twitch would have dramatic consequences. The upshot was painting of a new — and old — kind.

The *Cold Mountain* paintings are like Pollocks in slow motion. Pollock's dripped line flies. Marden's stroked line travels on foot. Both get where they are going, which is to interstices of incessant surprise — places where lines sail over and under each other and places where they jam up like too many people trying to use a doorway. The effect is literally phenomenal: not something that happened but something that is happening, becoming itself before your eyes. You see an accumulation of decisions that could have gone all sorts of ways other than the ways they go. Every move gives a little lurching sensation of sudden resolution conquering hesitancy. (Pentimenti of painted-over lines, like ghosts of error, haunt the backgrounds.) Marden's resolution is palpably attended by an irritable aversion to any form that might be expectable, anything like a cliche. I marvel at the sustained courage of pictures as big as the *Cold Mountain* suite, by far the largest single canvases he has attempted.

The work's success is sometimes a close call in terms of surplus energy — felt as lyrical profusion — left over from the struggle of satisfactorily composing impulsive marks over such an expanse. You may sense the sweat as, sitting in one of the director chairs thoughtfully provided at Dia, you watch the pictures. Though instantaneously beautiful, this is exceedingly slow art. It takes several minutes to grasp the personality of each picture, each being sharply distinctive in rhythm, color (pale tints amid the umber lines), and degree of vellum-like translucency, among other things. Whatever the attrition, all the paintings do triumph — and to my mind the best one, a terrific snarly fiesta, promisingly turns out to be the most recent. Then there is the bonus, after the exertion, of going into the rooms of drawings and prints, whose insouciant utter confidence and abandon made me feel I had been jumped by a gang of seraphim.

I suppose that Marden's apparent revival of the abstract big painting may be just a lovely illusion, a cunning hybrid without power to propagate. Certainly the comparison with Pollock, which he invites, is not exactly in Marden's favor. It reveals the relative modesty of his metaphor, his doubleness of life: a certain gawky mooncalf sincerity in tension with a certain courtly, elevated artifice. But when the worst is said of him, there remain those singing pictures full of qualities that had seemed long lost to contemporary art, qualities of individual soulful candor couched in a high public ceremonial idiom. This may be late work, at the mannered end of a tradition, but it shows, against the common sense of skeptics, that the end of the end is not yet. So I predict that Marden's achievement will go from strength to strength, in his own work and that of others heartened by him. Stranger things have happened, and when given a chance to hope, I am for hoping.

"WOMEN" BY WILLEM DE KOONING AND JEAN DUBUFFET *Pace Gallery*

WHEN A BOY WANTS TO FEEL LIKE A BAD BOY— most boys want to feel they are bad sometimes, some want to feel they are bad most times, and some are bad (beware these) — a reliable way is to draw a dirty or anyway derisive picture of a woman, or more likely of Woman. Bad-boy drawings may be caricatures of, say, a despised teacher, if the boy draws well enough that anyone can tell, but normally they take the most economical linear route to the double message "female" and "stupid." The graphic transgression momentarily relieves the boy's woe at being short, in all ways, on power. If the boy is a good boy, the drawing also makes him ashamed. The pleasure of being bad for a good boy is rarely worth the shame it costs, and he soon stops doing dirty drawings. Or he becomes an artist.

A grownup straight male artist is perhaps a good boy who has made a vocation of maximizing the pleasure of being bad while minimizing its expense in shame. He may dream of Pablo Picasso: full-time bad boy, shameless, who incidentally got all the girls and made the timorous badness in good boys weep with envy. But he is not Picasso, and he is never going to become Picasso. He has to face that. He makes drawings that might not look like drawings of a woman, or of Woman, though they sort of are. He makes art, or Art, in which furtive badness mysteriously feeds apparent goodness, or Quality. In his heart, pleasure and shame dance the old dance. Usually, this is the gist of his story, in which nothing dramatic happens.

A show at the Pace Gallery spotlights a moment in art history, around 1950, when the stories of two men hardly immature in years or powerless in their respective milieux took similar dramatic turns. Each man was deemed by some, including himself, the best contemporary painter in his art world. Independently of each other in New York and Paris, Willem de Kooning and Jean Dubuffet made series of dirty and derisive pictures of Woman more frankly vehement than anything comparable in big-time, cutting-edge art (not eccentric or a tour de force, but stage-center in its time) before or since. I am interested in why that happened. (There is a large difference in quality between the two artists, which viewers can see for themselves. It does not concern me here.) I am interested, too, in a consequence of that moment, which overloaded and thereby lastingly damaged conventions of Romantic sincerity in the art of painting.

De Kooning's "Women" (not his designation, but the common term) and Dubuffet's *Corps de dames* (the Frenchman's typically sarcastic title) were to some extent consciously destructive acts, involving in the first case what de Kooning called "the female painted through all the ages, all those idols" and in the second what Dubuffet denounced as the association of the female body "(for Occidentals) with a very specious notion of beauty." "Surely I aim for a beauty," Dubuffet said, "but not that one." Notes of liberation were sounded, in other words, but liberation from what? The beauty of Dubuffet's Woman pictures — in which the female form is a splayed, big-genitaled, tiny-headed, graffiti-flat totem — is mineral, an effect of textures sometimes fleshlike but mostly alluvial. The beauty of de Kooning's — in which the female has blindly staring eyes, one or more sets of ferocious teeth, and a massive body hard to locate in welters of paint — is virtuosic, a dazzling display of line and color simultaneously constructing and tearing apart the picture as the viewer watches. The overwhelming impression in each instance is of the artist's willfulness.

De Kooning's and Dubuffet's travesties of the female figure, revered central theme of Western painting since the Renaissance, still astound, partly because they seem so self-lacerating. A paradox of bad boy drawings of Woman is germane: the drive to reduce the female to a derisory cipher of sexuality invests it with devouring power, broadcasting the boy's sense of puniness. (Is that why the good boy is ashamed? Because he has made a spectacle of his fear?) De Kooning's female grows more fearsome the more he attacks her. The cliche word for his brushwork in these pictures is "slashing," but of course the Woman is made of the swipes he takes at her. The effect of a Pygmalion despite himself is generically comic, a self-mocking buffoonery, but you would have to be either very thick-skinned or hysterical to laugh at it. The fact of denigration — of Woman, of painting, of the artist himself — is so general that to get involved with the pictures is to incur your own taste of being denigrated, and it does not savor of mirth.

I remember bad boys, the older ones on the playground who used obscene language and gestures to intimidate us younger boys with their sexual knowledge and power (never mind that they were probably bluffing). I remember the feeling of awe and misery that I wanted to hide behind a cool mask but never could. Responses of inferiority from other boys are the bad boy's constantly sought bitter satisfaction. He doesn't care if he is tipping the hand of his own abjection so long as he can render others even more abject. Do I think that de Kooning and Dubuffet (like Picasso, who intimidated *them*) were motivated by bitter playground machismo? I do. It adds up when you know their career situations at the time.

They were older boys, for one thing, on competitive scenes where public attention was just beginning and pecking orders were being worked out. De Kooning, 46 years old in 1950, and Dubuffet, 49, were on the brink of fame after lives of grinding frustration. Make believe you are the more disaffected of the two, Dubuffet, until recently a wine merchant humiliated in your artistic ambitions two decades earlier by the disdain of art-world coteries. You are going to take no condescension this time, because it is your turn. You see younger artists in your war-groggy capital trying to revive high-taste School of Paris pictorial cuisine, and you think: pathetic. You will take the lads into the pissoirs and show them what their precious painting is about.

Now consider that you are de Kooning, with a well established downtown reputation as a painter's painter. Among other things, you draw like an angel. But just as you start to win the game, the rules change. With critic Clement Greenberg improvising theory for it, a brand of de-composed abstraction evolves and is promoted as the living end. It is tailored perfectly for Jackson Pollock, Barnett Newman, and so on who, among other things, can't draw worth much. You are threatened with being old-hat before you have gotten to be new-hat. At your easel, you commence to throw an expedient tantrum.

Why were the cockfights in question conducted so explicitly over the symbolic body of Woman? I surmise that the model of

Picasso, whose priapism raged on, was a factor, as was the recent reign of surrealism and its poisoned-sugar obsessions with the feminine. Such sexualizations of art were rapidly being suppressed in the time's newly respectable, intellectual, professional art worlds, in which working-class de Kooning and petit-bourgeois Dubuffet felt acutely uncomfortable. Maybe they figured they stood less chance in a discussion of aesthetics than in a bar brawl, and the fiercest bar brawls are over women (with whom they have little actually to do).

Whatever the reason, de Kooning and Dubuffet went and did it, hellbent to shock. They conflated creation and desecration in a way that every bad boy knows the desolate joy of, and the power of what they did remains as indelible as its awfulness. Like violence, their Woman pictures induce a state where you can't believe that something is happening, but it is, and you wish it would stop, but it hasn't yet.

ALLEN RUPPERSBERG: PERSONAL ART
Christine Burgin Gallery

In the late '70s a spate of winsome Conceptual art moved me to propose a new movement: Cutism. That was mean — meaner, for the joke's sake, than I meant, because I didn't want to condemn, exactly. I did want to mark work that filled austere self-referring forms of Conceptual art with cheery self-referring content of the artist's personal quirks and obsessions, as if art were a playpen for frisky narcissists. Somewhat a frisky narcissist myself, I had cause to go easy. What bothered me was just a little too much coziness in presumptions of mutual approval between artists and audiences.

It was a matter of degree. Some artists, such as Chris Burden and William Wegman, were spectacularly narcissistic in their work, but with enough attendant rigor, melancholy, doggedness (Wegman in more than one way), or pugnacity hardly to be Cutist. Maybe no artist could be purely Cutist. Cutism was simply the extreme of a collective drift toward theatricalized self-absorption. It was easy to insult. Critic Carrie Rickey wrote of "Naive Nouveau," Craig Owens of "Puerilism."

I now drop the past tense. Never having quite gone away, Cutism is back, tincturing work by perhaps most of the up-and-coming young American artists of an emerging '90s spirit. It precipitates regularly in the liveliest downtown galleries, including Feature, 303, American Fine Arts, Cugliani, Hearn, Gorney, and Andrea Rosen. Much of it is a variant — whose doyen is Mike Kelley — that I think of as Rancid Cutism, fascinated with the emotion of treacly stuff (stuffed toys are *the* early-'90s material) nudging over into revulsion. (Rancid Cutism eclipses the Cryogenic Cutism of, for instance, Jeff Koons, who vests treacly stuff with icy glamor. Expensive looks are insufferable to the new taste.) The strongest, so far unnameable trend, seen in the likes of Jim Shaw, Karen Kilimnick, and Jack Pierson, is toward shaggy autobiographical engagement with sexy and dire effects of American extended adolescence. All of it is Cutist to the extent that it needs complicit viewers and makes their complicity a work's main pivot of pleasure. Such art croons antic or husky undertones to seduce viewers into sharing its maker's smitten or, sometimes, appalled self-contemplation.

Economic recession helps explain the timing of Neo-Cutism. As during the draggy '70s, a down art market foreshortens the horizon for competition among artists. With fame and fortune largely out of the question, available career rewards shrivel toward in-group popularity. It might be the serious kind of popularity indicated by the phrase "an artist's artist." But Cutism is quicker. If in doubt, be fun. In times of fear and frustration, fun may be no joke. When taking demoralization head-on, art in a Cutist vein realizes the serious value of giving morale new footings. Such was the effect of a marvelous recent group show at American Fine Arts, imported from Los Angeles by curator Ralph Rugoff, with the Zen-Cutist title *Just Pathetic*. (The artists included David Hammons, Cady Noland, and Raymond Pettibon — three powerfully poetic souls I will call, because I cannot help myself, Trans-Cutists.) The imperative to ingratiate may be only good manners when people are depressed. And dedicated self-display, if the self in question is sufficiently interesting, can provide an exemplary public service when people are struggling for rudimentary senses of identity.

What launched me on this ramble is a show of five installational works, four from the '70s and early '80s and one brand new, by Allen Ruppersberg. Ruppersberg, born in 1944, is a Classic Cutist, perhaps, as well as something of an artist's artist — a veteran, perennially both esteemed and obscure, of an early-'70s generation that is coming in for timely renewed attention. Like Wegman and Alexis Smith, seen in current retrospectives at the Whitney Museum, Ruppersberg got his bearings in Southern California. He displays the distinctive combination of stringent Conceptual strategies and voluptuous self-involvement (part Marcel Duchamp, part Joseph Cornell) that used to make Los Angeles feel like the art culture of the future and now increasingly makes it feel like the art culture of the present. Unlike Wegman and Smith, and unlike Cutist eminence grise John Baldessari, Ruppersberg has never been at pains to formularize an eye-grabbing, crowd-pleasing style. Though given to flavorful nostalgias for decayed popular culture, arcane Americana, and beloved books — having once copied out in longhand the complete texts of *Walden* and *The Portrait of Dorian Gray* — he makes art that is strangely ascetic. (His opposite is Smith, who communicates similar nostalgic preoccupations with strenuous gorgeousness and the insouciance of a prom-decorating committee.)

The most interesting early works in Ruppersberg's show are two enigmatic "drawing projects," as they are termed in the gallery press release. *Great Acts of the Imagination: Volume I: World War II* comprises nine pencil drawings, apparently made with the aid of an opaque projector, from wartime photographs including shots of Hitler, Churchill, and troops of both sides in combat. Five actual photographs show a typewriter on which somebody or other has begun a memoir. "I shook hands with Adolf Hitler at a Party Rally in September, 1934," reads one. Another tells of walking with Churchill in London. All the pictures suggest alternate points of entry for a *You Are There* recreation of history. No even remotely coherent story devised by the viewer seems possible. The work's unifying factor is just the artist's temperamental preference for the viewpoints chosen. Considering the images and implied personae, I am left with a whiff of what it is like to cogitate with the mind, feelings, and imagination of Allen Ruppersberg — what it is like to *be* him. That's Cutism, of an itchy, under-the-skin, haunting variety.

Ruppersberg's new installation surrounds, with five silkscreen-printed, old cheap movie screens, a blank screen on which a 25-minute sequence of slides is projected to syrupy musical accompaniment (the score of *The Princess Bride*). The prints are from stills of antique educational films — 1,300 reels of which were lately rescued from a school basement by Ruppersberg, a connoisseur of cultural dreck right up there with Jim Shaw. The images include the title frame of something called *How to Remember* and an oddly lugubrious shot of a hand drawing a cartoon little bear. The desultory slide sequence, timed at a pace whose slowness is just short of exasperating, collates nature, culture, and abstraction in bucolic landscapes, melodramatic stills from the movie *Far from the Madding Crowd*, and frames of single flat colors. Running throughout are fragments of a quote from Jean-Luc Godard, given in French and awkwardly translated in English as "There is just a moment when things cease to be a mere spectacle, when a man is lost and shows that he is lost." And sure enough, as I watched (*The Princess Bride* oozing through my brain), the actors in *Far from the Madding Crowd* all commenced to look lost and the landscapes and colors seemed different kinds of place to be lost in. The apparent aim of *Negative Space*, as the slide show is titled, to leap by tacky means to sublime ends is definitive Ruppersberg.

The sublime is never reached, however, unless by Ruppersberg himself, dreamily playing with pictures in his studio. That's definitive Ruppersberg, too, as well as a general tendency in current art. Today many people's main first-hand aesthetic experience is of second-hand content, with a nagging sense of being always too late for, and everywhere peripheral to, a world palpably real. Some folks are more comfortable than others with this state of things. The more sanguine may deserve to be insulted. (Why should the rest of us be the only ones with hurt feelings?) Ruppersberg seems neither sanguine nor not sanguine, just uncannily resigned — mildly depressed and mildly piqued at being caught in a position of obvious weakness. His other '70s "drawing project" at Burgin includes himself, photographed stuperously supine on a couch, beneath drawings from a loopy old children's Bible-story book illustrating a cautionary tale of greed and ambition. The work is, in a word, cute, but with a cuteness about as light-hearted as the planet Saturn. Ruppersberg owns one particular existential response to the urgency of life: take it lying down.

JIM ISERMANN AND LILY VAN DER STOKKER *Feature*

Beauty and quality are terms disreputable in some recent criticism, and one has to wonder at so strange an impulse to deaccentuate the positive. We are talking about words that are incapable of being used pejoratively. (Try it; you can't, except by way of mocking someone else's usage.) Is this what offends certain of the critically minded, who are gloomy or pissed off on principle and resent anything impervious to gloom and resentment? It takes a remarkably strangulated rhetoric, in any case, to anathematize such deepset values. *Beautiful* and, in the sense of *high-quality, good* pop up in everyday conversation about every ten minutes even among off-duty intellectuals. When thinking caps are on, however, some make a virtue of shunning the vocabulary of joy that their own colloquial tongues endorse.

On the perverse playground of intellect that is art, where one must do especially what one is least supposed to do, the stage may thus be set for a rebound of beauty, quality, and other idealism-saturated abstractions lately scorned. A low-key dual show at Feature drops hints — subtly in the case of Jim Isermann, raucously in that of Lily van der Stokker — that an era of good feelings is dawning.

The shift points to a sunniness latent in the recently dominant, apparently downbeat tendency sometimes labled Just Pathetic or the New Low: work by artists like Mike Kelley and Cady Noland that, addressing contemporary culture's superabundance of ugliness and dreck, is arguably about failed beauty and failed quality, honoring beauty and quality in the breach. That refractory artistic strategy, an often anguished attempt to free aesthetic experience from encrusted tastefulness and other smothering expectations, may be paying off in a candid new appetite for sweetness and light, this dark cloud's prescribed silver lining. We will need more evidence for a trend than the tentative gestures of Isermann and van der Stokker, but both seem responsive to something significant in the air.

Isermann is a 37-year-old Los Angeleno known since the late 1970s as a retro master. He has made pictures and furniture in thrall to popular decorative styles of the '50s and '60s — everything from atom clocks and boomerang coffee tables to flower-power decals and supergraphics, sometimes rendered in works that are literally half painting and half shag rug. He plainly adores those signs of obsolete optimism for their own sake, with the melancholy edge of alienation from the present that such immersions in the past entail. Unironic in itself, his art has inhabited a realm of free-floating dismal irony: "beauty" and "quality" rather than beauty and quality, effects of the sarcastic light that an overlay of too much historical consciousness sheds on the here and now. So Isermann's new work surprises: four stained-glass windows without a whisper of any irony of any sort. They are stand-up beautiful and good, architectural elements for a never-existent graceful world that looms in imagination as they are contemplated.

The exquisitely crafted, richly colored, three-foot-square windows hang perpendicular to the wall, lighted so that one side of each is opaque and the other aglow. Their regular patterns of nested and overlapping circles and wavy bands, stirring no specific stylistic memories, radiate the ancient innocence of pure geometry. Isermann makes the most of a perceptual doubleness in any stained-glass window, as in any mosaic, between the pictorial image that adds up in the mind and the fragmented actuality that meets the eye. His target and grid motifs are immediately graspable, but to read them integrally a viewer must elide a riot of disintegrative sensation. Colors change across each leaded seam, and much of the glass is impregnated with brushstroke-like cloudy streaks that attract and hold attention. Readings of figure and ground, as between a grid of circles and the wavy bands that course through it, are endlessly reversible.

Though spectacular — and far too emphatic to register as "good design" — Isermann's windows are not drop-dead gorgeous. They are more die-a-little in their pleasure, a quiet and clear-minded, slow ravishment. They are sneakily novel as much in what they eschew as in what they embrace. They have none of the ecclesiastical or metaphysical aura, whether Christian or New Age, that would seem practically unavoidable in stained glass. Symbolic of nothing, they are absolutely secular satisfactions of the eye's appetite for beauty and the mind's for quality. They make it seem easy. Look around. It's not. For me, a quiet sadness attends Isermann's poised and lucid loveliness at the thought of how rare it is and, properly speaking, exceptional: a little island of finesse in a world of crap.

Van der Stokker, a Dutch-American relative newcomer who used to run a gallery on the Lower East Side, suggests insurgent optimism in work that is far slighter and more comical than Isermann's but will grow on you if you let it. She does things so apparently silly that, on first glance in a dignified gallery setting, you might expect them to physically vanish from sheer embarrassment. She joins a recent wave of artists, such as Jim Shaw and Pruitt & Early, who excavate febrile aesthetics of teenage obsession. She incidentally reveals by contrast how much of such art is a boys' club. Her stuff is stereotypically pure girl: saccharine cloud-bubble and rudimentary floral designs, in murals and the unbeatedably pathetic medium of markers on paper, with lettered evocations of "LOVE," "KISSES," "HAPPINESS," and, in sum, the "WONDERFUL."

Van der Stokker's colors are kicked-up Necco-wafer. Her drawing hardly registers as drawing, as if these images simply precipitated by themselves out of an ever-present archetypal pubescent mentality. They are to the utmost degree impersonal, then, while apostrophizing romantic sentiments that represent the personal in much of popular culture. They are signs of libido so engorged with puppyish goodwill as to be effectively sexless. Psychologically, the folk style at issue may split a difference between simultaneous impetuous urges forward to "mature relationships" and backward to kindergarten. Is it suffocating, grotesque, and stupid? Well, yes, and a drawing by van der Stokker suggests why: "NOTHING IS NEW EVERYTHING WILL ALWAYS BE THE SAME" goes the inscription in a flower as smaller flowers pipe up "THE SAME FOREVER." This is an unvarying, treacly realm without the grit of life in time.

Still, van der Stokker's pink-cloud cosmos is fairly awesome as a phenomenon, and she seems to approach it in a spirit of disinterested awe. In an interview with B. Wurtz issued by Feature she says, "Other people explore landscape painting and I explore love and friendly images." To view her works with an unprejudiced eye is indeed like exploring an exotic landscape, a rain forest of naive emotion that proves humiliatingly and hilariously easy to get lost in. Just such feelings of lostness often signal a cultural shift, the world suddenly unfamiliar. You know it is happening when mystery concentrates in the banal.

Determinedly trashy, van der Stokker's art relates to values like beauty and quality, as to love and kisses, as sentimental residue, though no less real for that. Isermann's assumes them as commonsensical principles. Both confront critical negativity with variants of an implied, simple, open-minded wondering: *why not?* They brighten the prospect of art's near future, when we may again be going to artworks rather than texts for the important information on culture's unfolding ways.

ANDREA MANTEGNA *Metropolitan Museum of Art*

"ANDREA MANTEGNA GIVES US AS MANY REASONS to dislike him as any great artist," Lawrence Gowing writes in the catalogue of this show devoted to a runner-up in the Renaissance popularity contest. I had decided as much before reading that line. The 15th-century master is remarkably easy to loathe, given how seductive he could be with his great big clarities of design and tiny delicacies of line and light. How could someone so dour hatch such loveliness? And why would his contemporaries put up with the effect, which is like being caressed by a fist? Some bitter thing, some spleen, seemed to drive Mantegna. He became one of the greats because of an epoch in which talent was forgiven anything. Artistic genius in Renaissance Italy can suggest a Groucho-Marxian club that would let in anybody.

The Met show occasions my first vivid take on Mantegna. It is exciting, as it always is to catch on for the first time to any of the true old masters — those deep-dish personalities simmering beneath the museum's dull crust, waiting for their turn to change your life. The experience is a sudden soulful expansion, a falling in love (or in hate, no difference) that reveals unknown possibilities of anciently rooted feeling and puts a new light on possibilities already known.

The image of Mantegna's that you know, if you know any, is the extremely weird *Dead Christ,* which did not travel from Milan to this show: defunct Jesus radically foreshortened (a newfangled trick at the time), his lacerated feet in our face. Most weird is how, having invented a grotesque motif, Mantegna hedged it, rendering the feet far smaller than the perspective called for. If this Christ were raised upright, he would take a shoe about size four. So we get a grotesquerie grotesquely qualified and a disagreeable sense of being manipulated. That's Mantegna: show-offy and high-handed. But come to close quarters, at the Met, with the paintings, and treat yourself to the miracle of their modeling, as if drifts of light clung to forms of rock-like density. That incredible touch is Mantegna, too, as is the rigorously thought-out architectural splendor of even his smallest compositions.

Once an image of his gets into your head, it is there to stay.

He is reputed to have been a major and maybe even homicidal sourpuss. (A certain rival mysteriously got dead.) I have loved learning that Mantegna's brother-in-law was Giovanni Bellini, the Venetian with the sweetest human spirit of any painter — if not anyone, period — who ever lived. What must the family dinners have been like? I imagine Bellini finding excuses to skip them. You may guess why from a portrait bust at the Met of Mantegna putting forth a look to make dogs whine and children cry.

It's perfect, though coincidental, that his favorite paint medium is called distemper. Tempera made with animal glue, distemper enables an inner glow of transparent glazes like that of oil paint, but without the melting sheen. Where not wrecked by posthumous layers of varnish, Mantegna's surfaces are as bone-dry as his soul, with an aura of pedantic control worlds removed from the emotional generosity and urbane brilliance of the oils Bellini was painting over there in Venice.

What ate Mantegna? He never lacked for success in a 60-some-year career from his days as a teenage prodigy in the university town of Padua to his death in 1506 in Mantua while under the patronage of Isabella d'Este — for whom he painted a preposterous allegory, *Pallas Expelling the Vices from the Garden of Virtue*, that belongs in the select category of artworks that are great without being good. He was criticized by some contemporaries, as by people ever since, for rendering humans as if they were made of stone. Was it defiantly, in his later years, that he made so many paintings — ultimate *faux* decor — of fantasized stone and bronze reliefs? He was terrific at depicting physical weight (look at how all his figures stand smack on the ground), a talent that, in painting as opposed to sculpture, it is easier to admire than to take much pleasure in. "He has deposited something angular and painful under the skin of European art," Gowing finely writes — going on to call Mantegna undoubtedly "one of the great archetypes," but "an archetype of what?"

I think Mantegna is the archetype of the jealous academic or professional mandarin who pursues mastery of a discipline not out of any selfless passion for it but precisely for mastery's sake. He wants to stick his pre-eminence to the world and to gain thereby an unassailable position. Let's say he succeeds. By any objective, professional, academic standard, he is the best. Like no one else, Mantegna put over in painting the revival of Greek and Roman antiquity preached by the Paduan scholars, nearly all of whom seem to have responded with poems of tribute monotonously comparing him to Apelles.

If the going standards dictate lyrical content, no problem — but no tenderness, either. A Mantegna madonna and child is like a lesson in the physics of baby-holding. The mandarin's relentless motive is to prove himself superior or, better, to prove everybody else inferior. His reward is cold comfort. He is a sore winner. No one of any sensibility can stand being around him, but when they speak of the field of his expertise they discuss him obsessively.

Lots of artists have a Mantegna streak, but at least in modern times the world rarely yields to them for long. Success for this type requires, to begin with, a personal power base, in touch with but independent of the uncontrollable metropolis. (Consider getting a bunch of professors on your side while marrying the sister of the current major art star.) More than that, success depends on an extraordinary historical circumstance of rapid cultural change, raising the stakes of artistic competition, and avid and fair critical aficionados to keep accurate short-term score. Needed is something like the Renaissance.

The key is a situation in which, for the people who matter, every question about art is wide open except that of its intrinsic and extravagant value. People only moderately in love with art might turn against an overbearing sort like Mantegna with little besides sheer novelty and quality to offer. But in such a situation — unlike our ulcerously skeptical present art world — sheer novelty and quality are a ticket to ride.

I have talked about Mantegna rather than about the Met's Mantegna show, which, more than half made up of things identified as possibly or probably or certainly not by the artist, is very largely a demolition derby for scholars and connoisseurs. I had fun kibitzing the tortuous wrangles that wend from wall label to wall label, especially dense in vast sections of engravings by, after, or *way* after Mantegna. (He is given in my dictionary as "painter and engraver," but now some experts think he never engraved at all.) The beady-eyed ardor of specialists when they emerge dusty from their lairs, blinking in the light of a major exhibition, can be poignantly entertaining so long as you remember not to care. Don't be distracted from making the personal acquaintance of this formidable character from the high noon of painting on Earth.

JOSEPH BEUYS: ARENA *Dia Center for the Arts*

GOING AGAIN TO SEE Joseph Beuys's immense 1970-72 photo-installation piece *Arena* before Dia shuts down for the summer, I reflected that I have never written anything exclusively about Beuys, though like most other critics I have referred often to the late German's spooky and benevolent eminence in art of the last quarter-century. I have waited to develop a clear take on him since he burst belatedly upon New York's consciousness in a 1980 retrospective at the Guggenheim. But unclarity — outrageous mystification, in fact — may be Beuys's essence, and I am inclined at last to make a subject of my own confusion about him.

Recent world events goad me. Beuys was a prophet of ineradicable powers of mythic irrationality in a postwar German culture that was hysterically certain of having eradicated those powers. Every sickening headline from Middle Europe, seeming to herald a new heyday of barbarism, increases the urgency of taking the mythic seriously, and in Beuys's dank, fecund aura useful thoughts may form.

I was in rooms with Beuys a few times and shook his hand once, but I never spoke to him. Charismatic types scare me, and Beuys, who died in 1987 at age 66, was the most charismatic man I have seen up close, with an electricity that doesn't come across even in all the seductive photographs of him with his beat-up fedora, fishing vest, and hound-dog glamour. He struck me as some sort of politician, regarding other people as the raw material of his ambition with that restlessly assessing glance politicians have. But what his ambition consisted in was plainly unusual. It had no odor of dominance.

With oddly courtly, shambling humility, Beuys seemed to put himself below rather than above others, as if he saw in others something that awed him. Charisma may be the ability to convince people that they have potential never suspected until the gaze of the charismatic one falls on them and winkles it out. Andy Warhol had that, too, though what his gaze conferred — roughly, star power — was superficial, whereas Beuys seemed to detect in everyone a mystic, funky depth.

Ah, Germany. (Or is that Uh-oh, Germany?) Beuys, the shameless shaman, functioned as a living symbol of rebirth after catastrophe, wandering into public in the 1960s out of the smoke of the '40s as if by a shock-dimmed and circuitous route from the wreck of the dive bomber in which, a Luftwaffe pilot, he had been shot down in the Crimea. The Soviet gunner who nailed that plane could not know that his bullets were authoring a legend that, as critic Rosalind Krauss once noted, smacks a bit of St. Paul's conversion on the road to Damascus.

Some people have doubted Beuys's tale of being saved from the snow and, in effect, brought in from the cold of history by Tartar tribesmen who wrapped his shattered body in felt and animal fat. (Annoyed by probing questions, he eventually began to downplay his wartime experience, even insisting that his constant use of felt and fat in his art was unrelated.) The literal truth does and does not matter.

The ragged tracks of suffering and survival in Beuys's countenance seemed real enough, and his conviction of truthfulness, as of vaguely apostolic mission, was persuasive. If his experience was not as he said it was, that just adds a grotesque touch to a persona that, functioning symbolically, is not subject to tests of fact. A German persona. In Germany, persons are forever vanishing into social roles and social roles into abstract principles. In conversation there you may catch yourself wondering not *who* but *what* you are talking to.

Beuys was a one-man masquerade ball of such self-displacements, embodying one obscure archetype or invented abstraction after another in acts theatrically calculated at once to rivet and to bewilder attention. His message was Utopia Now if only everyone, in imagination, would talk the talk and walk the walk he demonstrated. His political program as an activist for unorthodox education and the nascent Green party — freedom, democracy, ecological awareness — was impeccably liberal in its ends, though arrived at by metaphysical steps, including a bizarre theory of money, apt to elude nonbelievers in magic.

Arena (with a mock-Nietzschean subtitle, *where would I have got if I had been intelligent*) is a gravely beautiful and lurkingly funny collection of some 400 black-and-white photographs variously arrayed in 97 window-sized steel-framed gray panels. The sequence is interrupted and completed by three panels of intense monochrome, two of them blue ("for the cold clarity of the north," in the words of Beuys expert Caroline Tisdall) and one yellow ("sulphur and southern sun"). The mostly scrappy, snapshot-like photos — of multifarious objects, installations, and performances by Beuys — are grainy or blurry and often perfunctorily drawn or painted on. None of the indistinctly pictured works is in any way identified, and their chronology is thoroughly scrambled.

As documentation, *Arena* is practically anti-informative. Only deep-backgrounded fans will know what they are looking at. ("There is the iron plate he wore on his foot in *Explaining Pictures to a Dead Hare.*") It is all a bit like the memory-fed spectacle out the window of Dorothy's Kansas farmhouse aloft in the tornado. Eventually one may stop trying to read the montage of images and just surrender to its swirling pungence and elegance, sinking into the state of inchoate psychic arousal that is the Beuysesque.

All art objects by Beuys are in a sense souvenirs of his activity, and that makes *Arena* a souvenir of souvenirs, a dried garden of dried flowers. It succeeds in conjoining, for anyone willing to play along, a physical here-and-now with a mental there-and-then and even a mystical above-and-beyond, a firmament of flowing inspirations. I confess to playing along with Beuys only gingerly, wading rather than swimming in his art. My resistance seems to me fairly typically American, an effect of ingrained pragmatism fed by shallow historical and spiritual roots.

I feel the deep wildness of Beuys's promise — a wild faith in the coherence of existence on a plane of abstract idea and raw intuition — and I can't imagine why I would want to take him up on it. Still, I am grateful for the insight he affords into the nature of the totalizing compulsions always stirring in the depths of Germany, and not only Germany. I do believe that Beuys was an entirely positive force, a holy-clownish dispenser of benignly concocted antidotes to old toxins of fanaticism. It is just that when I reflect, with his aid and that of the evening news, on the persistence of those toxins, I tremble.

HENRI MATISSE: A RETROSPECTIVE
The Museum of Modern Art

THE MATISSE SHOW IS A CONTROLLED ORGY. It will let you know how much pleasure you can stand. I mean visual pleasure, of course — arousal of the eyes — but more as well. Matisse crosswires sight with other senses, sparking phantom thrills of taste and smell. He stimulates the mind to analysis, then slaps the mind silly with audacities. He activates the occult handshake of aesthetics and sex. He does it all with practically monkish discipline. Matisse's discipline gives a dignity, a grown-up permission, to our immersion in his art's polymorphous excitements. He makes a science of pleasing, as ruthlessly pleasurable in what he leaves out as in what he offers. He leaves out any sympathetic, messy engagement of the heart. He is monstrously cold.

I went to MoMA with a lot of accumulated ambivalence about this workaday sensualist, this yeoman of the armchair. I wanted to be hard on him — I dislike him, still — but it is not so easy to be critical while joyfully quivering. John Elderfield, the show's curator, is no help. I cannot recall any other exhibition installed with so blatant and successful an aim to addle intelligence with delight. The Matisse on view is a better artist than Matisse has been before or will be again. The man himself, if returned to life for the occasion, might be amazed: "I did that?"

The show starts slowly, like damp kindling smoldering into fitful flames. Fauvism arrives as a steady and merry though modest blaze. (It is striking how small those famous pictures are: portable parlor decor, often in overly ornate frames bespeaking the insecure taste of their early collectors.) Then in 1907 with *Blue Nude*, a body erupting with distortions that rawly energize and monumentalize the picture, all hell breaks loose. No artist except the contemporaneous Picasso ever had a run of pictorial invention like Matisse's in the subsequent seven or so years, and at MoMA we are along for nearly every whoop of the ride.

It is about decoration raised to a level of panic: representations slammed up to the surface with linear rhythms and color combinations registering as wilfully arbitrary pattern, every detail a surprise and the ensemble a riot. The freedom is stagger-ing. It is as if the most idle desire, the merest whim to see a certain motif in a certain way, were granted the power of a thunderbolt-wielding Zeus to make it happen. No Matisse imitator has come close to that quality of the big effect achieved through impulsive, speculative, almost nonchalant procedure.

As in every period of Matisse there are bad pictures, such as the obnoxious 1909 *Spanish Woman with Tambourine* that suggests egotistical complacency and the wonky 1910 *Girl with Tulips*. Most of his portraits and all his landscapes of the time flop, betrayed by his exasperation with fellow humans and unorganized nature. In this greatest of his periods, Matisse palpably burns with resentment for subjects that resist being schematized, and only inspired tantrums (for instance, the cancellation-like black arc in *Portrait of Olga Merson*) rescue some paintings. But the failures just prove that he took real risks. (And, come to think of it, Matisse's most endearing trait may be how generously he can fail.) He would not believe beforehand that anything was impossible, and when he brought off a major picture — *Dance (II)* (do you suppose the Hermitage will mind if we send them back *Dance (I)* and keep this one?), *Conversation, The Piano Lesson, Bathers by a River* — he entered into a chartless realm of wonderment forever.

In the late 1910s Matisse comes bumping down from those heights with morbidly obsessed pictures of the model Lorette, his dark lady of the sonnets. He painted her nearly 50 times, and nobody seems to know even her last name. (This biographical lacuna is typical of Matisse scholarship, still weirdly constrained by a sort of gentlemen's-club loyalty to the straying husband's secrecy.) Then he decamped to Nice, where in the '20s he churned out the self-exploiting style, the sensualist chic, that put modern painting over the top with the haut hoi polloi. Some people insist on deeming the Nice period underrated. It is not, though Elderfield diabolically improves it with grouped hang-ings that camouflage pictures' individual weaknesses by rhym-ing common strengths. To enhance the mood he even sneaks a potted plant into one room of these bourgeois baubles. I confess to being sent even by this part of the show, while clinging to a judgment based on several visits to a 1987 comprehensive Nice-period exhibition in Washington.

Matisse in Nice is drugged on self-absorbed, squirrely rapture. The artist in claustrophobic hotel rooms compulsively repeats his primal scenario of staring at nude or spicily costumed models. He hardly glanced at naked women, I think. He saw nude models, creatures clothed in nudity. He taught his sexual arousal not to narrow into desire but to dilate across a pictorial field, such that the least detail of decor is as eroticized as the model's body. His art is an engine fueled by sex, and it burns clean. Conservative types adore him for this. The relentless efficiency of Matisse's sublimation is a triumph of decorum under pressure. Of course he would have to have the young woman eventually — and you just know what a sensitive love-maker he must have been — but the painting that was there all the while, silent on the easel, would not breathe a word of it.

Matisse in his great period maintained the decorum of a single convention: that there should be pictures to hang on walls, never mind why. The embattlement of that decorum came not only from his biological drive but from all sides, from the global convulsion of modernity putting everything familiar in doubt. This Matisse can still make Western culture seem an excellent idea because so flexible and brave. The Nice (and nice) Matisse makes Western culture seem a take-it-or-leave-it deal entailing certain sacrosanct privileges. One Matisse is a hero, albeit aloof. The other is just a painter, albeit terrific.

After the '20s Matisse is essentially a graphic (at times supergraphic) artist, making design-y pictures dead flat and flashy in every format and medium. He rarely fails to grasp something peppy and satisfying, though his reach is not awesome. The late cutouts are overrated, as Elderfield frankly remarks in his well considered catalogue introduction. They are more winsome than wonderful, on the whole. But leave it to Elderfield to serve the cutouts with a slambang installation which, like the shoot-the-works finale of a Hollywood movie, sends a viewer out the door reeling. There has never been a better paced, more exhilarating, more refreshing museum show. Go soon. Have a friend with you so as not to appear insane when making involuntary noises.

HELENE SCHJERFBECK: FINLAND'S MODERNIST
REDISCOVERED   *The National Academy of Design*

HELENE SCHJERFBECK, OF WHOM I AM almost positive you never heard, is one of my favorite artists, and not just because she belonged to the happy few who start their last names "Schje." Of Swedish heritage (I am of Norwegian), she was a Finnish painter who died in 1946 at the age of 83. I have encountered her work on visits to Finland (my favorite out-of-the-way country), where she is cherished in cultural memory as a poignant figure of immense aptitude who endured a difficult life to eke out something fine. Hers is a classically Nordic authenticity: warmth in bleakness, winter light. So intense is her local appeal, there in Finland, that I used to suspect it could not travel well.

But it does.

This modest retrospective is the sleeper hit of the season, a surprise gift to lovers of painting and to anyone for whom past artists sometimes come alive as spiritual companions. Schjerfbeck is a minor artist, her achievement limited by blighting circumstances of her place and time, but so singular as to be archetypal of something. Call it the Schjerfbeckian, an extreme attenuation of the romance of self: self-conscious ardor and willfulness worn down to near transparency, like abraded silk, but intact. Other features are total commitment to art and ferocious personal honesty.

The Schjerfbeckian is purest in a series of self-portraits, done when she was very old, that are like nothing else in art: the painter's face rendered seemingly as much by touch as by sight, as if she sought herself in the dark. (Is there in all the world another *Self-Portrait with Eyes Closed*?) She discovers a skull ever more oddly shaped, at times like that of a newborn. Probing strokes bring out its battered oval — an oval trying to be an irregular polygon — within which blunt marks locate pinched, gaunt features. The always succinct technique varies widely, from line drawing to palette-knife impasto, as the artist marshals the repertoire of a lifetime to take the subject by storm again and again.

Schjerfbeck in these pictures (as also in a magnificent 1945

Still Life with Blackening Apples) is a stenographer of encroaching death. She dies bit by bit before her own eyes, under her own fingers. She is oblivious to an audience beyond herself. As viewers, we are voyeurs to a terrible privacy. The tone, which must be experienced to be believed, is exultant, an effusion of joy in abandonment to art's power.

Born in Helsinki, Schjerfbeck suffered a crippling hip injury at the age of four. Regarded as a prodigy, she received government scholarships to Paris, where in the 1880s she became a whiz at the then fashionable mode of genre naturalism. Her 1888 *The Convalescent,* which may be the most popular painting in Finland, shows a frail little girl avidly gazing at a sprig of budding greenery. It is amazingly painted, with Manet-like vigor and a mysteriously alarming effect I attribute to the peculiar color of the child's wide eyes: a grayed, lusterless blue. That practically subliminal touch, speaking volumes in a way strictly painterly, helps explain why the academic picture feels so ineffably *talented.* Like other early tours de force in the show, this work suggests the apprenticeship of a master.

Then Schjerfbeck's luck failed. Fate seemed to take an interest in hurting her. When she was 24, her English fiance broke off their engagement because, he carefully explained, her lameness revolted him. Her financial support ran out. She struggled with frequent painful illness to hold a teaching job in Helsinki, where her sophisticated art — increasingly modernist, with a lapidary concision catching glints of Whistler, Cassatt, Munch, Rouault, Matisse, and Japanese prints — often met with philistine rejection. In 1902 she retreated to a country town and lived with her mother until her mother's death in 1923. Thereafter she lived alone. She would never revisit her beloved Paris.

She was erudite, passionate, and shy. She was subject to agonies of self-doubt, but proud. She despised small talk. Rather than friends, she had soulmates and devotes. (One of the latter was an extraordinary art dealer named Gosta Stenman who nursed her career from 1915 until the end. Any artist should have such a dealer.) She pictured people in interiors, a "women's world," with tensile, cartooning line and zones of tremblingly moody color — an elegant style verging at times on chic illustration but almost always with something going on, something slightly or not so slightly demonic.

Her work absolutely must be seen in person to be appreciated. The key quality of her painting is lost in reproduction: a rousingly direct and physical touch, no matter how denatured or decadent the image.

The faces she painted are mask-like, and the paintings are masks of herself. In the late self-portraits she removed the mask. What was revealed is *sui generis*. It is beyond personal and nearly beyond human.

An earlier self-portrait, dated 1915, is a one-of-a-kind marvel and the most public of Schjerfbeck's works. When she was commissioned for it by the Finnish Art Society, where she had taught, she painted against a black ground her pale, rosy-cheeked face — a delicate apparition — craning upward like someone in the last row of a group photograph trying to be seen. Above her is her name in tombstone lettering nearly effaced, as if by weathering. The overall image is tenderly vulnerable and as vivid as a shop sign. She is a quiet woman who feels rather neglected, says the painting in a style that goes off like a grenade. For all its Northern austerity, this defiant self-presentation somewhat recalls Frida Kahlo.

Like Kahlo, Schjerfbeck derived strength from suffering. Also like Kahlo, she recommends herself to the present as a legitimate heroine of female selfhood against tall odds, whatever she intended. Schjerfbeck may be too chaste an aesthete to inspire a Kahlo-like cult, but a certain amount of cultishness would not be misplaced. Cults of rediscovery signal only that, in shadows of the past, something urgent and inarticulate is finding a voice and something nameless its proper name. Now having emerged for us, Helene Schjerfbeck should not, in any event, be allowed to reenter oblivion.

ANDRES SERRANO   *Paula Cooper Gallery*

A̲ɴᴅʀᴇꜱ Sᴇʀʀᴀɴᴏ'ꜱ ᴘʀᴇᴛᴛʏ ᴅᴇᴀᴛʜ ᴘʜᴏᴛᴏɢʀᴀᴘʜꜱ are so brazenly strategic they are beyond manipulative. The calculations practically line up with arrows pointing at them. First the subject: corpses in a morgue. Eeek. Then the medium: state-of-the-craft Cibachrome in four-by-five-foot prints silicone-bonded to Plexiglas. Wow. Then the form: closeups of body details composed like painted still lifes, with black backgrounds and washes of studio-type, often gel-colored lighting. Swoon. Finally the content: ambiguous! You decide! Tips for deciding might be found in a fashionably disaffected compendium of received ideas, as for instance: Americans — you know, *those* people — deny death. Unlike *us.*

Serrano's game could be called bait-and-switch-and-bait-again. He raises an expectation of shock so potent that I suspect some viewers come away feeling shocked without really having looked at the pictures. The switch, once you do look, is a prevalence of elegant, seductive, entirely artificial-seeming gorgeousness. (Only one image in the show, a man whose autopsied throat is laid open like a book, could not conceivably be approximated with makeup — and its appearance is so downright odd, with the exposed insides an unreal red, that the effect is less gross than engrossing.) A viewer's surprise and relief may then generate the infra-bait: a delusion of brave mastery of death, perhaps with a bonus sense of superiority to shallow, squeamish folk.

One can never rule out with an intelligent artist the possibility of a subtle, ultimate switch (or switcheroo) that makes fools of cynics. But Serrano's past work persuades me that, for all his evident intelligence, he is always coldly clever in his conceptions and anything but subtle in his meanings. He has made his career as a sort of advertising campaigner against supposed taboos. His project is passionate. By no mere fluke did he become a hero of the Bush-era censorship wars. But his passion does not inhere in his pictures, which seem less expressions than tactical gestures of his crusading bent. Serrano's invariably superb execution suggests an art director's workaday perfectionism, though in service to audacities. Most compelling for me about his new pictures is the simple thought of him doing them, doggedly coaxing beauty from shambles hour after hour amid the morgue stinks.

The photographs are definitely beautiful, as well as often sensationally poignant. Among their rare delicacies are the pale, pale yellow (and immaculate manicure) of the crossed hands of a female AIDS casualty and the entrancingly fine, alluvial texture of a black man's burned flesh. In paired pictures, two hands with stigmata-like wounds in their wrists appear to reach toward each other. The unseeing eye in the blood-smeared face of a woman "hacked to death" (says the title) seems a self-conscious homage to our last look at Janet Leigh in *Psycho*.

Most of the corpses are fresh. The calves of a baby dead of meningitis bear imprints of stocking elastic. (Was Serrano on call for choice new arrivals?) Two views of a hefty, tattooed male drowning victim are monumental landscapes of moistly gleaming gray flesh, suavely accented in one picture with reddish light. Locked in rigor mortis, the goose-pimpled arms of a "rat poison suicide" look poised for combat. A black cloth covers her face. She wears a lacy bra.

Once you start looking at these things, it is hard to stop. You know the subjects don't mind. The dead are infinitely obliging models, and Serrano reciprocates by focusing on their most interesting, if not exactly flattering, features. His relentless aestheticizing defuses the psychic mechanism of identification (*that could be me* or *that could be my loved one*) which can make pictures of the dead particularly unbearable. Liberated from fear and pity, contemplation may attain the dubious courage of schadenfreude. *They're dead. I'm not.*

Be it added, on this score, that a posthumous vulnerability — circumstances of death mandating a coroner's opinion or just negligible social status — landed these deceased ones in a morgue whose security proved nonchalant. The location is pointedly not identified, I imagine to shield whoever let Serrano in. Most of us probably can count on family and friends, when we retire from breathing, to keep us out of such slipshod facilities and thus off the walls of the Paula Cooper Gallery.

I do not like this show, though it seems entirely successful on its own terms — which are incidentally the terms of an honored gallery striving to regain avant-gardish cachet. Such cachet depends on mounting shows that abruptly reveal the aesthetic cogency, and naturally the marketability, of things previously more or less unthinkable. Cooper has done handsomely with and for Serrano. Given the task of validating a truly iffy artistic premise, the gallery's architectural grace and institutional dignity seem more than usually luminous. The show is an object lesson in what New York gallery culture is all about. (It's just that now and then I tire of New York gallery culture.)

With its blatant strategizing and commodity gloss, the show has a certain 1980s savor despite a theme and a vaguely political aura that are quite '90s. (The gallery press release is careful to establish the cadavers' rainbow credentials: "A cross-section of society was surveyed.") Serrano's death pictures feel late in comparisons, which they cannot escape, with prior major works by Cindy Sherman and Gerhard Richter. I am thinking of Sherman's several painting-like fantasy photographs of dead and/or mutilated characters — plus very notably a haunting series of body-part closeups shown at Metro Pictures in 1991 — and of Richter's profound grisaille paintings from news and police photos of dead Baader-Meinhof gang members, including morgue shots of Ulrike Meinhof.

For Sherman, whose formal practice rather thoroughly anticipates Serrano's, the aesthetic is a royal road to the verge of awful sublimities, such as death intuited and rehearsed in the mind. By playful means, she brings us to lonely, terrible, important places. Richter suggests that the aesthetic in face of death is intolerably trivial. His pitilessly dour Baader-Meinhof paintings invade art with the banal, numbing obscenity of real death in the real world.

In Serrano's new work, both fantasy and reality fall away, leaving only the aesthetic — the tug of visual curiosity and pleasure — to justify the exercise. It is an undeniable feat, this demonstration of pictorial art's power to triumph over harrowing circumstances, but it is not a feat likely to inform anyone's life. The ideal value of art about death may be precisely to interest us more deeply in our own lives, leading us to recognize our mortality and to assess our perishing selves. In this light, Serrano's show is not about death at all. It is only about art — art with an attitude — for those who share an insatiable appetite for novel, peculiarly spiced dishes of the stuff.

THOMAS STRUTH   *Marian Goodman Gallery*

TOWARD THE END OF THE 1970s I saw somewhere a startling black-and-white photograph of a Soho street, I think Greene. It was a view in fleeing perspective down several blocks, deserted but for a parked car or two under the off-white pie slice of an overcast sky. The focus was sharp throughout, etching even tiny details and making for a surfeit of information. I was fascinated by patterns of broken sidewalks and heaved cobblestones. I remember the sullen charm of the picture's castiron buildings, whose familiar architectural prose-poetry seemed more pungent for the fact of their marginality, like sidewalls of a stage, to a scene that centered essentially on nothing.

I also recall being rankled — made defensive, I suspect, in my pride of hipness to going pictorial styles — by the photograph's sensibility, which was strange to me. It was rawly, almost naively "realist" in a way and self-consciously "formalist" in some elusive other way, with a maddening lack of emphasis. It bothered me. Was this something to take seriously, to learn about? I concluded that the picture, though pleasurable, was probably insignificant. I am not sure why. I may have reflected that no one imbued with properly New Yorkish aesthetics (succinct, smart, punchy) would be caught looking at New York in so wide-eyed — so *gawking*— a manner.

If I thought that, I was right. The photo was one of a series done in 1978 by a 24-year-old West German visitor on a scholarship from Düsseldorf. My judgment was dead wrong, of course, blinkered by a parochialism then still barely possible for an untraveled and distracted New York art person. I would travel a lot presently, when the accumulated richness and overwhelming sophistication of contemporary European, especially German, visual creativity redrew the art-world map two, three, and four years later. But it took me over a decade to catch up on the author of the Soho street scene.

He is Thomas Struth, one of a generation of photographers whose work is the latest strength of a German art culture that seems to have no end of aces up its sleeve. Struth is showing new cityscapes, taken in the former East Germany, at Goodman and is represented by family portraits and huge Cibachromes of peopled museum interiors in "Photography in Contemporary German Art:

1960 to the Present," a survey at the downtown Guggenheim.

Curated by Gary Garrels at the Walker Art Center in Minneapolis, the Guggenheim selection ignores "straight" photographers except Struth and the terrific portraitist of bland young Germans at billboard scale, Thomas Ruff. (Glaringly absent is Candida Hofer, for one.) We will need another survey to demonstrate how a long fashion for artistic cannibalizing of photography is being challenged in Germany by foursquare photographic practices. As exemplified by Struth above all, these practices polish the tarnished notion that a camera can tell the truth in ways both cogent and important.

Struth studied with Bernd and Hilla Becher, the arch "typologists" whose deadpan, dead-on black-and-whites of old industrial structures are icons of photographic Minimalism. It shows. His urban shots apply Becheresque formulas of static, unpopulated (surely early-morning), shadowless views with a feel for the "typical" or "average" aspect of a subject. (As if in compensation, Struth's astonishing family portraits burn with human presence: each sitter vulnerably alone within an aura of shared intimacy. The portraits amuse and hurt in about equal measure. His museum pictures, meanwhile, are wittily theatrical apostrophes of the "art-space" situations in which they are displayed. They are also beautiful.) Struth's work has taught me to appreciate, in retrospect, the fecundity of the Bechers, who helped form the aesthetic and ethical alphabet with which their ex-student spells out sheer poetry.

Struth's East German streets have common features. Most of their buildings are pre-World War II — a condition rare in cities to the west, which took the brunt of Allied bombing and/or have been subject to insipid "restoration." The eastern sites are preserved by their neglect, apparent as slow-motion ruin in the foregrounds of the pictures and an ineffably soiled, sad quality farther away. As with most of Struth's cityscapes, there is an initial disorientation, a compound of absolute specificity of place and seeming arbitrariness in point of view. It is as if we were walking with a companion who abruptly stopped at a spot with nothing obviously special about it, facing ostensibly nothing much. Following his gaze, we slowly register that we are seeing, for lack of a better word, *everything.*

We see a space of passage formed by structures eloquent with history, culture, time, chance, and vernacular use. The deep-spaced structure of the picture inserts us into the scene, then lets us be. We must hatch our own explanations of what we are doing there, as we go to work on the information given. A conviction of meaningfulness, like a pressure in the brain, grows on us. It is not a matter of anything normally "interesting." The place is merely real. At the same time, it seems a rebus urgent to be read, as if it secreted evidence of a crime. We do not feel necessarily that the photographer knew the secret. He is not toying with us. It is rather as if he had a Geiger counter for meaning, whose meter happened to go crazy at this location.

One may begin by surmising. Did some miserable modern apartment blocks appeal to Struth because located in Weimar, where the Bauhaus fostered the architectural language here debased? Maybe, but discursive connections are swamped by a visual congeries of desultory patterns — molded-aluminum facade, beetle-browed balconies, sidewalk tiles, cobblestones, cars parked in tidy rows—that speak of "order" and "design" as mindlessly rampant as jungle growth. It is a kind of shock to see so completely, with such fierce clarity, what people who live in the buildings may never truly see, though it enters into the warp and woof of their being. One wants help to arrive. But what kind, how, and from whom? At last one quits looking, with a shudder. The image will not be forgotten.

I may overrate Struth somewhat because so starved, by psycho-politico-babbling trends in recent American art, for honest attempts at silent objectivity. If so, my intense enthusiasm for his work will abate with satiety. Meanwhile, why worry? It is wonderful to be reminded that the human organism features eyes in a head that also contains a brain to be served by them. It is wonderful to feel one's capacity for disciplined looking being pushed to maximum efficiency and even beyond it, into a vertigo or paranoia of active contemplation. Of course, other people's photographs do this as well. Maybe every photograph does it a bit. But count on a German to go to extremes. Walking in the city the other day, I was remembering the image, probably of Greene Street, that once detained my baffled attention, and suddenly I was seeing every street according to that omniverous, unprejudiced, hypersensitive model. I gawked, but not like a tourist. It was Struth out everywhere.

THE GREEK MIRACLE: CLASSICAL SCULPTURE FROM
THE DAWN OF DEMOCRACY *Metropolitan Museum of Art*

I NEVER GOT ANCIENT GREEK ART, not the way the Cradle-of-Civiliza-
tion pieties imply you are supposed to. At the Acropolis in 1965
during my only Greek sojourn, the sunlight hit me over the head
like a transparent hammer and I gazed with lethargy on the
bleached rubble. I was more stirred by the smelly, raucous Plaka,
where in a restaurant an impromptu dancer cut his hand slap-
ping a floor littered with broken glass and, still dancing, splurged
blood. That was great. I stumbled into a political riot and discovered tear gas, from which painful thrill kindly Greek strangers
helped me recover. I bought a knit beret and worry beads and
went native, in my dreams. I fell in love with Byzantine churches,
which still breathed kinship — as the Parthenon did not — to
the robust street. I was 23 and sided with the present.

I think a lot of people are ambivalent about the Attic thing,
target of more hype in Western cultural history than anything
but Jesus. A smarmy 19th-century odor hangs especially heavy
about the subject. That's when the British, among other sentimental rapists, liked old Greece so much they took it home with
them. Well, I sensed early on through literature the shocking
greatness of a moment that seemed insouciantly to think everything thinkable and to imagine everything imaginable. But the
whole business seemed so already-known and so encrusted with
obligatory opinions. In my enthusiasm-driven artistic self-educa-
tion, I more or less skipped Classicism.

Now the Metropolitan has the exhibition for me and anyone
else ready to outgrow adolescent resentments and to reconcile
with the West's tribal ancestors. A greatest-hits sampler, it is just
right for our vulgar need. I came out humming the tunes and
moving to the beat. The show might be titled *It's the Greeks, Stupid.* (Anything would improve on *The Greek Miracle,* which sounds
like an ethnocentric skin cream.) Some half-dozen pieces made
me intensely happy. It probably helped that I had just been writing about the Whitney Biennial, a show proving that long indifference to formal fundamentals has reduced the general run of

emerging American art to eclectic junk. That, not anything to do with politics, is the Biennial's bad news. In comparison, ancient Athens feels young and new.

The Greeks were plenty political, too. Only at a stretch does their politics yield a present sense of "democratic," a forced claim for a city-state whose majority was voiceless women and slaves. The art at the Met speaks of nationalism, theocracy, and militarism even as it does tenderly celebrate individuals, including women, children, and at least one servant. It is in the art's way of doing things that joy reigns. The keynote is ease. Everything seems a falling-off-a-log snap for these people, maybe because they rarely considered doing anything except from, with, and for love. Erotic rapture is practically their normal, civic attitude. How is it possible not to wish for what they had?

Bodily nuances as subtly known as the nape of your lover's neck deliver the goods, even in a battle scene. What remains of a naked warrior who may be Theseus (minus an arm, a hand, both feet, and his penis) is swordfighting a long absent Amazon. He seems to lunge forward with a very slightly slackjawed expression (this is fun for him), but you tell me which leg takes his weight. I swear he shifts back and forth as one looks. Present sports slang has the term for it: Theseus *jukes*! He is faking out his opponent, drawing her off balance as deftly as a star running back and with the same rangy bliss in his body's cleverness. The sculptor had to be inside that body somehow, to feel it twitch, as he carved the marble. To get the fullest blast of the piece's liveliness, take a head-on, appalled-Amazon view of it.

The most beautiful thing in the show is a four-foot length of the Parthenon frieze of horsemen. Four young riders and their galloping steeds bunch up three abreast in a relief that is just two and a quarter inches deep. The horses are fiercely spirited. The guys are loose, nonchalant, cool. The bottom of the picture, a forest of equine legs, is all machine-like clatter, while the top has a buoyant, swinging rhythm. Nothing in art is more like frozen music: pipes and drums, marvelous noise. Looking at it, I was along for the ride. Hooray for Athena! Three cheers for us.

The torso of a running nereid is the suddennest hunk of stone you ever saw. Her speed plasters her thin garment to her front with a wet-T-shirt effect, but she is nobody's babe. She is all fluid power and unbounded bodily happiness. She can run for days and will arrive, wherever she is going, like a thunderclap. Then there is the hardly believable Nike adjusting her sandal, the goddess doing something awkwardly human. It is an intoxicating carving of a body to which a dazzling carving of drapery is formed, all in one piece. The nereid and the Nike are adjudged decadent turns in Classical style, going for feverish virtuosity. They prove that the Greeks got decadence right, too.

The peak Athenian moment was soon over, mangled by war and plague. Sculptors who had worked on the Parthenon ended up eking out livings doing grave steles for the moneyed class. The result was some pretty amazing graveyards, where ordinary people got sublime sendoffs. One relief at the Met, picturing a dowager going through her jewel box with a servant, memorializes "a woman who loved pretty things and has left them behind in death," in the perfect catalogue description. Another shows a little girl bidding goodbye to her pet doves. I imagine the artist interviewing the family, asking what about their daughter had been remarkable. "Well, she liked those birds." Nothing partaking of affection was beneath the Greeks, and when they aimed high, wow.

I talked with someone art-knowledgeable who deprecated the Met show as "pretty." Her favorite thing in it, she said, is a pre-Classical standing figure in rigid Egyptian style. This struck me as a very modern sort of opinion, and it made me realize that my own long antagonism toward the Greeks belongs to a century-old educated contempt for both realism and idealism, opposites seamlessly joined in the Athenian sensibility. Might that prejudice be wearing out? It occurs to me that by far the best work in the Whitney Biennial, by Charles Ray, is a realistic nude sculpture — in full color, as we know the Greek sculptures were before weather and time. Not that we want a revived Classical look in art, necessarily. (Spare us another "neo-" anything.) But I wager that we do want something of comparable freshness and serenity, saying *yes* to life in common.

JOAN MITCHELL   *Robert Miller Gallery*

When Richard Diebenkorn, modern painter for people who don't like modern painting, died in California last month, his obit made the front page of the *Times*. That was more notice than Joan Mitchell rated when she died last October at her expatriate haven in France. I think her best paintings are better art than his — less fussy and more enjoyable, while at least as serious — though the point could be argued. He demonstrated more artistic range along with more of the genteel appeal that is apt to earn gratitude from *Times*-type, comfy-liberal culturati. Mitchell was a bit less virtuosic and way less reassuring. That she was female has something to do with it, though only in the sense that she was the wrong kind of female.

Times-types have made their choice of Top Art Woman of Diebenkorn's and Mitchell's 1950s generation. The Georgia O'Keeffe Memorial Trophy goes to Helen Frankenthaler for canvas acres of eye candy with attitude. You can bet Frankenthaler will be front-paged when she shuffles off. The O'Keeffe Trophy, which I just made up, recognizes with proud tolerance the sacred-monstrous qualities uncorked when a woman presumes to be independently creative. Certain brands of sacredness, perhaps flamboyant but never abandoned or actually aggressive, work best to soften the basic offense. O'Keeffe qualified, as did Louise Nevelson. Louise Bourgeois and Nancy Spero do not. Mitchell in her own way was too tough a customer for middlebrow mythification.

How tough was she? Anyone who knew her, as I did for a while, can show you bruises left by the blunt instrument of her sarcasm. A Chicagoan formed in New York by the two-fisted-alcoholic Cedar Bar scene, Mitchell might at a certain point have kicked back, trusting in others' esteem, but she did not seem to think it worth the risk. If you were in her vicinity and for the briefest moment vulnerable, she would wallop you. She was as vivid and predictably unpredictable as a cartoon terror, a Tasmanian Devil of art — except in her paintings, which though brusquely energetic are all blossoming generosity of spirit. Her vigor was untopped by anyone in her dead-end-modernist generation, including Diebenkorn, Frankenthaler, Sam Francis, and Jules Olitski.

This raises another problem for Mitchell's cultural standing. Who looks at high-style abstract painting any more? It is practically the definition of old-fashioned for the present generation of art students. It seems particularly unappealing to the heroine-seeking feminist constituency. Mitchell was thoroughly proud of out-boying the boys, and such afflatus is dated for people determined to value only games that dispense with boy rules. Fair enough. But even gender warriors might want to take a day off for Robert Miller's splendid selection of Mitchell's last paintings, done when the artist was dying of cancer and, typically, scorning the recommended treatments. Here is the stuff of a seasoned gladiator who went down swinging.

Mitchell's painting is inevitably called nature-based. One is indeed always in some sort of garden with it, a place of sunlight, flowers, moist air, and birdsong. But the bucolic rides in on her best art. It is not the vehicle, which is instead a most sophisticated and dashing way with formal elements of painting. The elements belong to an Abstract Expressionist catechism: big scale (even in the rare small canvas), improvisational stroke, exploded composition, and raw color. In a completely willful, hardly reflective manner, Mitchell made a more trenchant analysis of the Abstract Expressionist masters than any other member of the movement's so-called Second Generation.

Though Frankenthaler verged on it before going blowsily color-fieldish, Mitchell came closest to realizing the Second Generation's circle-squaring dream, which was to approximate at the same time Jackson Pollock and Willem de Kooning. She brought off Pollockian, muralistic abstractions in a way that allowed for local intensities of space-bending brushstrokes, de Kooning's Cubist bob-and-weave. Look at a Mitchell up close, then from a distance. See the in-and-out tussle of strokes, then the grand resolution. When Mitchell starts a swath with a two-inch brush you have no idea where it's going, but it arrives on time with your gaze as its passenger. It is a shape that is a line that is a shape. It is direction and location, both, while maintaining its integrity as a sheerly physical mark, straight from the shoulder.

Likewise brilliant, and harder than it seems in Mitchell's spontanous execution, is how her welters of strokes occupy the arena of the picture. She tends to leave much of the sized canvas bare. The whiteness is felt poetically as radiant backlight, though often with a grayish smudge here and there to double the ground's meaning with a hint of "atmosphere." (The variety and economy of her flirtation with landscape illusion dazzle.) Shoved forward by the light and weighed downward by their density, her painted areas nonetheless hover securely where they are put, with a relation to the canvas edges as casual and tensile as that of an outdoor hammock to the trees it is hung from.

Mitchell's paintings are declarations of instinctual independence. They refuse thought. They are all about sensation. Again, there is that abrupt, ineffably uncomfortable stroke — "like a bad back rub," a friend of mine hazards. Whatever else her garden may be, it is no place to relax in. Her not-quite-tube-fresh colors are like slaps in the face of a drowsing person. They insist that we wake up and be alive to life right this minute. No whining. Look. Feel. Feel anything at all, so long as it is strong. If you stayed up too late last night, you should have thought of that. Let's go.

Mitchell belonged to the last important artistic generation that assumed painting's centrality to art and abstraction's centrality to painting. She never faltered in the easy grandeur of that assumption — easy for her, because she lived it. Not for her the defensive modulation toward conservative taste that gave Richard Diebenkorn his soft-headed cynosure. With a deep self-honesty that just incidentally seemed to entail appalling social manners, she earned her aesthetic commitment day by day and canvas by canvas. A lot of people may be said to live for art, but with precious little liveliness. Mitchell really lived and really painted.

REE MORTON: WORKS FROM 1971-1974
Brooke Alexander Gallery

Rᴇᴇ Mᴏʀᴛᴏɴ ᴡᴀs ᴀ ᴘᴜʀᴇ ᴘʀᴏᴅᴜᴄᴛ of America circa 1970. When I met her around then at an art school in Philadelphia, she was an ex-Navy housewife in her mid-thirties with three children. She seemed a nice, warm person bedraggled with care and possessed, it quickly emerged, of intense artistic ambition all the fiercer for blooming late. She showed me some works. She may have fished them out of her pockets: scraps of wood with patterned markings. I remember being caught by them. They had something, a fetishy quality offset by sober formality. But the vulnerably eager Morton struck me as an unlikely type to become an important artist. Actually, she was a new type.

Morton died in a car crash in 1977 in Chicago, where she was teaching at the Art Institute. I was in Chicago lecturing at the Art Institute that day. I had not seen her in a long time. Judging from her ever more self-confident work — among other things, colorful swags and banners that celebrated "feminine" sentiments with ironic panache — she had become someone I perhaps did not know. She was expected at a party after my lecture. At the party I heard she was dead. The shock of that evening has not worn off for me. I still await my first distinct feeling about Ree Morton — unless, as I now suspect, numb anticipation is the feeling.

"She was Emily Dickinson in love with Raymond Roussel," said the late sculptor Scott Burton, who was great at summarizing people. That is, she was abstract passion in love with methodical eccentricity, enigmatic emotion crazy about enigmatic thought. How do you understand someone in deliberate flight from understanding? You don't. You attend the person's doings and their worldly context. Morton's context was an extended-family-like art scene friendly to the games of idiosyncratic creative personalities who would contribute to its group protocols. She did not live to transcend that rather soggy avant-garde — which could be as far gone on intuition as a more recent scene has been far gone on critical theory — but, like few others, she distilled its peculiarities into poetry.

The little retrospective of Morton drawings, constructions, and installations at Brooke Alexander, covering the first half of a six-year career, is a time-machine trip to the early '70s. During that recessionary, rudderless era, the serious American art world was an archipelago of schools and alternative spaces with fairly abundant public funding and scant public interest. The private-moneyed, big-audience '80s were far distant. Artists proved themselves, if at all, to their peers. Obscure, funky, ephemeral expression was valued by a milieu drilled in brainy Minimalist form and hankering for heart-felt content. Installations (called "environments" then) were the favored mode. Women were a growing presence.

All those period characteristics figure in the Morton show, a chunky palimpsest of history. Morton's main medium at the time was found wood: bits of used lumber and logs which she altered and arranged in quietly theatrical, mysteriously allusive ways. Mysteriousness is the work's strength and weakness. Vested in maps of unknown places and diagrams of incomprehensible ideas, Morton's hunger for meaning was its own object. She did not create art so much as conjure it, ritualizing a desire to make art. At the show, I was amazed by the persistent force of motives so frail. I was drawn anew into Morton's oddly rigorous, partici-patory narcissism, her intelligent and troubled, dreaming soul.

The earliest work in the show, a suite of manipulated wood scraps like those I remember, is the solidest. It is a display of pure aesthetic aptitude recalling Jasper Johns's famous prescrip-tion for art-making: "Take an object. Do something with it. Do something else with it." The combination of funk and formalism rivets because each extreme is so believable. Morton was really enamored, at once, of humble stuff and of art for art's sake. These pieces project a big psychological symbolism. They delicately suggest heavy-lifting spirit work: putting together the high and low registers of an ideal self, minus anything in the middle. They bracket wholeness.

Every beginning artist reinvents the wheel, producing art not yet differentiated enough to call for judgments of good or bad: art-in-general. Morton's is the extraordinary case of an artist whose tyro art-in-general occurred well into a life already rich in experi-ence. Her wood sketches are schematic but not tentative. They harvest ripe feelings. The feelings inevitably thinned out as she groped for agreement with her place and time, negotiating the middle of herself and her culture and what should have been the early middle of her career. But there are compensations.

Morton's most successful environment is *Sister Perpetua's Lie*, directly inspired by Raymond Roussel's plotless novel *Impressions of Africa*, which details bizarre ceremonies and amateur theatricals among the shipwrecked French guests of an African king. (A cult classic's cult classic, this book periodically pounces out of oblivion to change somebody's life.) Morton's three-part construction of drawings and wooden elements, connected by a black framing strip that meanders across walls and floor, is indescribable not because it is so complex but because each of the artist's decisions is at once so precise and so opaque. Thousands of words would be needed to detail it justly, and no number could explicate it.

Morton was indeed a vicarious soulmate of the divine Raymond, whose prose style of fussy incredibilities is vivid in the passage her piece centrally quotes: "To the question, 'Is this where the fugitives are hiding?' the nun, posted before her convent, persistently replied 'No,' shaking her head right to left after each deep peck of the winged creature." Aside from hazarding the fact that Morton had a Catholic upbringing, not even her most devoted critics have made much sense of her attraction to the beleaguered Sister Perpetua (who is, by the way, a mechanized statue in Roussel's telling). I think Morton gives a rather clear message with this symbol of a holy refusal to yield information. The message: don't ask.

I had a distant crush on Morton for a while. I think many people did. While being as toughly independent as a woman artist had to be, not to be patronized, she radiated a lovely combination of the maternal and the childlike, with somewhat more enthusiasm for joining the art world than the art world strictly deserved. The young-artist scene back then was a sort of collective holding pattern for disaffected, inchoately yearning refugees from sensible career choices. Something like that seems increasingly a style of the 1990s, which would explain why this Morton demi-retrospective feels timely. We may be into another era craving intimate heroes who will shift the polarity of an encroaching meaninglessness from negative to positive, depressing to festive. Such heroes must want to be artists as much as Morton did, which is as much as anyone can want anything.

CHARLES BURCHFIELD: THE SACRED WOODS
The Drawing Center

FOR MOST PEOPLE WHO HAVE EVEN heard of him, Charles Burchfield (1893-1967) may be a musty reputation from the crackerbarrel of pre-international American art. But he has a lasting, semi-cult appeal for others. Part of me has adored him ever since as a teenager I saw a reproduction of his *Ice Glare*. Owned by the Whitney Museum, it is an early-1930s view of a drab street wanly afire with winter light. The picture's bleak intensity thrilled me. It was so . . . interesting. I grew up in Midwestern small towns. Being interesting was not what they were about. The painter of *Ice Glare* got the stony heart of an American town even as he found a metaphysical glamor in it. His tranced concentration on raw fact struck me as illicit, not quite sane, and very satisfying.

Burchfield, from Ohio, lived most of his life near Buffalo, a spiritually tortured introvert who worked for a time as a wallpaper designer (cultivating a decorative knack crucial to his art). He gained success between the world wars with realist treatments of American places. Like Edward Hopper's, his finest realist works make no bones about the places' inclemency to the human spirit, giving access to some hard, empty, nonetheless brave, strongly solitary (not lonely) soul of the United States — at least, of the United States before television. Their quality of bottled-up emotion can affect like a lump in the throat. Burchfield had none of Hopper's tragicomic knowingness and rumbling sexuality, but in his small way, usually with watercolors, he could be as good.

But there was another Burchfield than the austere observor. He is seen at the Drawing Center in a perfect summer show, the kind that absorbs a wandering viewer in something peculiar that has a lot of incidental philosophical resonance. Depending on mood, this Burchfield can seem a miraculous visionary or one of the worst artists who ever lived. One's mood may be volatile. My own feeling teetered, when I saw the show, between rapture and contempt. Ecstatic, scared, relentlessly over the top, the work on hand, brought together by the Burchfield Art Center in Buffalo, locates a knife edge between communicative apotheosis and communications breakdown.

The pictures are nearly all landscapes in which something weird is occurring. The inevitable word is psychedelic. Trees shiver, light splinters, and skies burst. Sounds, of birds or thunder, assume visible form. Speaking as one of those who in the 1960s rolled our brain cells like dice in the pharmacological casino, I find many of the effects hallucinogenically correct — notably the various ways light is seen to become a physical force, a massy wind interpenetrating with, bending, and shattering solid matter. The sense of cogent zonkedness is most convincing when subtlest, catching the drift of those moments when confidence in the stability of the visible gives way to worried fascination.

But subtlety was a sometime thing for Burchfield in his pantheistic fits. Often he couldn't just look and feel. He had to interpret, commonly in religious terms. He flirted with the idea that what he perceived on his nature walks, a vibrating uncanniness, was really out there (rather than really in here, a psychic phenomenon) and proved God's presence. I imagine him sweating on a buzzing summer day with his watercolors gear, a nervous man caught between a chuckle and a sob. He renders a stand of trees in suspense — waiting for a telltale wobble in his perception, a fissure in the world through which something divine or demonic will announce itself in flowing pigments. His hunger for revelation is a lust in the head.

At his worst, Burchfield suggests a definition of artistic badness: travesty of the sacred, at once rousing and debasing profound yearnings. His images of wild oneness with nature, from insects in the grass to stars pinwheeling overhead, are too often forced illustrations. Terminally heady, they leave out the body (ourselves as nature, nature in us). They are less visions than animations, not so much Caspar David Friedrich as Walt Disney. But Burchfield at his worst can be amazingly close, a nextdoor neighbor, to Burchfield at his best, who keeps a taut connection between what he sees and his own exalted or morbid mentality — resisting the urge to, say, turn a forest into a Gothic cathedral.

The downbeat was his strong suit, artistically. He even had a specific symbol for "morbidness," a cat-eared shape shaded on top, part of a remarkable lexicon called "Conventions for Abstract Thoughts" that he invented in 1917. Other of the grim ciphers include two tall ovals for "imbecility," paired dark spirals for "fear," and a droopy shape, suggestive of a female pudendum, for "fascination of evil." The idea of one-to-one graphic equivalents for emotions is a choice bit of American pragmatism. And it works. Burchfield's "visionary" pictures can feel intricately programmed with particular manic-depressive states. To give yourself to them is to be invaded by this forlorn, excited, trouble-prone mind.

In the last two decades of his life, Burchfield calmed down. He solved his God problem by deciding that the divine is "separate from his creation." (He converted from pagan independence to Lutheranism — a colorless faith that, as someone brought up in it, I deem an astonishing choice.) While becoming bigger and grander, his work is still subject to close calls between bad and good, getting worse (in gaga celebrations of the seasons that, if backlit, would make nice pinball machines) and better. He brought off at least one masterpiece, *Solitude*. A brooding cliff face with shimmering waterfall and flame-like trees, this large watercolor was begun in 1945 and finished 19 years later. Deliberation paid off. Each detail speaks. Look at it for a long time. It is the map of a soul.

A gregarious painter friend of mine tells me that the Burchfield show is being fervently discussed in downtown studios and upstate summer retreats. This makes sense to me at the present moment of art-world demoralization, when the long insulted old metier of painting shows signs of revival, with cautiously rising hopes and sanely chastened expectations. Whether in painting or another medium, the next art that matters to people is quite apt to have something of Burchfield's primitive sincerity, homemade ingenuity, and iffy success rate, qualities opposite the shallow groupthink and facile theatricality that have been boring many of us lately. Burchfield knew that the way up is often the way down.

42ND STREET ART PROJECT
West 42nd Street between Times Square and Eighth Avenue

Early one morning in Washington, D.C., last week, I couldn't sleep and so went walking. Traversing the Mall in stagnant air that predicted a stifling day, I considered visiting Abe Lincoln's statue, but there looked to be about a hundred more steps to it than I remembered. I slouched into the Vietnam Memorial. Already another light sleeper, a woman, was taking a grease-pencil rubbing of someone's name. The Memorial did not move me, for a change. It felt inoperative, as if unplugged. I reflected that public art is art that looks futile without its power source, which is a crowd. The better, more sensitive the work, the more embarrassed it seems when deserted. You are not supposed to be alone with it.

Everybody needs love. So does each thing made by humans for other than strictly expedient reasons. Each such thing implies the thought, "They're gonna love this." When nobody loves it, the effect is mortifying. I had a moment of seeing as unloved even the wonderful Vietnam Memorial, where the touching sight of the grease-pencil woman palled a bit as she industriously piled up one rubbing after another. For all I know, there is a market in those things.

Is lack of love a present epidemic? It rages in the art world. This past season of shows was like an orphanage of the emotionally starved, some noisily complaining while most suffered quietly in corners. Many shows were likable — a condition peculiarly grave. Merely to like an art work is to acquire an awkward affection, as for a cute, not terribly bright cousin who is new in town with no place to stay. Likable art is more trouble than it is worth. I may have thought of all this in Washington because, the day before, I had seen an art show at Times Square.

On 42nd Street between Seventh and Eighth there are installations by over two dozen artists sponsored by the 42nd Street Development Corporation and Creative Time, Inc. Urbanistically speaking, the artists are crows to carrion. Like unrepaired leaking roofs, art works in otherwise idle buildings these days mean that the buildings are doomed. The deathwatch ensemble on 42nd Street is a long way from a federal monument whose supposed meaning is eternal remembrance, though in New York it makes sense to have our commemorations, like nearly everything else, on the fly. The show is mostly lame (as shocking as such an opinion may be to all you public-art nuts out there). However, a couple of things in it, by Jane Dickson and Karen Finley, really do commemorate something both special to the place and widely significant: dreams of whores and wishes of the ravaged, folk poetries of desolation.

"They're gonna love this" is not a thought ever implied by that perhaps over-famous block (whose edge on innumerable other such strips may be just its presence in a city chronically full of writer-flaneurs). "This'll open their wallets" is more like it. Itch and compulsion — a sin zone's arsenal — are considerations more practical than love, more predictable, neater. To make hay of them requires no creativity, just powers of observation and a heart of stone. The sin zone's romance, for those daringly susceptible, is precisely its cold travesty of natural need and yearning. Uncalculated and thus ignored, emotions desperate and tender hover about the scene like the foggy glow around neon signs. Half a snoot of alcohol, or whatever, aids the poignant mood, which can very easily get you mugged.

Dickson and Finley focus the drifting glow. I was immediately enchanted by Dickson's installation, which dragoons a large porn parlor into service as a showcase for bridal fantasies. I initially abhorred Finley's, which transforms the former Papaya World on the corner of Seventh Avenue with a passion-purple paint job and a mural of inept drawings and poems reeking of treacly adolescent sentimentality. Dickson's work has stayed with me. Finley's has come to haunt me, as I grasp its wavelength not with my sensibility but with the actual living and dying street. No names appear in the two pieces because 42nd Street keeps no files on its casualties, but communal loss throbs in these temporary monuments to temporary lives.

Dickson is a veteran realist painter of lower-class subjects. She has long lived near Times Square. The density of her experience gives weight to her installation, in contrast to the flimsiness of most other works in the show. (I include Jenny Holzer's familiar aphorisms recycled on defunct theater marquees; her very '80s media politics, reducing our troubles to effects of public rhetoric, suddenly feel as obsolete as the theaters.) Dickson has filled the windows of *The Bride* with backlit oval paintings on vellum of self-contented brides. Through the locked glass front door we peer into the cavernous Adult Video World, whose booths and counters are visible in subdued, rather elegant lighting. Stairs lead to a mezzanine where a spotlit, resplendent effigy of a bridal gown made of transparent material rotates, shedding glints of color like the rainbow hues of gasoline in water. Intense, silent dreaminess prevails.

Dickson's piece could be saying either that marriage is the dialectical opposite of prostitution or that marriage and prostitution are the same thing — if her piece were "saying" anything. I think she unjudgmentally touches on rankling confusions about sex and love, figured in two commercial institutions: porn parlor, bridal shop. Recreated in a museum, the installation would be terminally arch, but there it is on breathing, stinking 42nd Street with its double essences of peep and matrimony irony-free and pure in themselves while mutually lacerating in conjunction. Each viewer may take *The Bride* personally, brought to a lucid registration of cynicism or sorrow. The work offers no resolution more tidy than life is.

Dickson speaks in a public way to solitary woe. Finley whines and jabbers out of aloneness that has no notion of where it ends and public spheres begin. She is a remarkable figure in the culture. In performance, she combines astonishing charm with an incredibly irritating attitude, a me-me-me plaint of victimization. She is a doyenne of damaged lives, an avatar of every skeleton in every family closet, society's chicken come home to roost. To say she is authentic is to say the best and worst about her. She gives you two choices: stay or run away. I ran away from her Papaya World piece, but it has caught up with me.

The clumsy, flowery figures in Finley's mural are idealized, God-touched nudes of a man, a woman, and a child. They are accompanied by manic prose poetry of self-infatuation: "I am a polka dotted pony. Lollipops of cherry and grape adorn me. . . . I am a bouquet for all mankind." The intensity of the tone goes beyond typical teenage gush. It seems quite mad. The impression is not allayed when one learns (as I did from a press release) that the "lollipops" referred to are Karposi's sarcoma lesions, subtle representations of which speckle the figures.

The AIDS element of *Positive Attitude*, as it is blandly titled, is not spelled out on site, allowing the piece a more general resonance. The work's hysterical upbeatness evokes a corresponding negativity, the inky shadow of souls as deeply blighted as the mural is giddily exalted. Aesthetic distance collapses. Finley's installation becomes a sheer phenomenon, really happening in a real place habituated by real, terrifyingly injured young people whom she reaches toward with a certain presumption, but no condescension. Suddenly "art" seems a largely trivial issue. A viewer is knocked sideways out of critical detachment into awareness of common humanity in need of uncommon, indeed practically incomprehensible compassion.

The best that public art may offer now is a meditation in an emergency. The emergency is a vacuum of shared meaning — public meaning to which one gladly owes allegiance or private meaning that becomes cherished community property, no matter. We lack both kinds. Both kinds require that we enjoy feelings of selfless participation, the spending of surplus love. Whose heart today sufficiently overflows? Maybe ask Abe Lincoln, if you can stand the climb. Ask yourself. Keep asking. One way and another, we will return often to the emergency of present lovelessness, which is wrecking us.

THE VENICE BIENNALE

DEMOCRACY WRECKS ART. This unpopular truism popped into my head as I stood in a loggia of the Doge's palace (called by John Ruskin "the main building of the world") last week, complacently gazing down upon the little people in the piazza. Then I remembered that I am a little person, too, though a lucky little person to have come again to Venice, queen of the sea. Our sort overruns the old aristocratic sites of Europe every summer. We wear jeans and poke into sanctums of former power. We ogle paintings that confirm the artistic superiority of tyranny.

Democracy cannot produce a new Tintoretto, so it is nice to know that the old Tintoretto isn't broken. If contemporary art must get worse for there to be more democracy, fine. To regret the death of aristocratic standards, you would have to be confident that, things being otherwise, you would be among the aristocrats. You would also have to be able to enjoy that. What with liberal guilt, I can hardly handle the privileges I've got. Happily, the world possesses more than a lifetime of the great old things to look at, if mysteriously aggrieved folks like whoever planted that bomb in Florence last spring will refrain from blowing them up.

But we really have to stop acting surprised when big contemporary shows like the current Venice Biennale turn out to be stinkers — this despite abundant talent, curatorial skill, lots of government money, and bureaucratic effort on something like a wartime footing. It is huge, the XLV Biennale, with thousands of works by hundreds of artists in the national pavilions, the juried Aperto (open) of the up-and-coming young, and many collateral theme exhibitions around town (plus retrospectives of Marcel Duchamp and Francis Bacon). There are coups of pleasure, too, here and there, but they are tiny upticks on a skidding chart line.

Simply, it is in the genetic makeup of the big shows to stink from effluvia of good intentions. Political pressures for fairer representation of women, Third World countries, and so on are the least of this — tending toward liveliness, even, in Venice, as with an eye-opening show of recent painting and sculpture from

Senegal and the Ivory Coast. Democracy's breakthroughs can be brilliant.

It is quotidian democracy that palls, causing such swoons of authority as the present curatorial imperative *to serve the artist.* The artist is today's aristocrat by default, with full responsibility to decide what we the audience will see — as if artists, who are experts in how to do things, commonly have notions better than yours or mine of what to do. Tintoretto was not burdened with determining which theme to paint on which ceiling.

The one truly engaging, though miserably limited, thing an artist can do under such circumstances is to fulfill the audience's resentment by biting the serving hand. This is always easiest in the 28 national pavilions of the Castello Gardens, where the 98-year-old Biennale's history of nationalist promotion is a fat paw. Biennale team captain Achille Bonita Oliva tried to make it harder this year with his good-intentional idea of asking countries with pavilions to host artists of countries with none. But few national commissions complied, leaving to Italy, with its capacious digs, the role of mother hen to the developing world.

Besides presenting noisy, silly stuff by guest artist Nam June Paik, Germany has extended its reunified digits for this year's most mordant chomp, by Hans Haacke. Haacke takes on Germany's splendid and intimidating Nazi-modern pavilion. He has graced the entrance with a big photo of Hitler (looking bored) at the 1934 Biennale. Inside, he has broken up the marble floor, which, trod upon, yields a strange, wild music of clanks, clacks, and clunks under the block-lettered Italian for Germany, GERMANIA. Not known for leaving well enough alone, Haacke adds over the entrance the lame tendentious note of a plaque representing the Deutschmark, but this does not spoil his environment's violent, unforgettable theatricality.

Ilya Kabakov makes no mistakes with his even more violent alteration of the old Soviet pavilion, a czarist wedding cake of a thing built in 1914. He has surrounded it with a crude wooden construction fence and filled its darkened interior with a preposterous uncompleted and uncompletable remodeling that features grandiose staircases to nowhere in particular. Out back, a ticky-tacky structure painted with gaudy Soviet insignia blares tinny martial music. The whole symbolizes fantastic waste of fantastic energy, 70 years of Revolutionary delirium. It is terrifying and hilarious.

To become a major artist now, it seems, one should take pains to be born in a country with a totalitarian legacy.

Louise Bourgeois was born in France and is a woman, a combination that might make her choice as U.S. representative seem self-consciously virtuous were she not also very good. Bourgeois's mix of the gorgeous and the poisonous, the sculpturally consummate and the psychically raw, comes off wonderfully in the Georgian candybox of the U. S. pavilion.

I was told that a pair of European curatorial whangdoodles, lately under fire for slighting women artists, angrily challenged an American to say why Americans like Bourgeois so much. "Because she bugs you guys so much," the American might have replied but did not. Served by her own old-fashioned sense of ancient and Surrealist traditions, Bourgeois goes straight to the people, spurning the curatorial establishment's smarmy embrace.

GERHARD RICHTER
Marian Goodman Gallery

T HIS MAY BE A GOOD SEASON FOR PAINTING, why not? Everything else has had a chance. The general run of installational art, in particular, has been boring us stupid for what could be long enough. If there is any juice left in the theatrics of message-y environments, I will be surprised. If there is any really new juice in painting, that would be more than surprising, but it might not be necessary. Times of frustration and disappointment, when it seems that nothing changes, yearn for the consolation of philosophy: knowing that one knows something, almost no matter what. Painting is art's philosophical warehouse, stocked with visceral responses to Western culture's every big idea. "Painting is dead," a smart line for 30 years, is one such idea, which informs the paintings of Gerhard Richter.

Richter's new show is as beautiful as a toxic waste dump in the morning. Evil colors shimmer as if in mist, smolder as if in shadow, and burn as if in raking light. They are mostly normal, strong oil colors, such as cadmiums and ultramarine blue, in atonal, jangling combinations. The touch of evil owes to Richter's chance-generating ways of applying the paint and moving it around, with boards and scrapers. We get no sense of what and how the painterly events *mean*. A fiesta of chromatic and textural effects excites the eye while, with its hint that this is all a bunch of accidents, making wary the mind and heart. That a particular red occurs in one part of a picture can seem not much more significant than where a bug splatters on a windshield.

I am referring to the 13 abstractions in the show, most about eight feet square (a popular proportion lately, at the outer limit of "easel painting"). The works display a restless formal range from quilted grids to overall fireworks, with the tour de force of four coldly blazing canvases on which acidic lime-green grounds are splotched with blackish blue. There is also one small floral still life in the artist's "out-of-focus" Photorealist mode, a fiercely philosophical object that I will get to. The show's news is that Richter, since the sensation a few years ago of a suite of photo-

105

based paintings documenting the deaths of Baader-Meinhof gang members, has been happily producing ever fresh variations on his brand of slightly nasty abstract decorations that do not insult the intelligence. The variations are beautiful. Beauty is a bug that hits Richter's windshield time and again.

Richter's art marries a skeptical approach to an avid follow-through. Born in Dresden in 1932, he became in the 1960s an inventor of the brainy, astringent West German response to Pop art, ringing changes on Andy Warhol's chipper enslavement of painting to photographic reproduction. Richter painted from banal photographs of warplanes, murder victims, philosophers, soft-core pornography, cityscapes, landscapes, and still lifes of candles and skulls. He alternately mimicked, exaggerated, and trashed photographic content with handmade form, clearly fascinated by how stubbornly we credit the camera's pretension to truth even when we are looking at obviously manipulated paint. He became a virtuoso in debased genres, as if Toscanini conducted advertising jingles. With his no less generic abstractions, Richter segued to virtuosic cacophonies.

Richter's critical reception is an odd tale. His chilliness initially made him a far harder sell in the United States than his antic colleague Sigmar Polke. His reputation was taken up by poststructuralist and Marxist critics, notably his unlikely friend Benjamin H. D. Buchloh. Buchloh's attempts in an amazing 1988 interview to coax Richter into anti-aesthetic positions, beaten back by the artist, made for a cult classic among critical texts. (Dave Hickey wrote of it in a recent *Parkett* that not "since Cardinal Kajetan's interview with Martin Luther have two styles of moral seriousness collided so spectacularly with so little intellectual effect on either party.") So hypnotic is the irony Richter directs at painting that some people seem not to notice that this artist positively spews paintings.

Richter unquestionably loves what happens when paint meets canvas. That painting may be "dead" — a literally unbelievable, exhausted rhetorical medium — just allows him to dote on it the more deliriously. (I think of the beloved and irrepressible corpse in Edgar Allan Poe's short story "Ligeia.") Not having to add up, painterly phenomena can be piled on until the mind, persuaded that analysis is pointless, goes woozy with overstimulation. The effect is so far removed from representing nature that it rivals nature, triggering experience as primary as a sunset. Something like the old-fashioned Sublime occurs in brackets of a drily wised-up attitude. Intellect observes the turmoil of the eye passively, as if saying "Fancy that!"

We come now to the floral still life, a spray of white and yellow lilies and white and yellow daisies with a two-tone gray background. Richter inserts this lovely bauble in the show like a gambler dealing the ace that was up his sleeve. What it says in context is complex and open-ended: something about the character — the flavor — of our desire for representations, a desire at once scorned and tickled to fever pitch by the surrounding abstracts. The floral both panders to and cools the desire. Its photographic realism is of course intensified by the contrast, though its paint is palpably smeared to produce the "out-of-focus" blur. Illusion and the trickery that causes it register simultaneously.

Now notice something else, which makes of the show a very, very subtle instance of installational art. The larger-than-life lilies and daisies are hung at eye-level. We do not see the vase they stand in. A vase of the right proportion for the long-stemmed flowers would, by my estimation, have its bottom at about floor-level. Flowers and vase together would be human-body size, confronting the viewer. Imagine that the canvas is the mirror in a medicine cabinet invented by Lewis Carroll. Looking into the painting, you are viewing your own face, interpreted. You are a flower-head. You are a blooming mind arranged in the receptacle of your body. How do you look?

It seems faintly possible that Richter would reject my take on the still life. (After seeing what happened to poor Buchloh, I think I will not ask the artist — whom, by the way, I have never talked with.) But he would hardly deny that, in show after show, he has aimed to create a hypercharged ambience in which materialist matter-of-factness blends with practically surreal suggestiveness. This professorial German is a masseur of our aesthetic susceptibilities with scientifically educated magic fingers. If in our bliss we hatch outlandish theories about him, he can blame himself.

Richter plainly has no interest, while painting up a storm, in denying that the medium is used up. Painting being defunct, he gets away with murder. (There is no law on the books against offing a stiff.) He is not alone among current artists in such complicitous duplicity. The basic ironies, foreshadowed by Warhol and before him by Marcel Duchamp and others, have been art-world commonplaces for at least a decade, fueling a dead-painting strategy couched in terms of last-ditch decadence, as an "end-game." It is time to say that the game has gone on for too long to be an endgame. It even looks ever more robust, as witness this Richter show. Can we all just relax? We know that painting is old-fashioned and silly, but we *like* painting, okay? Painting will continue for as long as we crave knowledge that is a feast for the eyes.

GEORGE PLATT LYNES *Grey Art Gallery*

I HAVE A HOPEFUL HUNCH THAT the fracturing of the art culture on tribal lines has almost run its necessary course. Are we ready to be commonsensical about differences lately controversial? Might our various tribes, while maintaining their sovereignties, agree on the constitution of a United States of art? We — a shiny and mysterious new "we" that I propose to take for a trial spin — will see. A good test track is the Grey Art Gallery's George Platt Lynes retrospective, a very gay event that is an art event of a high order — an event, in fact, that has its mainstream feel precisely in aspects that are obstreperously homosexual.

Male nudes are the big news of the show. Many of us already knew that the modernist fashion, ballet, and portrait photographer, who died in 1955 at the age of 48 of lung cancer, cultivated a sideline in homoeroticism. Lynes was a figure in the loose circle — community? family? gang? club? — of gay artists and writers who, while often prominent in the straight world, made up a sort of shadow culture at midcentury. The culture was closeted, as it had to be, but for those privileged by wealth or talent the closet could be roomy and well upholstered. From Jean Cocteau in France to, say, Christopher Isherwood in Santa Monica, it linked a disparate cast of characters with a wink and a nod.

As I say, we knew that Lynes — while taking telling portraits of Cocteau (as advertised), Isherwood (radiantly sassy), and practically everyone else who was both gay and somebody — did nudes for his own and his friends' enjoyment. We did not know the vast scope, sometimes dazzling quality, and rampant peculiarity of this work, whose exhibition now bodes important revaluations in social and art history. A rethinking of Robert Mapplethorpe, who can be seen to start from where Lynes leaves off, is only the most obvious assured consequence. What interests me is a possibly exemplary role for certain tribe-specific art in relation to art in general.

The opportune trove of achingly cosmopolitan Lynes comes to us from some cardboard boxes in Indiana. This is not incidental to the work's history and even its meaning. About 600

Lynes photographs were collected by Dr. Alfred Kinsey for the study-materials archive of the Kinsey Institute. Having burned most of his professional bridges, Lynes in his chaotic last years eked by largely on sales to Kinsey, who thus figures as a sort of executive producer of the artist's braver images — the good doctor meanwhile fretting that Lynes did not provide him with "action" (that is, fucking) shots. The irony is delectable and creepy. Imagine a time when one's recourse against the terror of all-censoring, hysterical moralism was the condescension of all-condoning, nerveless "science."

Lynes was well ahead of his time, working for Dr. Kinsey's unbelievably disinterested archive. I fancy the photos in those cardboard boxes for 40 years as a beautiful captive in a wizard's tower, awaiting the liberating kiss of a prince. The prince has come in the form of social change. This is a nice story. However, we should keep in mind that it is the work, not the wizard and not the prince, that matters.

Lynes did not make sexological study materials. He made art, never more so than in pictures that focus on cocks and balls. Not only the frankest, these are in a true way his most dignified images. They are naked, beyond nude — while nude still, faithful to the artist's brand of Neo-Classical romanticism. (Don't look for Whitmanesque erotic democracy from Lynes. Only gorgeous types tripped his shutter.) The explicit nudes break free of his work's somewhat precious and dated standard mode.

Lynes's signature style is solidly modernist with an overlay of Surrealist vogue. It deploys a suavely limned monumentality — favoring sculptural bumps and hollows of light and shade — laced with the Cocteau-ish poisoned sugar of angelic archetypes and blank backgrounds toned to suggest a sky of dreams. While extraordinarily pretty, most of Lynes's work with fashion models, ballet dancers, and female nudes parades period mannerisms. (His best portraits are another matter: lightning flashes of idiosyncratic charm.) The vision of sexuality is circa Ava Gardner in *One Touch of Venus*, when desire somehow equalled acres of wind-machine-blown tulle.

The homoerotic nudes, with genitalia in some cases literally spotlighted, thus come as a welcome shock. They disarm criticism. Where is a subtext to analyze? The meaning is bang on the

surface. If there is anything unconscious about the pictures —
because so second-nature to the photographer's personality, taste,
and time — it is an amazing maturity, a casually grownup air.

Of whatever age, all of Lynes's models are men, not boys,
and know at least as much about their transaction with his camera as he does. A special proof is the free-and-easy dignity of his
way with black men, apparent in the free-and-easy dignity of their
way with white companions and with him. Was the midcentury
closet really, as it seems here, a less angry and predatory, more
liberally civilized place than today's unbuttoned world at large?

For me Lynes's masterpiece is a 1951 clinical view of a male
bottom against a literal cloud-feathered sky: a daylight moon.
Hugging his thighs, with his crossed feet in the air, the model
mimics the shape of a vessel, which he is. (He wears only what is
probably a chain-linked I.D. bracelet, at that time, I am told, a
sign of gayness.) Try arguing with this picture. It belongs in a
select class of the pornographic sublime with Gustave Courbet's
The Origin of the World and some of Mapplethorpe's more shattering images. Beyond actual pornography — because functioning
less to arouse than to emblematize the arousing — it is a fact
before it is anything else, and it stays a fact while attaining eloquent perfection of style. It is polemical, though in more than
one way open-endedly.

The picture argues the truth of homosexual desire. It says
that the truth comes down to tunnel-vision avidity for the physical apparatus that is on hairy, raw display. It says that the truth
radiates outward to inform abstract levels of experience. The
body's pose evokes a timeless language of form. The sky contrib-
utes an aura of lyric poetry. Everything hangs together. Everything convinces. Through its fearless candor and, at least as
important, through the pains it takes to be beautiful, the picture
tells an entire story. While arguing rhetorically, it neither preaches
nor pleads. It enfranchises every point of view on homosexuality, insuring only that all parties will sense the power of what they
are talking about. It puts homosexuality in play.

Lynes's moon illuminates principles that seem to me marching orders for art now: please us (the eight-cylinder new *uber*
"us") by declaring something real, and declare it by using with
the utmost economy the fullest technical and rhetorical resources

111

of pleasure.

This does not change the artist's standing orders — be gifted, be cunning, be true — but only points aptitude toward its proper job. (While I am at it: be adult, if that is not too much trouble. We have enough kid stuff for our present needs.) We in our turn will judge art by the strength of its conviction, regardless of whether the conviction is tribally or personally congenial. (Of course, art that agrees with you is always the hardest to judge.) Art of the future will disport itself at ease in realms of genuine discord, wanting no armor but beauty, or else art is over as a valuable preoccupation.

October 26, 1993

THE MORLEY SAFER AFFAIR

MORLEY SAFER'S ART-STUPID, television-smart emperor's-new-clothes number on *60 Minutes* has almost everyone in the art world upset. (If not roughly informed about the September 20 segment, welcome to the United States. Ask somebody.) Of course, almost everyone in the art world was upset already. These are hard times. Among Safer's crueler digs was an inference that the art world is wallowing in dough and successful hype, when it isn't. Where was CBS during the tulip mania of the 1980s? Back then, an art culture on a roll yearned to break through in the wider culture, which mainly sat back and gawked. The art culture of the '90s, dazed amid ruined fantasies of art as investment, tries to lick its wounds in peace, and here comes everybody.

In America, the way to get kicked is to be down. I hope this news does not shock sensitive readers.

The way to lose, when kicked in America, is to whine. Whining has been the response to Safer's kidney shot by a lot of art people who ought to be more cool. Either we have something good in contemporary art, which the rest of the world can take or leave, or what's the point? A dealer should say to bemused members of the *60 Minutes* audience, "We are open for business. We have the art. Come see for yourself." That is absolutely all a dealer should say. Let's practice some self-respect around here.

Beyond that, let us not circle the wagons without making distinctions among wagons. Safer's narrative hook was one of those slimy auctions at Sotheby's that do nothing for contemporary art except distract and degrade it. Am I to get indignant because a man was mean to *Sotheby's*? Come to that, am I to pretend that the art world is free of hustlers and idiots? Thinking the matter over calmly, I feel that in the art world there are innumerable people I might save from a burning building, but they could then find their own damn coffee and blankets. Not that any emergency impends. It is not as if the Gestapo is at the door. No one has reached for his revolver. It is just good old American booboisie philistinism, feeling frisky.

Morley Safer is a moron about art in the way I am a moron

about nuclear physics. He does not grasp that art is to be looked at with active curiosity, suspending prejudice, or to be left alone. I grasp hardly anything at all about nuclear physics, but I do not hold up to public ridicule people who are passionate for anti-matter. It is really that simple if art is Safer's subject, which it isn't. His impetus is the resentment that regular folk harbor for those who self-advertisingly spend money in apparently wasteful ways, such as for the mythic welfare Cadillac or, in this case, a cunningly decadent bauble by Jeff Koons. Also in action is such folks' endemic terror of being played for suckers, projected onto the shape-shifting and self-inventing, disturbing social sphere of the cosmopolitan.

If we must expend scarce nervous energy being mad at Safer, let it be for his fast one in superimposing the resentment onto the terror, implying that silly wealth and creative audacity come to the same thing. Most people of cosmopolitan spirit — including a lot of artists again, now that the '80s are over — must scuffle to get by, paying a price in security for their luxury of freedom. They should never complain. Win or lose and behind on the phone bill, they get more out of life than people whose intellectual stimulation consists in being spoon-fed vicarious adrenaline by *60 Minutes*. But it is no fun to be harshly reminded of your citizenship in a nation that, on balance, hates you.

Safer's superimposition of middlebrow rancors is naked in two putatively devastating sound bites he selected from his brain trust for the occasion, Hilton Kramer. Here is the first: "Just the act of spending money on an object makes [collectors] feel that they are collaborating in creating the art history of their time." And the second: "Many of these artists, as I well know, live in great dread of waking up one morning and finding that it's all disappeared, that somebody blew the whistle, and they're no longer going to be considered important."

Now, both of those statements are true. Art's present patrons feel they are collaborating in creating art history for the good reason that, like their historical predecessors, some of them are. As for the dread Kramer mentions, how many artists or just interesting people do you know who never suffer some variant of it? Ducks do not worry about being authentic. Modern human authenticity is wrested from anxiety. To be self-creative and self-honest is to be acquainted with an inward derisive whistle a lot scarier than the Cracker Jack prize Kramer has squeaked on for decades. By the way, a joke on populist viewers who may have let their hearts be warmed by Kramer is that he despises them.

Philistine attack cannot threaten those who know the philistine in themselves. Anyone with sensibility has an inner Morley, if not a grosser entity, that provides a painful reality check. I think of W. H. Auden's wonderful recommendation that "the internal Censor to whom a poet submits his work in progress should be a Censorate. It should include, for instance, a sensitive only child, a practical housewife, a logician, a monk, an irreverent buffoon and even, perhaps, hated by all the others and returning their dislike, a brutal, foulmouthed drill sergeant who considers all poetry rubbish." Something of the same should go for the thoughts in progress of someone serious about art. A jeering critic, let alone a television personality, ought to look like a pussycat compared to the demon of one's workaday self-doubt.

We should not imagine that the value of any art, never mind risk-taking new art, can be secured beyond doubt, out of earshot of the obscene sergeant. Some art worldlings have thought to dismiss Safer by merely observing that he scorned the work of, for heaven's sake, Cy Twombly. But how can the value of Twombly's or anyone else's pictures — Picasso's, Rembrandt's — be presumed self-evident? Every oil on canvas is just a swatch of cloth soiled in a certain way. The world divides between those who can and those who cannot do without the adventure of starting from scratch to discover for themselves the value of artworks, a value teetering in the momentary soul-state of the viewer and crisis of the world. People impervious to this trying joy should live and be well.

Of course, it is possible that such people are in a mood for malice to go with their life and health. There is a nasty tang in the air of culture, and not only on the Right anymore. Some liberals with free-floating loathing may be looking for politically safe, if not Safer, places to dump it. Safer showed the art world's advantages for guilt-free execrating: filthy rich, lily white, sufficiently male and straight, and bizarre. Will populist rage overcome the middle-class's deference to educated expertise? If so, we may see a genuine neo-booboisie that, like H. L. Mencken's original, wields its ignorance as armor against supposed corruption. It may have been a whiff of that possibility that stunned many of us as we watched Safer's lovable-curmudgeon turn. He seemed so proud of not knowing what he was talking about.

ROBERT KUSHNER   *Holly Solomon Gallery*
LARRY MANTELLO   *Jose Freire Fine Arts*

Lᴇᴛ's ᴛᴀʟᴋ ᴀʀᴛ and "decoration." Decoration takes quote marks because it is an idea that goes all strange when linked to the idea of art. The strangeness is a modern malaise. Before the 20th century, it was just assumed that art would be decorative along with everything else it was. Art made anything pretty. Then came avant-garde ambivalence about sorts of people that art had been pretty *for*. Artistic seriousness got associated with values hostile to mere visual pleasure. Abstract painters were notably gruff on this score, given their work's at times perilous resemblance to fabric design. But art's divorce from decor kept coming undone.

It was comical, how art tried to quit the job of glorifying upper-bourgeois parlors or penthouses or, at length, lofts. As adaptable as cockroaches, decorative fashion kept reforming around "difficult" aesthetics to the point, reached with Minimalism, of accepting the bare white space that is a passive adjunct to art — a pocket museum — rather than a domestic bower that art enhances. That point brought a real break. It was observed that the pocket museum, like the big kind, confers art-ness on anything within it. People started decorating with objects — stuff in space — in ways that subjected art and non-art to mutual contamination. By the '80s, artworks were name-brand accessories. You had your Sony entertainment system. You had your Kiefer.

Now back up to the 1970s and the misfired but intriguing movement, mainly in New York, called Pattern-and-Decoration. Among its leaders was Robert Kushner, whose present show at Holly Solomon seems to me his best. I will give Kushner credit and then salute the debut of a young Californian, Larry Mantello, who exalts a pointedly neo-'70s sensibility with post-Jeff-Koons, social-aesthetic cunning. Mantello shows where prettiness is now.

Pattern-and-Decoration rebelled against the visually grim avant-gardism of the early '70s. It sought a happy new deal, at once democratic and deluxe, with art's long-suffering public, a sybaritic communion keyed to an era when everybody seemed to be having sex with everybody else all the time. Embracing the

117

decorative also struck many as a tonic for the beleaguered art of painting. But the upshot was often a mishmash of overrich fabrics, ceramics, and so on and impoverished painting. P-&-D proved less successful in seriously elevating decoration than in insouciantly debasing art. It bore somewhat the relation to art that a lot of sex in the '70s did to love. It was accelerated fun with a depressing aftertaste.

Kushner was a '70s Pan. He was known to get naked and have others do the same, traipsing in swatches of cloth adorned with Matisse-y designs and sequins. Eventually he subsided into painting. It was a diminishment of ambition, but it turned out to be the right move. Kushner's painting has made ever stronger and subtler expression of a hedonism once glibly precious and gruellingly evangelical. What with floral motifs, gold leaf, and glitter, his current work is the same-old in a way, but the same-old with surprising gravity.

Kushner's big new paintings are divided into multiple rectangular areas, each area sharply different in color and painterly treatment. The pictures are unified by sprawling floral designs often in the form of overlay drawing. So intense are the disjunct local sensations that the unity of the work is rather miraculous — a miracle-in-progress that we are let in on, free to construct or deconstruct the image depending on how we regard it. The effect is generous and very sophisticated, a rewarding test of skill in looking at paintings. The more sensitive and discerning your gaze, the wilder your ride.

The pretty and its moody sister, the lovely — triggered by passages of elegiac darkness — are a consuming project for Kushner. You see him toiling at it. He uses the resources of painting as a toolbox, with great respect for the tools. The respect is an advance on P-&-D giddiness. You feel that Kushner knows the capacities of each technique, every brooding impasto or lyrical wash, to make meaning, even as he limits it to the task of pleasing. Decoration requires that every visible element pay its way in easy, immediate satisfaction. Kushner submits to that requirement with winning humility. He burns all manner of mastery to feed a little flame of bliss.

By being contained in painting, Kushner's decorative paradise is hypothetical, a theme park of the imagination. He thus accepts the defeat of the P-&-D fantasy of flooding life with visual splendor. Larry Mantello suggests why the defeat was inevitable: life at this end of the 20th century is already awash in visual splendor, though of a kind as likely to upset the stomach as to elate the eye.

Mantello has filled the Jose Freire Gallery with thousands upon thousands of giftshop and marketing-display tchotchkes. The ambience is complete with imprinted wallpaper, window scrims, and ceiling-hugging helium balloons; flashing colored lights; recorded disco music; and why go on? Simply, there is every useless thing you can and cannot think of that would be overpriced if given away. Here is the known universe of the tinselly in assemblages thematized by holiday (Christmas, the Fourth of July) and "exotic" locale (jungle, island), kitsch taxonomies within kitsch taxonomies up the gazoo. There is no irony. The artist plainly adores all of it. The effect is astonishing: absolute aesthetic weightlessness. Not lightweight. No weight.

Mantello's handling of contempo kitsch reveals its essence: colored air. The plastic or paper substance of these things only locates their surfaces in space. It occurs to me that something like this effect figured in Clement Greenberg's theory of last-word modernist sculpture such as Anthony Caro's. No wonder that theory felt laggard. Its mass-produced avatar had already begun to upset trade balances with Taiwan. Call it toxic modernism. The polymorphous product that Mantello celebrates is to art as carbon monoxide is to oxygen: a gas that the body thoughtlessly prefers, incidentally inducing the sleep of death. Being dead has advantages. As Woody Allen said, you can't beat the hours. Mantello's show is a seductive preview.

Fetishy junk assemblage is an old story. Its last generational hero was Kenny Scharf. Updating the story, Mantello dispenses with Scharf's druggy, funky Eros. In its place, he practices a Koonsian worship of immaculate newness (newicity? newitude?), the magic elixir of commodities before they are bought. I noted from dots on the gallery checklist that Mantello's assemblages are selling briskly. Good luck to their collectors. The first speck of dust will obliterate the art's defining perfection. Like Koons, Mantello recognizes newness as any commodity's aesthetic surplus value. Unlike Koons, he takes no pains to make mint condition durable in his work. He is true to the perishable reality of contemporary visual enchantment: here today, gone later today.

Like painting's loss of representational function to photography, art's loss of leadership in decoration is a modern given. Modernist scorn of the decorative, as of the representational, was always partly sour grapes — rejecting a role closed to artists in any event. To get over the scorn is to face head-on the juggernaut of industrialized aesthetics. Art in this fix has two choices. Dream in splendid isolation, like Kushner, of an impossible world. Or, like Mantello, exploit art's edge of self-consciousness to freeze what is the case in a spectacle of horrible gratification.

BILL JENSEN *Mary Boone Gallery*

THERE IS NO ART COMMUNITY, only more or less an art society. Community is about love. "If, out of a group of ten persons, nine prefer beef to mutton and one prefers mutton to beef," W. H. Auden wrote, "there is not a single community containing a dissident member; there are two communities, a large one and a small one." Society is about behavior. You can despise your host's choice of entree without social consequence, but if you throw it on the floor you will not be invited back. (In compensation, you may become a legendary hero to a community that shares your taste in food.)

Society is formal. Community is soulful. Many in the art world are so soul-starved they convince themselves of belonging to a community when they really don't. The art world is a fairly savage social zone where values are always in doubt and often in conflict. That's a function and part of the fun of the art world. It incidentally makes people very nervous.

Of course, there are communities within the art world, sects of passionate belief that put oomph behind values in common play. Art critics know that if they are flip about any art value, someone will feel like strangling them. The knowledge encourages thoughtfulness, or ought to. It may also incite sucking-up to in-groups and bashing of out-groups by slanting one's opinions of what the groups esteem. Art criticism's sorriest common fault is not obscurity, as rife and bad as that is, but cowardly or malicious *parti pris*.

Why do I think that Bill Jensen's show at Mary Boone is a good occasion for these thoughts? People are surprised to learn that Jensen, who throughout the '80s showed at the conservative Washburn Gallery, has joined Boone's once swinging stable, a byword for anathema in conservative circles. Jensen has been upheld by the likes of Hilton Kramer as a real, true artist in opposition to just about everything that I, among others, find lively and important in contemporary art.

This is not Jensen's lookout. He has any artist's interest in reaching a nonpartisan audience. I have yet to know of a good artist who is happy with being used as a weapon in communal warfare, though few artists feel they can be fastidious when it comes to support. Artists tend to be stoical, if not cynical, about the hobbyhorses of their critical champions.

So here I am about to form a shaky community with Hilton Kramer in liking Bill Jensen. It feels fine. If you never agree on anything with someone, check yourself for knee-jerk disorder. Jensen is an excellent painter who makes a conservative artistic case where it counts, on canvas. He proves that a style that would have been essentially conceivable 50 years ago can be practiced today with vigor. A capacity to nurture such continuities speaks as well for the health of a culture as a capacity to foster meaningful breaks with the past.

Jensen is an out-of-time Romantic whose virtual contemporaries include Alfred Pinkham Ryder, Arthur Dove, and Marsden Hartley — paint-obsessed visionaries of modern art in a provincial United States. (Other apparent influences are the eccentrics Myron Stout and Forrest Bess.) Jensen seems positively to hanker for that bygone time's soul-beleaguering isolation. His two-decade career in New York has seemed low-profile on purpose. With stubborn innocence and determined perversity, he likes art to be hard and to look hard. He projects a yen for tortured and tortuous splendor.

Jensen's style is a "homeless representation," to borrow a condescending phrase from Clement Greenberg. He paints abstract shapes as if they were objects and imaginary spaces as if they were atmospheres. He seeks to charge heady, vaguely heraldic design with emotional, sexual, mystical content — a generic sort of intention, which rarely comes to anything specific or clear. All in all, he starts in a deep hole with almost definitively corny and mediocre, hopelessly unintelligent motives for art. As often as not, he then claws his way out.

From Jensen you get raw belief in the higher reality of what happens inside the painting rectangle. You can't see around the belief, which meets your misgivings of thought and taste head-on. You must surrender or walk away.

Representing four years of work, Jensen's six small paintings at Boone include five that can be termed landscapes because they have horizons and suggest sky, mountains, and vegetation, all redolent of forlorn, crepuscular places. (The sixth renders an outlandish, floating body-like shape, a ponderous life-form pathetically equipped for existence only with lumps and stumps.) But you could go everywhere in the world and not find those places, whose geography is between the ears and whose topography is literal, made of paint. Clumped, buttered, splotched, scumbled paint-stuff is the tactile, all but smelly soul of this art. A Jensen is best viewed from a few inches away. Bring your reading glasses.

No previous Jensen exhibition has looked like this one. Widely spaced in Boone's elegant cavern and illuminated only by daylight, the pictures are as unlike each other as can be — in contrast to repetitive shows at Washburn that left me feeling that one Jensen was twice as good as two Jensens. Does this installation anticipate a more style-conscious, faster-track new audience for the artist? I think so. We get an object lesson in art's social positioning, the substitution of one myth of community for another.

Given pride of place is a tour de force: *Glare*, a vertical with a hectically smeared umber horizon separating a mud-colored soaring-bird-like form in a thick ocher ground below from scudding smears of tube-fresh yellow on a thinly mottled gesso ground above. The tawny work seems an anecdote of visceral exaltation that Clyfford Still neglected to paint. From the proper, nearby viewing distance, it becomes monumental. It wants to tease your soul out of your body for a stormy flight of imagination. Let it.

The other paintings on view are less dashing. Uncertainty seems their principle. "Where am I?" is their nagging, unanswered question. They look drab at first glance, but a long look releases sublimities of light and even color. Quite amazing is the slow chromatic punch of *Dim*, which presents a yellowish pear shape against a brown ground and a blue-green "sky" that contains a red-flecked halo or cloud outline. As you watch, the color starts to burn with ardor. The pear shape, bisected by a vertical line, could be an Edvard Munchian, autumnal tree, but it may also suggest an embrace of abstracted lovers. My heart bought the latter story. Beauty happened to me for a few seconds that reminded me why I love painting.

Any art, when it works, forms a fleeting community, a oneness with imagined others in pledging allegiance to something. Jensen's painting pledges allegiance to painting. His means are old, and his ends are easy to doubt. What is left is the sheer effectiveness of the artist's self-abandoning dedication. He so badly wants painting to matter that it forgets to be obsolete and obliges him. Like a rock in a stream, Jensen does not change the course of history, but he disturbs it a little. That's something.

LUCIAN FREUD *Metropolitan Museum of Art*
LUCIAN FREUD: EARLY WORKS *Robert Miller Gallery*

A LOT OF PEOPLE NEED LUCIAN FREUD to be a great artist. How else to explain the furor for the pretty good English portrait and figure painter? This is not a rhetorical question. I don't know the answer, though I am convinced it must go beyond the intrinsic charm of Freud's ultra-old-fashioned way of painting. The answer may involve exasperated nostalgia for artistical meat and potatoes (rich in vitamin PPP, for Painted People Pictures) as against the dietetic cuisine of most contemporary art. There may also be yens for the lovely old bedtime story of Genius — you know, the demiurgic, shady master at once fantastically better and somehow soothingly worse than you and me.

In any case, the sudden mania for Freud does not seem a conservative backlash, because too joyously aggressive for that term of embitterment. It's more of a frontlash. Everything's coming up Freud, naturally including commercial exploitation. Retroactively conferring "greatness" on an already high-priced artist transmutes inventories of his work from silver to platinum. At least three galleries besides Robert Miller — Matthew Marks, Brooke Alexander Editions, and Stiebel Modern — are now showing something or other Freudian. The competition for pieces of him is an art-business Oklahoma land rush. To which my considered first response is: phooey. A considered second response seems called for.

I keep having conversations with people, not all of them from the cherishable class of literarily advanced while visually challenged Brits, who swear by the grandson of Sigmund. My mind is pried open. Then I walk in on some of the paintings, and I'm back to where I started. (I saw the Met's show earlier this year in a claustrophobic installation at London's Whitechapel Gallery. It is better here, but not miraculously better. Though subtitled "Recent Work," by the way, it has a so-called "historic section" chewy enough to make it a semi-retrospective.) I have very little personal use for Freud's art, unless as an aid to reflecting on the psychopathology of everyday taste. When a wave of taste breaks this strongly, however, one must surf a bit or drown.

Born in Berlin in 1922 and brought to England in 1933, Freud became a cosmopolitan ornament in the post-traumatic-stress-syndromed London of the 1940s and '50s. He flogged his pedigree in early work — sampled at the Met and lavished at Miller — that marked him as a minor late entry in Weimar-era New Objectivism spiced with generic Surrealism and sugared with a formula of Keane-eyed pathos in portrait heads. (Other Americans undeniably akin to early Freud are Ben Shahn and Andrew Wyeth.) To excuse the gross sentimentality of the early pictures requires fancy special pleading, provided by Robert Hughes, John Russell, and others in a luxurious little book issued by Miller. The gist is a you-had-to-be-there evocation of postwar London's soiled, cold-water, alcoholic, ragamuffin glory. Want to know why Romanticism will never be abandoned? It works for *anything*.

The maturing Freud stopped doing big eyes and entered into a very English romance of pigment that looks the way shepherd's pie looks and smells. He paints really well in a realist vein, maintaining tension between the literal stuff and color of paint and the fiction of a subject's presence. Freud's color has a nice, dirty smolder to it. "Raw umber is to Freud as pink was to Matisse," Robert Storr once wrote. Freud's gnarled or buttery surfaces seduce the eye, except where a clotted buildup brags of how hard he worked to get a face, hand, or genital right. (I'm supposed to be impressed? I thought he was supposed to be a professional.) The main event in Freud is an inkling that oil paint and flesh are so similar that they might as well be regarded as the same thing.

To gauge the psychological charge of Freud's art, it helps to revive a musty buzzword of his grandfather's: neurotic. Neurosis suggests to me a tortuous means to an end, as in going from point A to point B via point Q. Point B for Lucian Freud is, I think, to size up and dominate other people. His point Q is painting, with which he invites the forgiving complicity — and ravening fandom, why not? — of strangers. This is not an unusual subliminal motif for painters. Freud just renders it unusually naked, in all ways. He wants us in on the sick excitement of playing with paint as if it were the substance, not just the image, of individuals self-abandoned to the sport.

I suspect that Freud may not overtly ask his nude posers (never professional models) to spread their legs but that he rejoices when they do. He dotes on vulnerability, which he treats with punitive indulgence or tender contempt. The mood is not sadistic, exactly. Call it sadistic, approximately. A notoriously randy straight, Freud paints almost exclusively women and homosexual men — the latter "because of their courage," he has said in a bit of patent balderdash. I think the reason is an elaborately defended illusion of superiority, expressed as seigneurial condescension to less privileged folks. His art as much as says, "I'm Lucian Freud — and you're not." The one person Freud renders as an equal is himself in ferociously agitated, incredibly unpleasant self-portraits not without courage. (A special case is man-mountain performance artist Leigh Bowery, who is so much more interesting than the painter that he steals the show in Freud's pictures of him.)

To tax Freud with misogyny seems pointless, given that he obviously despises and in some sense wants to fuck everybody, himself included. But his most telling paintings are those of naked young women, mostly blondes, in which his warts-and-all approach encounters no warts, only pulchritude. A question sometimes raised by nude painting — why is the artist depicting this desirable creature instead of having sex with her? — becomes acute with Freud, whose every brushstroke cops a feel. "Sensuality" is no answer. The effect is febrile arousal, sex in the head. Such sexuality seems so much more trouble than it can be worth that trouble must be the point. Freud's ultimate subject may be how personality diverts our animal natures and makes a vicious mess of our erotic relations.

There is no gainsaying Freud's authenticity and guts. The big problems arise with his paintings as artworks. His audacity with the brush is vitiated by academically fussy composition. (He could learn something in this department from New York's naked-meister Philip Pearlstein, or from Alex Katz.) The good perversity of his vision comes a cropper on the bad perversity of his great-artist airs, as in his injunction that all his paintings be framed behind glass. The late Francis Bacon enforced the same policy, sensibly in view of dead paint surfaces that are pepped up by the glass's simulation of glossy reproduction. The use of glass in Freud's case sacrifices juicy surface appeal in favor of swanky preciousness. For a laureate of humiliation, Freud lacks humility.

I believe the great-ification of Freud won't work. The already great-ified artists in the museums will look him over, chuckle, and bundle him off to his place among the century's honorable mentions. But today's push for Freud will itself go down in history as at least a symptom of a 1990s ache to rehabilitate "tradition." There may be something more and healthier to it, as well, if Freud's best quality — passionate candor about how actual life actually feels — becomes a cue picked up by a new generation. That he only shakily bridges a present abyss between contemporary art and common experience does not mean that the abyss is trivial. We should just wish for sturdier, more state-of-the-art spans.

DAVID SALLE

Larry Gagosian and Mary Boone Galleries

WE ARE LIVING IN THE 21ST CENTURY ALREADY. You read it here first. I stumbled on the news while wondering why nobody bandies the words *fin de siècle* any more. That phrase with an odor of apocalyptically tinged decadence was rife a decade ago. Of course! Leave it to the 20th century to rush the festival of its own demise like kids ripping open their presents before Christmas. To be 20th-century was to be too quick in all things, leaping to conclusions that promptly evanesced. Now we are making new kinds of mistakes, don't you think? (I mean, besides waiting for something that has already happened.) We won't go into it today. This is the 21st century, with all the time in the world.

So the 1980s were the last decade of the former century. They were a period of ripeness that proceeded to rottenness with the speed of a time-lapse film. Where they could overthrow political regimes, they did; elsewhere they overthrew optimism. In the art world, which became unusually keyed into the world at large, many of us found the speed exhilarating for a while, then sickening. When decadence goes decadent, it becomes something you hate to think of. Today the '80s are infamous for a mass poisoning of society by variously tainted money. But in art the decade began promisingly with keen efforts to revalue, suffer, and enjoy a century's accumulation of broken dreams. It saw phantasmagorias built from plundered wrecks of utopias, with a rainbow of attitudes from stonehearted pedantry to wild, faint hopes of last-ditch redemption.

David Salle made the definitive New York artworks of the early, better part of the '80s. His ferociously inventive paintings did everything that was needed, and nothing that was unneeded, to model the epoch's hungry self-consciousness. The pictures were one-man democracies of images drawn from many times and levels of culture, filtered through a sensibility whose strange hostility murmured of hurt feelings. The images (including objects, techniques, colors, styles, whole grammars of meaning) were convened in the field of the New York School big painting, Abstract Expressionism's heroic machine for harmonizing selfhood with the music of the spheres. Salle commandeered the machine as a processing plant at the end of everything.

Some of Salle's early-'80s works were better than others, but the weakest had something and the strongest were riddled with failure. That stood to reason. Things had to fail, in terms of values they once served, to qualify for Salle's lexicon. For instance, women had to fail as Woman, a romantic ideal. That Salle's female-nude images suggested misogyny damned him for those who did not care that his rage amounted to a confession: his dream, his nightmare, his hopeless vengeance. The qualification was trivial if, as some held, the personal is political. Others, including me, countered in Salle's defense that everything is potentially aesthetic. We argued for the amoral license of the aesthetic as a realm where only truth (including true falsity or sincere insincerity, not to mention authentic weirdness) counts. We lost. The 21st century is wall-to-wall moralistic.

Salle started to lose when he had to justify his share of an '80s style of success that came between artists and whatever they had done to earn it. He figured he could serve both a living art culture and the rootless constituency — a castle on clouds of vanity — of the '80s rich. But the rich of the '80s didn't just use art; they used it up. Salle exhausted his initial ambition and has not developed another. His show at Gagosian of quite good paintings and iffy sculptures (painted-bronze-and-whatnot assemblages that seem to me more trouble than they are worth) is so drained of juice either personal or cultural that it crumbles at a mental touch. His concurrent show at Mary Boone — comprising a 1982 classic, *Autopsy*, and three 1983 painting-constructions along with a couple of pleasantly frazzled new pictures — gives a contrasting whiff of the old, sulphurous Salle elixir.

Having learned a lot from Salle about the zombie science of animating dead aesthetic qualities, I could make a case for the "Early Product Paintings," a series at Gagosian that recycles 1960s-style recyclings of 1950s magazine advertising. The advertised products run to liquor, cigarettes, and sweets, evoking a virtual economy of addictions. (Sex is softpedaled. This is a kinder, gentler Salle.) Done in a wizard variety of techniques and insinuating pastel colors, the pictures bid to be addictive themselves.

Playing appearances of collage against facts of painting, they are suavely original. (People who see in them only imitation James Rosenquist have not truly looked at Rosenquist's work, to begin with.) A case for them is there to be made. It's just that no verdict in the case can matter as much as it ought to.

Be the new paintings either as good or as bad as is humanly conceivable, their game comes to the same thing: over, in any way that is important beyond the canvas edges. They don't do cultural work that needs doing. They apply lessons of early-'80s image consciousness that have been absorbed as thoroughly as, say, Barbara Kruger's epochal text-box-on-photograph graphic devices. Nor does Salle's current work convey any personal necessity more urgent than a drive to keep painting. There is no shame in that, but here is an artist who once cheerfully risked destroying painting by his manner of saving it. That audacity, fueled by obscure but infectious furies, has given way to essentially academic tinkering with big-painting conventions.

For the old edginess, consult *Autopsy:* a beautiful long canvas of pulsating geometric design — excruciatingly poised between exalting and ridiculing high-modernist abstraction — that abuts a canvas bearing the photograph of a naked woman who sits distractedly on a rumpled bed while wearing white paper cones on her head and breasts. The fusion of hypersophisticated aesthetics and goofy, seamy erotic play still shocks. It mounts a swing-barreled assault on any decorum or decency, either artistic or social, that wanders within range. It is a work of absolute willfulness and, at the same time, of candid self-abandon: the artist's heart, such as it is, laid bare. There is a sense of overflowing creative energy with lots more where it came from.

The 1983 painting-constructions at Boone are moody and clenched in feeling: *Cane,* a dark grisaille picture of an upside-down nude with, in the middle of it, a literal shelf supporting a glass of water in which rests the rubber-tipped end of a walking cane; *Man in a Hat,* whose eponymous subject broods behind a snarl of soiled copper tubing; and *Ugly Deaf Face,* whose title is lettered on the image of a heavy-featured face of indeterminate sex, with four small dimestore world globes dangling in front of it. These modestly sized works project a big scale, both physically and emotionally. They affect me with an enigmatic sense of fear

131

and loathing suggesting awful childhood secrets. I think they are permanent objects, which will never not haunt.

Salle can't rewind the world and himself to that giddy peak, as gone now as the 20th century's characteristically premature *fin de siècle.* Just to survive it would be a rare feat for him — as for anyone else likewise blessed and cursed by an art culture where early success, more often than not, is a cage locked inside and out and thrown off a bridge. What happens next for Salle will depend on his ability and courage to look at himself. His gifts give him a tremendous potential for putting into public aesthetic play widely and darkly shared feelings and intuitions: soul stuff. Those gifts are worth rooting for.

ROBERT MORRIS: THE MIND/BODY PROBLEM
Solomon R. Guggenheim Museum

IN THE 1960s, REVOLUTIONS came in bunches. We consumed seismic shifts of social and cultural form, style, and behavior. It was wild, but there seemed to be an inevitable logic to it. We were not necessarily happy with all the revolutions, let alone with the Revolution — the political big one, 8.3 on the Richter scale — that could seem to lurk somewhere over the stoned rainbow of possibility. This is worth remembering: certain brainstorms of the '60s struck some of us as lousy ideas. But what could be done about it? A tide was running. One was swept along. And even if one disliked the direction, the momentum was addictive, a hormonal jones: another day, another delirium.

Robert Morris was and remains a '60s hipster — infectious opportunist, macho surfer on the tide of change, Romantic cynic. I can't forget his sensational effect back then. He was always a half-step ahead in whatever artistic dialectic was the rage, from Fluxus-flavored Neo-Dada (making his first splash with an installation at Yoko Ono's loft in 1961) and Judson Dance Theater phenomenological performance through à la carte menus of Minimalism and Post-Minimalism to Earthworks, Bodyworks, and assorted Conceptualist bagatelles.

This is not to say that Morris was a leader. He was an extrapolator, a sort of action critic whose game consisted in beating other artists at what could be seen, cynically, as their games. He was a brilliant parasite, but a parasite. When '60s-type art gamesmanship collapsed in the early '70s, so did Morris's hot streak. His last coup was a 1974 Nazi-beefcake photograph of himself that appeared as an ad in *Artforum*: his sneering soul stripped bare, plus oiled. The ad inspired a counter-ad by Lynda Benglis, nude with a dildo, that graphically announced a whole new deal.

That's my Robert Morris story, which I know to be widely shared. A peculiar breath is drawn when Morris comes up in the conversation of '60s-art-world veterans: part awe, part contempt. You won't get this story from the huge, intensely dissatisfying retrospective at the uptown Guggenheim that promotes Morris as a straight-up great artist. (You won't get any story at all from the downtown Guggenheim's funhouse array of mirror installations by Morris that are, however, fun. Take the kids.) The show lays a trap for the credulous with a subtitle, "The Mind/Body Problem," calculated to change the subject from first-hand facts of art to figments of second-hand philosophy.

Because he is sheerly strategic, without a sincere bone in his head, Morris is a perfect foil for bellybutton-contemplating academic criticism. Except for a quirkily ambivalent rumination by David Antin, the show's densely texted catalogue is nonstop pompous woolgathering. Notable is an essay by Rosalind Krauss so relentlessly linking Morris's art to the writings of Samuel Beckett that you would think the artist were being certified as a literary critic. Few comparisons could redound less to Morris's benefit. The Irishman's anguished humanity humiliates the American's callous cleverness. Krauss seems to assume that emotional and spiritual significance comes along automatically, wagging its tail, when the leash of rhetorical analogy is twitched.

The content of Morris's art is smart, ruthless, college-guy cockiness, a winning hand in the '60s. Most of the other big-time Minimalists shared that luck of the draw, as did Frank Stella and, foremost among the Pop artists, Roy Lichtenstein (whose own Guggenheim retrospective recently was even more sterile than Morris's). It was put up or shut up. Arrogance ruled. Girls and sissy boys, except master demotic manipulator Andy Warhol, were out of the loop. In the era's incessantly revolutionizing culture, the trick was to act as if each zeitgeist zag was something you made up.

No one so regularly went to extremes in the pissing contest as Morris. He made a virtual fetish of snagging whatever was in the air while contributing nothing much. With a few substantial works he slipped into real artistry. His wire-mesh and slashed-felt pieces of the '60s are touchstones of Minimalism, delivering complex experiences of space and matter in dashingly economical, lucid form. (The same cannot be said for a later series in felt that forces silly sexual metaphors.) But most of his works, even from his best years and though often elaborately engineered, are essentially tossoffs. If he had never lived, the shape of art history since 1960 would be little different, an odd bottom line for an ace next-historical-step jockey.

As a rule, whatever Morris achieved was realized more solidly by someone else. The tortoises of committed Minimalists Donald Judd, Carl Andre, Dan Flavin, and Sol LeWitt steadily outdistanced his hare, and then a likewise disciplined next generation — Bruce Nauman and Richard Serra, among others — commandeered the track. Even Morris's fall-back status as a theoretician who thought too fast for his own creative good must take second place to the awkwardly synchronized but authentic genius of Robert Smithson. Morris outsmarted himself as an artist, with the consolation of becoming a pinup in academic lockerrooms where the nakedly smartass excites lust.

The main event of Morris's career since 1974 is an embarrassment: apocalypse-themed reliefs, sculptures, paintings, and drawings with which he apparently imagined he was finessing Neo-Expressionism. "In the early 1980s, Morris's thoughts turned increasingly to the possibility of global destruction," begins a hapless Guggenheim wall label introducing the artist's *Firestorm* pictures. Nor did Morris hesitate to exploit images of Holocaust corpses. Such colossal errors — to call them failures of taste puts it way too mildly — expose the Achilles heel of his hip presumption, a blindness to the difference between fooling with semantic structures and dealing with emotionally charged subjects.

Our horror at past crimes and dread of future doom are not off-the-shelf, readymade responses to be diddled at will. They are serious stuff, susceptible to being touched only by either a profound and tactful sensibility or by a spirit, serious in its own way, of literally hysterical comedy (as in *Dr. Strangelove* or *The Producers*). Morris has neither the circumspection nor the sense of humor to cope with themes truly meaningful to anybody.

Maybe he should have stuck with theater. Video projections at the uptown Guggenheim of early dance and performance pieces are tedious in themselves, being aridly pedantic recent restagings. (You had to be there.) But their then avant-garde elements of "task performance" and *tableau vivant* retain an air of discovery. More generally, Morris's facile type of talent is no vice in theater, where adroitly manipulated ideas do not sit around vulnerably, as in museums, for their shallowness to be found out. At any rate, this retrospective leaves the strong impression of a man greatly gifted for something other than art.

A THEFT IN NORWAY

A BLURRY SURVEILLANCE TAPE SHOWED two men schlepping a painting out a second-floor window and down a ladder. One man fell off the ladder. I had mixed feelings, watching this on network news. I would not have wept to see the thieves break their necks — some other time. But while the painting was at risk, I wanted them to be pulled-together cat burglars, not gravity-challenged Bozos. I wished the jerks finesse.

The place was the National Gallery of Norway in Oslo. The painting was Edvard Munch's *The Scream. The Scream* turned 100 years old last autumn. It is a terrifyingly delicate object, three feet high by about two and a half wide, that is made of oil paint, pastel chalk, and milk-based casein paint on a piece of cardboard. It is infinitely precious to me and, I think, to everybody everywhere forever, whether they know it or not.

Would the theft have become television news without the slapstick video? Days passed with no further word in any of the media, and the networks remained mute when, at last, newspapers reported hints that the painting was being held hostage by antiabortion fanatics. The ransom was to be propaganda: a broadcast on Norwegian television of the antiabortion shockumentary, *The Silent Scream.* It appeared that Munch's painting had fallen victim to the coincidence of its title in English.

The painting's fame also made it a target, of course, though the paucity of news coverage confused me on this score. Didn't anyone care? Then it occurred to me that in most people's minds *The Scream* is only abstractly, if at all, a unique, hand-made object. It is, rather, an *image*: that distended, flayed, wormish, homonuclear mask of absolute terror. Images can't be humped out of windows. They are everywhere and nowhere. You can't steal something that exists in thousands of reproductions, cartoons, joke greeting cards, and, lately, inflatable toys.

Many people find the image irresistibly comical, perhaps as an essence of over-the-topness: *too much.* Derision of it may be self-protective. A joke is the epitaph of a feeling, Nietzsche said. The feeling buried beneath amusement at *The Scream* is particular and universal dread. Who wouldn't resort to a callous chuckle to evade *that*? But you can't patronize the image when in front of the physical painting, because then it is no longer just an image. It is a fact. Step up to *The Scream*, if ever again you get the chance, and look long and hard. Laughter will die in your throat.

The Scream and other Munch originals changed my life when I saw them in a big show at the National Gallery in Washington in 1979. The experience confirmed me as an art critic. I wanted a piece of the difficult glory revealed by Munch, a power that can be wielded only through being shared. Like most Americans, I had had no idea of Munch's chops as a painter, really knowing only his prints (including uneven versions of *The Scream* with which he started the debasement of his own creation). Nearly all his paintings are in Norway. (Nazis sold off German collections of his "degenerate" work there during the war.) I have since been three times to Oslo and the cavernous museum hall, hung with his masterpieces, that is to me holy ground.

My sudden devotion was partly self-involved. My ancestry is Norwegian. People kept telling me I looked like Munch. I wrote a long essay on him and for a while almost fancied I *was* him. I got over the infatuation but not the romance, which gave me lasting instruction in how art works.

The Scream tells very exactly a truth of the easiest thing in the world to lie about: pure subjectivity. It culminated two years of Munch's constant effort to convey a personal event of 1891. In his words: "Stopping, I leaned against the railing, almost dead with fatigue. Out over the blue-black fjord hung clouds like blood and tongues of fire. My friends walked away and, alone, trembling with fear, I became aware of the great, infinite scream of nature."

Early treatments of the epiphany show a man hunched over the railing. Only the whiplashing red and yellow sunset and writhing landscape are active. Then it came to him, a figure formed of the rhythms of earth, sea, and sky: all of the nature in a person undulating in sync with a cruel universe. The self-consciousness of the person registers what is happening — ego-death, for starters — and reacts appropriately, venting a scream that never began and will never end.

Munch, 29 years old when he painted *The Scream*, was one strung-out young genius in the 1890s: alcoholic, agoraphobic, a compulsive traveler, a tormented lover. (He crashed in the 1900s, salvaged himself, and worked at reduced steam until his death in 1944.) He had a rock-star-like career then, especially in Germany, that only exacerbated the pressure he put on himself to be, as he said in 1892, "the body through which today's thoughts and feelings flow." The disasters of his reckless ways gave him sensational subjects that he distilled with care, augmenting his inventiveness with lessons from van Gogh, Gauguin, and other contemporaries.

In person, the rawness of *The Scream*'s savagely worked surface astounds. Nothing about it bespeaks "finish." But nothing suggests sloppy "self-expression" either. There is terrific, deliberated terseness in each element, such as the wrenching clash between the frontal, wavering bands of the sky and the hard lines of the railing in fleeing perspective. Space turns inside-out, near and far exchanging places. A killer detail is the pair of figures obliviously walking away, affirming that the scream is inaudible.

Munch penciled faintly on one of the painting's red stripes, "Only someone insane could paint this!" The picture is not personal. It is a pivot from the Naturalism and Positivism of the 19th century into a century of one damned thing after another. It is a beautiful work for its color and drawing, its fragility, and its discipline. It is like a flame into which the artist, mothlike, fed himself. The flame will keep burning while the painting survives.

As long as *The Scream* hangs somewhere on a wall accessible to the public, humanity will lack one alibi for being stupid about life, art, and the human cost of modernity — in a phrase of Kierkegaard's, "the dizziness of freedom."

There was the painting, a grainy gray rectangle on the television screen, coming out the window. The sight was like a kick in the stomach. It was crazy. It got crazier with the news that the perpetrators might be right-to-life. What sort of life do such people have in mind? To be preserved before birth for no end of barbaric abuse later? But it doesn't matter who they are, or what their reasons. They stole our picture and should fall from higher ladders.

SOL LEWITT: WALL DRAWINGS *Pace Gallery*

WHILE LOOKING AT SOL LEWITT WALL DRAWINGS "you can hear your blood pressure drop," a friend remarked to me. True. Little else so soothes the overwrought art-mavenish organism. "I was walking along thinking what a really good month this is for new art," another friend said, "and then I realized my thought was based only on the LeWitt show. This is actually another crummy art month, right?" Right. Go to the downtown Pace for what ails you and us.

LeWitt's wall drawings are a brilliant idea that yields a beautiful reality. Their brilliance and beauty are big-time significant. They make Western high-art culture seem a good and going concern, philosophically sound and socially positive. It is rare and wonderful to feel justified in saying things like this.

Your basic LeWitt wall drawing entails a set of written instructions for marking a wall of any size. A simple example from 1990 (not in this show): "A wall is divided horizontally into two equal parts. Top: Alternating horizontal black and white 8" (20 cm) bands. Bottom: Alternating vertical black and white 8" (20 cm) bands." This recipe cooks up an architecturally mighty array of rhythmic, fence-paling-like bars below and swift, barrier-like bars above. The room becomes a place of heraldic drama temporarily, until the installation ends and the wall is painted over.

Wall-drawings are sold and collected in the form of rights to their execution. (I don't think police knock down your door if you do a pirate version in your bedroom.) Though in theory anyone could perform them, in practice LeWitt employs flying squads of skilled executors. Despite the precision of his instructions, variables of hand and material inevitably enter in. No execution can be definitive.

As a work of art, a LeWitt wall drawing exists whether or not an execution of it exists at a given time. Where does it exist? Surely not "in" or "as" the instructions, which are just instructions. You can raise hairs on the back of your neck thinking about this.

Is a LeWitt wall drawing a software program whose hardware is the human body in an institutional matrix? Many things in the world are analogous. The rules of a sport, for instance. Choreography. Getting up, having coffee, and going to work. The wall drawing can seem a template of ordered human activity generally, just super-typical of our species. It aestheticizes a sort of thing we do without wondering why. The mind implied by the wall drawing doesn't wonder why, either. It declines even the question "why not?" It is benignly inexorable like an angel.

The angel hovers everywhere invisible in the air, ready to materialize as interior decoration.

So here we are in a gallery whose walls — palatially vast at Pace — provide the arbitrary dimensions of a number of fleeting LeWitts, from three rudimentary ones of penciled lines from the 1960s to a bunch of illusively solid geometries in multicolored, luminous ink washes. (I will not get into describing the images, an exercise of built-in tedium in LeWitt's case. It is enough to know that they are simply, dryly describable.) All of them delight the eye while causing funny stuff between eye and brain.

Scientists have confirmed what any painting-lover could have told them, that the optic nerve comes equipped with data-processing functions including memory — a sort of field unit of the brain. That's why eyesight is the fastest sense, delivering to thought huge complexes of information in apple-pie order in a flash. Normally we become aware of this automatic process only when, say, the glancing eye-brain, which lacks internal checks for plausibility, decides that a crumpled stocking on the floor is a small animal. Thought, upset, must then direct the eye to look again.

What happens with a LeWitt wall drawing is a persistent scandal for thought in the eye's report. Informed by other agencies that the drawing is a rote task performance, thought instructs the eye to recognize it as such, but the eye keeps sending back accounts of sheerly sensuous experience (with comments of praise scribbled in the margins). Empirical convictions of pleasure overrule reason — a marvelous joke for what would seem a hyperrational project.

LeWitt is a friendly ghost in the machine of Minimalist and Conceptualist art. He came on board in the mid-1960s as the most "systems"-oriented of a systems-happy generation of artists. He works out his cubic-lattice and other sculptures in advance from mathematical premises. There is often something gawky about the sculpture's physical presence, at which the sculpture as much as says, "Tough. I'm according to plan." Thus does the rationality of the plan register as irrationality — caprice, freedom — in the result.

Sol LeWitt is a very nice man, among other things a devoted supporter of fellow artists. This is worth noting given the prevalence among the Minimalists of bullies. It helps to explain the shift in tone, the sound of blood pressure dropping, when art fans speak of LeWitt, who has seemed a special case — a humane bonus — of the last prime-time avant-garde. I wonder if we can't just reconfigure our sense of the movement with him as king and the other fellows as squires. (LeWitt would be the Scandinavian type of royal who drives his own car.) This would even make critical sense.

Minimalism switched the polarity of Western aesthetics from the North of a fascinating object to the South of a self-conscious viewer. It reversed Renaissance perspective, funneling the world to a vanishing point in the perceiving mind. What makes this operation more radically plain than a LeWitt wall drawing? Nothing. The wall drawings reduce the metaphysical chaos of being-in-the-world to a delicate squabble between the ears, mediated by beauty. In the presence of the drawings, one grasps conditions and joys of cosmic citizenship.

"Irrational thoughts should be followed absolutely and logically," goes LeWitt's most famous quote. The same might be said, apropos a perfect democracy, of the irrational bundles that are human beings, with "respected" ("loved," even) in place of "followed." (Only in police states are citizens followed.) LeWitt is the last of the modern-art utopians who formed abstract paradigms of heaven on Earth. He is also the most practical. Here and now, in the world as is, his art exerts a lovely moral force.

BARBARA KRUGER *Mary Boone Gallery*

HOW YOU FEEL ABOUT BARBARA KRUGER may be how you feel about any anonymous public language, from advertising and propaganda to street signs and graffiti. Does such language get to you or not? I try to be perfectly stupid and numb when beset, like everyone else every day, by faceless voices of seduction and authority. To hand over personal brain cells and heartstrings to impersonal diddlers is to self-destruct, it seems to me. And so I resist Barbara Kruger, who does for the world's verbal-visual, manipulative racket what Richard Wagner did for the Teutonic unconscious, making it sing its insane heart out.

Kruger is a very, very good artist, though. I admit it, coming off a long, stubborn refusal to include her on my homemade short list of the right stuff in contemporary art. I have regarded her as too ideological, too theory-bound, too mechanical — too much on the side of forces she purports to fight, hostile to personal, soulful qualities that seem to me art's most reliable edge against engineered culture. But art has legitimate ways and uses beyond what I prefer. Kruger is an artist of tremendous achievement and really vast influence, and here I've been sitting tight, waiting for her to go away. This is embarrassing.

I surrender to the evidence of Kruger's influence on professional graphic style, her text-box-on-photograph motifs cropping up everywhere like dandelions. I have caught myself swelling with vicarious pride in her, for art's sake. Simply, she is among the most consequential graphic inventors since El Lissitzky, the stylistic codifier of Russian Constructivism. As also with Lissitzky, her style could not have acquired such clout but for serving the most dynamic political movement of its time, in her case feminism: message becoming medium becoming message.

Everything about Kruger adds up. Not incidentally with being feminism's leading propagandist, she is a grand master of art direction, perhaps the key — and least widely understood — consciousness-bending specialty in present mass culture. Art directors now may be practically what Shelley said poets were, "unacknowledged legislators of the world." Persuasive organization of visual-verbal information is the real, deep infra-information purveyed by the media, a sort of organic MS-DOS operating the brains of a managerial age.

Kruger got off to an Orson Welles-ish head start in art direction. By the age of 22 in the late 1960s, she was chief designer of *Mademoiselle*. Restlessly, she changed course and moved through book-cover design, poetry, and decorative painting to a period of intellectual woodshedding at Berkeley and other California places in the late '70s, re-emerging in New York with the epochally media-wise generation of David Salle, Sherrie Levine, Cindy Sherman, et al. She came into her own as a Robin Hood of layout and design, a principled outlaw stealing the secrets of the information-rich to serve the information-oppressed.

Is Kruger monotonous? I keep expecting to yawn at her red and black visual formulas and her decade-old verbal trope of a peremptory voice, sometimes named "we," that forever assails "you," whoever that is. But the jolt goes on. Kruger is repetitive in the way that, say, Donald Judd was, true to worldly analyses and aesthetic structures so fundamentally valid that they change slowly, if at all.

Is Kruger superficial? We are talking about American culture here. Next question.

Thus it is with the relief of a confessed admiration, though with temperamental demurrals intact, that I commend Kruger's new installation to whoever in New York did not turn up at the Boone Gallery one recent Saturday afternoon. I also viewed the piece on a sparsely attended weekday. Like any public art, it works best with a crowd, when your self-consciousness is atingle and you are not inclined to think too much.

The elegantly orchestrated environment, packed without clutter, comprises wallpaper of a grainily photographed mass of spectators, nine big "you"-bashing photo-text panels (varieties of masculine bad attitude bear the brunts), overhead printed messages of religious or ingroup-type bullying, and a marble-patterned linoleum floor inset with printing-plate-like tiles of variously satiric, mainly anti-evangelical thrust. Making the ensemble a theatrical four-alarm fire is a stentorian sound track of a gravelly male voice — part Don Pardo, part Jehovah — intoning abusive sentiments of generic misogyny and xenophobia to an expertly mixed accompaniment of applause, laughter, and screams.

Bring your own paranoia, if you mean to play along. Like most of Kruger's work, this chamber of psycho-social horrors runs a gamut from A to B: fear, anger. Blunt tyrannical menace ("Hate Like Us," "I slap you because it makes me feel good," "Get down on your knees and pray to the Lord") is met by needling fury of the oppressed ("Your con jobs. Your power trips. Your sob stories. Your spins."). The game seems an invitation to focussed temporary insanity — adrenalin-drenched self-identification with global guilt or rage — that may be cathartic for some people, for all I know.

My main response is a grudgingly thrilled fascination with Kruger's virtuosity. It's like how I feel at an Oliver Stone movie: impressed, but I'll be damned if I'll let him get to me. I dislike being damned and (when I can help it) being damning. Fighting fire with fire as a political strategy appeals to me less than fire control. On this score, I wonder at Kruger's use of stereotypical Christian fundamentalism as an all-purpose, evil Other, a handy garbage can for carefree hating. Granted, I am being awfully hypersensitive here.

The Ur-genre of Kruger's work is the political cartoon, not a medium for the tender-minded. She updates the photo-montage revolution in the genre achieved 80 years ago by John Heartfield (whose politics could be woefully stupid, by the way), giving it state-of-the-art tools along with a timely cause. That art directors eagerly plunder her ideas pays tribute to Kruger's originality, while calling into question the necessary relation of her means to her point of view. What can smash sexism can as readily sell soap. But the relation remains solid in Kruger's own practice, a triumph for art in the mainstream of social history.

CLEMENT GREENBERG 1909-1994

I CHANCED TO SHARE THE BACK SEAT OF A CAR with the Man Behind the Curtain for a couple of hours one winter night in 1981. Art criticism's Jehovah turned out to be a jowly imp who chainsmoked unfiltered Camels, giggled at his own audacities, and adored a fight. We argued zestfully. I told him Brice Marden was a better artist than his guy, Jules Olitski. He professed fascination that anyone could think so, and we went at it. I felt I won my case with room to spare, only later realizing that my seatmate had conceded nothing. Had he patronized me? It didn't matter. That was the only time I ever met Clement Greenberg, who died May 7 at the age of 85, and it took a weight off my soul.

To have come up as an independent art person in the 1960s was to know the intellectual terror of the "Greenbergian," a style of critical mandarins like Michael Fried, institutional pooh bahs like MOMA's William Rubin, and other art worldlings given to winning through intimidation. The style lacked Greenberg's too rarely noted, humble confessions of taste's subjectivity. Greenbergians used the wizard's theoretic fusion of ineffable transcendence from Kant and iron determinism from Hegel to warranty "quality" judgments carved in stone. Just try battling a position whose right fist can tag you as a yahoo and whose left can deck you as retardataire.

In terms of actual art, it was hard not to notice that the Greenbergians were out to lunch. The Color Field painting they had to regard as the living end (because it embodied the medium's "effects exclusive to itself," in Greenberg's formula) was vapid. Meanwhile, they snooted Pop, Minimalism, and most other signs of intelligent life in new art. Greenberg himself had withdrawn from the fray even before the 1961 publication of his great book of selected writings, *Art and Culture*. Behind the scenes, he took a dubiously active hand in the careers of his pet artists. He told them what to do. He chatted up collectors who bought Color Field by the acre.

Why couldn't I ignore Greenberg as nearly everyone in the '60s with smarts did? It was the majestic tone, the seraphic clarity, of his best writing, with its air of rigorous principles. He might be a rhetorical manipulator, with a T. S. Eliot-like pretension to be high culture's secretary of state, but he held himself to a standard of consistency that made his opponents look sloppy. I thought that as a would-be critic I should have answers to Greenberg, and I knew deep down it was hopeless. I felt that someone who wrote like that must be a superior being. Then came the car ride, and I had to laugh. I saw what kind of being Greenberg was: an artist!

Greenberg's *Times* obituary by Raymond Hernandez contains a nugget of psychobiography that is more than plausible, though awfully pat:

> He was the oldest son of a Jewish immigrant from Russia who owned a clothing store. By the time he was 4, he drew with great zeal, propelled by his own ability to bring objects and people to life.
>
> But his parents did not share his love of art or even appreciate it. Later in life, he described them as "barbarians," who threw away every scrap of his artwork and who perhaps unwittingly laid the foundation for their son's theorizing on the mutual antagonism between art and the average person.

This account has the minor virtue of explaining everything: an abused spirit taking vicarious vengeance on its abusers. But Greenberg, who early on taught himself Latin and German, plainly was going to do something or other dazzling, not necessarily involving art. He happened into art criticism the way everybody used to: by accident, because there was an opening. In the late 1930s, the *Partisan Review* crowd of New York intellectuals lacked a steady art voice. Greenberg, with a feel for the art scene via his friend Lee Krasner, accepted the role at a God-touched historical moment, when a few impoverished painters in downtown Manhattan were about to conquer the world.

He educated himself in public, he said. (I know how that works: painfully, but the lessons take.) His most famous essay, "Avant-Garde and Kitsch" (1939), makes much of a comparison between Picasso and the Russian painter Ilya Repin that, from ignorance, misrepresents Repin. To his credit, Greenberg preserved and called attention to the mistake when republishing the essay. It was a most un-Greenbergian blunder. To get the physical, formal, and stylistic facts of any art exactly right became the beginning and end of his method. If you can see what's there, he suggested, you will know what it's worth.

Greenberg's artistry arose in how he threshed the harvests of his honed eye. Redescribing art since Manet almost brushstroke by brushstroke, he fashioned ideas parallel to the new American painting's revaluation of the values of the European avant-garde. He was no mere commentator on the Abstract Expressionists; nor was he precisely a propagandist, unlike his eloquent rival Harold Rosenberg. He was one of the gang, just as truculently ambitious. (Did many of them despise him? They tended to despise each other, too.) His best work is to criticism what Barnett Newman's is to painting: a breathtaking simplification of a complex tradition, defying argument because in command of the details it combs out.

Try to pick apart any page of *Art and Culture* apropos Picasso, Braque, Leger, et al. It ain't easy. The point of view is narrow and the tone grossly arrogant. Greenberg might end an essay, "We can ask whether Braque has misunderstood himself since 1914." ("Misunderstand *this*!" I fancy Georges Braque responding.) But the analysis preceding the insult glints like machinery. Incidentally, a passage of the same essay applies to Greenberg's career after the early '50s: "a period of decadence, when personal gifts are no longer borne up by the circulation of new ideas and new challenges."

Greenberg's was a quandary common to New York thinkers of his generation: cheerleading the postwar triumph of United States culture, then confronting with horror that culture's true colors. It was one thing when Jackson Pollock used good old American pragmatism to trump Picasso, quite another when Andy Warhol and Donald Judd used it to shrug off avant-gardist compunctions and make an art cozy with the mass-cultural and corporate givens of American life. It was something still worse when avant-gardism reconstituted itself as an academic and institutional cartel hostile to personal aestheticism.

Greenberg cherished his own aesthetic pleasure as he did his Camels, which finally killed him with emphysema. I can identify in my more timid way, sitting here with my iffy passions and Marlboro Lights. Where I draw the line with him is against his rage for purity, which he theorized as an automatic tendency of modern arts. That theory, which lingers as the "modernist" strawman in a lot of "postmodernist" criticism, seems to me a mental disease. It is adequate to people's actual experience of practically nothing in the modern canon — except Color Field painting, which Greenberg as much as authored. Color Field is like the reductio ad absurdum of someone who, avid for ever sweeter foods, ends up devouring pure sugar. No wonder Greenberg's critical teeth fell out.

Fortunately for his immortal fame, greatness in or about art has little to do with being right. It has most to do with telling a story that imprints itself on the eyes and brains of your contemporaries. Greenberg's story of surface flatness and framing edges lent acute self-consciousness to an era of already intense, society-altering artistic events. He made people who hated him keener than they would have been otherwise and art that thumbed its nose at him more dashingly decisive. By saying some things about artworks, he changed the world. Take that, Mom and Dad.

NAYLAND BLAKE   *Thread Waxing Space*

The greatest sin we can commit against the Marquis de Sade is not to read him," goes a quotation from Nayland Blake in the press release for his show inspired by the Divine One's book *Philosophy in the Bedroom*. Oh great. Now I get to feel guilty toward the Marquis de Sade.

Not until now, in fact, have I reread de Sade since the early 1960s, when I plowed through a lot of him in hard-to-get Olympia Press paperbacks published in Paris with discreet green covers that bore the notice "NOT TO BE SOLD IN U.S.A. & U.K." Those were the days. I thought then that de Sade was a rotten individual and a boring writer, but liking him was not the point. The point was to scrape off my embarrassing Midwestern innocence, and a certain laboriousness seemed in keeping with the effort's importance.

Okay, I was snobbish, too. The marquis was over for me when he started popping up in college bookstores. I still associate him with the kick of the deepdish esoteric. This puts me at a loss with today's young folk who encounter him as sort of a special item among the Great Books. The challenge for them may be to take him seriously as other than a "case," and some, including Nayland Blake, rise to that challenge.

This is an interesting time for moral imagination. If public fascination decides, serial murder is today's up-and-coming career choice, right along with creative lawyering in defense of citizens who have done things it's hard to think about without trembling. A contemporary prophet is gaunt Jack Kevorkian, our John Brown dedicated to liberating people from living. Of course, everybody has excellent reasons for everything they do. We know that. It is less clear why the general appetite for hard cases seems to grow with each oozing feast.

The Marquis de Sade would adore it. As I confirm by again taking up *The Bedroom Philosophers* (Olympia Press's version), he was a dab hand at making the incredible sound almost reasonable. In the book, written in play form, seasoned libertines initiate a 15-year-old girl with windy speeches and hands-on instruction.

The speeches apply a single value — sexual intensity, upheld as godless Nature's only plan for humanity — to justify and, indeed, to exalt any abuse of one person by another who can get away with it. The girl proves her mettle at the end by taking the lead role in a group rape, torture, and mutilation of her mother, whose conventional morals enrage the libertines.

It may be a sign of my after all incurable innocence that I have trouble regarding de Sade as in any sense real. His work seems to me a one-note, utterly artificial entertainment on the order of Saturday-morning cartoons. But then, cartoonishness is a keynote also of Nayland Blake's bibliophiliac frenzy for the marquis. Blake evinces the cult fan's pride, which is to be interested beyond all measure — that is, *infinitely* interested — in the chosen object. His installation at Thread Waxing Space amounts to a combined cult chapel of Sadeity and academy of Sadeology.

You enter through an only somewhat menacing guillotine to behold a puppet theater designed for a production, never performed, of *Philosophy in the Bedroom*. The puppets are hardly functional-looking, surreal assemblages referring at once to the book's six characters and to 20th-century personages including erotic-doll artist Hans Bellmer and typecast Marx Brothers victim Margaret Dumont. The association of Dumont to the savaged mother in de Sade's tour de force exemplifies Blake's humor, which is witty without being terrifically funny.

There is a platform from which visitors are invited to declaim the book's text into a microphone; a curtained booth with a video scramble of Hollywood movies and porn so illegible that no one is apt to need the paper-towel dispenser Blake thoughtfully provides; reliquary objects containing burned, shredded, and pickled copies of the book; and an office where Blake, in residence during the show, pursues his scholarly researches and, when tired of that, can observe gallery visitors through one-way mirrors fitted with 18th-century-gaudy frames.

Speaking of cartoonishness, the gallery displays copies of a jazzy collaborative book, *Jerk*, by Blake and the writer Dennis Cooper. Blake's photographs of faceless hand puppets are pretty dry, but Cooper's puppet-script text about teenage serial murderers is amazing: the Marquis de Sade meets Beavis and Butt-head. It is a prose horror movie, in the verbal equivalent of TV-cartoon colors, whose hideous hilarity recalls the best (that is, grossest) Jacobean melo-dramas. At the same time, it freezes the blood with its more than plausible evocation of murder's slaphappy joys.

If absolutely free to do what you want, what will you want to do? De Sade's writings give the all-time most direct answer to that question: everything imaginable to increase *my* ecstasy. The historical de Sade, though a creep, pursued this end very largely within the limits of prose fiction even while not bottled up in the Bastille or an insane asylum. His is an elegant sort of fiction: aristocratic, based in courtly comedies of manners. Its humor of exquisite cruelty is a lost theorem. What happens when that elabo-rate embroidery on a theme of untrammeled privilege meets the yahoo literal-mindedness of American splatter-film democracy?

Blake and Cooper belong to a distinct trend in contempo-rary art toward staring into moral abysses that stare back into us. Mike Kelley, Cady Noland, and Robert Gober are others who expose sad and scary undersides of certain cherished values, notably including incautiously sunny views of freedom. If the trend is about anything in particular, it may be an ongoing, slow catastrophe of the liberationist tradition of the 1960s. Thinking of the way I read de Sade 30 years ago and of how Blake and Cooper read him now, I sense a vast, mean joke on my genera-tion. "If it feels good, do it," we said with leaping faith in human nature and a less than imaginative sense of what "it" could entail.

PICASSO AND THE WEEPING WOMEN
Metropolitan Museum of Art

DID PABLO PICASSO EXIST? It gets harder to believe. Think of him wielding pencil and pecker, astride a century. He rewired the world's optic nerves and imagination. He clambered through life on a junglegym of female flesh. "I'm God! I'm God!" he crowed occasionally to his umpteenth girlfriend Dora Maar in the 1930s. He was then still four decades short of receiving the universe's considered riposte of "I don't think so": his death. It must have killed him to die.

We no longer know what to do with Picasso now that ultravirility has become a nonvalue. The schoolyard envy of ordinary men for the priapic Spaniard used to be constant in writings about him. That leitmotif isn't entirely gone; it persists as vocational sheet-sniffing. William S. Rubin, Master of Mistressology, triumphantly opined lately that a famous 1923 painting, *Woman in White,* depicts not first wife Olga Koklova, as has been supposed, but American glamorpuss socialite Sara Murphy, a previously undetected Pablo playmate. Owned by the Met, the picture joins the present installation of the traveling "Picasso and the Weeping Women." Another William S., the Met's Lieberman, stubbornly identifies it as an Olga. Having weighed the evidence, I don't care.

Pabloid revelations keep coming, but their tone shifts from awed to academic. Not knowing what to do with him, we study him. "Picasso scholarship is still essentially in its infancy," curator Judi Freeman says ominously in the catalogue of this, her exhibition, which started in Los Angeles in February. Build a new wing on the library already groaning with Picasso tomes. Build a new library. Curtain off an Adults Only section. In 1928, Freeman tells us, Picasso "initiated" his newly acquired teenage lovetoy Marie-Thérèse Walter "into his preferred sadomasochistic sexual practices." That's all. No details. But surely somebody is computer indexing those practices as we breathe.

"Picasso and the Weeping Women," featuring the artist's late-1930s images of women going to oddly shaped pieces with grief and terror, is a great show. It covers a period of grueling brilliance, when Picasso kept junking and redesigning the female physiognomy like God the Creator with a stutter. The upbeat is antic grotesquerie; the downbeat is a preoccupation with something like absolute awfulness. As usual with Picasso, the particular emotion of the work matters little — far less than it ought to, somehow — compared to the mere fact that he was inspired.

He was simple in the ways that counted. People make the mistake of supposing that genius is complicated. It is the opposite. We regular folk are complicated. We are tied in knots of ambivalence and befogged with ambiguities. Genius has a primitive economy, like a machine with a minimum of moving parts, and the clarity of flat sunlight. Everything about Picasso came to bear with practically stupid efficiency when he drew a line. He was a line-drawing critter.

While commanding fantastic technique and formal acumen, he would make these silly little decisions, such as that an eye could be a chimney-thing in a tiny boat spilling tears, and then he would put them over with the full force of his talent. The effect is very simple and overwhelming. Observing his decisions image to image at the Met, and within each image, I experienced my familiar mode of Picasso-response: gasping like a beached fish. It's sort of horrifying how good he was, as well as how horrible.

Judi Freeman, whose catalogue is a model of telling organization and sharp writing, approaches the weeping women on two fronts. She relates the work in one way to the artist's rambunctious love life, juggling Walter and Maar as Koklova fumed offstage, and in another way to political events of the day, which makes sense given that Picasso's labor on *Guernica* — a fury of creation in May and June of 1937, readying the great mural for the Spanish pavilion of the International Exposition in Paris that summer — kicked off the main series of weeping women. Both connections are obvious but incidental to one's experience of the pictures.

Sure, Picasso was roiled by his women and upset by the rape of Spain. But to say that he "expressed" those feelings is too much. He never expressed anything in his life, except ironically or sentimentally. He was too self-centered. He put coded clues to his feelings in his work, which explains his appeal to the detective instinct of scholars. However, the emotional impact of these caricatural hints — faces of seemingly erectile tissue indicating Walter, for instance, or ravaged horses signalling Spain — is just about nil. Picasso was no more expressive than your average cartoonist.

He was repressive, really. Painting, he said in what has passed for a political statement, is "an offensive and defensive weapon against the enemy." I believe that for Picasso "the enemy" was the not-Picasso, everything in the world that demanded to be taken seriously on its own terms. His art maneuvers against that threat. What he couldn't ignore — or didn't want to, if it could be eaten, screwed, or otherwise delectated — he Picassoized. His main service to the political Left in the late '30s may have been to let them think what they badly needed to, that his heart was with them. In truth, his heart was a stone.

But oh my goodness, what he could do with a line and with color, as in the show's supreme masterpiece *Weeping Woman* of October 28, 1937, from the Tate Gallery. It is a splayed jigsaw of cubistic planes and surreal curves layed out in bright primaries plus livid green and purple and a deathly white. It describes a woman covering her lower face with a handkerchief and some-how simultaneously crumpling and biting on it. Her mouth full of grinding teeth shows through. She wears a jaunty hat, as if ambushed by tragedy at a party. Each detail, such as a racy blue flower on the hat, delivers a singular emphasis. Scanning the details is like being knocked down and getting back up to be knocked down again.

Picasso was antimodern. His art was one long combat of a primitive ego against the encroaching impersonal powers and teeming othernesses of modern life. That he seized on the very sensation of those powers and othernesses — alienating, fasci-nating, uncanny — to subdue them was his genius. It made him Mister Modern for visual art. But his thrust, in all senses, was that of a sheer refusal to yield prerogative (the right to exist, even, unless with his permission) to anything or anyone. Was he heroic? Ask Dora Maar, an intelligent woman, truly serious about politics, who got to watch her own nervous breakdown recorded step by step in an incredibly cruel sequence of Picassos.

To come to terms with him is not possible.

Catalogues

Text to be read in a quiet voice while the pages of Anselm Kiefer's book of woodcuts The Rhine *are turned; performed at the Museum of Modern Art, 1988.*

READING *THE RHINE*

I S THIS A BOOK? Books are issued publicly (published) for private consumption. Anselm Kiefer's *The Rhine* was made privately, by hand, for what turns out to be public display. It is a work of visual art, with affinities to music and film, that is about "bookness," among other things. It yields a theatrical experience having almost nothing in common with normal reading. The experience affords pleasures and meanings, peculiar to it, that we can discover.

The Rhine is wordless but for its title. It is not long on plot. Its cover and the first two of its nineteen spreads bear the same image of a place: a shadowy bend in a river presided over by a huge pine tree. There follow fourteen images of transit along a river like views from a passing train or car. (I am reminded of the train that travels up the Hudson from New York City, wonderfully close to the water.) Two of these images are repeated twice, so there are sixteen "traveling" spreads in all. Finally there is a last spread and the back cover, illegibly chaotic — the coda of a climax that involves the two repetitions, a general thickening of the black ink, and two nearly abstract images including a sort of zoom-lens closeup of the river.

Here we go.

Any book is a journey if you let it be, surrendering to its narrative or discursive rhythm. The title of this book that is not a book suggests a literal journey along a particular river. Do we believe that? The images might show any river in a northern latitude, or no river; they may be made up, imagined. Of course it doesn't matter. This is fiction. We will agree that we are traveling along the Rhine.

Aspects of this nonbook, *The Rhine,* have associations that most of us can share. The physical size and bulk of the thing project a magical quality of medieval tomes. The woodcut medium, simplest and most primitive of print techniques, has an archaism and a "Germanic" aura verging on banality. Then there is our common stock of myth and history about the Rhine, from picturesque castles to horrors of war. Finally, each of us will have unpredictable personal associations inseparable from our experiences of the work. I figured out recently that on the day Anselm Kiefer was born east of the Rhine in the south of Germany — March 8, 1945 — my father, an American infantryman, was dug in on the Rhine's western bank near Düsseldorf during preparations for the war's final offensive.

The pages as one turns them have a rough friendliness to the hand. They are coarsely fashioned and printed, objects palpably from the artist's own hand with a redolence, almost a smell, of the studio. Bits of straw and dirt adhere to some pages. A shoeprint shows that one page was stepped on. The whole is intimate in a shaggy country way like that of hewn furniture, woodsmoke, turned earth, and a hint of rain in the air of a late morning. There is the homeliness of hard but not especially exacting handwork. We sense the artist digging brusquely into the wood with sharp tools. Ink and paper wait nearby. The artist is driven by wanting to see something. What does he want to see?

He wants to see *light* of a kind produced by the contrast of black, black ink and white, white paper. He can't get enough of this glaring light. It gives him patience for the toil. He creates the light repeatedly with a satisfaction perhaps resembling ecstasy. Certainly I begin to be ecstatic, opening up to the light. I seem to remember things wordless and elusive but coming into focus. I remember light on water and light around water: any expanse of water puts light in the air. The artist seems to be encouraging me to remember light, forgetting everything else, until light suffuses me. I am hypnotized.

Do I want to let associations, collective and personal tones and fragments of memory, enter into my trance? I am free to do so. It is *my* trance. If I want to imagine the singing of Rhine maidens bereft of their gold, that's the work of a moment. Or the crash of artillery shells near Düsseldorf in March, 1945, why not? The book's almost negligent look, concentrated in making rather than representing, encourages me. The artist shows no care for realism about the subject — no description, no travelogue — or for elegance in the design. He is pleasing himself, not fishing for my admiration. Telling me that he cares only to make the effect of light, his indifference to everything else leaves everything else up to me. The book is a made thing, and if I opt to depart from the fact in favor of a reverie, this makes it *my* reverie.

When an artist makes a point of repeating an image or a type of image, one of two things is meant: the image, no matter how much repeated, is always different (think of Morandi); or else the image, no matter how varied in each repetition, is always the same (think of Warhol). I think that Kiefer's is the second way: iconizing, ecstatic, mantra-like. The book presents *the* Rhine, not "Rhine views." Against Heraclitus, in this case, you can step in the same river twice or a dozen times.

This is not the Rhine that will make you wet if you fall in it. This Rhine includes but is not limited to the wet one. As an idea, it includes but is not limited to rivers.

Everything in the images that does not represent water or sky is black. What does this mean? How does it work? The white, white light of water and sky advance from the page, mingling with your gaze. The rest — earth, shadow, vegetation — is a blackness you could fall into and keep falling. You will feel this at the moment when you surrender your common sense, which tells you that the black ink is physically nearer to you than the white paper. This surrender is the onset of reverie, a voiding of physical awareness. I remember light and forget my body.

Whether rendered in books, drawings, or paintings twenty feet across, all of Anselm Kiefer's landscapes are similarly disembodying. Always there is a doubleness between visual space of infinite depth and physical stuff that is out front, in your face. The order of space and stuff is unstable, subject to sudden reversal by a strong light that comes toward you. We might want to call the effect of exhilarating disembodiment "spiritual," but we are not obliged to call it anything. It is the opposite of normal landscape, which firmly locates the viewer in relation to its depicted space. Looking at any Kiefer, we are everywhere and nowhere.

The Rhine slides along. It flows always. To look at it is to sense its immemorial movement that has the awful sameness and persistance of all nature, of rivers and mountains compared to whose eternal existence our lives are sparks in time. To behold nature can be crushing because compared to her we die so very quickly, and she doesn't care. We won't be missed. Looking and looking at the Rhine, Kiefer contemplates his own death with evident calm.

As the journey proceeds, there are fewer thoughts, but the ones that remain, such as the thought of our death, are bigger and deeper. They are kept steady, made calm, by a certain consolation. What is it? The light. This Rhine trellises white light that reaches us in a steady outward stream. Like sound and smell, light is an aspect of nature that does not remain outside of our bodies, reminding us of our extinction. It flows inward through our eyes to become a principle of our consciousness and our inviolate livingness. Really to look — to look and look — is to elude time and mortality. So this is not a journey. Journeys have beginnings and ends, and transfixed by the light we do not understand beginnings and ends. They are absurd ideas.

What time is it, by the way? Is it day or night, sunlight or moonlight? Looking at the pages, I can convince myself of either. If the blacks and whites were reversed, as in a photographic negative, it would be the same. The reason is that the light of the page has no factitious source. It is not light to see by. It is light to see.

Try an experiment. Imagine that the river on the page, the Rhine, is flowing from right to left. I don't think you can do it without an effort of will that feels disruptive, even perverse. Left-to-right, the direction of Western books, is a vector we assume. It is a rule of "bookness" we obey without thinking while looking at *The Rhine*. It signifies a consoling dominance of culture over nature. The habits of civilization flow like a river from left to right.

Picture the map of Europe. The Rhine flows north from the Swiss Alps eight hundred and twenty miles, marking Germany's border with France as far as Karlsruhe, then through Germany past Mannheim, Mainz, Bonn, Düsseldorf, and Cologne and into Holland near Arnhem, at last disgorging in the North Sea. It passes about fifty miles east of Donaueschingen, the Black Forest town on the Danube where Kiefer was born, and roughly the same distance from the village where he lives now in the Odin Forest. Near Düsseldorf in March, 1945, my father saw his first jet airplane, a silvery German craft that dropped a single bomb which, missing a bridge, raised a flume of water in the Rhine. (Pieces of that bomb rest in the river's bottom.) The jet flew away so fast there was no time to do anything but marvel. With this glimpse of future wars, the war was nearly over.

Because the Rhine flows north in Germany and from left to right in the book, we are viewing it from its eastern bank, looking out from inside Germany. We face west. I enjoy this specificity. It lends a tingle.

The farther we go in the book, the more we are in the middle of a journey and of Germany, of history and of suspended time. The composition of the images supports a sense of middleness. How many of us, taking or making a picture of a river, would do it like this: dead-on, perpendicular to the flow? Wouldn't you, to show a river, instinctively angle your view upstream or downstream? (Probably upstream, the river coming to you.) To convey riverness, one tends to look along, not at. Kiefer's foursquareness feels folk-art-ish, iconic in a naive way — or else hypersophisticated, evoking modernist abstraction's uniform distribution of emphasis. In either case, the composition dilates the steady outward pulse of light.

I recall that Joseph Beuys performed an "action" in 1976 that involved being rowed in a boat across the Rhine at Düsseldorf. Beuys, the crash-prone Luftwaffe pilot, was a kind of father to Kiefer. I imagine my own father crossing the Rhine in March, 1945, the noise and stink of the crossing, and something leaps in me. A painful joy. I want to extract from Kiefer's *The Rhine* some consolation not just aesthetic and metaphysical, but historical and personal. But I can't. The book is too aloof, too alien. I start to feel estranged, impatient, and very American.

The actual Rhine is a busy river. Where, here, are the boats, buildings, and people? There aren't even any animals. No American would create so many landscapes and not put a few such things in. In a Dutch landscape, you can hear cows even when you don't see any. Kiefer is after all German in his view of nature. German conceptions of nature tend to be mineral and vegetable, purely. If they require a creature, it is probably an eagle, advertising exaltation. As an American, I do not have to stand for this. If I want to reflect that what I'd like to do with Kiefer's precious Rhine is waterski on it, that's my right and a way of getting even for the disappointment of my personal yearnings.

Maybe it is the monotony of the river images — at first hypnotic, but giving rise to restlessness — that has made me irritable. But now I notice that a perturbation is occurring also in the images themselves, as if pressures long building in the tranquil, gliding progress of the river were starting to erupt. The sequence stutters, undergoing flashbacks and a loss of coherence, as if clattering like film tangled in a projector. Patches of collage that appear throughout the book — added swatches of paper from separate sheets — become more frequent, sometimes overlaid on wet ink that soaks through with a greenish tint. We sense general disturbance, an air of disintegration and disaster.

The drifting middleness of The Rhine ruptures, exposing raw nerves of beginnings and ends. It is not that we are coming to an end of the Rhine or of a story. We might as easily be coming to a beginning, the onset of some maelstrom, some door to the river. Or maybe this is truly The End: death by drowning where the river loses itself in the sea. We are a long way from that serene bend in the river with its fatherly, comforting tree. The light of the last spread feels subaqueous, as if coming from overhead: dapples on a surface seen from a point of view sinking down and away. Confusion reigns in caves of the sea. The sea is confusion's empire.

What did you expect? Where did you think you were going? Who did you think you were?

REMEMBERED LIFE

I REMEMBER A PAINTING. It was a rectangular slice of hot stuff in a room where people were talking. In a mannerly milieu, it was a liberated zone governed by what someone — someone wonderful, naturally — wanted. Brought to it, ordinary desires for beauty and order were embarrassed by being overfulfilled, while extraordinary predilections — lusts, angers, audacities — descended like Visigoths puckering up for kisses from flummoxed citizens. The painting hung in a normal place and addressed the turmoil inside me as if to say, "That's all right. Your secret is safe with me. By the way, everybody knows it." Or perhaps, "Are we drunk yet?" The painting might be an archangelic de Kooning or a horny Rauschenberg, but it could be almost anything. The mere fact that somebody had thought to make a painting seemed a lot, to begin with.

Then I started forgetting it. Big, rumbling forces — this is a story of the 1960s — pushed skeptical gloom inward from the edges, and the painting dimmed. Partly there stopped being a normal place for the painting. Partly it became unbelievable that anyone, let alone anyone wonderful, even existed in a way commensurate with such delight.

Visiting Moira Dryer in her studio recently, I forgot to forget the painting. I became aware that here was something new, and something for me, though the awareness dawned fitfully. Finally it was something Dryer said, expressing an edge she has that I had not perceived, as I was looking at her work and trying to account for a quality for which the word "charming" was inadequate — but what else would do? I had asked her if she felt a commitment to abstraction (such being a byword among some current good girls and good boys of art), and she answered with sweet vehemence in the negative. "Not abstraction as a religious activity," my notes have her saying. "Not formalist or utopian abstraction where you look at it and are supposed to forget all your troubles, as with drugs. That kind of abstraction is about amnesia. I like to think of my works as artifacts."

An artifact! That's what the painting was that suddenly I re-remembered. Artifacts are materialized memory. I was looking at Dryer's paintings — which *are* paintings despite their dissembling tabletoplike objectness and, often, auxiliary components like tipped shelves, adding up to a self-deprecating matter-of-factness perhaps definitive of charm — and I was already remembering everything about them, as if from a former life. I was remembering the present moment. That reminded me of a painting, deep in the past, whose presence continues to burn.

The new thing in Dryer's work has been gathering quiet confidence in recent years here and in Europe among several artists, many of whom pay tribute to Ross Bleckner, as Dryer does, and steer by lonely lights of others almost famous for being hardly known, such as Ellen Phelan. It is a phenomenon *of* confidence, really — not of belief, the banner of the amnesiacs — and may boil down to responsibility to the notion that someone specific is going to look at the work: not "the viewer," that straw person, and not someone fellow-believing or in on the joke, but maybe anyone who could be "you" in the invitation, "Come as you are." It amounts to confidence in the stability of a world of rooms in which people talk, rooms with furniture in them, sites of normal troubles and yens for a familiar Eros.

Dryer again: "I like paintings in the here and now, allowing for irritation, tension, a little anxiety and conflict." Me too. Dryer was reminding me that intimacy, an anarchy of feeling protected by tact, can be a kind of cosmos. Art can't create intimacy out of nothing, but art can absorb fugitive tones of it and return them as song. Special about Dryer, working with tones that are faint and few, is how vast is the zone — mostly silent, of necessity — that she stakes out for intimacy.

Domestic Life is the vastly, calmly ironic title of a work by Dryer. Another work I was looking at in her studio is titled *Rustic Life* — an urban idea if ever there was one, I commented, and she agreed. "I'm not interested in landscape," she said, by which I understood her to mean that she is very interested in landscape, because in the zone of intimacy one is always interested, without regret, in whatever isn't there. Rivulets of rusty brown and pale blue in *Rustic Life* (Dryer is a startling colorist) commune with landscape as a New Yorker who never sees it communes with nature: abstractly, poignantly, in a way shared with others. Her studio is brightly lit and bare. Outside the window traffic labors into and zooms out of the Holland Tunnel. There is no end of things that aren't there, notably domesticity.

She told me she likes the short stories of Raymond Carver, vignettist of the ruins of American "domestic life," and that sounded right. She added that she thinks of any exhibition of hers as "a collection of short stories, where each story is different and has its own cast of characters and emotions, but there is a constant play between each and the next." So she is confident, like Carver, in the reality of a continuum of common life available for dipping into, all the more fitted for an art of memory by being full of gaps and fissures and failures. Memory doesn't even work unless something is gone.

The nine works in Dryer's present show include two with her device of a separate slant-faced unit, rather like the informational panel of a Museum of Natural History diorama, set beneath a painting on wood. (Her medium these days is matte acrylic, from which she coaxes the same hypersensitively tender quality of the casein she has given up, she says, because it proved all too literally fragile.) One work is titled *Old Vanity* and pairs a unit in leaden-looking steel with an awninglike pattern of wanly bright orange and beige stripes. I find its muteness, honed by the title, mordantly touching, as if it memorialized a life that had been folded up and put away. The other two-part work is in a darker and a lighter tone of livid green, streaky with a scalloped border above and neat with a "fancy" decorative motif of loops below. Dryer calls it a "portrait," suggesting that the absence in question is that of a particular person.

Without added parts, Dryer's seven single panels here remember, mainly, painting itself while generating the gists of stories with intently cultivated surfaces — if given sufficient cooperation by the viewer. (Must it be emphasized that any intimate relation is a two-way street? If you are passive to Dryer's work, not only will nothing happen, but the work will scarcely exist for you.) The paintings are about residue of passions like wetness left on a beach by departed waves. Painting itself may be such a wave (a big one), retrievable by association to something — almost anything — personal. Painting is summoned as a sheerly receptive membrane by the traces upon a surface of living emotion. Though naturally frazzled, the traces bespeak passion that must have been intense indeed just to have persisted. Dryer's title *Demon Pleasure* seems an understatement for whatever frenzy can still muster a noodle of bloody nail-polish red amid undulating forms doing their best to speak volumes with broken voices. ("I'm a wreck," the painting acknowledges in the tone you'd use to say, "It's Tuesday today.") *Sister Sadie* wants to tell about something so badly that it gets in its own way, trembling so with communicative excitement that you might want to hug it, which in your mind you may do.

Dryer delivers paint in runs and veils and smears with an impulse as vernacular as an accent. (Her studio ought to have a sign outside: "Painting Spoken Here.") She as much as delegates control of the picture to fluid dynamics and gravity. She thus stays out of the painting's way, while monitoring it to make sure it is up to something worthy and not to anything insulting her intelligence (such as some nonsense about landscape). "I like a feeling that the painting is taking over and making itself," she said to me. "Then the paint appears to be in motion, shimmering as if the picture were still in progress." That effect is straight from Abstract Expressionism, of course. Dryer proves to me, by reclaiming it, that painting can do all the dying that history wants it to — decades now of painting dead, deader, deader still — without losing the ethical majesty of such surrenders, those instances of letting go, of little death, of orgasm twinkling away. Dryer situates herself very far along the sinking curve of painting's historic diminuendo, finding the whole timbre of her art in faded tones. To put it another way, she accepts painting as a ghost of its former self, whereupon, sure enough, her paintings haunt us.

Through acceptance, then, Dryer bears witness to the reemergence from mists of memory of a room in which people, fit to be loved, are talking. You sense that it is a normal situation, life taking a sensible course. (And art is a rectangle of purposeful delirium.) Happy New Year, 1990. Artists since the '60s have done pretty near everything with and about culture except just inhabit it, such as it is and such as we are. Life, for so long an afterthought, could do with remedial rethinking. Is this the season to shelve Walter Benjamin and reread Jane Austen? Dryer's work evokes for me an Austenian spirit of serious comedy having to do with manners and morals, the priorities of a society "allowing for irritation, tension, a little anxiety and conflict" to accommodate human peculiarity within sturdy limits. Her paintings are about how to be. They are positively not about how to change or escape the world — options of amnesiac abstraction. They are artifacts of a crowded world that, since we happen to be in it, might as well be negotiated with sentience and grace as not. The paintings are about remembering yourself in the present, summoning yourself to live this very moment, so as not to keep piling up reasons to regret life. Never forget that your memory has a future.

MAN IN STREET (FOR R. S.) (POEM)

ASCENDING MARBLE HEAVENLY STAIRS toward mysterious streaming light was one idea. He had many ideas that did not survive in rooms where people chattered, crashingly ordinary people such as himself without an idea. Some days everybody was suicide fodder, fortunately too stupefied to know it.

Well into later life he retained a degree of innocence, a mist blurring the world slightly like nicotine or the dotted line in the air of a sweeter possibility that is real if you think so. He could think so though embarrassed continually by facts and continuously by the near certainty of being mistaken.

No, he said, I was not born yesterday. I was born this morning with a hangover, expecting goodness and resenting nothing. Gazes remind me that I exist. Once I encountered a rat in a midnight street and kicked at it. It reared up, fearless. It hated me. I was aghast with admiration. I want to be rat-like in that way, he said, though only if some people will still love me.

He pledged allegiance to the street and to the idea that it runs north and south or east and west with stoplights red amber green according to plan. In the city everyone has a plan or is in trouble or both, but the ultimate idea had to be unplanned. It was that you couldn't expect it. It was: as quickly as possible, don't think.

It was interesting to look at pornographic images denatured in the rendering just enough not to arouse. He liked pornography, as he explained nervously with his usual double intention to beg approval and to provoke, but quailed at its power. Dispassionately to regard one's own sexual emotion definitely was an idea, wonderful for a while and then interesting and then less interesting. It seemed important to guard this idea against an idea that it was not all right, but eventually no one cared any more.

He was always racing to give an answer before they got tired of the question.

People learn that sex is not an idea and violence is not an idea and, if they are lucky, love is not an idea, but love is apt always to remain somewhat an idea like quality or democracy that he wished would go away so he could miss it. The ultimate idea was never about "values" but he kept getting trapped into saying it was, as again the idea slipped away clean, dark, and inviolate.

Out there around the corner in the rain. Never far. There among moving shadows.

It was interesting to be an American without thinking about it in any detail, just abstractly magnetized by the idea "an American." The country's power was declining, what a relief not to feel guilty toward everyone everywhere, and the country was becoming poorer and more corrupt and not less stupid, and that provided a melancholy gravity. The only things truly interesting any more were things someone could be stuck with, such as sex and the Red River Valley, sex and Galveston Harbor, nostalgia for innocence and the Snake River. Only what was inescapable remained the same when thought about and when not thought about.

Everybody rediscovered stories. People printed and painted and photographed and telephoned and eventually faxed stories.

When did photographers stop saying "watch the birdie" and "say cheese," no longer saying anything but just presenting the lens's maw which reads "O"? "O" as in awe plus zero equals awe, only colder. Photographers moved in gangs over the earth killing everything into beheld-ness. Awe times zero equals zero, meaning photographers foolishly tried to multiply that moment that never changed. He drew a line on being over-emotional and promised not to be "touched" by photographs.

Sex and the Tennessee Water Gap, nostalgia for innocence and the Susquehanna River, sex and Lake Success. Death and the Mississippi River at night. Prairie. Prayer. His idea of God was the flatness of North Dakota. (Rain.)

He flogs his typical middleaged male self-pity for poetic effects. It works. Start with the available technology: the soft tuning fork of an ache in the chest or genitals. Shame adds heat: a burning face on which to warm cold hands. Gradually a moist music or spiritual steam rises, and in that vagueness appear shapes of what does not belong to anyone.

All right, get it out of your system. Get your system out of your system. Insert knife at your throat and yank down to your crotch. Pry open. Pull out organs and throw at the audience. It's what they want, isn't it? Actually it isn't. Tears ran down his face of embarrassment to have been so in error. Now he had severe physical problems.

Suddenly it became okay, and therefore boring, to insult communism. The "post" fell off "post-modern" and the "late" fell off "late capitalism" and the other wheels fell off the other words for a situation that turned out to be what it felt like: stuck.

Things were interesting and expensive. Money gave things consequence, making them inescapable in the way that is necessary for there to be ideas. Efforts were made to relate money to other kinds of value, but the other kinds proved optional and money stood alone. Then money fell down.

It began with a smell of turpentine and ended in odorless distances.

Stuck like a car up to its hubcaps in black mud after a thunderstorm, and they have no choice but to get out and admire the landscape. Stuck like lovers together. Stuck like a childhood crush that issues in fifty years of marriage and a photograph. (Greatgrandchildren.) Stuck like someone remembering these things. (Imaginary memories.)

In the streets postmen and postwomen wheeled their tricycle carts in which were publications with postage prepaid at the new higher rates. Prose in the publications indicated a rising level of discontent with the cultural hegemony of European-American males. He couldn't have agreed more. He couldn't have felt more uncomfortable, reading the publications in his apartment with sounds of the street entering from the late afternoon. He thought of males who were never comfortable, hegemony or no hegemony. He thought a new way of being uncomfortable had possibilities.

D. H. Lawrence roamed the world with the problem of himself, successively renaming the problem Italy, Australia, America, and Mexico. Lawrence enjoyed it though "it wore him to rags," as he wrote of an alter-ego.

Charles Baudelaire was forever "sharpening as I went / The knife of my mind against my heart." The idea of something hard honed by something soft, of a blade that wounds its whetstone, is wonderful and true. The mind grows more lucid the more the heart hurts.

Edvard Munch wanted to be the medium through which his day's thoughts and feelings flowed. He succeeded, dooming himself to obsolescence like a rock star, and made amazing pictures. Really to live is to be doomed to obsolescence, meaning death plus something nasty incurred by those who have scared people. In the street the gazes of the desperate and cunning covered him. He strolled in a crossfire of want that evoked the idea of a commensurate satisfaction that could have been the ultimate idea if he understood it.

Fakeness was another idea, though a small one. Or was it an idea? Was it possible to be fake on purpose? A real fake? The problem kept him occupied through one winter, until spring reliably shocked him with the recognition of everything he had meant to live and had not lived. Reality and fakeness do not apply to unlived things. The life he had missed ballooned over him like a night sky in the middle of nowhere.

The marble stairs streaming with unearthly light suggested triumphant madness. Did he want to be deracinated for a while? His friends would scorn him, and he would be laying in difficulties for future years. This had the sole advantage of being a plan, akin to testing fate by methodically crossing streets against the light without looking: rushin' roulette.

He thought that nobody gave him a break, either because they didn't think he needed one, which he did, or because the giving of breaks was against their intellectual religion. He couldn't believe they lacked the enlightened self-interest to help him be glorious. He helped others be glorious in order to set an example. Sooner or later it would be his turn, wouldn't it? Or maybe this was his turn the way it had to be, written in the book of giggling destiny.

He swooned whenever it was practicable, such as on the street when a cornice agreed to look perfect against a sky. It was the same with works of art, that little quick melting of tension that is swooning in action, though with art there was a backwash of thoughts whereas on the street there would be a quick, cold return of the drab and somewhat dangerous. Once he had an awful moment, thinking: I never swoon any more! So he experimented and found he had only been distracted, he could in fact swoon any time apropos almost anything. He was a cheap date of the universe.

Nobody talked about form and content. They talked about subject matter. They talked about other things for which he thought the word was "design," as in conspiracies and professional know-how. Some days he felt in imminent peril of believing he had a job.

Nostalgia for innocence and the Red River of the North. When that river is flowing from right to left in front of an American and the sun is on the horizon, the person is in North Dakota and it's dawn. Having been born by a river that runs north might have made him Canadian but instead it made him contrary. That and loneliness in which self-pity would not be contained but leaked in all directions, weeping for the poor world and sun and everyone. It was about the commensurate satisfaction. It was about the baby Jesus if he could believe in God, which he couldn't. It was about picturesque effects of sorrow.

A life is supposed to come to something. It never does, but it is supposed to. Do you know why we are put here? We are put here to suppose and to suppose. The last supposition is the end. That's all. The ultimate is death, and it was time he admitted it. The ultimate will bring him up short amid his ideas about the ultimate, making a sound to get his attention. Pencils down. Time not to be. Time to be gone. And what, besides the ultimate, is death? The best excuse. The others will have to make allowances. His empty chair.

He saw how some set out to be mysterious to others and succeeded only in becoming mysteries to themselves, immobilized like cars broken down along a highway where citizens zoom past with hardly a sideward glance.

He saw how some held back from the logic of their times, such as the logic of suddenly making a lot of money, and thereby lost the thread of history. He saw how others rushed forward with the logic of their times, and the thread of history strangled them.

He saw how the yearning for something to mean something was a proboscis that flailed through the world, attaching first to this thing and then to that and extracting substance that was perhaps delicious and perhaps nourishing. But the flailing never stopped. There were horrific moments when it parodied itself, waggling without an object as if futility were fun. It wasn't. It was embarrassing, and he became indignantly impatient for death to begin.

The Right aestheticized politics and the Left politicized art, and that about covered the possibilities except for the possibility of being alone. All around him people were joining something. He studied how to join himself, learning to search in the crowd of what might be himself for the face hot with shame of one whom the others shunned.

By and by, he cooked up a satisfying sense of imminent disaster, the world reduced to lurid silhouettes by phosphorescent backlighting. It was a painting from Berlin. Lots of people got to die while he wasn't dying, and it didn't seem fair. His ability to feel sorry for himself was getting spectacular.

And what of loving? He had loved. He continued to love. It was a suspension of his possibility, cantilevered protectively over the loved one's capacity for unhappiness. She will not be unhappy as long as I live, was the motto. It seemed crazy. Why should she be deprived of unhappiness? He concluded that love and craziness were one.

The night sky wheeled over the prairie. Tires sang along the interstate. In cities human beings engaged in behavior that, as children, they couldn't have imagined without screaming. Betrayal came and went like a fashion so perennial (the little black dress) that it might as well be legally mandated. He liked all the pretty fashions, the collars waxing and waning and the nubbly fabrics, the silk, the barely audible friction of legs in hose against something silken as she strode, the unknown one. He had a friend who went away. He had a love that continued like winter dusk. Lights came on in the buildings, blurred by the tears in his eyes until the night was one cold fire resplendently blazing.

He saw cruelty in the eyes of those who didn't exactly mean it. He saw kindness fluttering uselessly in gestures incompleted and unnoticed. He saw that it would be a good idea for God to push a reset button, starting everything over. With or without him, it didn't matter.

I want it on record, he said, that I like this planet, which is cherished by me from distant stars to the molecules of my perishing body. It isn't me, this body. Anybody else might as well have it, and the earth in which it will decay but not cease to exist, because nothing does really. He went on to claim oneness with some streaming brilliance, but his words were lost in the growing and finally deafening clamor of another day.

RALPH HUMPHREY: FRAME PAINTINGS 1964-1965
Mary Boone Gallery, New York, 1990

THROUGH THE FRAME (THE FRAME IS THROUGH)

THE TIME OF DAY OF RALPH HUMPHREY's Frame paintings is mid-afternoon of a weekday on which nothing in particular is happening or apt to happen. All paintings that are alive to feeling convey a time of the clock and the calendar. Up through the Renaissance the time is nearly always Sunday morning. Then Caravaggio invents Saturday night. With the Dutch, you've always just had dinner. With Goya, you've missed a meal and don't know which, because you can't tell whether it's night or you're in a sealed room. The Impressionists get up early in the morning. The Expressionists paint their landscapes fast, racing dusk. It is Sunday morning again for the Surrealists, only with rumpled beds. Malevich and Mondrian discover electric light. It's generally Friday night and Saturday (blowing the week's pay) for the Abstract Expressionists. Pop art stays up until dawn, in which it falls speechless.

Then comes the epoch of Humphrey, when an artist in a loft gazes at a blank canvas and wishes the phone would ring. It doesn't. Later, friends who visit notice that the artist's canvas is finished, and that it emits a steady pulse of gazing and wishing, the endless incipience of an afternoon on which it might or might not have been raining but was probably raining. They think they have rarely seen anything so forlorn and tender and so like the lives they are living without paying much attention to them. They will pay more attention in the future, if there is a future.

The Frame paintings are eleven large, unframed paintings made in New York in the middle of the 1960s. They comprise monochrome expanses within thin borders. They are historically important. Quite as much as contemporaneous work by Agnes Martin, Robert Ryman, and Brice Marden, they mark a sea change in the history of abstract painting, by which artists abandoned ideals of progress to seek in kinds of sheer presence a means for abstraction to survive as a necessary art. Humphrey's Frame paintings are tours de force of painting as criticism of painting, with the charm of emerging as gratifying paintings in their own right.

The mid '60s were a difficult time for the dignity, and an ominous time for the future, of painting. It was the peak moment of Pop (most tellingly Andy Warhol's) and Minimalism. You can feel the pressure of those witheringly reductive movements in the Frame paintings, which on first glance may look at once Pop-ishly racy in their blankness, like oddly shaped movie screens, and aggressively simplified in the way of Minimalist design. (Shibboleths like "framing edge" and "shape of the support" echo faintly, reminding us that that was the heyday, too, of Color-Field formalism.) Even as you sense impingements of Pop and Minimalism in the work's style, however, you can feel them being resisted in the work's intuitive color and execution. The Frame paintings are symbols of resistance to aesthetic cold-bloodedness by someone determined to retain painterly poetics — psychological dynamics, spiritual associations — that had been a miracle of Abstract Expressionism. The image of the frame, in borders functioning like internal bulwarks, evokes a state of besiegement. But there is trouble within the walls, too: the protected, central gray expanses poignantly broadcast *nothing*. Or, rather, *almost nothing*, a condition bleaker than the vigorous nihilism of cultivated nothingness. (I owe this and other suggestions to an essay on Humphrey by William S. Wilson in *Artforum*, November 1977.) The Frame paintings are worried pictures, unsure of their medium's capacity to subsist in a hostile environment.

It was usual in the '60s for new paintings to be unframed, just canvas on stretchers. People with no sense of the aesthetic issues may have felt that the point of it was shaggy and gregarious down-styling, like boys' long hair, and there was that aspect to it. Unframing put a painting in the room with you, another sort of body just there with your body. The time that passed as you looked was clock time, not "art history." We liked that in the '60s. Not being framed could seem a painting's way of not being tediously special in the manner of adults, museums, and other embarrassments. But a deeper crisis was afoot. In an era when Pop and Minimalism differently threatened to beat art down into equivalence with non-art, just another thing in a world of things, how could painting claim to be special at all? The question harbored a historical irony that Humphrey was one of the few committed painters then palpably to understand. The irony was that the deadliest challenge to painting's continuity had been incurred within painting itself by the Abstract Expressionists themselves, and most of all by the most poetic of them, Mark Rothko. The crisis involved elimination of frames.

A frame alerts the eye to the cessation of one world and the commencement of another. Pre-modern frames needed to be elaborate — wide swaths of ornate visual confusion — because the worlds they separated, the pictured and the real, were conceived to play by the same rules of appearance. Frames then worked hard to forestall the literal dis-illusionment that would result from a collision of the two worlds. The modern evolution of the frame paralleled the relentless course, in all areas of modern life, of abstraction, the drive to subsume more and more specifics of reality under more and more general terms. Apropos frames, the imperative of abstraction reached a point where the most vestigial strip of wood or metal served as "a word to the wise," laconically calling forth the protocol that let a picture be a picture. It was a point of triumph for abstraction — and of looming disaster for painting. Preachers of abstraction, such as Clement Greenberg, seemed to imagine that the process would somehow stop short of overwhelming the pictorial altogether. But who was supposed to stop it? What made the convention of bounded composition more sacrosanct than the convention of, say, realistic depiction? Frames were taken away. After a fleeting period of liberated glory, abstraction imploded.

Rothko wasn't the only Abstract Expressionist who made a point of presenting his work without frames, but he was the one who thereby realized the most flabbergasting effect: a nakedly objective presence of stretched canvas in growing tension — as you look at the picture, sinking into its hovering forms and excruciating color — with a subjective state of exaltation. It can make your soul go up like a skyrocket, that tension in the experience of a Rothko. But it entails a risky balance that Rothko himself could not keep up indefinitely. (By the '60s, his work had descended into somber hysteria. It is incidentally notable that when, with his late black-and-gray pictures, he managed to revive his art, it was with internal borders.) Meanwhile, Rothko had literally opened a physical frontier, formerly guarded by frames, across which the vulnerable illusion of the pictorial would face unequal combat with the real world. In the brutally pragmatic '60s, when "feeling" was a word often pronounced with scorn, objectivity spilled across the frontier and set about exterminating the soulful symbolization that had lived therein. It seemed for a while that only in the coldest, most mechanical formulations of picture-ness — such as the deductive designs on blocky stretchers rolling off Frank Stella's assembly line — could the pictorial retain any conviction whatsoever.

As is often noted of Humphrey — so often that he once titled a painting *Why I Don't Paint Like Mark Rothko* — he is an artist very much Rothko's heir, committed throughout his career to Rothkovian states of hypersuggestiveness rubbed raw by delicate perceptual friction. Few legacies could have been more difficult in the '60s, both because of the impasse that Rothko's innovations had come to and on account of the grandiose ideal Rothko had set for painting: no less than an individual's encounter with the Sublime. It had worked for Rothko — if the wrenching sensation, a kind of despairing joy, that I have felt in front of his art is what the Sublime is — but only fitfully and for a while. How could it avail for a painter in the historical crossfire of Vietnam and rock-and-roll? It could avail, Humphrey's Frame paintings testify, as a demand for emotional candor, striving to figure forth an artist's largest personal feeling that happens to be true. Thus the resounding *almost nothing*, the barely inflected, damply atmospheric dove-gray void, that Humphrey's borders frame. It symbolizes the state of a self existing only enough to know that it exists, a feeling bleak to the verge of despair, but Humphrey does not cross the verge. The truth of the feeling is inflected with the maximum acceptable hopefulness, the little hopefulness of a velleity toward beauty in the border colors of cooled near pastel, sometimes with traces of undercolors: a hint of tan in slate green, a simmer of red in pale blue. (The cooling down of usually warm hues — making for a chromatic charge that hangs back and hangs fire, exerting a moody attraction that can tug at the heart — is Humphrey's hallmark as a colorist, then as always.) The grayness is a wanly songful metaphor of subjectivity rendered homeless and drifting by loss of such security as a picture gains from a picture frame. The painted border is something lost that the grayness remembers or dreams of, and sings.

A prime characteristic of frames is that they aren't supposed to be looked at. They provide a condition for looking undistractedly into a picture. Like all forms open in the middle, frames are ungraspable, *as shapes*, by direct looking. To take one in, in its unity, you must gaze into the middle and grope outward with peripheral vision. Otherwise your gaze will always be perched or wandering somewhere around the periphery. Such is the effect of the borders in the Frame paintings, an effect of elusive form intensified — brought to a pitch of delicate frustration — by the irregularity and sheer attractiveness of color and facture in the borders' execution. Their brushy paint surface is raised relative to the flat gray centers (which however aren't absolutely flat but subject to thicks and thins of paint, apparent as shiny and matte areas when viewed obliquely). Their common edges with the gray centers are hand-ruled and uneven, with incidental transparent mixings of their colors with the gray. The Frame paintings are assertively human-made objects, though transfixed in their form by impersonal and artificial models. If they have any literary equivalent, it may be the "poor human prose" that, in his masterpiece "Howl," Allen Ginsberg advanced against the frigid glamor of a media-benumbed contemporary world. The Frame paintings put painting in the place of the spiritually alert individual. They just tell us that this has become a punishingly hard place.

Since I am remembering the mid-1960s now and how it felt to be alive in New York then — one felt very free, even groggy with a surfeit of freedom — I'll note one somewhat unusual feature, for the time, of the Frame paintings: all but one of them are in oils. They eschew the miracle plastics whose better-looking-through-chemistry pizzazz was, like unframing, a nearly obligatory element of the epoch's visual vernacular in any work that aspired to newness. You would have expected any painting that looked like the Frame paintings to be an acrylic. So that was an oddness, a subtle dissonance with the moment which amounted to a muted protest on behalf of something that the moment threatened. There was a sternness, too, about it, because (I recall) oils then did feel art-historical and grownup, an association-laden and unforgiving medium not for the amnesiac and inept. The combination in the Frame paintings of unframing and of oils may help to explain their still emphatic air of being at once unpretentious and dignified, down-styled and classical: seeming contradictions suspended in a faintly irritable, gently sorrowing emulsion of feeling. Like all art that endures, the Frame paintings are of their time and free of it, both. They are windows upon a temporary condition of the human soul that is always the same soul, whose symbolization in painting is ever old and new.

CHUCK CLOSE: RECENT PAINTINGS
Pace Gallery, New York, 1991

ANGELS OF A NEW BAROQUE

F EW ROOMS IN THIS WORLD are big enough to afford sharp perception of the images in Chuck Close's new paintings. In most spaces
one simply cannot get far enough away to lose sight of the work's
facture, its bravura shatter of visual information, in the representation it cunningly makes up. Looking through the wrong
end of binoculars would probably help. When I viewed Close's
new self-portrait at his studio, I hit on two other stratagems for
seeing better by seeing worse. Retreating as far as possible, I removed my glasses. Then I asked for a floodlight on the painting
to be turned off. Immediately the great gray face — cobbled of
gridded marks of black, white, gray, blue-gray, and umber —
snapped into sufficient focus for me to make out its expression
of open-mouthed avid gazing. The image came through the dim
loft to my slightly blurred eyes with a tigerish pounce, the roughly
eight-foot-high face taking on at a distance of perhaps fifty feet
the optical scale of a life-sized face shoved into mine. I felt less
that I was looking than that I was being benignly but very aggressively looked at. Replacing my glasses, then, and walking forward,
I watched the face loom and disintegrate back into its constitu-
ent pieces — thousands of little square compositions like thousands of discrete mini-paintings, row on row — and was again a
looking subject rather than a looked-at object, but a subject awed.
I knew myself to be standing in a field, radiating from the canvas, of representation-in-action. It was a Baroque sensation, physically enveloping and at once blatantly artificial and almost
punishingly lively. It felt very grand. Thinking about it put me in
mind of something about Velázquez.

You can play this game with any representational painting,
even a Vermeer or one of Close's maximally photo-realist early
works: move your eyes within the range at which an image is just
paint. Willem de Kooning once delighted in having a visitor examine details of a reproduced Norman Rockwell, of all things,
through a magnifier. "Look!" crowed the wizard of the Springs,
"abstract expressionism!" The abstractness of realist painting viewed

close-up is an incidental given of the hand-worked medium, a phenomenon so ordinary as to rivet the attention only of naive viewers and geniuses. Velázquez presents the classic case of conspicuous brushwork in tension with crystalline illusionism. The slip-sliding marks in the Spaniard's mature work, legible several feet away, will at some precise greater distance resolve throughout the composition, with a suddenness that can make you gasp, into speaking likeness. Test this with his *Philip IV* in the Frick, where seemingly identical off-whites daubed here and there abruptly announce, from an interval I have measured with baby-steps at thirteen feet, *lace! linen! satin! silver!* — the absolute quiddity of each of those substances, adorning a homely but satisfactorily regal fellow who just as abruptly is looking you coolly in the eye. Stepping back inside the sublime apparition, you may be lost in marveling at its ungraspable mechanism. (It is ungraspable because you cannot focus at the same time on marks and image, any more than you can study the typography of a printed word while reading it. Great artists make magic of the brain's frailties.) Chuck Close recasts this same mechanism into an original fusion of technique and meaning, inundating viewing space — in the atmospheric-architectural way of the Baroque — with dynamics fundamental to painting. By "original" I of course mean inventive, but also and more important *pertaining to origins*. At a time when it is common again to doubt the possibilities of painting, Close gives the old medium a jolt of primitive conviction.

This is great stuff, and Close plainly knows it. A sign of growing confidence is that he has edged away from his formerly reticent selection of laconic subjects — family and friends, regular people — to risk an elevation of theme. All the subjects of the new pictures are New York artists: Eric Fischl, Janet Fish, April Gornik, Alex Katz, Elizabeth Murray, Judy Pfaff, and William Wegman, some of our resident aristocracy of vision. All are portrayed doing what they do best: gazing. (Wegman is doing what he does best: gazing aslant, the sly dog.) There is nothing new for Close in the confrontational big-head motif. He has understood since the late 1960s the efficacy of a face that, looked at, looks back, organized from within (with the spontaneous attitude capturable only in photographs) by a personality that duels against the objectifying regard of the viewer. He has long made the picture plane a site of psychological head-on collisions. (In this he is, again, *original*, inventing a way to effect something that all paintings effect, only more so.) Different in the new work is a level of didactic metaphor, a poeticized artistic credo signaled by the use of fellow painters. It is all about seeing. Painters made of paint symbolize the will to vision that is the *original* motive of painting. Here are folks who just naturally and by training see better than we non-painters do. The elusive moment of catching their facial expressions, their *looks*, is thus attended by a peculiar drama. I feel a thrill of deference at the charismatic superiority of these gazes to my own. This metaphoric glamor, which sinks in when I begin to catch the eye of the subjects, is all the more compelling for being so baffled and delayed by the sheer size and ostensible crudity of the rendering. In-person perusal of the work is like an optical safari through jungles of paint in quest of hieratic Dr. Livingstons. The experience is tantalizing and, aesthetically, profound.

Is painting paint or image? It is both, and more than both. Paint itself becomes an image in the eye, and images complexly meaningful can seem to the mind as ductile as any pigmented stuff (such images constantly changing in aspect, always a jump ahead of comprehension). In the half-century since a general collapse of easel-painting conventions ruled out standard finesses of the image/paint conundrum, making self-consciousness about it mandatory, most strong painters have gravitated temperamentally toward one or the other pole. (Weak painters either fail to notice the conundrum's existence or, as with much color-field abstraction and mannered painterly realism, vacillate blandly in the middle.) Willem de Kooning is paint-as-image; Andy Warhol is image-as-medium. It is the rare painter — Jackson Pollock, Jasper Johns, Gerhard Richter, or Close — who revels in the conundrum itself, devising new ways to energize its opposite extremes simultaneously. Such a painter seeks a state of perception thoroughly incoherent, bollixing rational expectation and understanding, on all grounds except the formal order of painting, which by surviving the violent test strikes the mind with an effect of majesty. The formal order of painting, for such a painter, is never given in advance. It is what is left, an obdurate residue, when there is no other way to explain why some determinedly bizarre deployment of paint on canvas is not a mess. Close's violent test is an imposition on painting of geometric, scientific, and technological mere orderlinesses: grids, optical formulas, and photography. In terms of the subjective truth that is painting's cynosure, those objective systems don't make for order at all, but for chaos and entropy, a chill in the heart. Close's taciturn processes leave human interest and human feeling just two utterly disjoined refuges: the interest of somebody's face viewed in the fleeting instant of a snapshot and the feeling of a hand distributing paint over an incredibly long period of time. Between them, the lightning vision and the snail's-pace touch generate an artificial, impersonal, stunning effect: a revelation of the formal order of painting or, to use the old-fashioned term for it, beauty.

Beauty is a mental breakdown. It is a brick wall the mind runs into. I had a jostle with it at the recent Whitney Biennial when first glimpsing Close's wonderful *April* in the distance, through two doorways, upon entering the museum's second floor. *April* spilled across the intervening space its tawny and roseate effulgences, a complicated soft chromatic explosion in which, like the Rouen cathedral in a *Rouen Cathedral* by Monet, a substantial worldly entity ungraspably asserted its reality. The face of April Gornik seemed less to take form on the canvas than, by its expression, gently to will the painting into existence, modulating a dancing emission of color in order to have eyes, a mouth, and hair. Even at the distance, the image was somewhat blurred, just verging on distinctness — but actively verging, in a moment of becoming. This impression, like most experiences of beauty, was over in a flash. (I believe Kenneth Clark said you can't sustain aesthetic emotion for longer than you can enjoy the smell of an orange.) The experience was so lovely I thought nothing about it. There was nothing to think. In the context of the teeming Biennial, Close's paintings seemed at once toughly dignified and generously undemanding, comfortable with divided attention. They were like a car-crash survivor saying, "I'm all right. See to the others." Indeed, as a working critic I spent most of my time at the show grappling with work that had multiple problems — work that has since receded in memory, leaving high and dry just a few things emphatically including Close's. Beauty is a sleep of reason that begets angels. (Angels pass in silence.)

Close's angels pertain to a present worldly situation of art in which he is increasingly central.

As with art of the Baroque, Close's new works are paintings for palaces. They have a mission to enhance and expatiate on the grace and justice of privileged spaces, which in our day are definitively museums and museum-like venues. Close plainly works with such venues in mind. On an obvious level, only rooms engineered for optimum display of large works can fully meet his art's voracious space requirements. Lots of artists are similarly oriented, competing for the big rooms, but scarcely a handful possess Close's comprehension of the gestalt required by the contemporary palace: the exact balance of matter-of-fact physical presence and outer-directed dazzle, a blend of the imposing and the engaging that is convincingly infused with somebody's personal necessity. This last part is important. Western painting always symbolizes individual consciousness (even in the absence of any sign of it, which will automatically register as deliberate abnegation). What I term palace art arises with a ceremonious agreement, ratified in public, between individual and collective inclination, a lucidity about *what is wanted*. Simply, Close wants to make paintings that are satisfactory, up to the job that any painting must perform to justify itself now. That job, rigorously and subtly conceived, is his subject. The fantastic — the preposterous, the dumbfounding — labor-intensiveness of his style announces it, the more thrillingly because the effect attained is so light and clear, frictionless as sailing on a glassy sea. It is as if Close were driven by a titanic ambition to be responsible and modest, exalting little virtues. (I think again of Velázquez, who more or less gave up painting for the more desirable job of court decorator.) Close leaves to other contemporaries, including some of his rendered angels of art, the role of bending painting to this or that distinctive need or purpose. He will celebrate painting itself, painting's ordinary miracle. In the scintillating force-field of his new work you know where you are: in some sanctuary of a civilization that still hungers for epiphany and has not lost the capacity for producing people who can deliver.

POLISH HAIKU

WHITE DUCKS IN THE YARD of a derelict factory.

A workman with a hammer dislodges heaps of rust from an old lamppost. He seems curious to discover if, when the rust is removed, there will remain a lamppost.

Coal smoke in a powder blue sky.

"FUCK OFF" and "PUNK NOT DEAD" are prevalent graffiti. A young boy in a group of young boys, who surround him in postures of admiration, gives a passing train the finger.

Sunflowers!

Poland for an American making the first sojourn of his life to *Mitteleuropa* is a harsh place full of enchanting or disconcerting livelinesses. Understanding nothing, he collects impressions that he feels to be significant without knowing why.

Then he is in the presence of a Polish artist.

Miroslaw Balka is a big, strapping, open-faced guy 34 years old with a crewcut and pale blue eyes. He stands in a cramped, decrepit three-room house that seems far too small for him, as if it were a playhouse or he were a giant. It is the house in which he was raised. It became his studio recently when his parents moved to a larger, nicer house next door. "Now I can't imagine how we lived here," he says. He points to the corner that contained his boyhood bed.

Balka seeks an ashtray for his visitor, a smoker. Then he remembers that his ashtray is in Krefeld, Germany, as part of a sculpture. (A substitute is found.)

I first saw Balka's work, having heard nothing of him, in the Aperto of the 1990 Venice Biennale, and I was struck by the beauty of objects exuding a sense of poverty so pronounced that it made any *arte povera* I could think of seem a deluxe commodity by comparison. What was that quality? Now having been in Poland, I begin to know: the characteristic of found material where *junk* is a rare category because nothing may be so wrecked or forlorn as ever to fall from the grace of possible human use. When a thing breaks irreparably in such an environment, it is freed for employment as something else. Balka does not redeem his materials from desuetude so much as detain them from the course of twilight-dim careers in an economy of makeshift. In exhibition, his rusted metal and wizened wood seem shocked by their elegant employment, as abashed by ambient white walls and track lighting as an odd-job laborer thrust into a corporate boardroom.

Balka leads the way to his former studio, one tiny room of a two-room shed behind the house. The other room is full of tombstones, which his father engraves when not working as an engineer in a factory. Balka's grandfather, who died twelve years ago, was a mason who made tombstones — the local cemetery is full of his handiwork — and taught Balka's father to engrave. Sometimes Balka would be working, and the *chink chink chink* in the next room of his father's hammer and chisel would become maddening. He would flee. He credits his grandfather with making him an artist. He remembers with happiness accompanying the old man by horse-drawn wagon, taking tombstones to the graveyard. He recalls a grime-smudged album of photographs of his grandfather's tombstones, kept as a sort of catalogue for customers. The book was thrown away, and to hear Balka describe it is to feel the painful loss of some small, soiled Library of Alexandria.

In much of Poland as in any place that has been poor for a very long time, practically no location or object is quite clean or exactly dirty — *soiled* seems the overall word for a physical state as various in its types of soilage as the variousness of the words for snow conditions in Eskimo languages. One might learn fine distinctions there between soil incurred from without, as "dirt," and soil generated from within, as a byproduct of decay, with terms for degrees of each and combinations of both. One might study paradox. Is dirt "dirty"? Isn't it, rather, clean: cleanly itself, clean dirt? It can be immaculate when an artist finds an artistic use for it, as when Balka sets out a tray of ashes from the small, ancient wood stove that (very badly, he says) heated his former studio: soft gray ashes, of a subtle near-iridescence, fragile as gossamer. Resting in the ashes are lumpy balls of plaster that recall for Balka, he says, lumps of soap made by his father from salvaged slivers of nearly extinct soap bars.

Balka's materials teeter between the forms of their past and

187

possible uses and the entropy of their decay, their molecular disintegration. I think again of a functioning lamppost that is either rusted or made of rust.

The workman's hammer that will discover the truth about the lamppost may be a symbol of a new Poland. So, too, may be the work of Balka, an artist internationally resonant who says he is happy to keep working in the old Warsaw suburb where he grew up (while living in another, nearby area). The suburb, Otwock, figures in the early writing of Isaac Bashevis Singer. It was the last stop on a famous tram line from Warsaw and site of fashionable tuberculosis sanitariums. It is haunted by Poland's demolished bourgeois and Jewish pasts. In the much-vandalized Jewish cemetery of Otwock the sandy soil, long scavenged of sand for making cement, fails to cover protruding human bones. Balka's studio feels close to the center of a world anxiously contemplating questions of the persistence and possible transformation — destruction or redemption — of the human. It is something a visitor thinks about in Poland.

In last summer's Documenta 9 Balka showed a work incorporating stones from the grave that his grandfather planned for himself. The stones are terrazzo (pebbled cement ground to flat surfaces), poor people's marble. The family, having become relatively prosperous, deemed the material too humble. Balka's grandfather lies beneath granite. The grandson keeps faith with the grandfather, who in spirit follows his rejected sepulcher around the world.

"Something happens for you in your childhood, so strong for you that it never changes," Balka says. The minimalistic vocabulary and syntax of forms he has adopted — lingua franca of the world of international sculptural exhibition in which he is a rising star — is "just the visual aspect," he explains. An obviously Joseph Beuys-influenced lexicon of metaphoric materials (fleshy foam rubber, for instance, and salt for the primal human body) might similarly be termed just the semiotic aspect of Balka's art. (Another of Balka's Western affinities is to early Bruce Nauman, whom he recalls in taking a severe, ad hoc approach to what might be termed the problem of bootstrapping art: You are an artist in your studio, alone in space and adrift in time. Now what? Look around. What's there? What can be done with it?) Balka is not yet an innovator in sculptural aesthetics or poetics. He is prepossessing for his ability to make a learned language tell his story. The virtue of the language for him seems its capacity to sublimate — to render subliminal — charges of feeling otherwise uncontrollably powerful and contradictory.

Balka told me that in 1985, while still in school, he traded a bottle of vodka to a man with a broken nose for a small, crude figurine of Santa Claus that had a broken nose. For a student show, he arrayed many plaster casts of this pathetic object facing a pyramid of snow into which a rope descended. When the snow melted, the original Santa was revealed hanging by its neck. A lynching? "Yes, that is the word," Balka said. For another performance-like piece, he displayed a big papier-mache rabbit surrounded, and apparently threatened, by many sharp-toothed paper jaws. On consideration, Balka cut out for the rabbit a sharp-toothed mouth of its own for self-defense. The two installations seem self-explanatory as parables of the artist in an onerous world. I asked him how those startling works were received. "Fine," he said. "Nobody treated them as art."

Balka credits as a formative experience his reading, in English, of James Joyce's *Portrait of the Artist as a Young Man*. The book encouraged him to embrace his simplest and often most abject early experiences as themes for art. He was transfixed by Joyce's account of the sensation of bed-wetting: first warm, then cold. He made a sculpture about it. Emotionally charged bodily fluids figure in much of his work. Two rusted pipes close together and upright against a wall stop at eye-level. They are filled, Balka fancies, with tears. Short sections of pipe set in the floor are for him positive forms of the negative spaces made by the act, mysteriously satisfying to a boy, of pissing in snow.

In Warsaw I saw a sculpture by Balka in a Polish virtual shrine of contemporary art, the Galeria Foksal in the complex of an old villa used by the government. The Foksal consists of an office and a very small exhibition space with lovely oblong proportions, as if it were the scale model for a substantial gallery — and as if it were a pocket-sized working miniaturization of the panoply of a free international art world that until recently could gain no more purchase in Poland than this cherishable toe-hold. Memorable exhibitions have been held there of local and Western art (Giovanni Anselmo, Lawrence Weiner, Arnulf Rainer, Joseph Beuys, Tony Cragg, Anselm Kiefer) in the gallery's difficult history since 1966. Its director for all that time, Jerzy Barowski, is a tough sort of aesthete-saint who couches his passion in watchful, shrewd deference. Censors used to preview all Barowski's shows. Polish censorship wasn't so bad, he told me with a shrug: if the censors couldn't understand the art, they figured it was no threat and let it go. (The opposite policy pertained in Czechoslovakia, he said.) In the gallery when I visited was a Balka that incorporated a low-lying, narrow, rusted-steel trough, triangular in cross-section, holding a rivulet of dried salt. The trough was body-length, which made it a large object in the little space. But if one imagined it as a body lying down, then its situation seemed capacious, as if it were saying, "See, there's lots of room for me here." All of Balka's work, one way or another, may say something similar, intent on finding the minimum requirement of space and time in which *to be*.

Balka's world is wide now. So is Poland's, though in a country that needs practically everything in the way of infrastructure and whose currency features a *million*-zlotys note (worth eighty-some dollars last summer) the extent of the freedom rather dwarfs immediate prospects for making effective use of it. With Balka and his fiancee (now wife), artist Zuzanna Janin, I ate carp at a cozy restaurant in the Old Town of Warsaw, the Renaissance district which, destroyed like most of the central city in World War II, has been painstakingly rebuilt to its original appearance. The effect of the restoration is a bit Disneylandish, but promising in its energy. After dinner we sat at a cafe table in the night in the main square, and I liked being there with Balka and Janin, watching them watch the passing scene. Their scene.

We in the American art world have waited for something from the former Soviet empire, something new. Our eagerness for creativity from that quarter seems partly an expression of healthy curiosity and goodwill, partly a confession that our own artistic resources feel exhausted and in need of exotic transfusion. The pickings so far have been slim, and the best of them — as by Ilya Kabakov, as by Balka — tell us why. They also teach us how to square our expectations with what we are likely to receive. An "Eastern" artist must first master an artistic idiom of the West, because none of any sophistication, with a local accent, survived the long darkness. Then the artist must speak in that alien idiom of painful things, telling as with a stammering tongue, unused to speaking, of so many truths so long unspoken that they have sedimented like a river bottom. Only when all the layers of silence are dredged may we encounter the "new" in our frenetic Western sense.

Balka showed me an incredibly dilapidated old public trash container he discovered in Germany, and included in his show, when he first exhibited there in 1989. He had been very nervous about the show, he said. "But when I found this, I knew it would be all right." In Germanic lettering beneath the container's gaping mouth is the hungry, peremptory plea,

"Bitte"

ELLEN PHELAN: FROM THE LIVES OF DOLLS
University of Massachusetts at Amherst, 1992

DOLLNESS

IT WAS NIGHT IN LOS ANGELES and my little daughter was crying for her baby doll. Had we left it at the Avis office where earlier we rented a car? I phoned, and, yes, they had it. Returning there in a hurry, I rushed to the counter and blurted, "I've come to pick up a doll."

"Well," one of several young women behind the counter said frostily, "you have come to the wrong place!"

Carefully madeup in her tidy red uniform and "We Try Harder" button, she did look rather doll-like, come to think of it, even as she glared at me (flabbergasted-man doll) with vengeful rectitude. It was so funny I couldn't laugh.

Remembering that incident helps me think about Ellen Phelan's elegant and treacherous watercolors and gouaches of dolls — elegant in technique and form, an ongoing tour de force, and treacherous in content. She started making them in the late 1970s as gifts for friends and breaks from her abstract and landscape painting. In the mid 1980s they got out of hand. There are over a hundred of them now, an expanding doll cosmos. Phelan has discovered in her responsiveness to dolls, made communicable by graphic skills equal to any nuance, a royal road to her own and everybody else's unconscious. The work is consistently comic and just as consistently all but impossible to laugh at, because to get her jokes is to be trapped in them. Proper viewers of Phelan's doll drawings must be willing to regard themselves, among other people, in a light at once tender and ridiculous. I will try to follow my own advice here in my role of art-critic doll.

Life imitating a cartoon, my standoff with the Avis person was a moment of exquisite misunderstanding quite appropriately involving a double entendre of "doll." Dolls are materialized exquisite misunderstandings. They are dead things generating delusions of life. They are wish-fulfilling travesties meant to stir day-dreamy play. Just how various and subtle the field of that play might be, and above all how laced with specifiable ambivalences, I think I never suspected until encountering

Phelan's repertoire. But I always knew dolls are often derisive and often sentimental.

Common speech conveys the negative and positive feeling tones we invest in dolls. The Avis woman heard herself derided as a "doll" in the sense of plaything, less than fully human. But she would hardly mind a fellow worker, for instance, saying of her, "She's a doll," suggesting superhuman amiability. Here we have a major dialectic of dolls — caricature versus idealization — that whipsaws through Phelan's drawings, helping to explain the unsettling gravity of what looks at first glance, delightfully, like a toyshop come to life. Eventually one starts to suspect that Phelan's toys are disguised avatars of Goya's dramatis personae, with Edvard Munch supervising mise en scène and James Ensor cackling in the orchestra pit.

Phelan's scariest drawings are those in which idealizing dolls flip over into caricature, as in her *Blonde White Woman* series based on a Farrah Fawcett item radiating fantasies of long-haired, long-necked, pretty-woman perfection. Nudged by Phelan's watercolor brush, the image generates a kaleidoscopic rogues gallery of hyperfeminine monsters, each as instantly familiar as a remembered unfavorite aunt or the latest filthy-rich WASPette in the gossip columns. Conversely, among the most moving of Phelan's pictures are those that render dolls originally caricatural — especially blacks reeking of the old vicious Jim Crow condescension — with an intensity of feeling that hovers between adoration and sorrow, seeking in objects of scorn a solidarity with the absolutely human. Phelan is on dangerous ground with these drawings. On what other sort of ground should an artist wish to be?

With such exceptions as the Farrah Fawcett and an obscene and pathetic cameo appearance of *Bud Man*, Phelan prefers relatively antique dolls, whose remoteness from present fashion affords a strangeness congenial to imagination. She eschews strangeness-proof contemporary engines of gender indoctrination like Barbie and G. I. Joe. Socially conscientious rather than politically correct, Phelan is alert to stereotypes but leaves obvious targets and bloodless "criticality" to others. She seems less interested in "gender issues," for instance, than in what used to be called more reverberantly the battle of the sexes.

In her choice of models, Phelan emphasizes essential doll-ness, the quality of dolls addressed both to the eye and the hand: to be gazed upon, to be played with. Her images thus differ from other recent toy-based art, such as the coldly spectacular figurines of Jeff Koons and the touchy-feely stuffed creatures of Mike Kelley. If she shares anything with those contemporaries, it may be fascination with the unguardedness of our culture when it comes to toys, letting so much embarrassing information hang out in plain view.

Embarrassment is like an atmosphere, a sticky humidity, enveloping Phelan's dolls, which are helpless to keep secrets. When sentimental, like the brides and singers, they are desperately so, abjectly and plungingly sentimental. They are immolated in sentimentality like moths in a flame. The effect is sadness, with an upbeat of compassion. When derisory, like the drunks and some of the clowns, they are manically derisory, falling all over themselves to participate in their own humiliation. The effect is, again, sadness with an upbeat. A willingness to be ridiculous — rising to outright defiance with the kittens that flaunt their sexless sassy behinds — may sit well with a talent for endurance, turning energies of derision around and using them to ride out a bad moment. Make no mistake. Phelan's doll drawings are all moments to be ridden out, lived through, undergone. To resist their psychological tug may be to cast oneself as a stuckup connoisseur doll or an uptight bourgeois doll or something else delectably idiotic and perhaps kind of interesting.

The drawings are high-art bravura beautiful, the work of an artist justly celebrated (most tellingly, by other painters) for all but imageless paintings gracefully and gravely refined in sensibility. Phelan is as serious about art as anyone else I know, and it does not surprise her friends that she has often expressed a certain alarm at finding herself drawn into work that is, among other things, such *fun*. Here perhaps is a metajoke — Aesthete Ellen, caught playing with dolls — underlying the local jokes of the drawings. The happiness of it is the way Phelan's talent reacts to playing hookie from high endeavor. Her talent sings. With ravishing specificities of tone and texture, it transforms an idea that at first blush seems intrinsically illustrational into something mildly unprecedented, a species of still life crossed with figuration, cartooning taking an oath of naturalism, realism as chatty with poetic tales as the Ancient Mariner.

There is nothing else in art exactly like Phelan's doll series, though no end of things that are *almost* like it. Stylistically, the series is a prism catching glints of affinity with everything from Watteau and Fuseli to the work of innumerable contemporaries — and those contemporaries as variegated as the synthetic-naturalist Eric Fischl and the cartoon-wielding trickster Steve Gianankos. Indeed, the doll drawings somewhat resemble so much other art that they can end up seeming to resemble art in general, as if hitting on some primitive square-root theorem that qualifies something as art instead of as something else. In the context of a present art world bedeviled by uncertainty about what art is and what artists do, the upshot is altogether affirmative, a refreshing and reassuring demonstration of continuity in art's traditional means and ends.

For a moment in that Avis office, I was crazy about the woman who was looking daggers at me. Her blushing energy was terrifically attractive, as the daggers bounced off my innocence. The jerk she took me for would have said, "You're beautiful when you're angry." Fortunately, I was speechless. The man I had talked to on the phone came forward with the lost doll. I saw the woman realize her mistake and relax her hostility — *mistaken again*. I returned to the car and my weeping child, whose gratitude at recovering her pretend baby made me feel how lovely it is to be a daddy. Our nuclear family tooled off into the Los Angeles night — "Down Life's Highway," to borrow the title of Ellen Phelan's dazzling mouse-ification of weddedness. I know that road. It is unbeatable for going places, but it can lay some heavy distractions on your sense of what you are.

SCOTT BURTON: THE CONCRETE WORK
Max Protetch Gallery, New York, 1992

CONCRETE AND BURTON

1. CONCRETE

CONCRETE IS THE MOST CARELESS, promiscuous stuff until it is committed, when it becomes fanatically adamant. Liquid rock, concrete is born under a sign of paradox and does not care. It doesn't care about anything, lazy and in love with gravity but only half in love. Pour concrete out on the ground and it will start to puddle and spread, in rapture to gravity, but then will think better of it: enough spreading! Concrete can't be bothered; it heaps up on itself in lazy glops, sensual as a frog.

Concrete takes no notice of what is done with it, flowing regardless into any container; and the containers one makes for it, the molds and forms, must be fashioned with laborious care, strong and tight, because concrete is heavy and entirely feckless. Promiscuous, doing what anyone wants if the person is strong enough to hold it, concrete is a slut, a gigolo, of materials. Every other material — wood, clay, metal, even plastic — has self-respect, a limit to what it will suffer to have done with it, and at the same time is responsive within that limit, supple in the ways it consents to be used. Not concrete.

Concrete is stupid and will do anything for anyone, without protest or pleasure, so long as the person indulges concrete's half-love of gravity, its lazy mania to lie down. Concrete does not care if you respect it. It does not know the meaning of respect. Only give it a place to lie down, a place of any shape, and concrete will do your bidding.

Let concrete set, however, and sense the difference. Concrete hardens in the shape of whatever container received its flow, its momentary sensual abandon in thoughtless submission to half-loved gravity. Once it has set, what a difference! Concrete becomes adamant, fanatical, a Puritan, a rock, Robespierre. It declares like no other material the inevitability, the immortality — the divinity! — of the shape it comprises, be the shape a glopped heap on the ground or a concert hall, ridiculous or sublime.

Concrete that has set will have no thought, no monomaniacal obsession until the end of time, except this shape. No other material — not brick, not wood, not the very stone blocks of the Great Pyramid — forgets itself to such an extent. Bricks, planks of wood, and stone blocks whisper from their built configurations of their willingness to be disassembled and to become something else, on the understanding that the reassembler will respect their dignity, their compunction against doing just anything for just anyone. Whorish but ironic plastic holds back from a lasting passion for the form it takes, murmuring of its readiness if given heat, just some lovely heat, to melt into other forms. Likewise metal and glass. Not concrete when concrete has set.

Set concrete insists, insists, insists. It insists on the rightness, permanence, godliness of the form into which it flowed so carelessly. You must smash set concrete to bits if you would shut up the voice of its insistence, and even then the smashed bits will lie around insistently piping. I was in Berlin in 1990 and remember a thousand hammers banging away at the Wall, banging out "die, die, die!" The concrete of the awful thing was shrieking back "wall, wall, wall!" It took a long time for the hammers to win the argument, and even then the shattered corpse would not give in. I brought a handful of fragments home, and the ones that retained any flat surface shrilled "wall" in tiny voices, totalitarian for eternity.

There is something inappropriate, not quite right, about the notion of "working" concrete, finely finishing it, making its forms true, smooth, and pristine. It seems insulting to concrete's gross strength and simplemindedness, mocking concrete as one might a rough farm worker by forcing fancy evening dress on him. Unlike the farm worker, however, concrete is unmockable because impervious. Go ahead and make fun of concrete. You might as well. Concrete will never notice.

Concrete has no feelings to hurt. It does have feelings, as we know, but they are impervious, adamantine, fanatic, and untouchable by anything. Concrete is solipsistic. By contrast, clay is touchy, wood is as woundable as the flesh it is, and brick has a yeoman worker's pride, stolid and prickly. All have good reason to fear misuse and to exude sadness when misused. But kick concrete as much as you like, all you will hurt is your toe.

Concrete is among the world's best exercise devices for un-requited loving. You may love and serve it until your heart is worn out and be assured of no responsiveness, not a quiver in return. No loathing, even. Nothing! Concrete is like Don Quixote's Dulcinea, only colder. Coarse and stupid beyond com-pare, it combines these qualities with the froideur of a goddess, of Pallas Athena! It is a dominatrix blind, deaf, and dumb, dumb beyond anything.

Concrete has its one fleeting moment of slovenly sensual bliss, half-giving itself gloppity-glop to gravity, and then it burns coldly forever with its solipsistic thought, its idée fixe. You have to be a masochist to love concrete, enjoying the strength that your own capacity to love displays, until the strength is exhausted, when the loved one is a pitiless idiot.

2. BURTON

THE ABOVE DESCRIPTION OF concrete partly fits Scott Burton, too, as I remember him. I remember his densely sensual presence, his lazy humors — always with something animate about the humors, electric or volatile, not in the least concrete-like. But he definitely was half in love with gravity. He liked to lie down. He liked to sit. Not for no reason was he the best sculptor the world has known of places to sit down.

Most of all, Scott's imagination flowed like liquid and set like rock. He was always entertaining visions of form and func-tion and meaning, his erudite imagination liquid and flowing with possibilities, but once his imagination entered the container of a decision, that was it. To the extent that it was up to him (not always the case in architectural projects), there would be no fur-ther give, no leeway.

The form of any Scott Burton is monomaniacal, though with nothing arbitrary about it. Always there were reasons behind Scott's forms, reasons of history and principle behind reasons of function and beauty. Reasons upon reasons, as if some intelli-gent large force of inevitability working through time, some Hegelian demiurge, willed just this thing in just this form, like it or not. You were stuck with it.

You could not budge or shut up Scott's conviction once he

was decided, once he was set. It took death to suspend his insistence, smashing the wonderful imagination to bits. The bits are his works, insisting still. So I believe that Scott understood concrete and that his understanding had something of the spiritual about it, a sort of identification of the intelligent, animate man and the stupid, sluggish, slatternly stuff.

I maintain my belief even though Scott's active involvement with concrete was brief, during a period when he was interested in making furniture of all manner of building materials. (He experimented also with brick and glass.) Scott's concrete opus, conceived in the late 1970s and executed in the early '80s, comprises just three works: a group of 16 small, squat tables of various geometry, a single large conical table, and an inverted-pyramidal outdoor table with four stools in the same shape. The tour de force of the lot is the conical table, a feat of steel-reinforced engineering done with the aid of a master "cement man."

(I have been writing of concrete as if it were an unvarying substance, but of course it is human-made and variable according to the skill, care, and luck of its maker. Only people — never nature — could conceive a material so doltish, so merely useful, and only people can outsmart its doltishness to make it do splendid things.)

But the main and literally most Scott-like of the concrete works is the set of tables, a lexicon of geometries whose tendency to small-waisted, big-shouldered, squat proportions evokes Scott's body. Paired off two by two, the tables are like a dance party of Scotts. They were hard to do. Scott said he would have preferred just to pour them and let them be — just forms in "natural" concrete — but a look of "naturalness" in this unnatural material turned out to require the most strenuous artifice in finishing.

Scott kicked concrete, made fun of it, by treating it with such lapidary delicacy, dressing it up like the finest creature and escorting it to the dance of fine art. It is faintly preposterous to see Scott's concrete pieces in the fine rooms always prepared for art. "Why, isn't that *cement*?" someone might say. "Whoever invited *that*?" someone might say also. Be its forms ever so beautiful, concrete is an ugly duckling that becomes an ugly duck.

As well as slightly shocking and funny, with an admixture of mockery and perverse tenderness, the effect of Scott's exquisite working of concrete is to amplify the purity of his formal ideas. When he used marble, granite, and other fine materials — terrazzo, even, which is concrete in disguise, poor people's marble — Scott's pure form flattered the material by giving it worthy employment, and the material returned the flattery by giving the form a seductiveness that softened the severity of its idea. Pure form and fine material make an erotic unity that is sociable in the best company, perfectly mannered, seductive, and dashing. But pure form and poor, coarse, you-can't-take-it-anywhere concrete make a strange couple on the dance floor.

Concrete may be got up as fine as possible and still not fool anybody. But the pure form that has so condescended to concrete, with such heroic noblesse oblige, have we ever before quite appreciated its nobility? Look at it there with that impossible stuff, isn't it grand? When I see one of Scott's concrete pieces, I feel above all a pristine quality of high conception, as of a perfect drawing, though the thing itself may weigh half a ton. My eye and mind leap to the object to grasp it, then my grasp comes away, slipping from the object. My grasp brings away abstract qualities: purity of intention, ideality of conception, perfection of follow-through. It is a wonder to me in that moment that the concrete-ness left behind doesn't literally crumble.

Yet you know by looking at these pieces that Scott did love concrete, with the delighted masochism required for loving it. Not that he was going to make a habit of this. There is a limit. I think it took only those few pieces for Scott to touch bottom with concrete's potential for him. To do more would have been senselessly repetitive. It was Scott's way to do or say something very carefully and clearly, but only once or twice. If you didn't get it that was too bad; he was on to something else.

The quickest way of getting it, with Scott, is to concentrate on his choice of material.

THIS SPORTING LIFE, 1878-1991
High Museum, Atlanta, 1992

PROTOCOLS OF INNOCENCE:
PHOTOGRAPHY AND THE SPORTS FAN

He WAS RAWBONED AND TACITURN, the farm boy who was the best athlete in the high school where he was a senior and I was in seventh or eighth grade in the 1950s. A transplant from a large city, I could hardly distinguish him from the local louts whose answers to the problem of smalltown boredom included making my life a smalltown suffering. Then I saw a photograph in the school paper.

It was an action shot taken with flash at a track meet at dusk of him high-jumping, straining over the bar in the penultimate moment of the old scissors kick. He had no form or style to speak of, just strength and will. His face and limbs were contorted — sinews popping out in places I didn't know you could have sinews — as he made his body a slackjawed ungainly thing to clear the barrier. The high-contrast photograph was fearfully ugly, with livid whites of flesh bleached by the flashbulb and black shadows of muscles. It had a nakedness about it, and a bravery.

The photograph's use in the paper had to signify "school spirit," recognizing a feat on "our" behalf, and, indeed, I felt one of my occasional frail surges of loyalty to that town I hated. But the picture also unclenched wilder stuff: emotions of social alienation and yearning, perhaps, and sexual intimidation and fascination, among other syndromes of my adolescence. In streets and hallways thereafter I would furtively stare at him, trying to find the heroic aspect I had seen in the photograph. I couldn't. The violent glamor of the image remained an abstract attribute of his person, or else his person persisted as an awkward pendant to the image. Though the school was small, I never spoke to him, because I didn't dare, and he never spoke to me, because why would he?

I have begun this essay on sports photography with my memory of a successful sports photograph. In my case, you might say the photograph was freakishly successful. The photographer cannot have hoped for so extravagant an effect, but the effect was no mere fantasy on my part. All vocational photographers, like all artists and media artisans of any sort, angle to catch souls, whether they are conscious of it or not. Most are not conscious of it, mechanically using devices that, having once caught souls, linger as cliches. But even the tiredest convention may ignite somebody's spirit if, for instance, the person is young and grasps the convention's primitive content for the first time as if suddenly understanding something in a foreign language.

Part of my memory is a confused awareness of my participation in the power of the image: I was making it happen, somehow, even as it made something happen in me. (I couldn't actually believe this. I had to test it by looking for the whole cause of my thrill in the athlete.) That was a moment of initiation. I entered into an ordinary mystery, an open secret, of my culture, a protocol of innocence vested in the contemplation of sports.

The high-jump picture was a very American shot, in line with what might be called the *Sports Illustrated* paradigm: combining admiration of a particular athlete with connoisseurship of a given sport. Glance at any newspaper sports page in this country. What Americans like in sports photography is a fused double concentration on the dancer and the dance. The second baseman leaping to elude a sliding runner while turning a double play, the basketball player soaring for a dunk: images ever the same and new, like Byzantine icons.

What we don't like is anything extraneous to dancer and dance. Suppressed especially in the *Sports Illustrated* paradigm is any detailed presence of other observers, whose alternative angles on the action would spoil the illusion that we have the uniquely privileged view. Shallow depth of field, like fast film, is a technical given, presenting a thin slice of the world's space in a split-second of time. Nothing could be less like how humans normally see.

Unaided eyesight is approximate, a matter of constant, darting refocusings in space and, in time, of awareness that slides back and forth over the beat of the present: into the past, absorbing what has been seen, and the future, anticipating what will be seen next. Only the still camera can afford undistracted instantaneous vision, memorializing lightning-quick crises of action that we otherwise sense without actually seeing.

This superiority of photography to the human sensorium is the basis of its value for the sports fan. Is what I am saying true of any photography of motion? Yes, but minus the aspect of ritual that marks the work of the sports photographer (as, via television, that of the slow-motion replay director, whose decisions throughout a game can be a flowing lexicon of photographic conventions). The aspect of ritual binds pictorial craft to a practice of observation that is also an *observance*.

It has been said often that modern spectator sport is not just served by photography but is photography's creation. Such is plainly the case of *professional* sport, whose city-based franchises travesty the communal identifications that give people an emotional stake in amateur contests. (Of course, amateurism becomes ever rarer in fact than in name as our culture of spectacle burgeons; think only of the corporatizing of college football.) To be effective in mass culture — professional culture, made not by artists with passions but by specialists with job descriptions — sport must be mediated, because it is not in itself a medium.

Consider the experience of a fan at a ballpark. What I witness has features of theatrical performance (that of the circus, say), but unlike theater it is not structured for effect. It is not aimed at me. It is self-contained and self-directed, just baseball occurring — a children's game that grown men are toiling at, mostly oblivious to an audience. (Fans tend to resent players who showboat for the crowd, rupturing the game's containment; though certain stars, contained in their own signature auras, are indulged.) The game happens in a kind of transparent bubble from which I am excluded. My irrelevance to it is, in a real way, absolute. That I am a customer helping to pay the players' salaries hardly constitutes a bond; it is disenthralling, if anything.

For how long could I bear my exclusion and irrelevance if I had no relief from them? But there is relief. The next morning I open the newspaper and see the game I attended spread out in pictures, words, and statistics. I savor these slowly, sinking into the warm flow of irrational caring — innocence regained — that is fandom. Modern fandom is an artificial agreement of the individual with the mass, an agreement to pretend to care, in ways ideally indistinguishable from true caring, about something insignificant. The agreement would wither in a year if deprived of media irrigation.

What, then, of the mystery I found, and through memory can find again at will, in the high-jump picture? But for its tincture of "school spirit," my response to the image had nothing directly to do with fandom. No more then than I am now was I a fan of track-and-field events. It had to do with an aroused susceptibility of mine that, together with the craft and luck of the photographer, constituted the image as a symbol. In other words, the picture functioned for me like a work of art.

The memory gives me a mental pivot on which to turn from conventions of sports photography to the searching qualities of photographs in this show, which in quest of specific truths disdain to reinforce the fan's pretense to caring. These photographs reflect the nature of thematic art (work both really thematic and really art), which is to be inside and outside its subject at the same time. The picture I remember satisfied this definition, albeit accidentally, as at once a celebration of the high jump and an estrangement from it. It showed me the idiosyncracy of an athlete and the character — the technique, the ordeal — of a sporting event, but with detail transcending the event. The detail was intrinsically photographic, peculiar to a Weegee-like use of flash in darkness.

Photographs in the present exhibition achieve similar effects on purpose, identifying with some essence of a subject even, or especially, while distancing it. By being sports pictures, they do so with purity unavailable to other genres. Sport is an activity already, like art, aesthetic and gratuitous, though lacking art's forming consciousness. The serious photographer of sports must introduce that consciousness without destroying the innocent absorption, like a sleepwalker's trance, that makes sport interesting to photograph in the first place.

Consider one perfect picture, Steven Shore's 1978 view of New York Yankees star Graig Nettles practicing batting in the cage of a pitching machine. The immediate focus is on the resplendently uniformed player, fiercely concentrated in his batting stance. Note the straight diagonal line through his bat and down his left side to the ground. He is shifting his weight to his left foot in the first phase of a classically articulated swing. The figure might as well be an image razored out of the photograph of an actual game in a roaring stadium. Nettles could not bat more beautifully if the World Series were on the line. But the figure performs in autistic solitude amid a bizarre maze of pitching-machine cages, which in turn occupies an indifferent landscape. It is Fort Lauderdale, Florida: spring training.

These testifying data — someone to all appearances playing baseball, paraphernalia for simulating baseball, and a swatch of the wide world oblivious to baseball — are a laminate of realities. Fans and non-fans alike, I think, must respond to the strangeness of the image. Fans of a traditional sort may find it vaguely upsetting. Shore's eye for fissures among realities exposes what a fan of course knows but cringes from admitting: the meaninglessness of the game. (Speaking of fissures, remember the 1989 World Series, interrupted by an earthquake? The two games that followed the disaster, stripped to their triviality, were spiritless and grueling for all concerned.)

The style of Shore's photograph is exact to the late '70s, when younger American artists and intellectuals, with or without boosts from critical theory, became aggressively skeptical toward mass culture. The shift in sensibility fostered, among other things, David-Lettermanish hipness about popular genres, sort of "I-love-how-ridiculous-it-is-to-love-this." Shore's photography announces an end to innocence while leaving open a recourse of innocence to the protective coloration of irony, the facetiousness dissembling passion that is the common tone of sports talk among educated folk nowadays. Shore, an artist, got all of this in one disenchanted and riveted glance, and I am glad to pay tribute to a great photograph that has haunted me since I saw it reproduced at the time.

Shore helps me find another meaning in my high-jump picture. Like Nettles's uncanny focus on a ball popping out of a gismo, the preposterousness of the jumper's exertion, in clearing a barrier that bars no one, was part of the image's crazy appeal. No other worldly activity than sport, except maybe war, entails as a matter of course such desperate spasms of effort.

Shore's photograph is anti-heroic — deflating its subject from mythic status to skilled professionalism — in a way always increasingly typical of American sports fandom. Fans no sooner fixate on a star player than they seek to measure the mere person behind the reputation. American sports journalism sometimes seems a seminar in amateur psychology and character analysis. The scrutiny is rarely prying and malicious in the manner of celebrity gossip (though edgier tones have arisen with the growth of players' salaries and presumptions). Rather, the attention seems bent on democratically bringing down to regular human scale, if possible, incidental aspects of an athlete's personality, the better to contemplate with undistracted admiration the athlete's performance.

American fans adore (with due allowance for twinges of envy) the superiority of the star athlete, but fairly strictly on the basis of talent and of efficiency and grace in fulfilling the talent. Apparent exceptions — Babe Ruth, Muhammad Ali — entail larger-than-life individuals whose charisma spills beyond sport and disarms scrutiny. Such superstars invent the terms on which they will be regarded, leaving fans no choice but worship — we fans perhaps laughing with embarrassment at our subjection, but delighted nonetheless. Nicolas Muray's 1927 portrait of Babe Ruth, a primeval beast in a baseball uniform with phallic bat enfolded by huge paws, is a great document because, try as one might, one cannot avoid feeling that Ruth himself, not the photographer, authored it. More than one photographer who pointed a camera at the Babe got the best picture of his career.

For an instructive contrast to the American vernacular in sports photography, consider the 1941 photograph by Eugene Smith, *American Football*. The heroizing low-angled composition of a quarterback firing a pass while surrounded by hurtling bodies is like a frieze of Achilles launching a fatal spear. The picture's qualities of abstract and balletic form give it a chilly exaltation, at once gorgeous and, apropos American sport, all wrong. For an antidote, look at Garry Winogrand's eyelevel sideline football shot, dispassionately taking in the helter-skelter of a kickoff runback from behind the substantial rear end of a crouching referee in a crowded stadium on an autumnal Saturday in Texas, U.S.A.

The protocols of innocence in American sport, of which journalistic sports photographs are more or less calculated instruments and signs, depend on rigid separation of games from other spheres of life. But those other spheres may be freely projected

206

and reconstituted in the arena, the transparent bubble. My high-jump picture could function for me as a soul-stirring symbol — of masculinity feared, desired, despaired of — precisely because it was contained by rules of a sport and conventions of the sport's representation. The important part of the story, for me, is that I wanted and failed to reconcile the hero of the picture with the senior carrying books in the hall. (His name was Gale Sprute.) I had yet to develop the benignly schizophrenic American knack for enjoying mass culture, sports especially: a play of real feelings secured by the irreality of its object.

Like dreams, sports engage one's full emotions while underway, then dissipate to nothing. In calling this pattern benign, incidentally, I do not mean to gloss over its cynical exploitation. A lot is done with our feelings while they are in the molten projected state. Mostly, they are flavored with gross admixtures of commercialism. Less frequent are attempts to inject fandom with political content beyond occasional generic patriotism. The 1991 Super Bowl halftime show, replete with yellow ribbons for "our troops in the Gulf," was as politically charged as American sports mediation gets. While repelling some of us, it wasn't exactly Leni Riefenstahl, whose apotheosis of Hitler's showcase 1936 Olympics was high art in the worst cause imaginable.

In art that involves photography, we are emerging from a period obsessed with exposing mass-cultural manipulations. Much of the work of that period, naively skeptical, both belabors the obvious (not lost on mass culture's seasoned consumers) and misses its point (the consenting-adult transactions I term protocols of innocence). But some work brilliantly reveals triggers of our dreamlike collective pleasures without imposing tedious judgments.

Such is the art of Jeff Koons, whose altered Nike advertising posters of basketball stars are undeservedly less well known than his sculpture. Koons's posters, rendered with the same printing screens by the same commercial firm that did the originals, employ sumptuous oil dyes instead of inks on snowy linen instead of paper. The subliminal effect of these substitutions is to kick up the seductiveness of the posters just enough to send it over the top of a viewer's habituated resistance to commercial blandishment, exciting the mental reflexes that the ad campaigners counted on.

By amplifying rather than deconstructing the American blurring of fandom and consumerism, Koons affords no refuge of a detached point of view. To look at his posters is to experience at full force and in untippable balance the tug and the repulsion of the media pizzazz that plays so finely on our feelings to such crude ends. Thus humiliating viewers' pride in their immunity to kitsch, this artist has often been condemned in the way of a messenger blamed for the message he delivers. We would do better simply to swallow Dr. Koons's medicine of queasy consciousness, say thank you, and get on with our grievously equivocal lives.

Having begun this essay with reference to a sports photograph in a Midwestern town, I end with another, David Graham's *The Post Bulletins Practicing at Graham Park, Rochester, Minnesota,* 1988. A decidedly unformidable gridiron team takes posture instruction from an off-camera coach in an industrial neighborhood crowned by a corncob-shaped water tower. The salad of realities somewhat recalls Steven Shore's Graig Nettles picture, except that in Graham's shot the disjunctions are far from crisp. The amateur players approximate professional, let alone mythic, ideals of football only wishfully, in their own minds. (They are adorable.) They are not spiritually separate from the background factories, whose workaday quiddity defines them more than their helmets and pads do.

Graham's centering of his composition on the water tower pronounces an ambiguous judgment: *corny.* This is a corny culture whose pursuits can only be corny. How we feel about that — in what measure alienated, amused, or resigned — is a choice given by the picture's ambiguity. The choice is anything but rich or dignified, but it represents freedom of a sort that must satisfy those of us determined both to share in our nation's available joys and not to insult our own intelligences more than we absolutely have to.

There is something to be said for this. The willful foolishness of immersion in sports culture harbors an always present potential of transcendence when some reverberating truth — some symbol — bursts clear of ordinary contingency. One of Graham's desultory footballers may on a given afternoon do or experience, in ragged play, something unforgettable for which he has no word or model. Or some such thing may register in the eye of an onlooker. Some such thing may even emerge in the tray of a photographer of the event, an image to set the blood racing. A lover of sport, as of art and ultimately of life, can make no preparation for such epiphanies except jealously to preserve an appetite for awe.

SYMPATHY FOR THE DEVIL

To HEAR SOME PEOPLE TALK about Jeff Koons, you would think he is the Devil. In fact, he is not. Those people are hysterical. They should calm down. Koons is only a subaltern demon, a Beelzebub: the Devil's minister without portfolio and ambassador at large. Koons attends to practical details of Satan's plan for the world.

Satan, who is mutability, plans a period of meaningless change that will leave no one and nothing what they were before — change in accord with no one's hopes, not even for change's sake but for no sake, going nowhere. It will be a fine period for art, as usual when Satan comes knocking.

Satan is an electrician in the basement of a building, rewiring every connection. He doesn't care what new connections are made so long as they are arbitrary. Now the flick of a switch on the third floor may turn on a lamp on the second floor or turn off a television set on the fifth. Just so, Koons's art is arbitrary in exact ways. Its causes and effects are as plain as an electrical plan that has been methodically deranged. The building served by the plan is culture. The plan changes nothing about the building but only makes its operation self-conscious and interesting.

This is no time for conventional art criticism. It is an unconventional time when the art that matters, such as Koons's, acts in a void.

During conventional times, artists are courtesans of history. (Art critics are whores of art history.) Artists accept the positions in which history arrays them and perform, perform, perform. They try to make history come in them. They are nymphs to history's Zeus. (Satan, Zeus: a miscellaneous mythology for a miscellaneous time.) Be the whim of history ever so perverse and even vicious, artists will flatter it as irresistibly exciting.

When history is stabilized, not fundamentally changing, its wants are conventional. (History was relatively stabilized for four decades until recently.) Then the courtesanly service of art to history is predictable and easy to learn. It becomes almost respectable. But when history is changing deeply and thus withdraws from ordinary consciousness, a principle arises to which I give the name Satan: incessant arousal, always about to come and never coming, when any performance may serve but no performance is ever consummated.

Koons is neither conservative nor avant-garde. He is radically reactionary.

Both "conservative" and "avant-garde" mentalities in art hanker after reigns of Zeus. Conservatives want conventions, nostalgic for the past. Avant-gardists want anti-conventions, nostalgic for the present. Conservatives dream of a respectabilization of art's concubinage, a marriage with history. Avant-gardists scheme to be favorites in the harem. Both conservatives and avant-gardists desire what cannot be had when history is deeply changing, when Zeus is absent and Satan takes charge. (Conservatism and avant-gardism meet on common ground at last: now both are ridiculous.)

By "radically reactionary" I mean that Koons reacts against history as movement in time — any movement at all, never mind "progress." His political model seems to be the state of culture in Europe during the centuries of royalism: a rigid hierarchy that bound classes with ascending ties of fealty and descending ties of noblesse oblige. Consider Koons's series of liquor-advertising posters (printed with the actual posters' original screens, but in oil dyes on linen for an amplified seductive jolt), each ad targeted by market research to a specific social-economic stratum.

Koons has offered precise analyses of the liquor ads' class appeals, from blatant images of luxury for the lowest classes to luxurious images of nearly total abstraction for the highest. Koons does not complain of the ads' covert manipulativeness. He deems the manipulation splendid because not covert at all, because generously revealing. The manipulation reveals what we are — poor, lower-middle-class, middle-class, upper-middle-class, rich — according to our aesthetics of intoxication.

Koons wants all people to know and embrace their social determinations, their places in the class structure, seeing how pleasant it would be if everyone did so. As a good American he does approve upward mobility, though as a bad American he identifies upward mobility with "stardom." All in all, he tempts the citizenry with the ultimate allurement: what is the case, the way things are. (Satan smiles.)

If Koons is not complaining about society, neither is he cynical. Complaint and cynicism are historical attitudes, differently confident that history's march will alter an offending society in ways specific to its offense. Complainers hold out for the alteration, waiting to be on history's side; cynics impatiently exploit what they despise, saying "After us the deluge." Today history has withdrawn, leaving people no intelligible political future either to direct or to repel their passions. Koons suggests how pleasant it would be to regard society's given state as immutable, embracing its arbitrary order and incidentally delivering human passions up to sheer mutability, making of society Satan's playground.

Koons is chaste. He may have made a literal exhibition of himself having sex with Ilona Staller, but in relation to history he is virginal. His relations with Satan are submissive but Platonic. The Devil's goatish reputation is undeserved. Satan is the figure of incessant unconsummated arousal, which is practically the same thing as impotence. Koons delights in history's withdrawal, not to be obliged to serve history's wants. He is freed to serve his own wants, which are sterile.

Koons's career is the story of his exploitive, ambivalent relation to the institutional order of the art world.

Koons's first mature works were vacuum cleaners encased in Plexiglas. They are monuments to sterility. They are poems, hymns, paeans to sterility and shrines to the primitiveness of bourgeois manias about cleanliness. ("Cleanliness is next to godliness," goes an awful old Protestant saying, and from that angle, in a certain light, the two qualities are one.) The vacuum-cleaner works are melancholy because, like everything else on a dirty planet, they are imperiled by dirt. They rely on the institutional order of art, especially the mechanism that assigns them a market value, to preserve and protect them. They pray anxiously for the permanence of the institutional order.

Similarly Koons's basketball-suspension tanks. These works demand constant maintenance. The proper flotation of the balls (symbols of potency sustained in impotence) is a sign that someone still cares enough to keep adjusting the fluid as required to

212

carry the tanks' unnatural state of nature into the future. The fluid symbolizes "art space," specifically the imaginative space radiated upward by a sculptural pedestal. (Koons has returned the pedestal to sculpture while retaining the outer-directed aesthetics of the Minimalist revolution that once banished the pedestal.) More generally, the fluid of the basketball tanks stands, again, for the institutional order of art, the invisible cultural medium that buoys up so many assumptions and presumptions, so many complacencies.

To this point, Koons had not significantly departed from Marcel Duchamp. He was still a courtesan of history, though a frigid courtesan. History could look but not touch. (Such was precisely the case with Duchamp — a pure exhibitionist, a sacred dancer in the harem.) Only in the middle 1980s did Koons become a virgin.

With his stainless-steel kitsch figurines and drinking paraphernalia, accompanied by his liquor and basketball posters, Koons began to abandon the institutional order of art as a sustaining medium. He prophesied for this order a dead, deadening fate, which he welcomed joyfully. His art became funerary: immortal because deathly. With stainless steel — "poor people's platinum," he said, a material that efficiently simulated the one quality (expensiveness) that everybody associates with art — he made an indestructible model of social hierarchy in terms of its dreams of taste.

Every dream of taste (kitsch being defined as the dreaming of taste) is an unwitting dream of art. It seeks unknowingly to emulate a real person who once really loved a real artwork — the person, occasion, and object lost but for the faintest of auras that lingers, no one knows how, as a folkloric ectoplasm. The most ignorant people can recognize it. Sensitive dogs may smell it. The poignance of the dream of taste, mysterious compensation for a mysterious lack, transfixes ordinary folk and leads them as if sleepwalking to buy atrocious things. That is, the things are "atrocious" to educated eyes, but what can education teach of the poignance, the great lack? It is a huge power, that ravenous worldwide lacklove. Koons understands it.

In the middle of the stainless-steel phase sits *Rabbit*, the divine bunny reflecting and accepting the world's entirety. *Rabbit* was

Koons's first masterpiece. His second is *Puppy*, the 40-foot-high Scotch terrier of growing flowers which, in a town near Kassel, stuck its tongue out at Documenta 9. By conjoining the low animal with high human artifice and merging kitsch with art, *Rabbit* and *Puppy* activate at a stroke the whole conceivable spectrum of ahistorical life. That is why they are masterpieces. *Rabbit* is mutable from without, by promiscuous reflections, and *Puppy* is mutable from within, by natural growth. Each is satisfied with and satisfies life as it is (that is, life as it *is not*, identified with the great lack). Neither waits to be impregnated by history.

Koons speaks of his 1988 exhibition of ceramic and wood sculptures as "the banality show." The show brought the sociological poetry of the stainless-steel pieces to fruition in colorful, big, immaculate objects which, yes, packaged banality in refined symbols of class sensibilities. For me that show was thrilling and depressing: my mind raced, my heart sank. At the time I wrote that "Koons symbolizes the apotheosis of corporate culture, the increasingly sacrosanct authority of money, the eroticizing of social status, and other emergent diseases. . . ." I was mostly wrong because hysterical, fancying that Koons was at one with certain obnoxious social trends. I did not yet grasp that he stood against all trends, all movements in time. ("Eroticizing of social status" was correct, though.)

Koons's art is about eroticism without distance, with no physical space or interval of time between the desiring one and what is desired. At no point in the loop of his art does desire begin and at no point is it consummated. A viewer is free to hold back emotionally from identification and to say, "I do not desire that. That desire is not mine." But the viewer cannot say without hysteria, "I do not recognize that desire. That desire is not real." The desire — for love in the guise of fetishes — is recognizably very real, the engine of the mass world. Koons's ceramic and wood sculptures are not in themselves fetishes. They are erotically cold and dead (that is, they are contemporary art), and each of them symbolizes the fetish-creating human hunger for love totally, as a whole.

Professional art people keep misunderstanding Koons because complacently expecting to grasp the essence of his art that only professionals can understand. There is no such essence.

There is a quality, or set of qualities, growing from modern-art history and from aesthetics of Duchamp, Pop, and Minimalism. But to grasp the professional art-ness of Koons's project is to hold an empty shell. No privilege is gained thereby over the most vulgar or naive, uneducated perception. On the contrary, perhaps.

A connoisseuring eye that correctly detects in *Puppy* a sculptural principle akin to Richard Serra's can miss the piece's richer content, which was not lost, when I saw it, on children who played around the flowering animal with delight. Even viewers who laugh with stupid derision at *Puppy* have an authentic response. There is stupidity aplenty in the work, carefully provided for the pleasure of stupid people. The only really disfiguring stupidity possible in the face of a Koons may be the presumption to a specially qualified comprehension, the vanity of art professionals.

The Devil adores all presumptions and vanities, because they lead humankind astray.

To the extent that Koons specializes in comprehending his own enterprise, he is capable of self-betraying vanity, sharing the misery of the professionals. He is ever in danger of losing touch with the grace of brute simplicity. He succumbed to this danger, I believe, in his series of computer paintings and sculptures of himself with Staller. The pieces in the series made too much sense intellectually as classless images of happy sensuality offering shameless permission to every class and had too little presence as artworks. Koons's idea has an impeccable precedent in Baudelaire: "Fucking is the poetry of the masses." But the idea was undercut by the factitiousness of the two merely individual persons rendered. Like the staged photographs of himself that Koons used to promote "the banality show," the images with Staller function best as advertisements for a definitive body of work which, in their case, does not exist.

Puppy proves that Koons has regained his balance, proceeding on his fated course out of the art world and into the world at large. He is proceeding along a line that may be tremendously fruitful: "public art." Normally either a political lie (under state tyrannies) or a contradiction in terms (in democracies), a truly public contemporary art seems realizable by Koons as by no other living artist. This is because he, like no one else, gives the term "public" a weight at least equal to that of "art." "Public" is no simple modifier of "art" for him, but the very medium — the source, the genius — from which his art arises and where it finds a home. There ought to be a Koons sculpture in a park or plaza of every city. The planet would not improve, but it would be more vivid. Count on art professionals, threatened in their standing, to oppose the spread of Koonses.

The Satanic will rule in culture of the near future because something must always rule, and because no political imperative (or none that is constructive) promises to generate ruling power anytime soon. At such a time civilization feeds on itself, digesting its own contents. At such a time the world of meaningless human behavior, which is Satan's incubator, is the only world. One is free to despise it. One is free to mourn, to resist, to destroy. But one will be obliged to live out every day of the epoch, and to do so with accurate consciousness may be better than to do so with hysteria. I would not recommend Koons as a hero to anyone. I do introduce him as a person (if "person" is the word for him) useful to know.

HOW TO BE ALIVE

Aʀɴoʟᴅ ᴇɴʟɪɢʜᴛᴇɴᴇᴅ ᴍᴇ ᴀʙᴏᴜᴛ Tɪᴛɪᴀɴ and I enlightened him about Bellini and we increased each other's enlightenment about Rembrandt, if memory serves. Arnold and I are a two-member old-master fan club. When he painted a portrait of me looking hauntedly anguished, which I decided is how he would feel if he had to be me, he draped a swatch of silk brocade over my shoulder for a 17th-century-Amsterdam-ish effect, he said. It ended up more Spanish-seeming, but then we were raving about Velázquez.

Most painters do not want even to think about Velázquez, the way most poets do not want to think about Shakespeare. It would make them wonder why they bother. As a rule, artists who permit themselves to dote on the past great are resigned to failure. I know I take a masochistic pleasure at times in thinking about, say, Shakespeare, my pride beaten down to the wormy satisfaction of gauging my relative misery as a writer. But then, I would never attempt a Shakespearean technique. The Bard has nothing to teach me except humility. For Arnold, who now and then emulates Titian in a positively collegial spirit, things stand differently.

Old masters for Arnold are companions who reassure him intimately of a vast continuity. He does not revere so much as gratefully respect them as highly advanced vocationals useful to know. His archaic glaze technique is neither conservative nor not conservative. It is not even archaic, in his hands, but a thoroughly practical idiom. With chiaroscuro he can make the masters who stand at his elbow clear to himself and himself clear to them. The technique is a protocol for dealing with colleagues who require tactful consideration, on account of being dead, when the occasion is beauty and desire whose object is similarly disadvantaged: remote, never had, never attainable, while in its very absence present, reliable, inviolable. Arnold is on easy terms with things vulgarly considered to be *not there*.

Arnold at one time was something of a protege of Agnes

Martin, America's Tantric genius of present absentness, and I have come to consider his spirit remarkably close to hers, with a difference that is major but less decisive than it may appear. Martin empties. Arnold fills. She renounces worldly appetite. He wallows in appetite for sensual luxury, for sexual love, for things rich and warm. He is a heretic to Martin's religion, but a heretic in good standing. He puts a different mask on the same god of the Ungraspable, an image of congested mortal yearning in place of Martin's pale wind. The god moves no nearer and no farther away for wearing the image. The god is already and always infinitely near, infinitely far, and serene.

Arnold will not stop dreaming of sensual worldly bliss. Just won't. Don't ask him. He would freak, making you sorry you asked. He will want, want, want. He *will* be impure. He will bring his gang of Renaissance Venetian cronies and work you over. He will not bear insult to any lovely thing. He is an appreciator. And yet his spirit is absent-minded of physical existence. Left to itself, it disinterestedly soars. It likes the sky. On a cruise in the Mediterranean last summer, Arnold took maybe a hundred photographs of watery horizons. They are what his spirit sees in its spirit mirror, a motif variously adapted to be the background in all his paintings, whether of big heads or little birds. A trick of the paintings is that the background is emotionally more immediate than the subject it is visually behind.

Painters paint because in the whole world there fails to exist something they need to see. They make good the world's oversight. Arnold needs to see a poignantly beautiful and strong male face that sees *him*. Arnold matter-of-factly adds this face to the sum of what is. It is massively, dramatically, overwhelmingly real while, to the same degrees, unreal. The face's reality and unreality are aspects of a single quality for which there is no word (and thus must be a painting) but only a flat-footed explanation: the face sees not the viewer but the painter. The same goes in a succinct, cherishable way for Arnold's small paintings of flowers and of parakeets: modest symbols of life, presented by the painter to himself, calmly riding out storms of the spirit's at once deathly and deathless watery sublimity.

Another Arnold (Matthew) said all culture is about "how to live." Knowing Arnold (Fern) has enhanced my education in this department, with a special emphasis that might be termed "how to be alive." It is about a confidence of being that is doubly anchored: in self-forgetful attachment to fleeting things and in self-forgetful apprehension of changeless things. Between, as in protective brackets, freely roil the self-aware passions of fear and yearning, anger and love, terror and delight, whose unashamed expression proves that someone is not wasting the opportunity of being alive. The passions pour from Arnold's paintings without a trace of either irony or hysteria, but with sweet, high artifice and sweet, honest faith. I pity anyone — I pity myself, in my frequent distraction — unable to recognize the message of this art as absolutely contemporary. Arnold's art is here to help us, if we let it, and of course to be beautiful, because beauty is only good manners in art.

THE FAITH OF DAYDREAMS

Did you hear about the insomniac, dyslexic agnostic?
He stayed up all night worrying about Dog.

— Anonymous joke

THE LAND OF "WILLIAM WEGMAN" lies under an enchantment: the idea of art. It is conditioned by the idea of art as countries are conditioned by geography and climate. The topography of "William Wegman" is low-lying and swampy, like Florida. The air is Arizona dry. The temperature hovers just above freezing, as during late November in New England. Atmospheric events include cumulus clouds, dust devils, and aurora borealis. Visitors must not be in a hurry. Even if they make headway in the soft soil, they find no roads or directional signs. To be lost is unavoidable. Visitors should pretend to enjoy being lost until, with practice, they become good at it.

The economy, social structure, and government of "William Wegman" are those of daydreams when the daydreamer is a serious child. Such a child muses not on superheroes and fantastic adventures, but on visions of reality: technical feats of engineering, perhaps, and other mysteries of adult behavior. When dogs play roles in "William Wegman," they are enacting the real as best they can. They look out at the viewer as if to say, "Is this it? Have I, in this instance, comprehended life accurately?" In paintings that render the landscape of "William Wegman," daydreams of industrial development and exotic geography work hard to convince the daydreamer that the world is knowable and, by him, known. In drawings, the daydreamer tests his belief that all interesting statements obey the formula "strange but true."

If one met people in "William Wegman" — as one does in a way determined by "if" (they are subjunctive people) — they would be polite. Their entire conversation would consist in telling you that their names are William Wegman. At times they would vary their utterance with a rising inflection, this way: "My name is William Wegman?" A visitor should not respond with incredulity or impatience. It would be most tactful to shrug one's shoulders. Shrug enthusiastically! Lyrical expressions of honest bewilderment are the poetry and song of "William Wegman."

The religion of "William Wegman" is austere, without ritual. Its religionists wonder constantly how they stand with God, if there is a God. In "William Wegman" it is possible to contemplate God whether God exists or not. This is a local ability, but it can be acquired. To learn it, first worry about something actual (your debts, say, or your health). Are you worried? Now remove from your mind the object of your anxiety. Make sure that there is nothing concrete in your mind. But continue worrying, meanwhile adding to your thoughts the possibility, rather faint, that everything will come out all right in the end. If successful in this, you may be a congregant in the bemused church of "William Wegman."

Though immaterial, "William Wegman" is materially based. It is manifest in communications media both expensive, such as paintings, and moderately priced, such as the catalogue you hold in your hands. This land has emerged from a twenty-five-year public career involving one artist aided by dealers, curators, publishers, technicians, friends, lovers, critics, and dogs. It is made possible by commercial and governmental institutions motivated to earn profits or to fulfill duty by pleasing their respective audiences. Indeed, a defining feature of "William Wegman" is its sensitivity to the character of the worldly agencies upon which it depends.

William Wegman, the man officially responsible for "William Wegman," is a court comedian and sorcerer of the professional art world since the late 1960s. He is an artist's artist, whose subtle parodies of the artistic vocation stir rueful laughter in sophisticated colleagues. He is also a popular (not Pop) artist, maker of images that are delicious to people not normally attracted by contemporary art. He has no rivals for his odd eminence. His sensibility is as rare as a desert flower that blooms once a year by moonlight. And yet he is a hard-working, sturdy entertainer, the equivalent in pictorial art of a rock'n'roll band that revives its popularity with each new generation.

Wegman was born in 1943 in Massachusetts. As a boy, he thought he would become a magazine illustrator. (For practice, he painted many images of a girl in advertisements for Breck

Shampoo. This girl reappeared in his first return to painting, the "manifesto" picture *Hope*, in 1985.) Around age 18, he was "struck hard by a late-teenage urge to become 'deep.'" (All quotes here are from a recent conversation I had with the artist.) He contemplated "the Void" and painted "Existentialist-Abstract-Expressionist triptychs." But by then he was at an advanced art school, exposed to the clash of strong artistic movements that marked United States culture in the early '60s: triumphant but declining Abstract Expressionism, triumphantly rising Pop Art and Minimalism. "I was in the class right before every student had to choose sides, deciding whether to be Pop or Minimal."

I am Wegman's age and well remember the New York art world of the '60s and early '70s, when like him I frequented the New York art bar Max's Kansas City. There some leading Minimalists, such as Carl Andre and Robert Smithson, drank in the front, while Andy Warhol and his entourage would be found in the back. I usually went to the back. It was like passing through a den of scowling intellectual gangsters on the way to a degenerate children's birthday party, or through a grainy black-and-white film to a movie the colors of lipstick and neon. Wegman lingered in the front at Max's during visits from his then center of operations in Los Angeles. (He would long be regarded in New York as a "California artist" — a dubious but carefree status, shared by the likewise eminent Bruce Nauman and Edward Ruscha, that excused one from soldiering in Manhattan art-gang wars.)

At school, Wegman had soon imbibed the youthful aesthetic doctrine of the 1960s, whose slogans included "painting is dead." To be "deep" was unimportant. To be "original" was everything. As a student and teacher at several colleges, he developed an "aversion to Surrealism and Expressionism," wanting to participate in the severe Minimalist romance of pure self-evidence but not its dogma of abstract form. (Not until 1979, incidentally, would he succumb to the very non-Minimalist vulgarity of making a photograph in color: a picture of the dog Man Ray displaying paws embellished with red nail polish.) "I got estranged from myself in order to be unique. I worked with non-art materials. Dropping things off buildings. Using strips of cellophane and bits of mud and hair. I never knew when a piece was finished."

Wegman came to photography through documenting his

ephemeral works. The notion of the preconceived photograph as an independent artwork struck him suddenly, he says, at a party in 1970. He had gone to the party after idly drawing little circles on the back of one hand. While there, he picked up a slice of cotto salami. He noticed that the peppercorns in the meat were the same shape and size as the circles on his hand. It was an epiphany of structure. He recreated the sight for his photograph *Cotto* and proceeded over the next several years to produce a multitude of photographs in which strictly formal resemblances unite wildly disparate realities. The idea of art is the perverse hero of these pictures, which are like the experiments of a mad scientist oblivious to common sense. Wegman soon enlisted the ideal laboratory assistant: his dog Man Ray, for whom no task was too hard or silly to be executed with yeoman dignity.

A good moment for Wegman and for art occurred in 1969 when, at a college in Wisconsin, he borrowed some video equipment and experimented with the then fashionable but usually unavailing new medium. That was an epoch of excruciatingly boring videotapes by artists. Working alone, Wegman put himself in front of the camera and improvised small performances partly inspired by "little stories by Jorge Luis Borges — Borges's parables of circular time." (The idea of circular or "crystalline" rather than "linear" time was being brilliantly theorized then in the writings of Robert Smithson.) "I decided that the trick of video was how to get into and then get out of the frame." Wegman's devising of organic length, shape, and closure for units of video was a small but all-important achievement. Among other things, it drew the first distinct frontiers of "William Wegman."

Consider four of the early tapes.

— The camera is on the floor. The artist, on hands and knees, backs away from the camera, dribbling milk out of his mouth. He backs around a corner, having left a trail of milk on the floor. From around the corner comes a dog (Man Ray) lapping up the milk. The tape ends when the dog bumps into the camera.

— The artist, grinning, says that he was treated for depression with electric shock therapy. Since the shock, he says, this grin has been frozen on his face. Everybody thinks he is happy, but he is still depressed. "I don't know what I'm going to do," he concludes with a hint of menace.

— A book with a cover photograph of Jorge Luis Borges lies beside a dead fish. A text by Borges about an ancient Egyptian myth of divine fish, which swim ahead of the Sun-God in a circular voyage over and under the Earth, is recited by a voice that appears to come from the fish, whose jaw moves in synchronization.

— The artist critiques Man Ray's spelling. The words "park" and "out" have been spelled correctly, he says. The dog watches him intently. Then he explains disapprovingly that the word "beach" has been misspelled "beech." Man Ray whines. The artist says comfortingly, "Well, okay, I forgive you, but remember it next time."

Each of these brief tapes involves a childishly transparent artifice, a self-evident trick. Each is played out with perfectly grave deliberation. In the total self-consciousness of the exercise, a mental window is thrown open on the character of any and all performance. The urge to perform is nakedly revealed in a way usually definitive of failed, embarrassingly bad performance. (As a rule, few things in life are more unbearable than watching someone on a stage trying in vain to be affecting or funny.) But since the revelation of performance effort is the whole point of Wegman's videos, "failure" becomes the mark of his success. This strange-but-true success unleashed an extraordinary power of significance in the early 1970s.

The U. S. art world at that time was a zone of collapsed boundaries and meandering energies. Two avant-gardist decades had left in their wake a culture accustomed, or resigned, to artistic permanent revolution. But there can be no revolution without opposition, and nothing in U. S. society any longer offered coherent resistance to even the most radical changes in the form or focus of art. The actions of the young artists crowded into newly constituted "alternative" art institutions met with growing public numbness. When in 1973 Wegman's contemporary Chris Burden had himself shot in the arm with a rifle as an artwork, the event was prominently noted in *The New York Times*. As I recall, no one mustered the energy to denounce it.

The early 1970s was a period of roomy, drab interior spaces — either drably new, in the case of recently built art schools, or drably old, in a fashion for unimproved loft studios. Artists everywhere did visually unappealing, strenuously theorized stuff

— or "projects," as the works tended to be termed — under loose headings of "conceptual" and "process" art. Socially the mood was casual and democratic, if only because competition for worldly rewards seemed pointless. (A national economic recession had wrecked the art market.) The artists worked for each other and a free-floating cohort of hangers-on and aficionados. It was in this dispirited milieu that the name of William Wegman first began to be heard.

I do not recall where or when I first saw photographs and videotapes by Wegman, but I can hardly forget their impact. It was as if a miasmic atmosphere had been pierced by a ray of light. The photographic images and videotaped comedy routines were very funny, of course — hilariously laconic in a vein reminiscent of Buster Keaton with a touch of Woody Allen. (Wegman's writing often displays an Allenesque, cracked cogency. For example, "My video work can be likened to Plato's *Dialogues*, only my work is primarily with dogs.") Most of all, though, I remember a feeling of bizarre comfort. As a viewer, I was being engaged directly and matter-of-factly. There was no "artistic" posturing, but rather a deeply informed satire on all such posturing. The satire was not angry, but it made room for anger. It made room for whatever I or any other viewer happened to be feeling. It offered simple companionship in realms of grotesque complexity.

The modest gesture of Wegman's photographs and videos of the '70s carried serious weight because, in a fundamental way, it was a gesture of historical despair. It concluded a young artist's desperate ambition, pursued with extreme talent and tenacity, to seize upon the idea of art. Avant-gardism had held out the once-and-for-all conquest of art's essence as an ever-present possibility. Wegman had tried naively to believe, to assimilate, and to advance the Minimalists' aim of reducing art to its foundations. But he was too late and too intelligent for this last of the modernist Utopias. The absurdity of the effort pressed upon him. He commenced to make work of the absurdity. The idea of art escaped upward like an unknowable, Protestant deity, hovering above Wegman's acts of precise, careful futility.

Wegman's art has a "Northern" pathos, the emotion of an isolated individual hungering for meaning in a world where action, driven by the notorious "work ethic," is always plentiful and meaning is proportionately scarce. He made a comedy of this constant plight, burlesquing it with actions of spectacular meaninglessness in which the wish for meaning persists tirelessly — doggedly! — despite everything. Wegman's solitary studio theatrics resonated deeply with U. S. culture at large. By the late 1970s his work was being broadcast nationally on *Saturday Night Live* and he was making large-format photographs with equipment offered to him by the Polaroid Corporation. His lonely crisis with art turned out to accord with a vastly shared crisis — a catastrophic loss of faith in the meaningfulness of any medium, any image — in the wider world.

Wegman's unexpected rise to celebrity brought personal difficulties. His life grew disorderly. When his dog Man Ray died in 1982, he was devastated. Pressured from without and within, the refuge and laboratory of his studio became joyless. Partly he was facing the problem of any successful avant-gardist — what to do when embraced by the bourgeoisie — compounded by the irony of being post-avant-garde, an artist who had gone forward with the idea that going forward was impossible. When Wegman painfully reconstituted his life and art, the result was a split that still pertains: highly professional photographic entertainments, of which his recent fairytale books *Cinderella* and *Little Red Riding Hood* are marvelous examples, and highly individualistic paintings, belatedly fulfilling the teenager who yearned to be "deep."

"At night, before going to sleep, I would have these visions," Wegman told David Ross (in *William Wegman*, 1990, Abrams, p. 15), speaking of his transition in the '80s. "In this dreamy state, the Lord told me to start using my God-given talents. I interpreted this to mean painting." Thus did the elusive deity of "William Wegman" show a smiling aspect. It is an aspect that had always flickered in Wegman's drawings, which are like lightning raids on the artist's stream of consciousness: fugitive thoughts that, no matter how slight or foolish, deliver a startling force of authenticity. (One laughs at them with a shock of recognition, suddenly aware of one's own normally unheeded mental processes.) With his paintings since 1985, Wegman has immersed himself in that stream, going to the source of hopeful imagining that never ceases to flow below and around anyone's conscious mind — bubbling wellspring of the routine courage that keeps us equal to the ordeals of living.

Wegman begins his paintings with sponged washes of acrylic paint. Literally daydreaming in these abstract fields, he picks out and develops images with oil paint and small brushes. The general procedure is a familiar tactic of Surrealism, but with an emphasis that undercuts the Surrealist glamor of unconscious inspiration. What Wegman discovers in his reverie are not personal obsessions or collective archetypes but culturally processed, sociable emblems: cliches, in a word. This is the cosmos of the serious child, who daydreams to lay hold of a reality conceived to be stable and ultimately accessible. It is reality according to a children's encyclopedia, which alphabetizes the universe in tidy, enchantingly illustrated segments.

Wegman's paintings are vertiginous in their refusal of both irony and sentimentality. Their little airplanes in painted skies and boats in painted seas fly and float with the sole authority of having been once, by someone, wholly believed. They assert the serious child's whole trust, whole faith, in the reliable truth of images. Is it astonishing that Wegman, a prophet of Western culture's loss of faith in images, should now advance so ingenuous an identification with timeworn representations of people, places, and things? It is, but the paintings derive their effectiveness precisely from his long habit of skeptical irony. We deal here not with a contradiction of skepticism, but with a residue. When intelligence has done its most and worst to abolish faith, faith nonetheless endures with the feckless patience of water wearing down rock.

We may finally identify the exact real-world place and time in which exists the land "William Wegman": right here, right now. "William Wegman" is not a domain alternative to the actual. It is the actual considered as a gift. Just as daydreams are gifts given by the mind to the mind, to make living more bearable, Wegman's art is a gift of transparently created phenomena to the given phenomena of the world, to make reality more bearable. At root, perhaps all of art intends to be just that. But we live in times alienated from the trust that this transaction of art requires. With a humble humor that goes as far as art can to propitiate doubt, Wegman offers healing communion. With profundity whose touch is as light as a feather, he guides us toward an available grace.

227

WILLEM DE KOONING AND JEAN DUBUFFET

Pace Gallery, New York, 1993

THE PATRIARCHS

The oldest hath borne most; we that are young
Shall never see so much, nor live so long.

Willem de Kooning's paintings from the middle 1980s are lyrical events in slow motion. They are as pure as birdsong long drawn out, labyrinthine, and serene. It is a very sophisticated and considering bird, this warbler in red, yellow, blue, and white. It starts and stops, trying this and that like a rehearsing musician (I fancy a clarinetist). But its mood is not familiarly human. The author of the paintings appears to harbor no particular concerns or intentions, driven by an organic inclination, an instinct, for unhurried, endless, and all-forgetful joy.

The last paintings of Jean Dubuffet are plenty human, bristling with consciousness. They are unusual in their own way. They are like music thrown into reverse, song unsinging itself, melodious sound devolving into stutters, gurgles, and rales. It is as if an orchestra's finale were a passionate tuning-up. The effect is preposterously generous. The orchestra is tired of having the conductor select from its bag of tricks. It dumps the bag in the audience's lap.

These are wonderful paintings by two of the last commanding figures in easel painting's reign as the queen of Western arts. The works unfurl themselves in a historical void. They have met with silence in the art culture of today, a dumbness of people, notably including most critics, who have forgotten how to expect marvels from paint on canvas and how to talk about them when, very rarely now, they occur. The paintings embarrass our wizened era. They do so with their confidence that selves emptied out, lives thrown away, into the receptacle of the painted picture are kept in a safe place and persist indefinitely.

The paintings are beautiful.

They are modern.

They have a tragic air.

Start with the tragedy, mild but with a bite to it. We have

here the work of old men. The men were warriors when modern art was a war of the authentic against the false, the fresh against the stale — back when cultural orders could still settle in for long enough to grow false and stale. (How odd to feel nostalgic for that!) De Kooning and Dubuffet never lost their spirits of opposition, even decades after there was anything really to oppose. At last their struggles traveled orbits around themselves. The point is that they struggled still. Growing old, they kept changing, bereft but also freed of any pretense that their acts might move the world.

"The wonder is, he hath endured so long. / He but usurped his life," it is said of King Lear at the end of Shakespeare's play (meaning roughly "he outlived himself"). The incandescent moment of *Lear* occurs when, at death's door, the irascible patriarch attains something like moral perfection:

> Come, let's away to prison.
> We two alone will sing like birds i' the cage.
> When thou dost ask me blessing, I'll kneel down
> And ask of thee forgiveness. So we'll live,
> And pray, and sing, and tell old tales, and laugh
> At gilded butterflies, and hear poor rogues
> Talk of court news; and we'll talk with them too,
> Who loses and who wins; who's in, who's out;
> And take upon's the mystery of things,
> As if we were God's spies; and we'll wear out,
> In a walled prison, packs and sects of great ones
> That ebb and flow by the moon.

Lear's beatitude alters nothing of the disasters that led to it, nor can it ward off the murder of Cordelia. Except for Cordelia, only stonehearted enemies attend the moment. (Edmund's response to perhaps the loveliest speech ever written: "Take them away.") Lear's last-minute grandeur is impotent and pointless, in any consequential way. It arises like an immaterial menhir in a real desert. Likewise, though on an entirely other plane of reckoning, the late works of our two artists — works of intense ease, of pleasurableness terrifically grave — are monuments out of time.

De Kooning and Dubuffet leave no successors, only survivors, in the tradition of the easel painting. From the *Mona Lisa* to *Woman I*, that tradition was a touchstone of Western arts. It became the proving ground especially of modern art, which wrote finis to rival traditions of architecturally integrated painting for church or palace. The easel painting has functioned in language as a symbol of creativity in general. To apostrophize the creative, it used to be sufficient to mention Rembrandt or van Gogh; and you don't have to be very old to remember when the words "art" and "painting" were more or less interchangeable in common speech. (I wonder if an etymologist could trace the lifespan of that curious conflation.) Today "art" is apt to connote an academic department or a business, at any rate a professional field. "Painting" may evoke an awkward vocation, both grand and wanting: the specialty of a meritocracy exiled from significance. What happened?

There are more than enough answers to that question. One answer is simply that modern art happened, an acid bath of self-consciousness that ate away dispensable conventions until finally it dissolved painting's indispensable, bedrock fictions. "The only certainty today is that one must be self-conscious," de Kooning wrote in 1949. Like Dubuffet, de Kooning embraced the destructiveness of the modern even as he gave it something toughly resistant to work on. To put it another way, these two potlatch chiefs munificently squandered painting's historic capital, which could not be saved. As their working lives ended, they were still feeding painting and themselves into their ceremonial bonfires, now in solitude.

It will not do to yoke de Kooning and Dubuffet too tightly. They are mutually antagonistic figures, all the more so for their numerous similarities: born three years apart at the start of the 20th century, both "northerners" by heritage who gravitated to "southern" abandon, both individualistic late bloomers in their careers, both abstractors magnetized by the figure, both competitive males fiercely ambivalent toward the feminine. Nor do their most obvious differences account for the acutest discrepancy between them. De Kooning is the more classical painter, one of the all-time masters of the craft. Dubuffet ironized painting, identifying it with the God-touched ineptitude of the primitive, the insane, and the renegade. The Dutch-American culti-vated the flowers of his extraordinary gift. The Frenchman ripped his own extraordinary gift out by the roots. But these are inci-dentals in our present story.

The true distinction between the two is a matter of tempera-ments assigned opposite roles by culture and history. De Kooning played the Apollonian modernist in the youthful revolution of American postwar painting. Dubuffet played the Dionysian ras-cal in the weary devolution of the School of Paris. History counts in our comprehension of artists of this magnitude. They worked with culture at their backs, peering over their shoulders at the decisions they made. Their decisions, not their gestures. What they did in painting, not what they did with painting. The fiction that painting is a discrete world of cause and effect, intention and consequence, remains barely but functionally intact in all their work.

Not for them (except sometimes for Dubuffet, as in his envi-ronmental pieces) the shape-shifting by which postwar painting flirted at times brilliantly but in the end suicidally with resem-bling other things — walls, flags, sculptures, billboards, photo-graphs, common objects — on its way to tumbling out of specialness into the ordinary. The edges of pictures by de Kooning and Dubuffet are still threshholds, like the entrances to temples. What happens inside the threshholds is, as always, a keen regis-tration of physical, mental, and moral energy. It is also, in this late work, an immolation of habit, the final precipitations of the body-memories of men for whom painting was living. Recall Lear's last words: "Look there! Look there!"

The de Koonings are slow and sensuous. They are about draw-ing. The Dubuffets are fast and thorny. They are about marking. Each picture is the summation of an old male body attached to a brush, caressing or roughing up the body of painting. De Kooning feels around like someone seeking an object in the dark, or like someone in darkness touching the contours of something and wondering what it might be. Drastically less patient, Dubuffet fills the pictorial air with peremptory gestures, forming a net to capture whatever — maybe something, maybe nothing — is lurk-ing there. De Kooning's mood is bemused curiosity. Dubuffet's is giddy exasperation.

These were masters. What is mastery? It is an unfailing sense, put to exacting tests, of what a given medium requires for its minimum integrity, its survival. A master is like an adventurer who deliberately gets lost in a forest for the gratification of finding his way out again. The first stroke of a brush on a canvas destroys the canvas's unity. The last stroke restores the unity. This is true of any painting. It is a matter of degree. The degree of destruction incurred, of lostness risked, in a master's work is hair-raising. We sense that there was a moment, or more than a moment, in the work's execution when any other artist would have been paralyzed with fear. The master proves himself, then proves himself again, to be our leader, our only guide through the wilderness of his making. He constellates an idea of the heroic father.

Is the father wayward? Never mind. The father need not explain himself. There is only one father. This is a way things used to be, which has been collapsing in Western culture. (Lear today would be a reprobate, trashed by Regan and Goneril on the talk shows. Cordelia would be steered to a codependency counselor.) De Kooning and Dubuffet are figures in the penultimate stage of the collapse of fatherly pathos. Alternately magnificent and childish, sardonic and foolish, defiant and cajoling, they lived out the frenzy of competitive triumph in a game — the gladiatorial order of masters — that disintegrated around them. They helped to insure that painting would suffer historic eclipse by so thoroughly identifying it, through their own efforts, with primordial male initiative, most unguardedly in their respective Women paintings. What happens in their late paintings isn't even an endgame. It is after the endgame. Out of time.

They painted to keep themselves company in old age, when friends become few and troubles swarm. It is well known, and needs to be considered, that de Kooning in the middle 1980s was suffering severe memory loss. (I recall my last conversation with him, several years earlier. "I don't remember so good any more, d'ya mind?" he said in that delightful Dutch-accented patois he never outgrew. I said I didn't. "Good! Let's talk!") The elusive object he seeks in the paintings is himself, what it was like to be himself, a master mapping his being on the body of painting. The knowledge comes and goes. It always did for de Kooning, with his famous "slipping glimpse." Only now the forest is inescapable. Searching must be for searching's sake.

These de Koonings are amazing demonstrations of pictorial negative space, never so dominant even in the watercolors of Cézanne. Their active color is bright, flowing white. It is metaphysical, God-like, Moby-Dick white, a color that is everything and nothing. It disgorges organic-seeming shapes and swallows them up. Lines atop the white seem not to touch it, as if they flew across it like skimming seabirds. The always distinctly feminine shapes take their contours from the white, which is brushed over a multitude of now invisible — forgotten — possibilities. The shapes emerge like insistent memories. For me they have a haunting redolence of de Kooning's work from fifty and sixty years ago — back when he was assimilating the influences of John Graham and Arshile Gorky, his charismatic artistic uncle and tragic artistic brother.

A beautiful and poignant effect in these paintings is the dragging of a red or blue stroke or a yellow effulgence over the white, which bleeds through. The strong colors are paled by the white's stronger light. The work's hero, this light seems capable at any moment of bleaching away all color in blinding haze. Everything in the pictures happens at the sufferance of the white. The white lingers over the shapes, lines, strokes, and colors, touching them with frail tenderness, turning and arranging them, picking them up and letting them fall. The exercise is indeed as thoughtless, though also as uncannily contemplative, as birdsong — the song of the mockingbird, perhaps, that toys with snatches of what it has heard, building and unbuilding arpeggios in an endless afternoon in a distant summer that invades and displaces present time.

To turn here from de Kooning to Dubuffet is a jolt. It is as if a truck — a big and old one, smoking and rattling, spewing parts of itself — drove into a languid afternoon trailing clamorous night. The ground of our experience goes from white to black: a night sky for Dubuffet's potlatch pyrotechnics that blaze in primary colors that are jangling, atonal, sulferous. As his end approaches, Dubuffet shoots the works. He, too, tries to remember himself. Unlike de Kooning, he succeeds with painful clarity. He remembers someone obsessed with painting, planning paintings, cataloguing paintings, painting feverishly as if against a divine deadline that, always approaching, never arrives.

Dubuffet's marking of a surface is like an animal's marking, with scent, of its territory. He records not his feeling but his existence. Proof of one's existence is never concluded. Each new instant disbelieves it. Thus the incessant piling-up of marks by Dubuffet: not horror vacui (empty space is not the problem) but horror of cessation (empty time, time in which one isn't). This constant meaning of his work was never more naked than in these paintings. A cunning strategist, he was always at pains to frame his activity as a set of performances. He worked in series, each with its title and rationale, its synopsis. No such tidiness pertains here. There is no time for it. Dubuffet performs in a theater that is burning down.

The Dubuffets are all verb, without nouns. Their subjects are adverbial. The artist, painting, takes notice of how he paints, entering the effects in some of his titles. He paints fluently (*Fluence*). He paints dramatically (*Dramatique*). What he notices, and we notice it with him, is how his mood interacts with the architectonics of the canvas. The pictures tell stories of how easel painting's formal tugs, its hypersensitivities to relations, impose order on mark-making riot, turning convulsions into dances. "Howl, howl, howl!" Lear cries in agony, and it is the most splendid music because he cries metrically. Easel painting is the iambic pentameter of the pictorial, as field painting (post-Jackson Pollock) is the free verse. Relational composition is a parachute that did not fail to open for Dubuffet when he threw himself from precipices.

"Why do I keep doing this?" de Kooning said to me wonderingly when last I saw him. He was gesturing at his studio crammed with work in progress. "I don't need the money!" He shook his head in antic disgust. Of course, he kept painting because it was what he did, what he was. Out in the world, the climate for painting grew ever more inclement. He couldn't help that. He couldn't help himself. Nor could Dubuffet help himself, whose boundless worldly ambition increasingly went unrequited but whose spirit never succumbed to bitterness.

When Willem de Kooning would stand before a blank canvas, that was a moment of Keatsian "wild surmise" marvelous to conjure up: the medium of Titian about to be taken for yet one more exquisite ride. As for Dubuffet, it is hard to imagine any canvas staying blank for more than an instant in his vicinity. He plowed through the muddy world bespattering every accessible surface with manic glory. Like Lear, these patriarchs outlived themselves, at last speaking luminous monologues in paint without use or call and defenseless to a shortsighted art world that responded, if it responded, "Take them away."

FRANK STELLA: BLACK PAINTINGS
Musée de l'art contemporain, Bordeaux, France, 1994

HIPNESS VISIBLE:
STELLA'S BLACK PAINTINGS IN THEIR TIME

IMAGINE A MENTAL STATE IN WHICH icons of doleful stasis can thrill. I am thinking of mania, where feelings of confidence and optimism verge on dread. The manic subject hurtles without brakes. A vision of immutable repose may exude pathos for this subject — overwhelmingly so if the static vision is itself a sign of euphoria, perhaps as a product of revolutionary invention. A rising class of the educated young in the United States at the end of the 1950s was such a subject, abruptly self-aware as a generation granted seemingly inexhaustible prosperity and limitless freedom. Was the world in any way dissatisfying? The world would be changed! Frank Stella's black paintings, a widely felt shock when shown at the Museum of Modern Art in 1959-60, added an enchanting coolness to the growing excitement. To this day, those dour artworks retain for some veterans of the era a nostalgia as poignant as a song tinged with erotic memories.

To be receptive to Stella's black paintings in their time was to receive a gift of control. Like carbon rods inserted into a fissioning nuclear core, the works served a generation's sense of power by absorbing excess radiation. They hinted at mastery not just within art but *of* art, and beyond that of history, culture, and life itself — history, culture, and life being the negative, shadow terms of the pictures' positive stasis, barbarity, and deathliness. Deathliness a positive term? Life a negative? When control is the issue, yes. Stella signaled his self-consciousness on this point with an astoundingly barbarous title, *Die Fahne hoch* ("The Flag on High") — a marching song of the Master Race. The signal was partly a hip joke, playing on an American penchant to call any appearance of extreme orderliness "fascist." Beyond that, the title broadcast a conviction of licensed innocence, a liberty to exploit the expressive resources of any moral territory without qualm.

Stella was a young man, a young American, a graduate of Princeton University and earlier (as a fellow student of the sculptor Carl Andre) of the elite Phillips Academy in Andover, Massa-

236

chusetts. This was then an unusual background for an American painter of avant-garde proclivity. Unusual at that time, too, was Stella's lack of training in such traditional crafts as figure drawing. His extensive studio education had been "progressive," almost strictly in abstraction — a preparation more strategic, one might say, than tactical. He was something new on the scene, but right behind him came a generation of the similarly prepared who would make his artistic profile the norm. The epoch of Stella saw a triumph of academically oriented specialists — in production, mediation, and analysis — as hierophants of the aesthetic. It was a time of priestly professionalization that continues to this day, hard to keep in view because so pervasive. The professionalization was just beginning in 1960, when the American art world was still fundamentally bohemian.

I will not engage critical theories that came to the support of Stella's early work. I will proceed as I have begun, exploring the significance of the black paintings in psychological and social terms that seem basic to the most successful art of that time. The American art criticism, usually termed "formalist," that flourished in the '60s was of a piece with the time's American art, part of a rhetorical onslaught, a generational power play, determined by historic openings. But the criticism often argued one thing while the art, more authentically, argued another. Clement Greenberg and his followers marshalled the period's most sophisticated analysis in service to the period's most irrelevant movement: Color Field, which did not include Stella. Michael Fried, the most gifted of '60s critics, labored quixotically to reconcile Stella's work with Greenbergian theory. Donald Judd championed Stella in ways brilliantly lucid while transparently self-serving. The story of American criticism in the '60s can fascinate, but it is a sideshow.

The story of American art in the '60s was worked out not by critics on the page but by a collective enterprise of sensibility more or less in the street. Commerce and fashion were the fulcrums of change, but the lever was operated by a shifting cohort of amateurs. A sort of Darwinism on amphetamine governed the scene, with novel species of art appearing and perishing in a moment. Still, a shared sense of history and a commitment to recognizing the cogently new imposed a certain order. Engineers have a saying that any mechanical system works with maximum efficiency just before it breaks. Such was briefly the case with art in America. For a few electric years, until 1968 or so, art advanced through reciprocal action between artists and a keenly responsive audience that included other artists. The audience included critics, too, but was collectively smarter than any indvidual. For instance, no prominent critic articulated a judgment that was common coin among young observers in New York in the middle 1960s: the two artists who mattered were Stella and Andy Warhol. This judgment was not argued. It was too obvious for words. It was hip.

Hipness, born in jazz culture, exploded through America in the '60s before collapsing into cliche with the hippie movement. Hipness marked a period in modern annals of youthful malice against elders perceived to represent a repulsive status quo. In individuals, hipness recalled 19th-century dandyism as a shape-shifting, spectacular means of dissimulating insecurity by causing insecurity in others. As a group allegiance, it looked forward to its present-day antagonist, political correctness. Today the p.c. young drive former hipsters crazy by pronouncing rules of attitude and conduct. Such matters, for the hip, went entirely and almost superstitiously without saying. But hipness in its indirect way knew how to intimidate; it, too, was terroristic. It imposed an instant authority harsher than the old authority it opposed. Its keynote was suddenness. Art history would show Stella displacing previous artists in a stable art sphere. The truth is that Stella helped to colonize a new locus and language for art. The sphere he occupied came into being along with him.

In the comprehensiveness of their visions, Warhol and Stella were overqualified for the movements — Pop and Minimalism — with which they were quickly identified. A word for their overqualification is hipness. They were mordantly worldly. Warhol was hip to new facts of popular culture and demotic behavior. He would become the world's premier media artist. Stella was hip to new facts of academic culture and institutional behavior. He would become the world's premier corporate artist. Young observers in the '60s knew instinctively that both artists rode a single wave that was obliterating conventional structures. What Stella and Warhol inherited — or, rather, skimmed — from the high moderns, specifically the Abstract Expressionists, was only what pertained to and advanced a sense of power. Power is always in the present tense. Power practically *is* the present tense, action too self-secure to bother about precedence and consequence. The moment of Stella's and Warhol's full power was brief, a seismographic spike, but it left a permanent mark.

Conventional art critics in the early '60s haplessly tried to relate Warhol to Dada and Stella to past geometric abstraction, when the only historical models that truly counted for both painters were the most unprecedented, virginal aspects of work by Jackson Pollock, Mark Rothko, and Barnett Newman: large scale, synoptic image, symmetry, repetition, all-over facture, emphasized flatness, and the rest of the radical catechism of New York School painting. Warhol and Stella concentrated Abstract-Expressionist tropes into rhetorics of instantaneity, semaphores of the new. Their effects stabilized and exalted young viewers' sense of historic election, a generational hubris laced with panic.

The hip delights in setting snares for the square. Art hipsters of the '60s rejoiced when critics hostile to Stella's black paintings — the work, wrote one distraught party, of "the Oblomov of art, the Cézanne of nihilism, the master of *ennui*" — fell into the trap of describing the paintings' imagery as "white pinstripes." This reading exactly mistook the observable fact, which is that the pictures comprise freehand-painted two-and-a-half-inch-wide bands of black enamel separated by thin gaps of unpainted canvas. The reading of "pinstripes" betrayed the blindness of the critics to what was there in the paintings, an error all the more delectable in that the critics probably began by complaining that there was nothing in the paintings at all.

To view black bands as visually positive and white lines as negative, upending a habit of Western seeing, epitomized a visual hipness recalling jazz music's orientation to the off-beat between normal rhythmic stresses. The hip style of art writing in the decade of "formalism," which Stella's black paintings initiated, was a detailed, uninflected language of description, scorning the hazy approximations of impressionistic prose. Another of the time's square solecisms, akin to the sighting of "pinstripes" in Stella's black paintings, was the often repeated presumption that Warhol "painted soup cans," when anyone exercising a little rigor could see that Warhol silkscreened images of soup cans or, better, photo-mechanical reproductions of images from advertisements for soup. To confound literal-minded citizens then, one outdid them in literal-mindedness. Any hint of interpretation, let alone of detachable "literary" meaning, was taken as pitiful evidence of an obsolete mentality.

And yet Stella left essayistic meaning in plain sight with the titles of the black paintings. The title of *Die Fahne hoch* was a tour de force (cleverly apt for a brutally heraldic painting), as was, for instance, *Turkish Mambo* (a self-mockery of this painting's wobbly execution, taken from an innovative piece by jazz pianist and hipster's hipster Lennie Tristano). The most telling group of titles refers to places in the depressed black Brooklyn neighborhood of Bedford-Stuyvesant (*Tomlinson Court Park, Arundel Castle*) and to notoriously shady nightclubs (*Zambesi, Club Onyx*). As for *Jill*, using an innocent-sounding woman's name, Stella was quoted as explaining that "Jill was involved with some of those places" — a mild remark that suddenly makes a simple crisscross abstract design a sexual spider web or a radar screen for dark impulses. The titles' brand of hipness belongs to an era of beatnik literary fashion, with special redolence of Norman Mailer's contemporaneous pamphlet *The White Negro*.

The master title, and perhaps the master painting, of the black series is *The Marriage of Reason and Squalor*. "Reason" seems an ironic reference to the work's misleading appearance of geometric regularity. "Squalor" takes on in context a hint of French *nostalgie de la boue*. (The black paintings do indeed look *muddy*, like striated wet loam.) An influential short story of the period by J. D. Salinger was titled "For Esmé — with Love and Squalor." "The Marriage of Heaven and Hell" is one of the greatest poems of William Blake, a particular hero of the Beats. Plainly such contemporary breezes played on Stella's youthful sensibility as on an Aeolian harp. Hip observers got the overall drift in a flash. Squares, notably including art historians, did not get it, and still do not. (However, latter-day squares may draw support from Stella himself, whose work has been insulated from both social and artistic currency, the academic output of an eccentric academy of one, for most of the last twenty years.)

The power at issue in the black paintings when they first appeared was all-American, saluting the peak moment of the American Century. The debt of the black paintings to Jasper Johns's *Flags* is well known. An anecdote recounted by William S. Rubin tells of the time when Stella, still at Princeton, was experimenting with stripes in partial emulation of Johns. Struck by the resemblance and as a joke, Stella's teacher Stephen Greene scribbled "God Bless America" on one of his student's paintings. Stella was "furious at his teacher's temerity in defacing a painting," in Rubin's words. Also involved, I surmise, was a generational clash definable in terms of hip and square — keeping in mind that the hip is a state of always incipient irony that is destroyed, becoming an empty apothegm, when revealed. Greene was square in making explicit a content that for Stella could function only and exactly in being tacit: national identification, a personal assumption of American imperial potency. Nothing makes the young loathe their elders more than violations of intended subtlety.

Stella's most striking feat in the black paintings was to render sheer subtlety sheerly blatant. He used the radiantly vague inference that is pure abstraction to an effect that is ice-cold and matter-of-fact, a phenomenological slap in the face. Approving critics at the time spoke of the work's "mystery." Any mystery of the work, I think, resides in the fact that there is absolutely no mystery about it. The work is truly matter-of-fact, truly a result of self-evident calculation. The work's original meaning arose not from some ghostly essence but from a material evolution of art in the world. The new world, suppressing the bourgeois parlor of easel painting for institutional public space, would have great use for abstraction's machinery of inference and no use for any particular meaning inferred. Outright Minimalism, from Donald Judd to Richard Serra, would be the mode of art most congenial to the advanced taste of the new world, but Stella's early paintings were its first fully mature prophecy.

"What you see is what you see." Stella's most famous remark, made in a 1962 interview, exercised a coercive hold on American aesthetics in the '60s that is now hard to credit. The remark is one of those modernist oracles or koans, such as "ornament is crime" or "less is more," that superficially sound like nonsense while being profoundly ... nonsense. This particular oracle clamped itself onto its time's thought as a non plus ultra of artistic probity. "What you see is what you see" shamed Stella's contemporaries in their penchants for reading emotional content into visual form — as if sentimentality were the only, zero-sum alternative to brute beholding. Sounding mightily demystifying, Stella's statement in fact mightily mystified its own major terms, "you" and "see," as the mere agent and the mere agency of a visuality sufficient to art — as if "seeing" could ever be extricated from the thousand processes that constellate personhood ("you"). To regard Stella's statement as magically right was to share a period madness.

I recently saw several of the black paintings for the first time in years. The works were in a room with paintings by Robert Ryman and Agnes Martin and a 1967 steel-mesh modular sculpture (four cage-like units fencing a square of floor) by Robert Morris. The black paintings were terrifically imposing and, if anything, even more aggessive than in my memories of them — partly in contrast to the delicately nuanced nearby Rymans and Martins. (Meanwhile, the black paintings seemed on fraternal terms of hip insolence with the splendid Morris piece.) I was struck anew by the shocking, quite sensational deadness of the black paintings' facture, despite fallible handwork that leaves filmy smudges and tremulous wavers in the gaps of blank canvas. The facture is dead because overruled by the hieratic design and overwhelmed by the looming blackness. A viewer is shown gestural signs that would normally be poignant and is forbidden to respond to them. That's the shock.

Looking at the work in the same room by Martin (penciled lines on white fields) and Ryman (brushmark-inflected white fields), I saw how both these artists learned from Stella while correcting his work's overbalance toward design and color by valorizing touch. The sign of handwork, assassinated in the black paintings, is a living hero in the works of Ryman and Martin — works that are vulnerably unpowerful, though a power of feeling may arise in their viewer. Invulnerable, the black paintings assure that the viewer can have no feelings except those appropriate to a confrontation with power: awe, resentment, masochistic glee. I could not help but judge that the Stellas were greater art than the Rymans and Martins. At the same time I found myself wondering at this quality of "greatness," suddenly rather disgusting to me. I realized I was glad that the '60s, with their worship of the overbearing, were long gone.

In the '60s, many people liked to think they worked "dialectically," from extreme to extreme in a way that built by destroying. They enacted a disproof of dialectics. In the end, there was mainly destruction. A given process of contradiction might be exceedingly precise at a given point — Stella's black paintings being such a point, an exact hinge of history — but overall the processes of '60s art moved by more or less random means to entropic ends.

The best text of American art in the '60s was written piecemeal toward the end of the decade by Robert Smithson, that rarest of sensibilities: a hipster with a tragic sense. He understood the entropy of dialectics. He enjoyed it! He finely assessed Stella's contribution to the profligate disaster that Smithson saw as his era's legacy to the future. With reference to all of Stella's paintings up to 1966, he wrote of "purist" surfaces that harbor a "contamination":

> Like Mallarmé's "Hérodiade," these surfaces disclose a "cold scintillation." They seem to "love the horror of being virgin." These inaccessible surfaces deny any definite meaning in the most definite way. Here beauty is allied with the repulsive in accordance with highly rigid rules. One's sight is mentally abolished by Stella's hermetic kingdom of surfaces.

Sight "abolished" by paintings! Stella's was a monumental, monumentally perverse achievement. It came triumphantly to nothing, one might say. Certainly it started in the black paintings with a nothingness positively militant — a "darkness visible," in John Milton's description of Hell. The manic historic energy that called forth this vision of intoxicating deathliness is lost to time. But the vision endures to bemuse indefinitely.

ON OUTSIDER ART

I have seen things that other men only think they saw.
— Arthur Rimbaud

HERE ARE MARVELOUS THINGS made without permission. "Outsiders," their makers are termed. Who terms them that? Insiders, of course. Us. Experts, functionaries, fans. Fluent in the language of art exhibitions, we are the institutionally and professionally trained and mannered, the housebroken, the plugged-in. We are a permanent floating committee of the tribe of Western culture, assigned to sorting and explaining valuable visual artifacts. We know that the artifacts are valuable by the fact that we sort and explain them. Our choice of what to sort and explain, made with tribal license, is value's very criterion. What we regard is valuable; what we don't can't be. What value did the objects in this exhibition have before any of us chose to sort and explain them? The question is meaningless.

I have opted for a sour, edgy tone here to avoid the sweetly reasonable expertise that is usual in catalogue introductions. I see nothing sweetly reasonable in Outsider art. (To define: Outsider art is art produced by a culture consisting of one person.) Rather, I see poisoned charm: efforts to ingratiate laced with loneliness, resentment, and fear. Outsider art introduces into the field of my professional competence something obdurately comfortless and untamed, not a fine artist's disciplined exploration of nether consciousness but an eruption of nether consciousness more or less per se. I cannot directly serve such content in the introductory-essay form. I can only indicate an edge of the form and say that beyond the edge, over there, lies wildness.

The wildness does not occur on the face of Outsider art, which commonly bespeaks a passion for order. The Outsider is a decided type, taking joy in decidedness. With remarkable consistency, Outsiders strive to be absolutely accurate to content that they perceive to be absolutely plain. Though often hermetic — perhaps casting their revelations in grandiose styles or self-protectively opaque codes — they do not deal in "mystery." They deal in what they know. Though often burdened by life with chaotic experiences, they do not deal in chaos. They deal in what gives them refuge from chaos. Straightforwardness and coherence — however outlandish, however embedded in absurdity or banality — govern the forms of their activity. Unlike fine artists who deliberately slip the leash of conventionality, Outsiders struggle to leash — to stabilize and conventionalize — themselves.

They seem to want what we have.

Educated reception of Outsider art tends to be riddled with patronizing sentimentality. The sentimentality can seem defensible because it shakes hands with the Outsider's passionate faith in the power of visual-art conventions. Do Outsiders not realize that they are employing conventions, stumbling on history's inventory of proven motifs, reinventing the wheel? How cute! And how cunning, the accidental originalities and delirious excesses of their serendipitous process. So like Gaudi or Picasso or Klee, in a way — and yet they never heard of Gaudi, Picasso, and Klee! (Simon Rodia, creator of the uncannily Gaudi-like Watts Towers, was shown photographs of the Catalan master's Sagrada Familia cathedral. Said Rodia skeptically: "Did he have help?") Those adorable people prove how authentic our conventions are, don't you think? And above all how desirable. They want what we have. See the monkeys act like humans!

I have caricatured a sentimental view of Outsider art to make it repulsive to, among others, myself. Resisting the view requires some vigilance, because it answers an Insider's heart's desire. We yearn to be reassured and flattered in our educated dependence on received forms and structures. In return for Outsiders' unwitting reassurance and flattery of our visual sophistication, we bestow our approval upon people who can have little or no understanding of why we are so worked up. If anybody is "mysterious" here, it is us Insiders, with our hysterical approbation, in Outsider eyes. I believe and hope they distrust us. We are almost certain to betray them because certain to be unnerved by their actual motivation — if, indeed, we even take note of it. The sentimental transaction occludes loneliness and resentment. It disavows fear.

The edge of Outsider art's wildness is invisible. It is at the onset of the visible, in the signal from brain to hand that yields the first mark or word on a surface or the first joining of one object to another — the first stuttering step of a will to articulate. Is this step like the first word or image formed by a child? Somewhat. But the child rises, wondrously, to the articulate from a tumult of innocence. An adult typically well advanced in years, the Outsider rises, fearfully, from a tumult of experience. Some particular congeries of events and conditions, probably harrowing, planted the seed for that seemingly spontaneous bloom of making.

Celebrate if you like the Outsider's endurance, buoyancy, and optimism. Outsiders celebrate these things themselves. The Outsider says: *I survive. Praise God.* Or else: *I persist. Praise Me.* Go ahead and join the celebration. But do not presume to comprehend the loneliness, resentment, and fear of the life thus taken in hand. Something injurious midwifed the Outsider's creativity. Something punished him or her into song. This thing that we have to thank for the loveliness of the art made the artist a failed member of whatever community he or she came from. Outsiders are social strays, even pariahs (or else they are not Outsiders, but either folk artists or a naive species of fine artists). Do not presume to make an Outsider welcome. Unwelcomedness is his or her necessary state. Amid the charming eccentricities and felicitous fancies, something howls.

"Artists of Vision and Purpose," this exhibition is titled. The word "purpose" provides a nice distinction. Unlike fine art, to which our tribe issues a license of gratuitousness to set it apart from mundane labor, Outsider art palpably has jobs to do. The jobs may be as simple as the routines of a self-appointed public entertainer or they may be arcane, perhaps of a priestly or shamanistic character: tasks vital to maintaining right relations between this world and another. The Outsider often feels vested with a magic role and a magic responsibility. The feeling might have a psychological basis: art-making as a defense against personal despair or worse. I have a sneaking hunch that Henry Darger's labor-intensive nightly flights of imagination, for instance, spared this world the acting out of a dangerous lunatic.

"Vision" is dicier. It is too glib a compliment, somehow, for visualizations that may differ from the norm — the perceptions, anticipations, dreams, and occasional hallucinations of regular citizens — mainly in point of quirky form and surprising intensity. If we must name a quality in which strong Outsiders are superior to the rest of us, let it be *candor*. They cut to the quick of obsessions and spin out powers of invention that we dimly recognize as potentials of our own that some fear or shame — some socialization — prevents us from realizing. In this sense, Outsider "vision" is just a direct access to things we all share.

Right here, I think, is where the unique value of Outsider art begins: in the necessarily fearful recognition of something that is missing in the artist, some normal component of personality that, along with its positive functions, checks the free flow of "vision." To confront Outsider art is to venture into an anarchic neighborhood of the mind and to be met by a denizen who is perfectly and expansively at home there. Does it make you nervous? It should! Your degree of safety in the situation is precisely the degree of your inadequacy to what is going on: your denial in yourself of compulsions that are regular street smarts in the Outsider's shadowy alleyways.

I think it is best to consider this show a walk on the wild side of oneself. Both understanding and a degree of respect may result. What would I have to be like to have made the work myself? How does that likeness feel? In my typical experience, Outsider art first elates me with a sense of all-bets-off freedom and then flips into a sense of oppression. The Outsider is anything but free. He or she is as doomed to the specifics of a single "vision" as a bird is fated to trill always its one song. Don't we know yet that wildness is not freedom but iron determinacy? (Tameness is the parent of choices.) Outsider art is a nearby threshhold of the wild, maybe our most direct possible exposure by daylight to the untranslated language of the mind abandoned to its own resources. Do not heap self-congratulatory praise on this raw evidence. Looking upon it, humbly reflect.

IN MY EXPERIENCE, AN ONSET of beauty combines extremes of stimulation and relaxation. My mind is hyperalert. My body is at ease. Often I am aware of my shoulders coming down as unconscious muscular tension lets go. My mood soars. I have a conviction of goodness in all things. I feel that everything is going to be all right. Later I am pleasantly a little tired all over, as after swimming.

Mind and body become indivisible in beauty. Beauty teaches me that my brain is a physical organ and that "intelligence" is not limited to thought but entails feeling and sensation, the whole organism in concert. Centrally involved is a subtle activity of hormonal excitation in or about the heart — the muscular organ, not a metaphor.

Beauty is a willing loss of mental control, surrendered to organic process that is momentarily under the direction of an exterior object. The object is not thought and felt about, exactly. It seems to use my capacities to think and feel itself.

Beauty is never pure for me. It is always mixed up with something else, some other quality or value — or story, even, in rudimentary forms of allegory, "moral," or "sentiment." Nothing in itself, beauty may be a mental solvent that dissolves something else, melting it into radiance.

Beauty invariably surprises me even when I am looking at what I assume to be beautiful — a sunset, say, or a painting by Giovanni Bellini. There is always a touch of strangeness and novelty about it, an element that I did not expect. The element is usually very simple and overwhelming. In the sunset, I may identify something I never realized before about color. In the Bellini, something about mercy.

Sometimes the object of beauty is not just unexpected but bizarre, with an aspect I initially consider odd or even ugly. Such experiences are revolutions of taste, insights into new or alien aesthetic categories. When I first "got" an Indian temple sculpture, it was as if my molecules were violently rearranged. Something similar happened when I first "got" a painting by Jackson Pollock, say, or Andy Warhol — any strongly innovative artist. As a rule, what had seemed most odd or ugly became the exact trigger of my exaltation.

An experience of beauty may be intense, leaving a permanent impression, or quite mild and soon all but forgotten. But it always resembles a conversion experience, the mind's joyful capitulation to a recovered or new belief. The merely attractive (pretty, glamorous) and merely pleasing (lovely, delectable) are not beauty, because lacking the element of belief and the feeling of awe that announces it.

The attractive or pleasing enhances the flow of my feelings. The beautiful halts the flow, which recommences in a changed direction.

Beauty entails a sense of the sacred. It surrounds something with an aura of inviolability, a taboo on violation. I am mightily attracted to the object while, by a countervailing and equal force of reverence, held back from it. I am stopped in my tracks, rooted to the spot. Beauty is a standoff.

Beauty has an equivocal relation with taste, which at best guides me to things I will like and at worst steers me away from things I might like if I gave them a chance. Taste may sharpen beauty by putting up an initial resistance to its object, making keener the moment when my intellect lays down its arms in surrender. Taste that is not regularly overridden forms a carapace, within which occurs spiritual asphyxiation. But to have no taste at all is to have retained nothing from aesthetic experience. Taste is residue of beauty.

In line with recent breakthroughs in neurological brain research, I fancy that one day the mental event that is an experience of beauty will be X-ray photographed. I predict that the photograph will show the brain lit up like a Christmas tree, with simultaneous firings of neurons in many parts of the brain, though not very brightly. It will show a suddenly swelling diffused glow that wanes gradually.

There is something crazy about a culture in which the value of beauty becomes controversial. It is crazy not to celebrate whatever reconciles us to life. The craziness suggests either stubborn grievance — an unhappiness with life that turns people against notions of reconciliation to it — or benumbed insensibility. The two terms may be one.

"Beauty" versus beauty. Platitude versus phenomenon. Term of sentimental cant versus dictionary word in everyday use. I want to rescue for educated talk the vernacular sense of beauty from the historically freighted, abstract piety of "Beauty."

A dictionary says beauty is "the quality present in a thing or person that gives intense pleasure or deep satisfaction to the mind." Now, the idea of a "quality present in" external reality could do with qualifying in this case. Overly confident identifying of experience with its object can foster rigid projections, such as "Beauty," that repulse the playful, exploratory, even skeptical vitality of aesthetic perception. Speech should distinguish beauty as a quality more volatile than, say, the color blue. The sky's reputation of being blue has never yet, that I know of, incited a rebellious conviction that it is orange. But anything's reputation of being beautiful is guaranteed to recommend itself to some as a theory, if not of the ugly, of the boring. To argue that beauty is real is unnecessary. To argue that it is interesting requires making room for the position that it is "all in the mind."

Meanwhile, can there be any possible problem with "intense pleasure or deep satisfaction to the mind"? I know those experiences, and I like them. I believe that others know and like them, too. For people without the comfort of religion, and even for many who are religious, the experiences may provide a large part of what makes life worth living. Any society that does not respect the reality of "intense pleasure and deep satisfaction to the mind" is a mean society. Respect for something begins with having a respectful name for it.

Many of us talk too little about our delights and accord other people's delights too little courtesy. This is especially so in these days of moralistic attack on things that make life tolerable for many: a cigarette and a drink, even, to ease someone's passage — perhaps also to shorten the passage, but that is no one else's business. Beauty, too, is an intoxicant. So, too, is moralism, if moralizers would only admit it. Baudelaire said it best: "Always be drunk. Get drunk constantly — on wine, on poetry, or on virtue, as you prefer." Today many people drunk on virtue harass people who prefer wine or poetry. You can't argue with the harassers, of course. You can't argue with drunks.

No one is without experiences of beauty. "You can live three days without food," Baudelaire wrote. "Without poetry, never." By poetry, I think he meant beauty in its thousand forms and tinctures, some of them common to all lives. "Fucking is the poetry of the masses," he said by way of amplification.

Moralizers take as their business the pronouncement of who gets to take pleasure when, where, how, and in what. The very word "pleasure" can be embattled now. I read an intellectual debate somewhere in which someone defended a respect for popular culture on the basis that it is pleasurable. To which someone else objected, "So is heroin." I suppose the objector meant that popular culture is an opiate of the people. He was one of those who think the people should not have opiates.

Socially invested "Beauty" has sins to answer for. (I recall a little usage lesson from my childhood: "Women are beautiful; men are handsome.") But the idea of beauty need not be imprisoned by its former uses. Indeed, the conviction of timelessness that is instilled by beauty recommends that the word constantly be shorn of period-and-place-specific connotations, even as it constantly takes on new ones.

The notion of anything being "timeless" is rationally absurd. But such is the lived sense of beauty, which Baudelaire identified as a flash point between the fleeting and the eternal. This is a healthy absurdity, which makes palpable the limits of thought's poky categories. Baudelaire stumbled upon it everywhere. In 1846 he noted the fashion of the black frock coat, whose "political virtues" as a symbol of democratic leveling were not inconsistent with its "poetic beauty, which is the expression of the public soul — an immense procession of undertakers' mourners, political mourners, mourners in love, bourgeois mourners. All of us are attending some funeral or other."

Anyone who cannot find an analogous poetry when surveying the parade of a contemporary street is an unfortunate person.

❧

Do experiences of beauty today fall within the purview and function of art? Not necessarily, and certainly not all the time.

Forty or so years ago J. L. Austin wrote that it was time for aesthetics to quit fretting about the single narrow quality of the beautiful. He recommended for study the dainty and the dumpy. Though without intending to be, he was prophetic. Since pop art, minimalism, arte povera, and conceptualism, artists have devoted themselves to all manner of aesthetic sensations exclusive of beauty — to the point where it seems vital to think about beauty again, though hardly to reduce the focus of the aesthetic back to beauty alone.

Loss of necessary connection between beauty and art seems another of the baleful effects of modern technology, which can simulate, so readily and in such abundance, experiences which once were hard to come by. Visual beauty has been escaping from visual art into movies, magazines, and other media much as the poetic has escaped from contemporary poetry into popular songs and advertising.

Beauty's value as a profound comfort, a reconciliation with life, inevitably wanes when ordinary life is replete with comforts, notably including less frequent exposure to the ugly. The beautiful meant more before indoor plumbing.

Another reason for the progressive divorce of beauty from art is the institutional order that governs most activities involving art. Servants of this order, like minions of an established church, naturally try to rationalize their functions. They are temperamentally averse to irrational and, especially, indescribable phenomena. If I had what I believed was a mystical experience, probably the last person I would report it to would be a priest or pastor. Similarly, I do not discuss beauty with curators. It would only discomfit them and embarrass me.

❦

Anyone can tolerate only so much beauty. Some years ago a doctor in Florence announced his discovery of the "Stendhal Syndrome," named after the French writer. Stendhal had reported a kind of nervous breakdown after a spell of looking at masterpieces of Renaissance art. The doctor noted a regular occurrence of the same symptoms of disorientation — ranging, at the extreme, to hallucinations and fainting — in tourists referred to him as patients. For treatment, the doctor prescribed rest indoors with no exposure to art. It occurs to me that contemporary art is hygienic in this regard. I have never had the slightest touch of the Stendhal Syndrome at a Whitney Biennial.

Beauty is not to be recommended for borderline personalities. It is perhaps most to be recommended for those who, quite sane, most resist the notion of surrendering mental control, such as certain intellectuals who insult aesthetic rapture as "regressive." They should come off it. The self you lose to beauty is not gone. It returns refreshed. It does not make you less intelligent. It gives you something to be intelligent about.

Entirely idiosyncratic, perverse, or otherwise flawed experiences of beauty may be frequent. There is nothing "wrong" about them, and the distinction between them and "real" experiences of beauty is murky (requiring quotation marks). Unusual experiences may constitute a pool of mutations, most of them inconsequential but some fated to alter decisively a familiar form. Of course, such alteration, like the distinction between familiar and mutant beauty, is moot unless a cultural sphere exists in which subjective experiences are openly revealed, compared, and debated.

An experience of beauty entirely specific to one person probably indicates that the person is insane.

❦

"Beauty is Truth, Truth Beauty"? That's easy. Truth is a dead stop in thought before a proposition that seems to obviate further questioning, and the satisfaction it brings is beautiful. Beauty is a melting away of uncertainty in a state of pleasure, which when recalled to the mind bears the imprimatur of truth. I do demur at Keats's capitalization. Truth and beauty are time-bound events. Truth exists only in the moment of the saying of a true thing, and beauty exists only in the moment of the recognition of a beautiful thing. Each ceases to exist a moment later, though leaving a trace.

Are there canons of beauty and truth? There are. Everybody has one, whether consciously or not. In social use, canons are conventionalized imaginary constructs of quality and value which, at both best and worst, are abstract rating games for adepts of this or that field of the mind. Battles over canons should be passionate and fun. Something is wrong if they are not fun. Usually the cause of the disagreeableness is a power struggle in disguise.

Nothing makes for worse art and more trivial politics simultaneously than *Kulturkampf*, a symbolic fight over symbols. Art is given misplaced concreteness as the bearer of realities it is taken to symbolize. Politics becomes fanciful. Righteous blows are struck at air.

Quality. We need this word back, too. It has been abused by those who vest it with transcendent import, rendering it less a practical-minded rule of thumb than an incantation. Quality is a concept of humble and limited, but distinct, usefulness. It is the measure of something's soundness, its aptness for a purpose. I want a good-quality picture to hang on my wall and a good-quality wall to hang my picture on. I will be the judge of what sort of quality — or, better, what combination of quali*ties* — is appropriate. I will be delighted to discuss my judgment with you, and you may enjoy the discussion, too, so long as I refrain from suggesting that my preference somehow puts you in the wrong.

In matters of quality, aptness is all. The best airplane is no match for the worst nail file when your nails want filing. Meanwhile, there is also an order of quality pertaining to purposes in themselves. It does not matter how well something is done if it is not worth doing, or if to do it is evil.

Much resistance to admitting the reality of beauty may be motivated by disappointment with beauty's failure to redeem the world. Experiences of beauty are sometimes attended by soaring hopes, such as that beauty must some day, or even immediately, heal humanity's wounds and rancors. It does no such thing, of course.

Much resistance to the reality of truth suggests a potential of truths that the resister fears.

Much resistance to the reality of quality, as a measure of fulfilled purpose, bespeaks the condition of people who either lack a sense of purpose or whose purposes must, by their nature, be dissembled.

Insensibility to beauty may be an index of misery. Or it may reflect wholehearted commitment to another value, such as justice, whose claims seem more urgent.

When politics is made the focus of art, beauty does not wait to be ousted from the process. Beauty deferentially withdraws, knowing its place. Beauty is not superfluous, not a luxury, but it is a necessity that waits upon the satisfaction of other necessities. It is a crowning satisfaction.

Peter Schjeldahl was born in North Dakota in 1942 and has lived in New York since 1964. He is a columnist for *The Village Voice* and a contributing editor of *Art in America*. He has worked as a regular art critic for *The New York Sunday Times*, *Vanity Fair*, and *7 Days*. His books include *The Hydrogen Jukebox: Selected Writings 1978-1991* from the University of California Press, and *The 7 DAYS Art Columns*, The Figures, 1990.